About the Author

As the published author of her memoire, 'Hoosier Hysteria' and an instructional book about making art quilts, 'Create Landscape Quilts', Meri is an internationally recognized, award winning art quilter and teacher. Besides writing science fiction, her other passion is music. As a child, she dreamed of singing with a professional Gilbert and Sullivan theater company, and she was thrilled to be able to do so in the 1990s with the renowned San Francisco Lamplighters. Meri currently lives in central California with her family and two rowdy felines.

You can see her quilts at www.meriartquilts.com.

The Sisters of Caliban

The Valhalla Stories Book I

Pegasus

PEGASUS PAPERBACK

A CIP catalogue record for this title is
available from the British Library.

ISBN 978 1 80468 056 8

*Pegasus is an imprint of
Pegasus Elliot Mackenzie Publishers Ltd.*
www.pegasuspublishers.com

First Published in 2024

**Pegasus
Sheraton House Castle Park
Cambridge England**

Printed & Bound in Great Britain

To all of the struggling writers out there. Never give up!

A Note About Valhallan Pronunciation[1]:

Valhallans speak 'Norsk', a blend of the ancient Scandinavian Languages of Old Earth, including Norwegian, Swedish, Danish and Icelandic. For those who are interested, the following guide may be of use:

ä – *ah* as in 'jacket'

å – *oo* as in 'poor'

æ – *eh* as in 'bet.'

e – *eh* as in 'bet', except before 'r' when it is pronounced ah (thus: '*Jeg er* = *Yeg ahr*)

ö – *uh*, with the lips pursed, as in the French 'deux'

j – *y* as in 'yet'; never pronounced as in English.

kj – *sh* as in 'share' but softer, similar to the French 'je'

r – is never pronounced as in English, but is always given a quick flip, similar to Spanish

---

[1] My humble apologies to my Scandinavian friends, relatives, and readers! In trying to imagine how the various beautiful Scandinavian languages might have become intermixed and fused together over the centuries on an isolated Fringe planet called Valhalla, I have taken the authorial liberty of mashing them up together, hoping to create phrases and expressions that might be somewhat intelligible to English-language readers.

I.

Janne

1.

Imagine a sky full of stars... Not 'full' in the way it looks from the surface of a planet with several miles of atmospheric interference between yourself and it, but full in the way the sky looks from the observation deck of a starship or from one of the dome worlds: inky black, with millions of stars burning fiery bright in every direction. At least that's the way it looked to me while I was on University VII – and I eventually came to believe that this was how I would always see it. Never again for me the hard deep blues, the fragile pinks, or opalescent whites of a terrestrial sky. Or so I thought...

I was living at the time in the South Polar Dome on University VII in self-imposed exile from my father's house.

Anyone whose home world belongs to the Concorde Alliance will surely have heard of University VII: that small, airless planetoid dedicated by its founders to the admittedly grandiose ideal of 'the pursuit and preservation of all sentient knowledge'. But unless they have actually toured University, they might not be familiar with its layout.

University VII was constructed as a system of interconnected domes linked together by underground tube shuttles. The original Old Domes were provided with artificial atmospheres and landscaped with specimen plants in an effort to make their residents feel 'at home'. Included in the Old Domes are the Technical and Humanities Institutes, the College of Fine Arts, the Law School, and the smaller but extremely famous Music School, which is set somewhat apart from the other campuses.

Eventually, as more room was needed, the New Domes were added at either pole, but in quite a different style. Since anyone stationed in the New Domes is either an astronomer, a scientific or medical researcher, a robotics designer, a cataloguer of some sort, a mathematician, or a statistician like myself, the Founders assumed that we would either require an unobstructed window into space, or else that we would be so focused on our interfaces and laboratories that we would be oblivious to anything that exists beyond our work stations or living quarters. At any rate, these are the standard reasons given to explain why both the North and South Polar Domes are enveloped in perpetual night.

When I told my father of my decision to leave our homeworld, Caliban, and accept a five-year research grant on University VII, he seemed to age a little right before my eyes. His handsome face beneath its close-cropped cap of black hair appeared to sag and I noticed for the first time the tired creases in the corners of his shrewd, grey eyes.

"Oh, Janne, have we hurt you so badly that you want to retire from public life?" he wanted to know.

But I had no ready answer.

"Won't you reconsider?" He asked this quite gently, yet there was such sadness in his voice.

I shook my head, not trusting myself to speak.

"Can't we talk about this?"

Again, I remained silent.

"Very well – if you must go there, why not apply to the Music School instead? Music has always been your special love, and Director Andebar is a close family friend."

"You know it's far too late for that!" The moment the words were spoken, I regretted my outburst: in preparing to make my announcement, I had vowed not to let anger get the better of me.

"But you're only twenty-two, Janne, twenty-two!" He passed his hand across his eyes in a familiar, tired gesture, but then went on more calmly. "The Music School accepts qualified musicians of any age. And Cristan Andebar has a personal interest in you: he's encouraged your musical studies ever since you were a child."

"I'm quite aware of that."

"Then why not take advantage of our connection? I'm sure he'd be delighted to allow you to…"

"No! I won't have him doing favors for me. I won't have *anyone* doing favors! From now on, I intend to take care of myself."

"Isn't there something I can say that will change your mind?"

"No. I've made my choice."

And thus ended our conversation.

How could I possibly explain that the Music School would be too painfully full of life and activity for my peace of mind? How to make him understand that all I wanted was solitude and the safety of numbers: cold, fixed bits of data which I could manipulate and which could not manipulate me?

There were no words for what I felt just then.

And so I went away to the South Polar Dome. And each 'day', as I walked through the pedestrian tubes on my way to work, and each 'night' as I walked back to my room, I looked around at the impersonal, monolithic slabs of the Research Institute buildings and then up at those countless stars.

And I felt, at last, a kind of peace.

2.

It wasn't until my fourth year on University VII that I finally yielded to my father's frequent pleas to return home. By then the thought of visiting Caliban was no longer quite so disturbing. Besides, my sister was touring University VII. Why not accompany her home, my father wanted to know – and I was unable to think of a good reason to refuse.

TiAnn is a lovely, willful girl-child (at least she was back then): her white-blonde hair and aristocratic features lent her an air of timeless, ethereal beauty. But looks can be deceptive, and beneath that frail façade she's as tough as cerosteel. Furthermore, she knows how to use the discrepancy to her best advantage.

Another thing which isn't obvious from her appearance is that she's a brilliant lawyer, and although she was only twenty at the time of her visit, she had already been training for several years with my father's associate Drexel, a man considered by many to be one of Caliban's finest advocates. Recently my father and Drexel had decided that TiAnn would benefit from advanced studies at University VII.

However, with typical stubbornness, she balked. Yet she did consent to visit University VII so she could observe the Law School in action and make her own assessment of its possibilities. After all, Drexel had offered to pay for the trip, and TiAnn has never been one to refuse a gift.

My schedule was unusually busy just then: I had several projects I was anxious to complete before I left on vacation. As a result, and despite my best intentions, I had very little time to spare for my sister – in fact she had been on University VII for nearly a week before I was able to arrange to even take her out to dinner. By then she was thoroughly bored, a feeling she did not bother to hide, and I must admit that I was relieved when our rather strained outing was over.

Several days later, when she called on me in my quarters, I was trying to set the place in order in preparation for our departure to our home world,

Caliban. But it was distracting to see her there, a warm, vibrant presence in the midst of my living space expressing her distaste for the University Law School with familiar, passionate intensity.

"…The professors are incompetent. Their lectures are a joke, and the casework and assignments are a travesty," she was saying. "And the students! They're as insipid a bunch of morons as I've ever had the misfortune to meet!"

"That's too bad," I responded, suppressing a grin. She certainly hadn't mellowed with time. "Would you mind stepping aside so I can get to my desk?"

I edged past her and sat down before continuing, "I'm really sorry you don't like the Law School. I was hoping you'd want to study there. It would have been fun to be able to see each other more often than we have these past four years."

"If two hours once a week is all you can spare, I might as well stay on Caliban!"

"Come on, TiAnn, I spent more time with you than that! And I told you I was going to have to work especially hard to get ready for this vacation." Even as I spoke, I was sorting through a large stack of work slates: a difficult task under the best of circumstances.

"I'm no more impressed by your so-called projects than I am by the Law School," she spat back.

Rather than argue, I steered for what I hoped were calmer waters. "Well then, tell me what you *did* like about University. Surely there must have been something."

"Ha! Everything about this place is pale and grey and dull. Just like this room. Just like *you*!" She picked up the slates I had so carefully arranged and slammed them back down on the desk, sending several of them clattering onto the floor. She leaned towards me, palms flat on my desk, her eyes blazing a challenge.

And I stared back, struck by the sudden realization that this tall, graceful girl, this beautiful young woman – my little sister – had become a complete stranger.

Abruptly, she turned away. "How can anyone stand to live like this?" she muttered, more to herself than to me, yet I felt every word as if it was knife-edged. "Sleep, eat, work – sleep, eat, work. Day after day – year after year – locked in a cell. No sky, no fresh air, no people, no parties – nothing to do. It's disgusting!"

Her shimmering, sky-blue dress made emphatic sweeps across the faded grey plasteel floor as she paced back and forth in a restless circuit. She was so full of violent energy, like a caged animal, that she made my tiny cubicle seem far smaller and drearier than it had ever felt before.

"Don't be so hard on my life, TiAnn!" I attempted a smile, struggling to suppress my hurt feelings. "This place may not appeal to you, but I like it here. And there's plenty of interesting and important work for…"

"Oh, please!" A stamp of her silver boot. "What kind of work is this? You can't tell me it's worth doing! And this certainly isn't living. No one could ever have made *me* come here!"

"No one made me. I chose it."

"Fled to it, you mean!"

I stopped smiling, too angry to even formulate a reply.

At that moment, the comm console chimed its cheery greeting in jarring contrast to our harsh words. Clenching my hands into fists to keep them from shaking, I strode over to answer, fighting for self-control.

"Message for Statistician Janne Trellerian," the metallic voice of the University AI issued from the console.

"Trellerian speaking." I was proud of myself for somehow managing to sound equally dispassionate.

"As per your request, this is a reminder to report to Shuttle Bay 24 in thirty minutes standard. The shuttle will commence boarding at sixteen hundred local."

"Message received." I switched off.

My sister's words, coming from behind me, broke the tense silence. "I guess we'd better be going." She sounded relieved.

"I guess we should," I agreed, equally happy to be able to avoid further conflict. Yet there was an uncomfortable tightness in my chest, and at that moment I realized with awful certainty that my visit to Caliban was going to be a total disaster.

"Your luggage, Janne!" TiAnn suddenly exclaimed. "Don't tell me you haven't packed yet!"

"I most certainly have." My reply was curt enough to make me wince.

Even after all these years, why must we fight nearly every time we were together?

Did it have to be that way?

"Where are your travel bags?" TiAnn demanded.

Without deigning to respond, I reached for my guitar case.

"You aren't still lugging that old thing around, are you?" She forced a smile, obviously hoping to ease the tension.

"I am."

Without another word, I shouldered my modest travel pack and headed for the door.

"Is that all?"

"Yes."

"You're joking!"

I turned back. "Well, as you yourself pointed out, I don't have much space in my living quarters for collecting things." I didn't attempt to hide the scorn in my voice.

With a shrug of her silky blue shoulders, TiAnn stooped to retrieve her two stuffed-to-the-point-of-bursting enormous carryalls and bulky travel pack.

Seriously overburdened, she staggered out after me.

I didn't offer to help.

3.

Once aboard the shuttle, I was surprised to discover that I enjoyed having nothing more important to do than to settle back in my seat and watch the grey, crater-pocked, dome-studded sphere that was University VII drop out of sight below us. In the aftermath of our argument, it seemed that neither my sister nor I felt much like talking.

However, as luck would have it, conversation was unnecessary: we had been assigned front row seats in the shuttle's forward passenger section with a marvelous view of the cockpit and crew, framed against a backdrop of velvet-black void, pinpricked by billions of stars.

Our 'crew' consisted of a pilot and co-pilot: a man and a Soolian.

Although all member races of the Concorde are humanoid, Soolians are definitely among the most exotic in appearance. With their multi-faceted eyes, flat snaky hair, gracefully sinuous torsos, and long double-jointed fingers, no one would ever be tempted to call them human-standard. Furthermore, it's common knowledge that Soolians are a home-loving and secretive race. It was quite unusual to see one in so public a capacity. Still, Soolians were nothing new to me: by what seemed at the time to be simple coincidence, my supervisor at University VII also happened to be one of those rare Soolian extroverts who was willing to consort with outsiders. Daily contact had long since cured me of my initial fascination.

But TiAnn was another story. At twenty, she had seldom been off-planet, and although Caliban is located near the Galactic Hub and therefore caters to a multitude of tourists, our visitors are for the most part human-standard. This was undoubtedly the first Soolian my sister had ever encountered, and from the moment she set eyes on him, she was captivated. Face alight with interest, and suppressing an occasional shudder, she kept her attention riveted on the alien.

I must admit that I, too, was preoccupied – but it was the human who intrigued me.

He appeared to be thirty or so – the sort of man the Space Guild loves to feature in their travel ads: tall and lean, and oh-so-handsome in his formfitting, silver-grey flight suit, pale blonde hair cropped regulation close to his symmetrical head, steely blue eyes, shapely nose, square chin, and thin, expressive lips that suggested either fierce determination or else a tendency to stubbornness. From where I sat, I could even see the faint purple traceries at his temples where the pilot-to-ship AI interface contacts were implanted.

However, it was not his appearance that caught my attention – although strapped into his seat with the ship's AI link encircling his brow like an exotic crown, he was certainly Space Guild officer personified.

But what impressed me were his hands. Graceful, long-fingered hands – hands with a life of their own performing an intricate dance across the control panel: competent hands doing their job well. I appreciated the professional efficiency and many hours of training those hands represented – as fit and agile as any highly-skilled musicians.

His voice, coming suddenly over the cabin speakers, startled me out of my reverie. "Welcome to shuttle flight 1630, outward-bound for University Seven's Gemini Space Station. Our estimated flight time is sixty-seven minutes standard, and we'll be docking at gate FN Seventy-One."

As far as I was concerned, this was standard flight information and could just as easily have been delivered by the onboard AI – as it should have been. I could only suppose that our eccentric pilot preferred the personal touch.

"And if you've just discovered that you're not going where you thought you were," he was saying, "I'm afraid it's much too late to do anything about it."

Behind us, the other passengers chuckled, apparently amused by this frivolous banter.

What was the fellow trying to prove?

"And now I'd like introduce myself and my co-pilot," he said. "Starship Captain Eirik Sanderson, at your service – and this is my flight engineer, Prelakiel dar Arien."

This announcement brought startled murmurs from those seated behind me. Even I was surprised. Everyone knows that starship captains and their crews don't fly shuttles, they fly starships.

It was Captain Eirik Sanderson's turn to chuckle, and he made it seem a reassuring, captainly chuckle. "Believe me, I'm as surprised as you are to find myself serving in this capacity," he confided. "But let me assure you, there is a simple explanation – and it isn't that my flight engineer and I have both been demoted."

The reaction was all too predictable: another ripple of good-natured laughter.

"You see, like many of yourselves, Prel and I are tourists here at University Seven, and when we requested shore leave our superiors apparently decided that as long as we were going planet-side they might as well get their money's worth out of us. And the next thing we knew, they'd assigned us to crew this shuttle."

Although this so-called explanation was patently false, there was an undercurrent of credulous noise from the ranks behind me.

Flight Engineer dar Arien grunted something to Captain Sanderson.

"Yes, I suppose you're right, Prel," the captain replied. "Folks, my colleague has just advised me that it's always best to tell the truth… So I guess I'll go ahead and confess that the real reason he and I are flying today is that we wanted to see University Seven and we didn't trust anyone else to get us there and back!" He turned all the way around in his seat to offer up a supercilious grin.

My fellow-passengers rewarded him with more appreciative laughter, but I was outraged. Why had this man interrupted his elegant flight maneuvers to deliver a silly comedy routine?

Just then Captain Sanderson, still smiling like a fool, happened to glance in our direction, and what he saw obviously disconcerted him.

There we sat in the front row: TiAnn staring in goggle-eyed fascination at the flight engineer; and me, scowling at them both and feeling that I would be only too happy to slit their collective throats – if it wouldn't mean that we would never reach our destination.

For several seconds the captain stared back at us, his expression shifting from amusement to confusion and finally to hot embarrassment. He turned back to his companion, his face flushed an unnatural red, and I was close enough to hear him mutter, "Why don't you say a few words to these nice people, Prel?"

After that, to my considerable relief, without wasting another moment on inane pleasantries, he retreated to the haven of his flight controls.

When the Soolian began speaking in the gluey, thickly-accented voice of his species, I tuned him out and instead returned my attention to the impersonal, midnight-dark sky. However, it was quite a while before I managed to recover my composure, for I was haunted by thoughts of the captain. It was disturbing to discover that he was so vulnerable.

Weren't starship captains supposed to be impervious to the scorn of mere mortals such as myself?

I was greatly relieved when, an hour or so later, TiAnn and I were able to disembark from the shuttle without further incident and lose ourselves in the bustling crowds that hurried through Gemini Space Station.

4.

"Well, this *is* a surprise!" It was Captain Sanderson.

We were standing in the passenger lounge of the starship *Solar Eclipse*, not far from a tastefully quiet ensemble of Cristan Andebar's omnipresent Journeymen and Journeywomen musicians, headed inward from University VII towards the galactic center. It was our first 'evening' out from Gemini Space Station, and therefore the occasion of one of those tiresome social functions which every starship in the fleet seems to feel obligated to put on its schedule, and which most passengers – myself not included – seem to enjoy.

I was there at TiAnn's insistence, and so far I had spent most of my time studiously avoiding the other guests, and concentrating on the music. As for my sister, she had somehow managed to corner the Soolian flight engineer, and they were engaged in an intense conversation at the far end of the room.

"I beg your pardon," addressing the captain, I was uncomfortably aware of his height – I seldom have to look up at anyone – and he met my gaze with an unsettling mixture of cool appraisal and very masculine self-confidence. In addition, I thought that he was standing a bit closer than was socially acceptable: it implied a certain intimacy, however unfounded on fact. "Were you speaking to me?"

"Imagine running into each other like this!" His smile didn't quite reach his eyes and there was something else as well – could it possibly be a challenge? – although I certainly couldn't imagine what it might be.

"I haven't the slightest idea what you're talking about." I knew it was brusque – but why bother being polite after he had made such a fool of himself on the shuttle? "I don't even know you. In fact I believe you must be mistaking me for someone else."

I started to turn back towards the musicians.

His response halted me in my tracks: "Impossible. You're eminently unforgettable. But you're absolutely correct: we haven't been properly introduced. Madam…?" Now there was a definite twinkle of humor in his eyes that was at odds with his serious expression.

"I am not 'madam' anything," I cut in before he could say another word, thinking that perhaps if I was rude enough, he would go away and put an end to this farce. "I am Sera Janne Trellerian of…" Abruptly I ceased speaking.

After all, why divulge unnecessary information? And on second thought, he undoubtedly already knew my name if he'd bothered to check the passenger manifest.

"Pardon me, Sera Janne Trellerian of," he parroted back, deadpan, but with a definite ironic twist to his lips. Then he bowed. "Captain Eirik Sanderson at your service. Welcome to my starship."

"Pleased to meet you…" I mumbled, while in my mind I was frantically searching for a socially acceptable escape gambit.

"You can't imagine how surprised I am to find you here," he was saying, yet somehow I doubted his sincerity, "because even though you don't seem to remember me, I must confess there's no way I could have forgotten *you*!"

I knew I was blushing. I could only hope that he would quickly tire of this preposterous game – whatever it was – and leave me in peace.

"How odd: you don't have anything to say," he persisted. "Why is that, Sera Janne Trellerian? You aren't shy, are you?"

Silence seemed the most prudent response, yet I could feel myself flushing hotter by the moment. If I didn't figure out a way to end this embarrassing confrontation, and soon, I suspected that before long my face would rival the security team uniforms in brilliance.

"Funny: you didn't seem the least bit shy the other day," my tormentor pressed on, apparently undeterred by my continuing lack of response, "which, needless to say, is why I haven't been able to get you off my mind."

"Really, Captain, I…"

"Aren't you even a little bit curious to know why a starship captain has been obsessed with you for several days?"

"Not rea—"

"Of course you are! You know, ever since I saw you on that shuttle, I was delighted to discover that you'd booked passage on my ship because I've been hoping we'd have a chance to talk, even if it was only for a few minutes. Just long enough for me to ask you one simple question."

My stomach did an uneasy little flip-flop. What could this irritating man possibly want with me?

"To be perfectly honest," he was saying, "from the moment I set eyes on you, I had the distinct impression that I'd done something to offend you. And it's strange: I'm still getting that feeling right now."

"That's the most absurd—"

But he went on as if I hadn't spoken: "Which, I confess, is why I haven't been able to forget you. So what I keep asking myself – what I've been dying to ask you – is this: what can I, Eirik Sanderson, possibly have done to antagonize a total stranger?"

"I assure you, Captain, you're very much mistaken," I said with as much dignity as I could muster. "I am not offended. In fact, I barely even noticed you."

"Hey, wait a minute!" He caught my arm as I turned to leave. "You can't just walk off like that!"

"Look, this is all a stupid mistake," I said, shrugging free of his hand. "Can't you just forget it?"

"A mistake? What kind of mistake?" His expression brightened. "Oh – you mean it's a joke! So that's it! I thought it had to be something like that. Okay, who put you up to it? Was it Carter?" He stood there, watching me expectantly.

"That's not exactly what I..." Any further attempt at words died unspoken.

He waited me out, his arms folded across his chest.

I sighed. Obviously, this was a tenacious man, and all the wishing in the universe wasn't going to make him give up and go quietly away.

"Really, Captain, it's nothing personal," I said at last. "It's just that the other day I..." I faltered, suddenly feeling very foolish. How could I possibly reveal my fantasies to him? I looked away, unable to meet his eyes.

"Oh, come on," he urged, "it can't be *that* bad."

"Can't you just forget…" I began, but then, without warning, my temper flared. How dare he put me on the spot like this, even if he *was* the captain of this ship?

Very well: if he was going to insist on a confession, I'd give him one he'd never forget!

"Well, Captain," I began, "since you're so determined to learn the truth about the other day – I'll tell you…

"I certainly wasn't expecting to have that shuttle piloted by a starship captain, but I wasn't going to complain about it either. I enjoyed watching you fly – I really did. Your training is superb. You handled that ship as if it were an extension of yourself… And if you must know, I admit that I was fantasizing about dashing Space Guild officers. The guild must wish they had a thousand more like you. And then…

"And then you had to go and spoil everything with your ridiculous monologue and those dumb jokes. They made you seem so terribly human!" These last few words came out in a rush, and my face felt positively incandescent.

Captain Sanderson was grinning with boyish glee. "Gee – I was afraid it was much worse. I really *was* awful, wasn't I?" He didn't sound the least bit contrite. "But you'll have to forgive me: it isn't every day that I get to fly a shuttle. And I guess I did get a bit carried away. Sorry I ruined your fantasy."

"You don't have to apologize—" I began, but he interrupted.

"You know, I suspect that what you're really trying to tell me is that I'd be a whole lot better off if I kept my mouth shut and concentrated on flying my ship and looking handsome."

"Well… I wouldn't have put it quite that way," I said, struggling to suppress a smile and feeling very foolish indeed.

He burst out laughing.

I stole a furtive glance at my sister. Fortunately she was so taken with the Soolian that she never even looked our way.

The captain must have been watching me closely because his response was immediate. "If you're checking up on your sister, don't worry: she's far too involved with Prel to pay attention to us. And if you're wondering: I introduced them."

"How did you know?" I blurted out, and then I hated myself for falling into such an obvious trap.

"Know what? That she wanted to meet Prel, or that you're sisters?"

"Both."

"Well, naturally I was curious to find out who you were, after the reception you gave me on the shuttle – now don't interrupt… So as soon as we reached Gemini Station, I checked the passenger manifest. I guessed about Prel."

"Then it's as I suspected: you already knew my name before you began talking to me!"

"As the old saying goes: 'Rank has its privileges'." He grinned. "And I suppose you might call it cheating if you feel so inclined, but it seemed a much better way of starting a conversation than asking you right off why you were so annoyed with me."

"You're probably right about that."

His smile was disarming. "In any case, I'd already guessed you were sisters. There's quite a strong family resemblance."

"I don't agree!" I felt myself freezing up all over again, and wished it wasn't happening. "My sister looks quite a bit like our mother, and I take after our father." I hated myself for sounding so churlish – and that made me angry with the captain all over again.

"Nonsense," he was saying. "No one would ever doubt that you were sisters. I can't imagine two more beautiful women."

Disgusted with myself for having almost forced him to pay me a compliment, I bit back another angry retort. And because it was obvious that I wasn't going to be able to get rid of him any time in the foreseeable future, I resolved to steer our conversation away from personal matters. Besides, there just might be a way to get even with him…

"For your information, Captain," I said in as mild a voice as I could manage, "looks can be deceptive. What you can't possibly have anticipated when you so thoughtfully introduced them, is that at this very moment my innocent-looking sister is undoubtedly picking your flight engineer's brains about the intricacies of Soolian tribal law. And I know from personal experience how touchy Soolians can be."

The captain winced, and I knew I'd scored a hit. "Prel's far touchier than most." His eyes shifted uneasily from my sister to me, and then back again. "Perhaps we should stroll over there and…"

"Of course," I continued, "there's another thing you can't possibly know about TiAnn just by looking at her… That lovely head of hers is packed with knowledge about Concorde law and customs. She's been trained by the finest legal minds in the Concorde, and she knows every trick in the book about the art of cross-examination."

To my considerable satisfaction, the captain looked, if anything even more uncomfortable.

"So don't worry about your Soolian – or TiAnn," I concluded. "She'll extract the information she wants with a brain surgeon's skill and he'll never suspect a thing."

For a moment longer the captain looked uncertain, but then, unexpectedly, once again he grinned. "All right, you've made your point: we've now established that your sister can take care of herself." His eyes narrowed. "Which brings us back to you."

That wasn't at all what I'd been hoping to accomplish!

"So: tell me about yourself, Sera Janne Trellerian. What brings you to University Seven?"

"I live there."

"Ah. Are you a student or a teacher?"

"Neither."

He waited, but I was determined not to reveal any more about myself than I had to.

"I see. Well, perhaps you'd like a drink," he said at last. Without waiting for my reply, he reached past my shoulder, and with practiced skill removed two glasses from a passing robo-server. Handing me one, he saluted me with his glass. "Here's to the mysterious and taciturn Sera Janne Trellerian."

There followed several moments of blessed silence.

"Obviously you don't want to discuss University Seven," he began again, "so let's try another subject. My research has revealed that you're ticketed through to Caliban. Since nobody lives on University Seven forever, may I take it that you and your sister are going home?"

Before I had to answer, we were confronted by a fat woman in a hot-pink mini-sarong. The poor thing had coordinated her makeup and dyed her hair to match as well, and her equally fat escort sported a skin-tight jumpsuit of the identical unfortunate color.

"Oh, Captain, can you spare us a minute?" she simpered, batting thick false eyelashes that were perched above her heavily kohl-ringed eyes like tipsy pink spiders.

"Why certainly, madam," he replied, turning on his professional charm. "What can I do for you?"

"Didn't I tell you what a nice man he is, Corrie?" she enthused with barely a glance at her companion.

"You certainly did!" he responded heartily, yet he seemed ill-at-ease. "But maybe this isn't a good time for a chat. I'm sure the captain would much rather be talking to this lovely young lady."

With deliberate insolence, the captain turned to slowly inspect me, one eyebrow raised in exaggerated skepticism. But before he had a chance to form a reply, his garrulous admirer hurtled on.

"Oh, I promise we won't take up too much of your time, Captain Sanderson," she hastily interjected – clearly she had no intention of allowing her quarry to escape. "It's just that I was telling Corrie here about meeting you this morning when my group toured the control room. It was so thoughtful of you to join us in the observation area, when I'm sure you have much more important things to do than entertain your passengers."

"On the contrary, madam, greeting passengers is one of my most important responsibilities." Somehow, he managed to deliver this deadpan.

Delighted with his gallantry, Captain Sanderson's flirtatious fan fluttered her pink spiders at him and rattled on, "You were explaining about jump sequences. Or maybe it was hyper-jumps? Remember, I told you about that, Corrie?"

He could have said 'yes' or 'no', and it wouldn't have made the least bit of difference, for she immediately continued: "And you told us that when the flight engineer and the ship's AI plan our jump sequences, they have to work out our exact position on star charts to make sure we don't get trapped in one of those weird hyperspace – uh – Clobber-You Dementias…" she proudly finished, then rounded on her skeptical-looking counterpart. "He did too say that, Corrie!"

The captain winced. "Actually, they're Calabi-Yau Dimensions," he corrected, sotto-voce, yet I heard him quite distinctly.

I strove to keep my expression neutral, well-aware that the Pink Lady wasn't really interested in learning about the intricacies of starship navigation. Rather, she wanted to be able to tell her friends back home that she had had a personal conversation with a Real Starship Captain.

I took the opportunity to escape.

I felt a little bit sorry for the captain, but not too sorry. Mostly I was thankful that we had been interrupted before I had been forced to discuss anything of a more personal nature with him.

5.

However, Captain Sanderson was apparently not the sort of man to give up easily. During the week that followed, the *Solar Eclipse* hosted a series of social events which TiAnn and I dutifully attended, and on each occasion I had the distinct impression that he was purposely, although unobtrusively, seeking me out. We were seldom alone for more than a few moments, and his conversation was never again personal or anything other than scrupulously polite, yet neither was he aloof. It was my impression that he was on his good behavior, perhaps hoping that I would come to appreciate his finer qualities.

His crew certainly liked him, I couldn't help but notice. A spirit of camaraderie, of trust and professional pride radiated from his people. There was no doubt they respected him. As the daughter of a planetary ruler, I was aware of the subtleties of leadership without coercion – of inspiring subordinates to want to do their jobs well. Captain Sanderson definitely possessed this quality, the mark of a true leader.

***

I adapted quickly to the ship's routine which was, after all, not so very different from life at the South Polar Dome. In either place, there was a constant bustle of activity, lights were on 'day' and 'night', and it was up to the individual to establish his or her own personal routine. If passengers desired food, exercise, entertainment – musical or otherwise – companionship or sleep, the appropriate places were provided to satisfy their needs. My life at University was similarly shaped, and on the *Solar Eclipse*, whenever I felt the need for privacy, all I had to do was find the nearest observation deck where I could usually count on being alone for as long as I wished, watching the infinite procession of stars.

For the most part though, the trip was rather tedious and I soon began to wish it would end. However, Caliban is on the opposite side of the galactic lens from University VII, and the *Solar Eclipse* was a luxury liner, so we had to work our way in towards the center, and then back out again via the established trade routes in order to drop off and pick up passengers and cargo, and to re-provision the ship. And the closer we came to the Hub, the shorter the jumps we could safely make. As a result, the sub-light flights into each solar system seemed to take forever.

Many of the planets we encountered offered interesting side-trips, from several hour jaunts to days-long excursions, depending upon the visitors' schedules and inclinations. To relieve our boredom, my sister and I began taking advantage of these stopovers, going planet-side to see the local sights: shops and museums, floating cities and famous landmarks, botanical gardens and architectural wonders. Before we reached Caliban, TiAnn and I had seen all of this and more.

On our first outing, I was startled when Captain Sanderson joined our group of sightseers, but after several such appearances I began to expect him to show up, and was surprised and – if the truth be told – even rather disappointed when he didn't put in an appearance.

Many of the planets we visited were apparently familiar to him, for he frequently added his own commentary, both perceptive and entertaining, to that of the official tour guides. His presence was certain to make the day more interesting. And with each excursion, without quite realizing that it was happening (and perhaps this was his intention), I came to know him a little better – so that by the time we reached Arcadia, my opinion of him had mellowed considerably.

Arcadia is a Concorde Preserve: one of those rare worlds that the Powers-That-Be have designated as being so unique that it is proscribed to all 'settlement and planetary exploitation'. Of course, I now understand that there is more than one kind of exploitation, but in those days I accepted without question the official Concorde propaganda that prohibiting the development of a planet's natural resources spared it from ruination.

However, although Arcadia was officially neither settled nor exploited, it was quite rigorously 'managed' by AdventureWorld Ltd., one of the richest and most powerful conglomerates in the Concorde (in fact, AdventureWorld operates most if not all of the Concorde's Nature

Preserves). And it was AdventureWorld's practice to offer an extensive array of tours, tailored to the prospective visitor's interests and time limitations, on each of its 'lovely virgin' planets.

Having nothing better to do while the *Solar Eclipse* was docked at the Zenith Space Station, TiAnn and I decided to tour Arcadia. Neither of us had had the opportunity to visit a Preserve, although I for one had always wanted to do so.

Our credits had barely cleared the Net before we found ourselves aboard a sleek AdventureWorld shuttle, heading away from the space station and towards Arcadia and Nexus 172, one of a series of domes which are scattered at regular intervals across the planetary surface, and whose purported function is 'to protect Arcadia's fragile ecosystem from xenobiological contamination'.

In transit, we were plied with food and drink and a lengthy multi-media presentation describing the wonders we could experience – including a number of 'not-to-be-missed' luxury resorts – should we be inspired to extend our stay.

Thoroughly propagandized, we were finally deposited at our destination, a bright mini-dome the size of a small city which sat, glittering like a soap bubble, directly on the margin where a dense tropical jungle met a vast, semi-arid savannah.

There, AdventureWorld employees sorted us out into our various tours: jungle, savannah, or some combination thereof, depending upon how much time and credits we visitors were willing or able to invest in the experience. My sister and I had opted for the eight-hour savannah trip, and although I hadn't noticed him on the shuttle, I wasn't really surprised to discover Captain Sanderson among the thirty-odd persons in our group. The Pink Lady from our first evening's soirée and her companion Corrie were also in attendance.

Our transport was a low-slung, torpedo-shaped vehicle with a transparent roof and sides, and – as we were enthusiastically informed – the latest in hover suspension technology. Before long, we were gliding across Arcadia's pale mauve plains on a cushion of air, our bodies comfortably enthroned in plush swivel chairs, refreshments and digital binoculars supplied by an efficient swarm of robo-servers, always ready to indulge our slightest whim. Although it never occurred to me at the time, we might as well have been watching a holo-vid in an entertainment bar, for all of the actual contact we were allowed to have with reality.

As was his custom, Captain Sanderson had seated himself in the very front of the vehicle. I caught the occasional word as he chatted amiably with the young man who was serving as both our tour guide and driver – at least they chatted during the intervals when the driver wasn't using his comm to point out local sights to the rest of us passengers.

And really, the savannah was breathtaking. It had been advertised as reminiscent of the ancient African veldt or the Great American Plains of Old Earth, and judging by vids I had just been shown, this was certainly true. Vast herds of animals roamed freely across the wind-swept pampas, grazing or traveling in slowly-moving processions, each with its own kind. Our guide pointed out the various species and told us how they lived and behaved. Seen from the haven of our transport, from afar or even close-up, most looked innocuous, but our host assured us that this tranquil scene was an illusion, there were many predators about as well as prey.

At the halfway point, we stopped and a meal was served, although by that time most of us had consumed so much in the way of snacks that few had any appetite. However, it was pleasant to find ourselves stationary, privileged to witness this eternal landscape and way of life. It made me feel very small indeed.

"Aren't you even curious?" Captain Sanderson was asking our driver. He was still up front, but now he was standing, his long body leaning, relaxed, against the forward door-lock as he gazed outward. Both men were eating: two of the few people in our vehicle who were taking advantage of AdventureWorld's culinary bounty.

"Wouldn't you give anything to be out there? Feel the sunlight on your face. Smell the grassland? Hear the sounds?" The captain's tone was bantering, yet I sensed real intensity beneath his breezy façade.

"Not me. Too many things out there that might decide I'd make a tasty snack – and I'd much rather be the one doing the snacking." Grinning, the driver took a hearty bite of his energy bar.

"What makes you think they'd be interested in alien protein?"

"You never know, Captain – and I for one am not willing to take the experimental approach to finding out. Besides, even the supposedly peaceful ones can be quite dangerous if they get upset."

"You've honestly never wanted to go outside?"

"Never."

"Does anyone go out?"

"Some guys do: daredevil types who sneak out just to impress their girlfriends and prove they're macho."

"Oh, Corrie, will you look at that!" the Pink Lady enthused, her shrill voice carrying over the general buzz of conversation.

Everyone fell silent as two dozen or more tremendous beasts hove into view, breasting over a steep rise in the terrain which had not been readily apparent from our vantage point. They plodded steadily along, more or less parallel to our position, as if they had some definite goal in mind, and the closer they came, the more awesome they appeared.

Their skins were a pale dun color mottled with dark grey patches. Their rear legs rivaled the columns that support the grand portico of Caliban's Opera House, and because their front legs were so very much shorter, they walked with an odd lurching gait, as if they might pitch over onto their blunt noses if they attempted to move too quickly. A long bony ridge protruded above thick mobile lips, sweeping upward past the eyes to form a flaring crest that terminated several feet above the crown of the head. Splashed with red, yellow, orange and iridescent blue-green, the crests were a riot of gaudy color on an otherwise somber animal.

"Well, what do you know!" our guide said in a hushed voice as he thumbed on his microphone. "Believe me, you're some lucky folks: we don't see these critters every day."

"What are they?" the Pink Lady immediately piped up. "They weren't mentioned in the travelogue."

He turned to her with a smile. "No, they wouldn't be. In fact, they're so shy, many of our staff xenobiologists have never so much as caught a glimpse of one in the flesh. As for what they are: well, they have some sort of fancy scientific name, but we guides call them Honkers – and if you wait just a couple of minutes, you'll probably find out why."

The words were barely out of his mouth when the strangest, most eerie sound filled the air. It began as a vibration so deep that it was more of a physical sensation than actual sound, shaking the floor beneath our feet. Then it swooped upward in pitch, from bassoon, to oboe, to flute range – and then impossibly higher, until my teeth felt as if they were rattling in their sockets. Abruptly, mercifully, the noise cut off, only to be followed a heartbeat later by second blast.

"Usually it's the males who honk," our driver informed us as the last echoes died away. "We think it's some sort of territorial warning – something like: 'Keep away from my harem if you know what's good for you!' They make that sound by forcing air through passages in their crests. The males also use their crests to attract females, and for fighting – shoving matches mostly. No one's ever heard a female honk, even though they have all the right equipment, but they *are* very protective of their young."

"Are those the babies?" one of the other passengers asked, pointing. "They're awfully big."

"That's right: the ones in the center. Whenever they travel, the adults escort them there, for their safety we presume, although as far as anyone knows they have no natural enemies."

The Honkers slowly drifted to a halt and several of them lowered their heads and began to graze.

"Now if you folks will excuse me, I've got work to do," our driver announced. "It's time to check in and get a fix on our next heading. Enjoy the Honkers. We'll be moving out in about five minutes."

That was good news. I hoped we would be on our way long before the male was inspired to do any more serenading.

"Oh look, Corrie!" the Pink Lady cooed. She had abandoned her seat and now stood on our side of the transport. "Isn't it adorable?"

She was referring to the smallest Honker, which had left the herd and was meandering, apparently aimlessly, in our direction, every so often glancing backward over one shoulder as if expecting a parental recall. And youngster though it was, its eyes would have been on a level with mine, had I been standing up in the transport: eyes that were full of curiosity and a disconcerting gleam of alien intelligence.

Passengers crowded the aisle and there was an excited babble of conversation while everyone admired the baby Honker.

"That's weird," the driver muttered from the cockpit. "Really weird." He spoke so quietly that I wouldn't have heard him if I'd been sitting even one row further back.

"Is there a problem?" Captain Sanderson immediately asked, coming to stand beside him. His voice was low and carefully neutral.

"I'm not sure. I've been trying to uplink with the nav-sat system, but I'm not getting any response."

"Are you sure you're keyed in correctly?"

"I've checked three times. The system isn't responding – it's almost as if the satellites and the Net don't exist."

Both men lowered their voices, and I leaned forward, straining to hear.

"Any idea what could be causing the trouble?" Captain Sanderson was asking.

"No. But what I do know is that we aren't going anywhere until I can download our next heading."

"Can't we backtrack?"

Glancing briefly up from his console, his face drawn in a worried frown, the driver shook his head. "I've lost that too."

"Do you think it's the system or your equipment?"

"Don't know. I'm running a diagnostic."

"Oooh!" Exclamations and delighted laughter erupted from my fellow passengers.

The baby Honker had at last reached our vehicle and was cautiously snuffling the siding with its rubbery nose. Apparently satisfied that we merited further investigation, it rose on its hind legs and began running its delicate lips and tongue across the transparent canopy.

Momentarily distracted by its antics, I watched as, absorbed in its tactile explorations, our alien visitor traveled the entire length of the vehicle. Rounding the blunt rear end, it continued up the far side – only now it was shielded from its own kind, although its every movement was eagerly observed by its human admirers.

A sudden blast of sound made me cower in my seat, reflexively jamming both hands over my ears in self-defense as I glanced out the window.

There was a surge of movement within the Honker herd as a lone figure and then a second, larger one detached themselves from the others. Together they came hurtling towards us at incredible speed.

"Get down!" the driver yelled. "And strap yourselves in!"

Pandemonium reigned as people threw themselves into the nearest seats, vacant or otherwise. The transport rose, shuddering, on its curtain of air and then lurched drunkenly forward as the driver slammed it into gear.

Something struck us amidships like a battering ram. A blizzard of unsecured missiles – bodies, refreshments, and robo-servers went flying as our vehicle rolled over on its side with a sickening crack like the sound of a giant eggshell breaking. But by some miracle, its structural integrity otherwise held.

Another blow, this time accompanied by human screams that rivaled the Honker's enraged bellows in intensity, and the transport skidded sideways, rolling halfway over onto its back before returning to its former position.

It was all over in a matter of seconds: the male Honker lowered its enormous head and bashed us one final time for good measure before collecting his skittish female and their meekly-submissive offspring, and escorting them from the battlefield.

In the comparative silence that followed, I took stock.

TiAnn and I were among the lucky ones: since we had never left our seats, our safety harnesses still held us in place with our legs dangling awkwardly, mid-air.

Many others weren't so fortunate. I caught glimpses of arms and legs sprawled every-which-way across what used to be the opposite wall of the transport but was now the floor. And that 'floor' was chaotic: personal belongings were haphazardly strewn about interspersed with food, feebly struggling robo-servers, broken crockery, and trash. There were muffled groans and whimpers as people began to stir among the wreckage.

"Stay calm, everyone," Captain Sanderson's voice cut through the babble. "No need to panic. Is anyone hurt?" Levering himself out of his front row seat, he glanced around, assessing the situation, and then quickly made his way over to our driver.

I released my own safety harness, dropping down to what was now the floor.

The driver had apparently been struck on the head by a heavy piece of luggage that someone had stowed in the overhead racks. The captain knelt, gently checking the pulse in his neck.

At his touch, the young man's eyes fluttered open. "What…?" he grated out.

"Honker smashed us up pretty good." This was said in a matter-of-fact voice. "Knocked us over onto our side."

"Oh, shit – the communications equipment!"

"No – don't try to sit up. You need to stay down."

"But I've got to…"

"You don't have to do anything. Assuming the worst – that we can't use the comm link – does this vehicle have an emergency beacon?"

The driver started to nod, then winced. "Sure. It should have been activated when we got hit, but you may have to turn it on manually. I think I'm feeling well enough to get up and…"

"Not so fast, pal." The captain put a restraining hand on his shoulder. "You stay right there. Just tell me what to look for, and I'll check it out."

"But what if you can't…?"

"Hey, I have my own personal transmitter that the Space Guild insists all their personnel carry. So I promise you, someone will come looking for us before long… And in the meantime, don't worry: I'll take care of everything. All you have to do is tell me where the beacon and the med kit are."

"Well, at this point, it's not as if we need a driver," TiAnn commented, cautiously levering herself out of her seat and coming to stand beside me, while the captain was still rummaging through the debris in the driver's cockpit. "If you ask me, it doesn't look like this thing is going anywhere any time in the near future."

The captain immediately looked up. "Keep that thought to yourself," he bit out. "No point in frightening the others." Standing, he surveyed the scene, his lips compressed in a grim line. "Has anyone here had first-aid training?" he asked, raising his voice over the increasing tumult.

"I have." I fervently hoped that it was someone else, and not me, who had volunteered this information.

"Good." He handed me the med kit. "Follow me." Then turning back to TiAnn: "Keep an eye on the driver."

Boot soles crunching on refuse, he preceded me down the length of the transport.

Those who had been standing and were unable to find seats were the worst-off. Some had suffered only minor cuts and bruises, but a number of others had more serious injuries, and the Pink Lady's partner Corrie was by far the most badly hurt, with a horribly twisted right arm. The Pink Lady herself stood beside her companion, howling inconsolably.

"Get me a blanket," the captain snapped, pointing an authoritative finger at her.

Her howl cut off, mid-crescendo.

"Excellent," he said as she complied like a sleepwalker. "Now hold this." Snatching the med kit from me, he shoved it into her hands, exchanging it for the proffered blanket as he squatted down beside Corrie, whose lips were turning an unnatural blue. "Go through that kit and hand me anything that has 'anesthetic' printed on it."

I had to look away when the captain began examining Corrie's arm. With remarkable skill, he first anesthetized his patient, then went to work improvising a splint to immobilize what looked, even to my untrained eyes, like severe multiple fractures. As soon as the medication had started to take effect, he dispatched me, Pink Lady in tow, with the remainder of the medical supplies to tend to the other victims, instructing me to advise him if anyone else had been seriously injured.

Fortunately, my limited training was sufficient for the task and the Pink Lady, given something constructive to do, proved to be an adequate assistant. By the time we returned to him, the captain had finished working on his patient.

One look at her injured companion, and the Pink Lady began to whimper again.

Captain Sanderson stood up. "That won't help Corrie," he said firmly, placing both hands on her shoulders and turning her around so she had to face him. "And he definitely needs your help."

"But what can I do?" Teardrops hung, glittering, on her eyelashes and her full lips trembled. "He's unconscious."

Putting an arm around her broad shoulders, he said quite gently, "That doesn't matter. He still needs you...You never told me your name."

"Betana."

"Corrie still needs you, Betana. You'd be surprised what people can hear, even when they're unconscious... So I want you to sit down and talk to him. He needs to know you're here. And you can take this cloth and water bottle," placing both items in her hands, "and wet his lips whenever they seem dry. If he starts to wake up, or if you need me for any reason, just have someone come get me. I'm going up front now to check on the driver."

I trailed after him, still clutching what was left of the med kit, stopping whenever he paused to offer calm reassurance to those who seemed to require it.

TiAnn watched us approach. Slumped below our former seats, it was impossible to assess her mood.

"Get up," the captain told her without preamble. "I want you to go around and take stock of our supplies. Organize the food and any bedding you can find. Get the able-bodied passengers to help. Make sure everyone has something to do and that people are comfortable. We may be here for quite a while." Without waiting for her answer, he turned aside and focused his attention on the injured driver.

***

Outside our transport, shadows were lengthening as evening approached. Over the next few hours, Captain Sanderson alternately chatted with the driver, making sure he remained prone and awake, and made the rounds, leaving me in charge of the young man while he assured the other passengers that help was on the way.

By the time our rescuers arrived, I'm sure there wasn't one single person in our transport who wasn't as impressed and grateful as I was for his steady presence.

6.

After our experience on Arcadia, it was hardly surprising that both my sister and I lost our taste for sightseeing. And not long afterward, there came a day when we were finally outward-bound, heading away from the Hub and towards Caliban. Stopovers were fewer and farther between, and I found myself with more and more time on my hands and less and less to do. I became increasingly restless, and was only able to quell my inner demons by devoting long hours to practicing my guitar, or attending some of the many the musical offerings that Andebar's Journeymen and Journeywomen regularly provided in the ship's luxurious lounges.

Of course, if I so desired, there were the usual social functions to attend, the same boring cocktail party conversations, the same opportunities to make superficial contact with people I would never see again – but this was even less appealing to me than they had been before Arcadia.

At this point, Captain Sanderson seemed to be deeply involved in his duties. I seldom saw him at gatherings, although now I might actually have enjoyed talking with him. Yet somehow his absence seemed appropriate: we were nearing the end of our journey – and I too was quite preoccupied, wondering how I was going to react to seeing my father again.

Then, a little more than a day out from Caliban, our monotonous shipboard routine was interrupted by an extraordinary incident…

TiAnn and I had been gradually adjusting our schedules to coincide with Caliban standard time, and on that particular 'evening' we were in our cabin getting ready for bed, slowly undressing as we compared notes about what was the first thing each of us wanted to do when we reached home. She had friends she was anxious to contact, and I told her I wanted to take in as many cultural and musical events as I possibly could.

She had just begun describing the new Performing Arts Center, which had been constructed during my absence, and I was asking if she knew if anything of particular interest was scheduled to take place there during my visit, when our conversation was rudely interrupted.

Without any warning whatsoever, the ship took a sudden sickening lurch and the floor seemed to skitter sideways and drop out from beneath my feet. Moments later, before I could fully recover either my wits or my balance, the ship staggered a second time, and I was thrown to the deck.

In the same instant, a red light on our comm unit began flashing, and somewhere down the corridor a siren came to life, its shrill ululation immediately blotting out any possibility of rational thought.

"Attention, all passengers!" a harsh young voice barked over the inter-ship comm link in rising counterpoint to the sonic chaos in the hallway. "Attention!"

Shaking my head to clear it, I glanced up at TiAnn, who was lying in a crumpled heap on her bunk, her face chalk-white.

"Lieutenant-Commander Devron Bork here," the voice continued. "This is an emergency! All passengers and off-duty personnel should strap themselves into the nearest bunk or acceleration couch. I repeat: this is an emergency!"

There was an angry buzz of voices in the background. Whatever had just happened seemed to have sent the entire crew into an uproar.

In the eternal-seeming minutes that followed, neither TiAnn nor I said a word – we just remained where we were, staring at each other. I for one was too stunned and frightened to move, in fact I scarcely dared to breathe, afraid of what might be about to happen next.

Out in the corridor, the alarm droned mindlessly on.

"This is Lieutenant-Commander Bork," the voice came back on suddenly. "The flight engineer has asked me to apologize for the shaking up you've just experienced. He reports that we seem to be having some difficulties with nav-con that's caused a glitch in our grav-gen system. The captain should be in the control room at any moment to... Oh, Captain!" The young man's voice cracked with emotion and relief.

"Thank you, Mr. Bork." The familiar voice sounded cool and in control. "Shut that damn thing off!"

Mercifully, the mind-numbing racket in the hall outside came to an abrupt end.

Captain Sanderson resumed: "Ladies and gentlemen, I'm terribly sorry you've been subjected to this unpleasantness. We seem to have run into a bit of sub-light interference back there – perhaps we hit the wake of some other starship coming out of hyperspace. I'm sure you'll be relieved to hear that we're not expecting a repeat performance. However, for your own safety I'm asking you to remain where you are, and to stay strapped in for just a little while longer. Be sure to call the sick bay if you or anyone you know of is injured. I'll be back with a status report as soon as I have something more definite to report. Sanderson out..."

The comm link gave a faint click but failed to shut off completely – instead it continued to hum with background noise: the uneasy hubbub of agitated crewmen and women all talking at once.

I crawled up onto TiAnn's bunk.

"Are you okay?" was her anxious question.

"I think so. Are you?"

Before she could answer, we were interrupted by Captain Sanderson's voice, speaking with quiet intensity and completely unguarded.

"All right, Devron: report. What the hell happened back there?"

"I-I'm not sure, sir. No one saw anything beforehand, but the recording of the shock wave looks like it may have been an explosion – it's almost as if we hit something solid."

"Prel?"

"Yes, Captain."

"You were on the scope back there. Is that how you read it?"

The Soolian started to reply, but we never heard his answer.

"What the hell! Who left the bloody comm on? Devron, that was your respon—"

The comm link suddenly went dead.

Twenty minutes later, the captain came back on to release us from our confinement, and to explain that the mystery had been solved: apparently the navigator had miscalculated slightly coming out of our last jump sequence, and this in turn had caused us to run over one of the navigation buoys that mark the approach to the Caliban Sector.

He was apologetic and really quite convincing – and I felt nothing but admiration for his bland, easy lies. I knew that no guild navigator who was licensed to fly a starship would ever make a mistake like that. Furthermore, if we had run over a navigation buoy, then we must have run over two of them.

No one else I talked to then or later seemed to be the least bit suspicious of the captain's explanation, and I refrained from voicing my misgivings to TiAnn, who had taken a heavy-duty tranquilizer and gone straight to bed.

***

Sunlight reflecting off the water below caused the shuttle window beside me to go partially opaque.

Caliban!

There was a tightness in my chest, and I realized only then that I had never really intended to ever return home. However, it was far too late to turn back now. Already I could see the shoreline and the spaceport on the outskirts of distant Sycorax City. The water rushing past below us was the purest of blues: as pure and deep as the sky. The beaches were silver, the grass and foliage were the freshest of greens. And beyond, shining like an earthbound star, its fairy-tale towers festooned with aerial walkways as fleets of sky-taxies darted between the buildings, Sycorax City was an enchanting sight.

"Ah, Caliban, jewel of the pleasure worlds." I sighed.

"What was that?" TiAnn asked.

"Never mind. I was just thinking out loud."

She regarded me quizzically, but didn't press the issue.

I glanced back out at the view, and then forward towards the cockpit where Captain Sanderson was once again at the helm. What kind of starship captain was he, I wondered, that he spent so much of his spare time flying shuttles?

Realizing that this would be my last chance to watch him at work, I settled back in my seat to enjoy the experience – but thoughts of my impending reunion with my father kept intruding.

What could I possibly say to him?

And what would he say to me?

The flight was over all too quickly, and soon we were releasing our safety harnesses and standing up to leave. Moments later, I was following

TiAnn down the aisle, past the captain, who was talking to the co-pilot, and out onto the extensible bridge that linked the shuttle to the terminal.

"Sera Trellarian?" Although I hadn't been aware of it, he must have been right behind me as I stepped from the shuttle.

"Welcome to Caliban, Captain Sanderson," I said without much enthusiasm, for I was in no mood for pleasantries. But then it suddenly occurred to me that he might in fact be useful, if only as a distraction from my bleak thoughts. I forced a smile and teased, "Are you here for another tour?"

"May I walk in with you?" he asked, dodging my question.

"Of course."

Matching his stride to mine, he accompanied me across the bridge. I was peripherally aware of the graceful spires of the city beyond the terminal, and without consciously looking for them, I also located the government buildings and our family residence, Government House. It was strange but also achingly familiar to breathe once again the fresh sea-scented air of my home world. I squinted against the hot, summery glare and blindingly blue sky. If I chose to look for him, I knew that I would probably see my father waiting for us at the arrival gate.

Instead, I turned to the captain. "Are you planning on sight-seeing?" I repeated, determined to concentrate on the immediate present. "I could recommend some interesting places."

"Well actually I was hoping…" he began.

"Father!" TiAnn called out. Several steps in front of us, she was waving eagerly. "Over here!"

"TiAnn!" a deep, familiar voice answered. "Janne!"

And I had to look.

There he was: my father, Prime Minister Arram Trellerian of Caliban. With a pang that I had not expected to feel, I noticed how his dark hair appeared much lighter now, streaked with grey. His beard and mustache had gone all silvery too, but he still looked strong – very strong.

"Father," I said, as we joined him, my voice disconcertingly husky. "It's good to see you."

"You've been away far too long," he said, embracing me. Did I detect a quiver in his voice? "But who is this: a friend?"

Belatedly, I realized that the captain was still there, patiently observing our reunion, and I knew that I was blushing. How dare he meddle in my family's business?

But the next moment I felt a flood of relief. Here was something safe to talk about: a distraction to grab onto.

I introduced the two men.

"Captain of the *Solar Eclipse*," my father mused. "Weren't you involved in that beacon incident?"

"Yes, sir – I was."

"Then I suppose I should thank you for bringing my girls home safely. By the way, what exactly *did* happen out there?"

The captain's intense blue eyes shifted uneasily from me to my sister, and then back again. He cleared his throat but didn't speak.

"Oh, come now!" my father cajoled. "Surely you're not reluctant to talk in front of my daughters?"

"Excuse me, sir – I'm not sure this is the appropriate place to…"

"Of course," my father interrupted. "You're quite right: no need to discuss it here. Would it be convenient for you to accompany us back to Government House? We can talk there."

"Thank you, sir. I'd be pleased to do that."

My father turned to us. "Very well, girls. Let's go claim your luggage. Our transport is waiting."

"I'm not going home," I blurted out, astonishing even myself.

"Not going…?" he began, and then his expression hardened when he realized what I meant. "Oh, Janne, not that again! Still the same old argument – after all these years?"

I glared at him, my jaw clenched tight, biting back an angry retort.

"Is there a problem?" Captain Sanderson asked, his face carefully neutral.

"Janne, you're impossible!" TiAnn spat out, her voice shrill with annoyance. "Now I suppose you're going to start in about the Tourist Center."

"Tourist Center?"

"Yes," I told the captain with icy calm. "You see, the government – my father – has always believed that it's a good idea for everyone…"

"Not everyone!" my father protested, but I went on as if he hadn't spoken.

"…For everyone who arrives on Caliban to be delayed at the Center for some period of time while their credentials are checked out."

"Janne, I'm sure Captain Sanderson isn't interested in hearing about this," my father interjected.

"Well, he should be! According to Caliban law – the law *you* sponsored – he's supposed to be detained there too."

"Nonsense! You know the Tourist Center is a mere formality, and that more stringent measures are only applied when necessary. The Tourist Center is a pleasant place – not a prison."

"Tell that to someone who's being incarcerated there!"

My father chose to ignore this incendiary remark. Rather, he said, "Of course I'm not going to have Captain Sanderson detained, Janne. Nor you either." Suddenly, he sounded very tired.

"But, Father, I'm no longer a resident of Caliban: I'm an expatriate. Surely that makes my motives for returning all the more suspect."

"Stop acting like a spoiled child and come home!" he snapped.

"I'll join you there later – after I've served my time!" I picked up my guitar and travel pack. I hadn't known that I was actually going to go through with it until the words were out of my mouth, but by then it was far too late to undo the damage. My stomach churning with anger and embarrassment, I entered the long line of visitors who were waiting to board the transport that would take us to the Tourist Center.

No one tried to stop me.

***

An hour later, I stood alone in the middle of the small cubicle which the State had assigned me, thinking how different this room was from my cell on University VII – and also how similar. Some thoughtful person had placed several scenic holos and a small vase of flowers on the simple gray cube that served as a table in an effort to make the room seem a bit less sterile.

My thoughts turned to my father, recalling the tired lines that creased his face and his graying hair. And suddenly I felt so alone.

Why, oh why had I behaved so badly at the spaceport?

Choking back a sob, I reached for my guitar, hoping to find solace in my music. It had always helped before.

Sometime later, my door panel chimed. Rising, I went to answer, not really aware that I was holding my breath, hoping against hope that it was my father, come to make peace with me. But to my dismay it was that pesky captain!

"What do you want?" I asked, not caring in the least how ungracious I sounded. And then I turned quickly aside to hide my tears.

"Was that you playing?" He remained standing in the doorway, his military cap in his hands. "It was beautiful."

I took a surreptitious swipe at my damp cheek. "Did my father send you here to convince me to come home?"

He laughed. "Not a chance! Your father says you're every bit as stubborn as he is, and there's no point in trying to talk you out of something once you've made up your mind to do it. And I was able to assure him that I know from firsthand experience how right he is."

I looked down at the floor, struggling to hide my embarrassed blush.

"Very well, Captain Sanderson, you may as well come in and tell me why you're here," I said, once I had recovered my composure. "I doubt it's because you were anxious to hear me play my guitar."

Still he hesitated, standing awkwardly in the doorway, twisting his cap in his hands. Despite his height, he suddenly looked like a young boy who suspects he's about to receive a thorough scolding.

"I promise I'll be on my good behavior." I offered him my most disarming smile. "*Now* will you come in?"

He didn't budge. "Yes, well umm… It's just that I uh… Well, I was wondering if you might, you know, be interested in…" His voice trailed off.

"Interested in…?" I prompted.

"In going out somewhere this evening," he mumbled, keeping his eyes averted. For someone who was usually so poised and in control, he seemed remarkably flustered.

In spite of myself, I was intrigued. "With you." It came out as something between a statement and a question.

"Well, yes. That was the general idea."

"I see…" The next moment, I astonished myself by replying, "Certainly. Why not?"

Our eyes met, and I caught a look of sheer amazement that flashed across his face before he could smother it. Then, with a laugh, he strode into the room and took possession of my only chair. "Why not, indeed."

"However, there *is* a slight problem, Captain Sanderson." Drawing what was left of my dignity around me, I came to stand before him.

"I wish you'd call me 'Eirik'," he said rather wistfully.

"Well then, Eirik, there *is* a hitch."

"Which is…?"

"Inmates of the Tourist Center aren't allowed into the city proper until they've received their clearance papers. I might not be free until tomorrow morning."

"Oh, that." He stood up and began rummaging through the pockets of his flightsuit. "No problem. I've already taken care of it." With a flourish, he held out a small, Government Issue slate. "Your official clearance, SeraTrellarian."

"You *did* work it out with my father!"

"I did not!"

I glared at him, daring him to come up with a reasonable alternative explanation.

"In case you don't know it," he flared, "starship captains are quite capable of pulling their own strings!"

He stared me down until I had to take the damn thing from him so he'd stop looking at me like that. Sure enough, my release had been authorized by the local Space Guild representative, and not by my father.

"So, now what?" I demanded rather sourly. "I suppose you have a plan."

"I know it's none of my business, but don't you think you should go home?"

"You're right: it *is* none of your business!"

But suddenly, I didn't feel like fighting with anyone anymore. Striding over to the comm console, I asked to be connected with Government House. Shortly thereafter, my father's face appeared on the holo-screen. He looked haggard, and also quite surprised to see me.

"I'm coming home," I announced without preamble. "I've been cleared."

"So soon?"

"You can thank Captain Sanderson for that."

"I certainly will, the next time I see him."

The captain stepped up to the comm console. "Hello, sir. I'll escort your daughter home now – if she'll allow me to. I've asked her to spend some time with me this evening and she's accepted – with your approval of course. I realize that you haven't had an opportunity to see her yet."

Although his eyebrows shot up another notch, my father quickly regained his composure. "You have my blessing, Captain. Thank you for your help."

"Thanks aren't necessary."

"Nevertheless, I'd like to return the favor. Where were you planning on going?"

Eirik looked over at me.

"I don't know where we should go!" I snapped, feeling my face go hot all over again – unfortunately the captain seemed to have that effect on me – and hating to have to admit it. "As you very well know, I've been away for several years."

"Then may I offer a suggestion?" my father asked, his voice bland, ever the diplomat.

Eirik waited patiently in silence until I gave a nod.

My father recommended a favorite restaurant of his. "My treat. I'd also like to reserve a pair of concert tickets for you: our old friend Cristan Andebar is playing tonight at the Performing Arts Center, Janne. How fortunate that you've come back in time to hear him."

No matter how irritated I might have been by my father's interference, he knew as well as I did that I would never pass up any opportunity to hear Andebar play.

Saying that he would make all the necessary arrangements, my father cheerfully signed off.

And thus my fate was sealed.

Eirik called a sky taxi, and on the way to Government House, he said that he would pick me up there later that evening. In the meantime, he told me, he had to return to guild headquarters to file an official report concerning our 'incident'.

By the time the taxi touched down on the Government House grounds, I was fuming. I cursed myself for my moment of weakness, hating the captain for having talked me out of my resolve to remain at the Tourist Center, hating my father for organizing my evening with the captain, and hating myself for having accepted the captain's invitation in the first place.

I was sure it was going to be a miserable evening.

7.

I had intended to go straight home, soak in a long hot bath, and unpack afterwards. However, by the time I arrived at Government House, I was far too agitated to do anything more constructive than pace around my room, haphazardly taking things out of my travel pack while I struggled to sort out my feelings about Eirik Sanderson.

There was no doubt about it: he was an attractive man, and the attraction wasn't just physical. Yet I hated to admit that I was susceptible to his charms. Other women would not have had such a conflict, I was sure.

Handsome, charismatic, and a Space Guild captain! I scoffed. *What more could anyone ask? He must have women throwing themselves at him wherever he goes!*

And that being the case, why was he interested in me? In his presence, I had frequently been childish and downright rude: not the kind of behavior that would ordinarily inspire a man to pursue a woman. In fact, his reaction should have been exactly the opposite – and that made me question both his taste *and* his motives.

Preoccupied with my thoughts, I happened to glance over at my reflection, which was mirrored in my dressing room doors. What I saw was a tall, rather pale woman whose figure was a little too full for my taste.

Too much sitting around all day in a cubicle, I chided myself.

Reaching up, I fingered the thick cascade of red-brown curls that fell almost to my waist – this was definitely my best asset, I decided. Otherwise, in my opinion there was nothing particularly unusual or striking in what I saw. I doubted that the captain was after me for my looks.

With a shrug, which my mirror faithfully reproduced, I gave up. If I didn't understand myself, it seemed unlikely that I would be able to figure the captain out, no matter how hard I tried.

***

After a brief, restorative shower, I was surprised to discover that I felt remarkably calm and ready to take on whatever the evening – and Eirik Sanderson – might have in store for me.

Four years earlier, I had left almost all of my formal wear behind on Caliban on the assumption that I wouldn't be attending any state dinners on University VII. As a result, I actually had more of a choice of things to wear here than I did where I now lived. Selecting a gown that suited my mood – an unsettling mixture of anticipation and dread – was a challenge, and I lingered over my toilette, considering the various impressions I might wish to create. Which was more appropriate: the low-cut black dress or the virginal white, the warm, sensuous gold or the haughty silver?

I could have gone on playing dress-up indefinitely: it was certainly an entertaining way to avoid facing both reality, Eirik and my father – but at last there came a moment when I knew I had to stop. It was getting late, and my father was probably wondering what had become of me.

It was my father's custom to spend most of his private time in his spacious ground floor study, and this was where I expected to find him. But upon reaching the downstairs hall, I caught a glimpse of someone else: a moderately tall, solidly built person, swathed from head to foot in a long, midnight-black cloak. Even more peculiar, our unknown visitor was striding rapidly away from my father's study, hood up and cape drawn tightly around his body as if to minimize his chances of being recognized. If there had been any shadows, I felt sure he would certainly have joined them, stealthily blending into the surroundings.

Upon arriving at the far end of the corridor, this strange apparition hesitated, and in that instant I caught the barest hint of a profile. But the next moment, whoever it was vanished from sight around the corner.

For several long moments, I stood outside my father's study trying to conjure up elusive connections. There was something tantalizingly familiar about that half-seen face.

At last, failing to reach a conclusion, I approached the door. Unless it had been one of his regular undercover spies, surely my father would be willing to enlighten me.

Chuckling at the absurdity of the idea, I knocked and entered.

"Janne!" My father glanced up, startled – and for the briefest moment, I could have sworn he looked rather guilty. "What a pleasant surprise."

But he couldn't possibly have been any more surprised than I was – for there, leaning forward with both hands on my father's desk as if he had been interrupted in the midst of an urgent declamation, was Captain Eirik Sanderson! At the time of our parting, he had agreed to pick me up before the concert, but it had never occurred to me that he would show up in my father's study.

Somehow I managed to stammer out a greeting.

"We're almost finished here," was my father's far too casual reply. "Just give us another couple of minutes."

Grateful for the reprieve, I beat a hasty retreat to the other end of the room, where I pretended to be engrossed in a holo-map that was projected above his worktable. Yet I was much too rattled to even notice what it represented. Instead I just stood there, struggling to regain my composure. Still, flustered or not, I couldn't resist sneaking a surreptitious peek at the two men.

Actually, it was fascinating to see them together: one middle-aged, compact, and muscular, the other tall, slim, and in his prime. Yet despite their physical differences, there were also definite similarities. Each carried himself with an undeniable air of authority and command; both expressed themselves with forthright confidence, and neither seemed to be deferring to the other as a superior.

I found myself wondering about the captain's personal life: where he had come from and why he had chosen a career in the Space Guild. What experiences had he had with men of power that allowed him to hold his own, apparently totally at ease, with a man like my father? And for that matter, why was he here so early? Was it simply to tell my father about the disturbing incident that had marked our arrival in the Caliban system – but hadn't that particular interview taken place earlier, before Eirik had come to retrieve me from the Tourist Center?

In an unlikely gestalt, my thoughts skipped to my father's mysterious visitor. Was there somehow a connection between this person and Captain Sanderson's report? Once again, I recalled that shadowy profile. I felt more and more certain that this was no stranger.

But before I had time to pursue that intriguing line of thought, the men finished their private conversation and came over to join me.

"You look lovely," Eirik said, regarding me with undisguised admiration.

"Ah, my favorite dress," my father said. "That shade of green really suits you."

"Where I come from, it's our wedding color," Eirik informed us, "the color of life and continuity."

Aware that I was blushing – we redheads are cursed with both a tendency to do so and the inability to hide it – I gave them my best approximation of a smile and changed the subject.

"Father, a few minutes ago I saw someone in the hall outside your study. Did you have a visitor?"

"Well, yes, I…"

"Cristan Andebar!" I cried, finally making the connection. "It *was* Andebar, wasn't it?"

"As a matter of fact, it was."

"What was he doing here?"

His hesitation might have been imperceptible to someone who didn't know him as well as I did. "Janne, you know that Cristan always stays with me when he's performing on Caliban."

"Of course. How could I have forgotten?" But although I didn't voice my doubts, I certainly didn't recall ever having seen him slinking out of Government House like a thief!

"Too bad you didn't join us earlier – he just left for the Performing Arts Center, and unfortunately he won't be back here after the concert tonight. This is his first stop on an extensive tour, and he's on a tight schedule. In fact, he has to leave Caliban almost immediately after he's finished playing. I know he'll be sorry he missed you."

"I'm sorry too. It's ridiculous: I never seem to find time to visit him on university, even though we're practically neighbors."

I turned to Captain Sanderson. "I hope you had a chance to meet him. He's quite a remarkable person."

"Well, yes, I… I did speak with him just now." And then, he too faltered, his eyes shifting rapidly to my father's face, and then back to me. "Actually, I already know him."

"Oh?" Suddenly, it occurred to me that Eirik's excursion to University VII might not have been for the purpose of sightseeing, as he'd pretended on the shuttle. Had he gone there to meet with Andebar, or was I reading more into everyone's actions than was reasonable?

At this point, there was a rather awkward silence.

"Well, I suppose you two must be anxious to get going," my father said at last.

"Whenever Janne's ready."

"I'll call an air taxi," my father hastily suggested.

"That's very thoughtful, sir, but we're really not in that much of a hurry. And since we have plenty of time, I'd rather walk. That is, if it's okay with you, Janne."

"Certainly."

I was pleased to note that in my dress shoes, I no longer had to look up at him, and I felt a sudden surge of anticipation. The next few hours were bound to be a challenge.

***

The early evening air was soft and summery.

"TiAnn says Weather Control has scheduled rain for later tonight," I told Eirik. "Are you sure you wouldn't prefer to take a taxi?"

He laughed. "After all the time I've spent in space, rain will be a pleasure! But are you sure you don't mind?"

I shook my head – and then, on a sudden whim, I vowed to say as little as possible.

Let *him* carry the burden of our conversation!

"You know, I can't remember the last time I had a chance to take an actual walk," he was saying, certainly unaware of my resolve. "Unless you count those sight-seeing tours you and your sister were so fond of booking…"

He sighed. "These days it seems like the only walking I ever get to do is pacing around the control room." He offered me an amused smile. "All I ask is that we don't reach our destination too quickly."

Rather than reply, I led him through our formal gardens and out of the government compound. When we reached the city proper, my only remark was to ask if he'd like to continue on at street level, or would he prefer to take in the view from the aerial walkways?

"Definitely the walkways," was his immediate response.

It was the best time of day to take the Aerial. From our vantage point, high above Sycorax City, we could see all the way out to the ocean where smoky-pink clouds marked the setting sun. Air taxies zipped past, close enough for us to catch the occasional glimpse of well-dressed passengers, while below our walkway, lights were coming on here and there like earthbound stars. We swooped down towards them, and then back up again as the slidewalks carried us along.

"Caliban certainly deserves its reputation as one of the most beautiful planets in the Concorde Alliance," Eirik said after a while. "Did I mention that this is my first time here? It's hard to believe that in all my years of guild service I've never had a chance to visit."

He said nothing more until we were back at street level. "Unless I'm mistaken, we ought to head over that way." He gestured in the general direction of the central plaza.

When we began walking again, I found myself wondering if my silence bothered him – or for that matter, if he even noticed it.

"This is good," he said presently, and I wasn't sure whether he was referring to our walk, the beauty of the city, or our being there together. Perhaps it was all three.

"I'm glad you like to walk," he went on. "At home it's the most common way of getting around – air sleds and riding beasts are mainly used by invalids, for hauling loads, or if we need to get somewhere in a hurry." He glanced over at me. "I don't suppose you've heard of Valhalla?"

"Valhalla!" I exclaimed, startled into breaking my vow of silence. "Isn't that way out on the Fringe?"

"Yes: Valhalla is a Fringe planet. In fact, it's so remote that, unlike Caliban, we hardly ever get any tourists. Our only distinction is that we were originally settled by colonists who believed they could trace their ancestry all the way back to the Scandinavian Alliance on Earth. I suppose it's just a backward little place, but sometimes I miss it terribly."

"Have you been away long?"

"Eight years."

"You haven't ever gone back?"

"No."

"Why not?"

He shrugged. "Stubborn pride, I guess. The same reason you went off to the Tourist Center this morning."

To cover my embarrassment, I quickly asked, "What's it like? Valhalla, I mean."

"Green. Valhalla is mostly forest – at least the part where my family lives is mostly forest. I bet you didn't know that you're out walking with the last Thane of Hawkness."

"Thane? Of Hawkness?" One look at his face and I could see that even the mention of it was painful. "What's that?"

"Hawkness is the home of my ancestors. It used to be mine too…"His voice trailed off.

To keep the conversation going, I told him that I thought I remembered reading about Valhalla when I'd studied galactic history. "Your form of government is supposed to be quite ancient, isn't it?"

"So they say. According to the records, when the first colonists arrived, they divided the planet up into holdings, something like the way historians think they were organized in Old Scandinavia. They even used some of the same names: Reykjavik, Oslo, Uppsala, Trondheim." The lilting syllables rolled pleasantly off his tongue, as if he was savoring their taste. "But they added new ones too: Hawkness, for example."

"I like the sound of that," I told him: as non-committal a remark as I could think of – anything to keep him talking.

"We have a feudal sort of arrangement, with what we call a *Hövding* – you might call him a chieftain or high lord – over everyone, and Thanes to run each major estate, and people who work the land. But it isn't exactly like ancient Scandinavia either, because estate-holders have a great many obligations towards the others and can't do absolutely anything they please…

"The power of the *Hövding* is the most arbitrary," he continued. "He *can* do just about anything he wants – and to anyone. Only common sense restrains him – and there have certainly been *Hövdings* who lacked common sense! My Uncle Einarr, our current *Hövding*, for one."

He was silent and brooding for several moments.

"And Hawkness?" I prompted.

58

"My family has lived at Hawkness for fifteen hundred years. At the time of my father's death, I became Thane." Without seeming to be aware that he was doing so, he fingered the intricate black necklace of twining dragons that encircled his throat. "And now that I've left, our line will finally end."

"Why did you leave?"

"Wait!" Taking my arm, he turned me aside into a less busy street. "I think it's down here."

"But this isn't the way to the Performing Arts Center."

"I didn't want your father to plan our *entire* evening." And now his tone was bantering. "So I did some research on my own, and found out about a nice cafe where we can sit and have a drink before the concert."

The search that followed put an end to our discussion, but eventually we came to a small establishment that hadn't existed when I'd last lived in the City.

I had hoped Eirik would continue his story, but once we were seated and had placed our orders with a robo-server, we were suddenly awkward again. Our eyes met for one brief instant and then both of us looked quickly away. Unfortunately, it seemed as if it was easier for us to communicate while we were on our feet. As our drinks arrived, I searched my mind for something to carry us through our impasse.

"You didn't answer my question," I reminded him at last.

"Which was?"

"I asked why you left Valhalla."

"Oh. Yes." He stared into his glass as if expecting to find the answer there. "Personal reasons."

"I'm sorry, Eirik! I didn't mean to pry."

He looked up quickly. "I didn't think you were. I was just trying to find the right words."

"If you'd rather not talk about it…"

"My personal reasons?" he mused, ignoring my offer of a reprieve. He sighed. "Well… Before I left home, when I was still a young man and really quite green, I was living with my *kjæresta*: my childhood sweetheart. She died unexpectedly." This was delivered in a matter-of-fact voice. "After that, there didn't seem to be much reason to stay, so I left Valhalla and joined the Space Guild."

"I'm so sorry," I repeated.

"Don't be. It's no longer important."

We sipped our drinks in silence.

When he finally spoke again, his voice was harsh. "I suppose there are some who would say that I ran away – I'm sure there are many back home who think so." His eyes, when they met mine, were a stormy blue-grey. "And why not? It's probably true."

"Eirik, please don't! I didn't mean for you to…"

"It's okay." As he said this, the pinched lines around his eyes and mouth eased. "Somehow I don't mind talking about it tonight. Not with you. There really hasn't been anyone to tell…

"You see, we Valhallans believe that each of us is destined to find the person who is our *kjæresta* or *kjæreste* – how would you say it? – our soulmate for life. And once this happens, after a time of living together, the couple has children to ensure that their families will go on. We also believe that there is seldom more than one *kjæresta* or *kjæreste* for any person – which means that a lost lover is almost irreplaceable… So what reason did I have to stay? I had no children to carry on after me, and I myself had become a sort of untouchable."

"That's ridiculous! Similar things must have happened to other people. You can't be the first Valhallan to lose a lover."

"No, not the first. But we're very strict about limiting each pair to having only two children in order to keep our population small. And there's very little disease among Valhallans, so such a loss is quite uncommon: even the *Hövding* might have a difficult time finding another partner if he lost his *kjæresta*. Besides, there was no one else I wanted."

"So you left home. Funny: in a way what happened to you isn't so different from what happened to me…"

But I didn't wish to pursue that particular subject, and since it was nearly time for the concert to begin, I suggested that we finish our drinks and leave.

***

The Director of the Music School is a brilliant musician. My father, who calls him friend, says that Cristan Andebar has the black heart of a scoundrel – but Director Andebar has been my idol since childhood. In fact, he's the reason I fell in love with music. And that love has never failed me, even during my most difficult times.

When Andebar performs, he often gives part of his recital on the ancient instrument called the guitar and it's no coincidence that I too own one. The night Eirik and I heard him, he devoted the entire first half of his concert to guitar music, playing first solo, and later with several of his talented Music School Journeymen, much like those I had encountered in my starship travels, in an ensemble. The second half was performed on the synth.

At the beginning of the concert, Director Andebar walked out onto the stage dressed in black, as always. He thanked the audience for coming to hear him and mentioned that he was honored by the presence of several close personal friends.

My father, who was seated in the front row with his entourage, stood up and bowed graciously: first to the director and then to the audience.

When the applause died down, Andebar spoke again. Since this was a special occasion, he said, he would like to present a special program. Briefly, he went on to describe the guitar's origin on Earth and before each piece, he told us something about its composer and unique qualities.

Early in his career, my father says, the director was frequently criticized for the informality of his concerts: for talking to the audience as though he was having a private chat with one of his students, and for changing his program as he went along in response to his own mood and audience reaction.

But that was long ago. Nowadays, no one dares to criticize Director Andebar about much of anything. He has long since earned the awe and respect, and in some circles perhaps even the fear, of the public and music lovers alike. In fact, he has become a living legend.

Besides, my father says that the director has so many students, graduates, Journeymen and Journeywomen scattered throughout the Concorde that even a whispered word about him is sure to eventually reach his ever-alert ears – and perhaps that's part of his mystique.

That night, although Andebar performed brilliantly as always, I was less attentive than I would normally have been. Even while he was playing, my thoughts kept returning to the tantalizing bits of personal information that Eirik had divulged. In spite of my reluctance to get involved with him, or for that matter with anyone else, I wanted to know more.

After the final curtain, by mutual agreement, we decided to skip the crowded post-concert reception in the Performing Arts Center's Green Room although I knew that both Andebar and my father would have welcomed us. Instead, after hailing an air taxi, we were soon speeding across Sycorax City, heading for a late supper at my father's favorite restaurant.

On the way there, neither of us had much to say – and that mostly concerning Andebar's impressive talent. And no sooner had we touched down in the tasteful entry courtyard, than the maître d' hurried forward to greet us effusively. Within minutes, our obsequious host was escorting us to a cozy nook with a wonderful view of City Park and the Bay.

"Your father's favorite table," we were proudly informed.

Even after the fellow had left us in peace, we continued to chat about the concert. It seemed the safest topic.

"I'm really glad you enjoyed the music," I said. "Director Andebar is someone I've always admired. He and my father have been friends for years."

"I really can't understand why you and your father have such difficulties with each other. You're lucky to have him," Eirik suddenly blurted out, and then his face flushed red. "Excuse me – I apologize. I know it's none of my business."

"It's okay." I offered him a rueful grin. "You'd have to be blind not to notice."

"Then you're not angry with me?"

"I've been really awful ever since we met, haven't I?"

"Well..."

"It's okay. I know I have..."

And then the words came pouring out. "But Eirik, please try to understand... The whole time I've known you, I've been on my way back to Caliban – and you have no idea how nervous that's made me... My father and Caliban: there's so much hurt and anger inside me about both of them that I haven't really been in control of my feelings ever since I left University."

"I suppose I'd feel the same way if I was returning to Valhalla." He offered me a sympathetic smile.

Just then the waiter – since this was an exclusive restaurant, it boasted actual human servers – arrived with our food – but I scarcely noticed. At that moment, it seemed vitally important to say something that would make Eirik think better of me: something that would prove to him that I wasn't the spoiled, temperamental Prima Donna he must surely believe I was.

"What you told me about yourself earlier…" I said, as soon as our waiter had retired, "I understand – better than you know… You said you were living with someone – well, so was I, although he certainly wasn't any sweetheart, childhood or otherwise! And I'm sure you know what I'm talking about when I say that being the oldest daughter of the Prime Minister of Caliban carries with it certain obligations."

"I can even tell you what they are," he said, his lips compressed in a grim line as he ticked the points off on his fingers: "To marry well – to produce the requisite number of offspring – to behave responsibly and set a good example for others… Oh yes, I'm quite familiar with all of that."

"Exactly. So when I was eighteen, my father arranged a marriage: I was offered to the eldest son of one of Caliban's most prominent families. I suppose I should give my father credit for that – at least he didn't ship me off to some godforsaken backwater planet. Instead, he used me to cement a local political alliance…

"The only problem was that the young man in question was a beast: vain, vulgar, stupid, and incredibly cruel. Still, I persevered for almost four years, believing that my father, in his infinite wisdom, must have seen some merit in the fellow – something I had overlooked. And every day of our life together, I hoped that I would somehow miraculously find a reason to fall in love with my partner."

Although he was watching me intently, Eirik made no comment, so I continued: "During our third year, he was killed in a flying accident. Needless to say, I didn't mourn him. Fortunately, there was no child, and I was free to return home. I went back just long enough to collect my things and make arrangements for an internship at University Seven – which is where you found me…

"So you see: I've made a place for myself there, just as you have with the Space Guild. And it's a comfortable, impersonal place where I don't have to watch the sun come up every morning and wonder how I'm going to make it through the rest of the day until the man I was yoked to drinks himself into a stupor and falls sleep, hopefully without having laid a hand on me."

"And you blame your father for your failure to find happiness?" He seemed genuinely curious, if a bit skeptical.

"Of course not! But I *do* blame him for using me."

"Life has a way of using us all," Eirik said with oracular seriousness. "And the more prominent your place, the more surely you will be used."

"I've given up my prominence."

"That's running away."

"Look who's talking!"

He actually laughed. "You're right, of course." He raised his glass. "Let's drink a toast to Janne and Eirik: fellow escape artists."

After that, the rest of our dinner was pleasant. We chatted easily and kept the conversation light. It was as if by some unspoken agreement, we had decided to put our personal problems behind us. And now that each of us knew the other's story, we were far more comfortable together.

By the time we left the restaurant, a light rain had begun to fall. It was a refreshing change: a surprising sensation after four years at the South Polar Dome where, of course, such a thing never happened – and I told Eirik so.

He laughed with delight as we drew our coats around ourselves and stepped out into the warm night.

"Where are we going?" he asked. "You walk as if you had a purpose."

"Let's go to City Park. We can wander around there all night if we want to, talk ourselves hoarse, and catch terrible colds, and no one will make us come in."

The night was filled with the smell of damp, newly-cut grass and the perfume of hundreds of flowers. In the daytime, there were always people out and about enjoying the gardens, but on that particular rainy evening, we had the place to ourselves, for not even the Park's many gardeners were on duty.

"This reminds me of home," Eirik said as we strolled along the carefully tended paths. "But home is so much wilder. Aren't there any wild places left on Caliban? Any untamed mountains – any woods or meadows?"

"Of course not! This is a civilized planet."

"I suppose it is." He actually sounded regretful. "What is it they say: Caliban, jewel of the civilized worlds?"

"Pleasure worlds," I corrected.

"Ah yes: the pleasure worlds. Everything here is planned. But don't you sometimes wish for something a little bit less controlled?"

"No. At least I don't think so."

"Of course not. Still, I think you might enjoy Valhalla. You might like a change."

We walked on, and even though both of us were soon wet, I didn't want to go home and end our evening together. It was so long since I had found someone worth talking to, and I suspected Eirik felt the same way.

Briefly he took my hand – his was warm, long-fingered, and strong – and tucked it into the crook of his arm. "The girl I told you about earlier… My *kjæresta*. We were never properly married because she refused to bear our child."

"Why?"

"She said it would tie her down too much. She was what we would call in Norsk a '*vandrare*' – in Galach you would probably say 'a wandering spirit'. A gypsy. It didn't matter to her that I was a Thane, or how many generations of us there had been. She felt that having a child and becoming part of my family would be too confining…

"But if she had agreed, I would have given her this," once again he touched his black dragon necklace. "And on my world that would have constituted a vow on her part to carry on my family's line. It would have been a vow between us too – one of working together towards certain goals. It would have brought her many responsibilities such as those you and I discussed earlier tonight. She refused them. And because I loved her, I lived with her anyway, always hoping that she might eventually change her mind."

"I wonder if she would have," I mused, "if she'd lived."

Although I was deeply engrossed in our conversation, I was also acutely aware of the distracting pressure of his arm against mine, and of the rise and fall of his chest beneath his uniform jacket.

"At the time I was sure she would relent, but now I'm not so certain. After all, I'd known her since we were children, and she was a wild one even then…" I could see the white flash of his teeth as he smiled at me in the semi-darkness. It seems that I'm attracted to stubborn women."

"Stubborn, foolish women," I muttered, suddenly feeling very awkward.

He stopped and made me turn to face him. "And you? What are you attracted to? Obviously not to power. To your freedom?"

"Not always," I replied, confused and trying to figure out why he seemed so terribly desirable just then.

"Then I think I should kiss you." He sounded so serious, even though he was still smiling. "That is, if you'll promise not to be offended."

"I promise…" I started to say, but he lowered his lips to mine before I could finish.

One kiss and then he held me away from him, studying my face. When we kissed again, I felt the length of his long, lean body against mine.

"I never expected it could be this way for me again," he murmured. "We really don't know each other very well, but my feelings for you are strong. I want you very much. Do you want me?"

"Yes." It was all I could manage to say.

"However, I refuse to make love to you like an animal here in the park." A definite note of teasing had crept into his voice. "Will you come somewhere with me?"

I nodded my assent.

"Where should we go?"

Was this really happening? I couldn't seem to think clearly. "To the guild barracks?"

He threw back his head and laughed. "Why not the Tourist Center?"

"Oh, all right then – we'll go back to Government House. I know how we can sneak in."

"I thought you might."

So we found the nearest station and called for an air taxi – and all the while we waited and all the way home, he kept one arm around me, a strong reassuring pressure, as he looked with silent laughter into my eyes.

8.

I awoke the next morning to bright sunlight flooding in through an open window. Somewhere in our gardens a syrinx began to sing. I looked over at Eirik. He was still asleep, his handsome stranger's face withdrawn into the privacy of his dreams.

How odd it was to be there with him, although it also felt as if it were the most natural thing in the world! Yet in nearly four years we had lived together, I had never once allowed my former partner to cross the threshold of this room.

Which made me think about the night just past...

How gentle and considerate Eirik had been: almost as if he had somehow known of the thoughtless, brutal way Karle had used my body to satisfy his needs, regardless of my wishes. But last night had been different, very different, and I was grateful to Eirik for having considered my pleasure as well as his own.

And now the warm light of the new day filled me with hope and a subtle sense of promise. With a contented sigh, I snuggled back into the pillows, my eyes seeking out the details of my once-familiar room.

I was a very different person from the tormented young woman who had last resided here, yet my room was essentially unchanged and achingly familiar. Still, after more than four years in a tiny cubicle, it seemed almost oppressively large and opulent with its jewel-toned, richly colored rugs, the fine art glass pieces that I had so lovingly collected, and its unobstructed view of the Government House gardens.

Beside me, Eirik stirred. "That was very nice," he murmured, his lips curving in a sensuous smile. His sleepy eyes seemed to smile too, alight with some private joke.

I sat up. "I think I'm supposed to be embarrassed to find you here. But I'm not. And you're right: last night *was* nice."

"Then why are you getting up?" he asked, reaching for me.

Laughing, I eluded his grasp, slipping out from between the cool silk sheets, and placing both feet on the heated tile floor.

"Breakfast." I stood. "We all get up early here so we can spend time with my father before he starts his work day. You may as well come along. Somehow I don't think he'll be surprised."

Eirik chuckled.

I turned away, looking for something to put on, and he watched me from the bed, his hands clasped behind his head.

"You're very beautiful."

"Flattery has already gotten you about as far as it's possible to go," I told him.

In my dressing room, I pulled on a morning robe. Out in the bedroom, Eirik said something that I didn't quite catch.

I returned to the room. "Sorry. Did you ask me something?"

"Nothing important," he replied a little too casually. "I just mentioned that I'm thinking of taking a vacation. The guild really owes me: I haven't had an extended shore leave in nearly eight years."

I began brushing my hair, all the while watching his reflection in the mirror. "You mentioned that last night, but it didn't sound as if you were about to go rushing off on the next starship."

"Well, right now it's just an idea." His voice was carefully neutral. A moment later, he added, "You said you're on vacation too. Until when?"

"I have to return to the university by the end of the month. Why?"

"It's just that I was thinking of going back to Valhalla. To see how everyone is…" Again, he hesitated. "If I did, would you consider going with me?"

I suppose I should have been surprised – but I wasn't. Somehow his request seemed a natural consequence of our night together. At the time, it never occurred to me to question how very quickly everything was happening.

"Well… How about it?" he coaxed.

The thought of my father and TiAnn brought a guilty pang. Would their feelings be hurt if I left Caliban again so soon after I'd arrived? Of course they would! And what was I going to tell them: that I was so infatuated with Eirik Sanderson that after spending a single night together that I'd agreed to run off to some out-of-the-way Fringe planet with him?

Yet despite these perfectly reasonable misgivings, I heard myself answering, "Okay. After all, it isn't as if I've had time to unpack."

"Wonderful!" Apparently satisfied that the issue was settled, he got out of bed and came over to plant a lingering kiss on the nape of my neck. When I pushed him gently away, laughing, he grinned at me and headed for the bathing room.

"Hey – wait a minute, Eirik!"

He halted mid-stride. "Yes?"

"You haven't told me when you plan to leave. And how do you know the guild will agree to release you right now, on the spur of the moment?"

"I know they will because I've already asked."

"What!"

"Yesterday afternoon, after I finished filing my flight report. I'm off-duty as of then. Now don't look at me like that…"

Forcing a laugh, I realized that I was mildly annoyed. "Eirik Sanderson, you're certainly sure of yourself! *I* didn't even know this was going to happen."

"Neither did I, but I thought there was no harm in asking for leave – just in case."

He retreated to the bathing room, and a few minutes later I heard him singing in the shower.

***

To my chagrin, my father didn't seem the least bit surprised to find Eirik sitting at our breakfast table – and by my abrupt change of plans. And if his feelings were hurt, he certainly didn't show it. Instead, he merely suggested that we might want to spend a little more time on Caliban before leaving for Valhalla. Then he smiled at me across the breakfast table, and patted the back of my hand the way he used to when I was a child.

TiAnn sulked her way through breakfast, which as I recalled was nothing unusual, although she did manage to come out of her funk long enough to remark, with little real conviction, that she hoped we would have a good time on Valhalla.

Before breakfast was over, my father was telling Eirik to be sure to come back to see him again, whether or not I was with him. Apparently I wasn't the only one who had succumbed to the captain's considerable charm.

***

And so it came to pass that three days later I found myself once again embarking upon a journey – only this time I was sitting in the co-pilot's seat of a small intergalactic flyer, watching as always with pleasure Eirik's sure hands moving across the control panel, even as he silently communicated with the shipboard AI.

"Request permission for take-off," he told the guild controller.

"For your safety, the Space Guild has issued a warning that all traffic entering or leaving the Caliban system should be on the lookout for possible flight hazards – exact nature unspecified. The guild requires anyone sighting objects of an unusual or suspicious nature to report them immediately on our emergency frequency."

Eirik and I glanced at each other.

"It's because of the mines – or whatever they were – that we almost hit, isn't it?" I whispered.

He winced. "Was it that obvious?"

I nodded.

"Captain Sanderson, do you copy?" the controller wanted to know.

"Affirmative."

"Good. You're cleared for takeoff. Have a safe trip."

It wasn't until we had left Caliban's busy traffic pattern behind and were outward bound that Eirik seemed to relax. He assured me that he could hear me quite well in spite of his AI link which he once again wore like some weird sort of crown – but suddenly I felt shy, realizing how very little we actually knew about each other.

What would the next few weeks be like, I wondered? Would we enjoy our time together? Did we have anything at all in common besides our mutual physical attraction?

Never in my life had I ever done anything this rash!

"Having last-minute regrets?" Eirik asked, reaching over to cover my hand.

"Not really," I lied. "But I was thinking that I don't know what to talk to you about – what your interests are."

"But that's good! It means we have a great many things to discover about each other. As for my interests... Well, there's traveling of course, exploring the Concorde's many cultures, and one small, very green planet called Valhalla. It's going to be fun showing it to you. Can you believe that you're my first off-world visitor?"

For a while we flew on in silence.

"If you don't mind," he said at last, "before we leave the Caliban system, I'd like to take the time to backtrack a bit and check out the area where those mines turned up. I have the coordinates, and it should be interesting to see if there are any more surprises waiting for us out there."

My mouth went suddenly dry. "Are you expecting something definite?"

He glanced over at me. "I'm not sure we should be discussing this, but... Well, you *are* Prime Minister Trellerian's daughter..." He brooded for a moment and then apparently reached a decision. "You won't repeat anything I tell you, will you?"

"Of course not!"

"Hey, no offense intended. I know I can trust you – but this information isn't public knowledge. I'm only supposed to discuss it with people who have the highest-level security clearance."

"You have my word – if that helps."

"It does. The government wants to keep this very quiet."

"To keep *what* very quiet?"

"There's been a rash of similar incidents occurring all over the Concorde these past few months."

"I had no idea!"

"You aren't supposed to."

"What kind of incidents?"

"Two or three ships vanishing without a trace, six more mines found in the Caliban sector alone, and several others in locations scattered across the Concorde; a couple of occasions when whole satellite networks have gone down without any apparent cause – similar to what happened to us on Arcadia. Some public disturbances. Things like that..."

"The Space Guild is investigating – quietly. So is your father, but he's doing so independently. And mixed in with all of that, there's a persistent rumor of some really strange sightings. No doubt it's nonsense, but some people claim we're being watched by aliens: an unknown race from another galaxy."

I suppressed a shudder. "What does the guild think? What do *you* think?"

"The guild isn't speculating. They don't really have any hard evidence, so their official position is that they don't have an official position. Personally, I think the idea of an invasion by evil aliens from outer space sounds like something straight out of pre-Concorde mythology. So if there *is* trouble, I willing to bet just about anything that it's being caused by real live Concorde troublemakers – not by little green men."

I laughed, as I'm sure he'd intended. His viewpoint seemed eminently practical.

We spent the next few hours cruising the outer planets, but found nothing unusual. Admitting that a further search was probably pointless, Eirik turned his attention to the AI and the complex calculations that were necessary for plotting the most direct yet safe series of jumps to Valhalla – none of which can be done without the help of the onboard computer.

Because Valhalla is located on the outermost edge of the Concorde Alliance, in an arm of our Home Galaxy that is commonly referred to as 'The Fringe', we would have to backtrack through some of the same territory we had covered on our trip from University VII to Caliban. But since we had no intention of stopping anywhere besides Valhalla and could therefore avoid passing directly through the Hub, this trip would be much faster. Thus, linked to our ship, Eirik was able to consult with it to plot longer jumps, dropping out of hyperspace just long enough for the AI to take the necessary star fixes before we jumped out again.

***

As he had accurately predicted, Eirik and I learned a lot about each other in the time it took us to reach our destination. We entertained ourselves by playing chess and making love, and I also spent many enjoyable hours playing my guitar. At my request, Eirik started teaching me some elementary principles of navigation; he also let me attempt a few of the co-pilot's duties. It was fun, and for the first time since I had left University, I began to relax.

In our time together, Eirik told me more about his home. His maternal uncle, Einarr, was presently Valhalla's *Hövding*, but his policies had so antagonized Eirik's deceased father that the two families were not on good terms.

"My father's goal was to liberalize government policies. He hoped that Valhalla would move towards some form of democracy, but what he failed to take into account was the fact that Uncle Einarr is a true despot. Power means everything to him and nothing short of death will ever convince him to give any of it up. Eventually, my father became so discouraged that he moved us out of Hawkness House, our traditional residence in the government complex, and went into semi-retirement.

"At his request, I helped him build a new family home – at first he insisted on calling it Hawkness Sanctuary, although eventually we shortened it to the Sanctuary. It's on the northern edge of our lands, overlooking Valhalla's famous wildlife refuge…

"And once our new house was completed, he devoted what turned out to be the rest of his life to studying the Sanctuary's creatures. He spent a lot of time cataloguing and sketching them – incidentally, he was quite an accomplished artist – and for the first few years, I worked with him…

"But we never gave up our dreams of a new and better government, although in the end we had to shelve them, temporarily we hoped. Anyway, we were so busy with our building project and our studies, and then running our new homestead, that getting out of politics didn't turn out to be such a terrible blow. In the end, my father was very proud of what we'd accomplished at the Sanctuary. I'm anxious to show it to you."

"Is that where we're going?"

Eirik nodded. "There's more to my family saga, if you're interested…"

"Of course I am!"

"Well, about ten years ago, after my father died, Uncle Einarr called me to him. By then he was over fifty and still childless although, heaven knows he'd tried hard enough to get an heir – and not just with my Aunt Helga. But that's another story…

"Anyway, he offered to make me his successor because by then he realized there weren't likely to be any little Einarrsons or Einarrsdotters coming along. But we were never able to reach an agreement. Before our discussions were finished, he accused me of having caught my father's sickness – democracy, that is. And because I didn't want to pay the price for his endorsement – because I couldn't bring myself to lie and tell him that I'd carry on as he wished – he dismissed me as hopeless."

Then Eirik's lover had died, and after that his uncle had had no use for him whatsoever since he was almost certainly doomed to be childless too.

When Eirik left Valhalla, the matter was still very much unsettled. Eirik was curious to find out who his uncle had chosen. He said he hoped it might be Magnus Egilson, the man who had been his closest friend.

Before we had time to become bored with ship-bound life, our last jump had been completed, and we were entering the Valhallan system. We sat together in the cockpit, watching the flyer's forward holo-screen: a jewel-like, blue and green globe seemed to be gliding towards us through space, growing larger and more richly-detailed by the minute.

"Home," Eirik said with a sigh that was either wistful or sad. Then he adjusted his temporal link in preparation for our long, gliding descent.

9.

'Green. Valhalla is mostly forest', is what Eirik had told me our first evening together on Caliban. At the time, it hardly seemed like an adequate description, yet as I peered through of the flyer's viewport, I could see right away that it was actually a concise summary of a very obvious fact.

Luxuriant plant growth poured out onto the tiny airfield from every direction like a living tide that was attempting to drown the pavement. It had never occurred to me that there could be so many different shades of green.

A dilapidated wooden flyer hangar stood, or perhaps it would be more accurate to say leaned, off to one side of the field where a veritable tidal wave of vines whose masses of vivid chartreuse flowers engulfed its sagging roof, threatening imminent collapse. I recalled Eirik saying that Valhalla seldom attracted visitors, and the wretched condition of the airfield underscored the truth of his statement.

As our flyer's airlock cycled open and we stepped out, squinting, into the blazing sunlight, I gasped as the thick, heavily-scented air slapped me in the face like a soggy towel. Between one instant and the next my clothing went from comfortably dry to sopping wet.

"I'd forgotten how warm it is here," Eirik said, tugging open the collar of his flightsuit. When I gave him an incredulous look, he retorted, "Well after all, it *is* summer."

Side by side, we began walking towards the hangar, but I had difficulty concentrating on where to place my feet: it was all I could do to keep from gagging on the moist, fetid soup I was inhaling. Eirik caught my arm when I stumbled over a clump of weeds that was practically exploding from a jagged crack in the pavement.

A young man in a sleeveless shirt and shorts emerged from a small building beside the hangar. He was still straightening his rumpled clothing as he reached us, then quickly executed a stiff little bow with both hands extended, palms towards us.

"*Goddag.*" That said, he promptly switched to Galach. "Excuse me for not meeting you promptly, sir..." His eyes darted nervously over the insignia on Eirik's flightsuit. "I mean, Captain. We don't get many off-planet visitors and I'm afraid you caught me napping, what with this heat and all."

"No need to apologize." Eirik studied the youngster's face. "Aren't you Harald, Gunnar Egilson's boy?"

"Why yes. Do I know you, Captain?"

"*Jeg er Eirik Sanderson frå Hökness.*"

I could easily guess what he must be saying, but although the words were spoken with a smile, the hurt expression in his eyes betrayed his true feelings.

"*Thane Sanderson! Förlåt!*" The young man's distress was painful to see. "*Eg...*"

"Speak Galach, Harald. We have a guest."

The young man rolled his eyes at me like a skittish colt, but he began anew. "Forgive me, Thane Sanderson! I-I didn't recognize you."

"There's no reason why you should have. The last time we met, you couldn't have been more than eight or nine." I realized that Eirik was trying to put the boy at ease, hoping to end this awkward moment. But it was no use.

"No one told me you were coming!" The youngster looked like he was about to burst into tears. "No one said to expect you!"

"That's because no one knew." Eirik's voice was calm and reasonable. "It's okay, Harald. It's not your fault."

"Someone must be notified... Your uncle! If you'll wait just one minute, I'll run inside and message the *Höv...*"

Eirik caught his arm as he started to bolt. "No need to get excited, lad. My uncle will find out soon enough."

"But..."

"No 'buts'! And there are plenty of other things you can do for us... First of all, I'd like to introduce you to Sera *Janne Arramsdotter frå Caliban.*"

I had to suppress an amused grin at Eirik's Nordification of my name.

Harald bobbed his head at me in his best approximation of a bow. Under the circumstances, I thought he did it rather well, considering that all the while we were talking, Eirik was marching him briskly across the field, keeping a firm grip on his upper arm.

"Now, Harald, Sera Arramsdotter and I plan to be here for several weeks. Do you have room for my ship in your hanger?"

"Certainly. Right now the only flyer parked there belongs to the *Hövding*."

"Good. Do you think you could manage to put mine in there as well? We'd like to go on ahead to Hawkness."

The boy's face lit up. Obviously, he hadn't expected to be entrusted with such an important responsibility. "Yes, sir –*Thane Sanderson!*" he answered with gusto, his eyes kindling with the dazzled gleam of hero worship.

By then, we had reached the edge of the airfield, arriving at a place where a narrow path disappeared into the dense foliage. To my relief, it was much cooler here, although the air was still unbelievably humid.

"Now, Harald, if you'll just keep Sera Arramsdotter company for a few minutes, I'll go fetch our things from the flyer…" And he was off, retracing our steps across the broiling pavement.

The moment he was out of earshot, Harald began chattering happily about what an honor it was for him to be the first person on Valhalla to welcome Eirik Sanderson home. Gleefully, he speculated that no one would believe his story that the Thane of Hawkness had finally returned. But then his expression clouded over, and his guileless face grew troubled. "Excuse me for asking, Sera, but Thane Sanderson *will* contact his uncle right away, won't he?"

"I'm sure he will," I said in as earnest a voice as I could muster. "Although I believe he has several important matters he has to attend to at Hawkness first."

"I hope he doesn't wait too long. The *Hövding* has a terrible temper!" The boy was actually trembling.

"Don't worry, Harald. I'm sure Thane Sanderson won't do anything to antagonize his uncle or get you in trouble."

At this point Eirik returned with his military carryall and my travel pack slung over one shoulder and my guitar case in his other hand. He made an elaborate ceremony of thanking the young man for his help, giving me a conspiratorial wink when he thought Harald wouldn't notice. And that poor boy just stood there, shifting uncomfortably from foot to foot, trying to be patient with his elders when it was obvious that all he really wanted to do was get his hands on Eirik's ship.

Our leave-taking completed, Eirik handed me my guitar and escorted me onto the trail. Immediately the trees closed in around us, blotting out all traces of the airfield as totally as if they had swallowed it up.

***

The woods stank: an unfamiliar pungent odor, redolent with the scent of decaying plant matter and ripe vegetation, of damp earth, and the perfume of a thousand exotic flowers. The air hummed with the noise of insects, and unseen creatures called high up in the trees. The light that filtered down to the forest floor was greeny-gold, patterned with shifting shadows that made the narrow trail difficult to see.

Abruptly, without any warning, everything around me – the trees, the shadows, the leaves, and the very air I was breathing – came pressing in on me, seemingly intent on crushing the breath out of my body: a body which, for some reason, had become its own worst enemy.

My sweaty skin itched and crawled. Every step required an almost superhuman effort, as if gravity had suddenly quadrupled. I had to consciously pull air into my lungs and then force it back out again – air that was so sickeningly wet and viscous that it was like breathing water.

Why wouldn't my eyes focus properly?

Was that roaring in my ears really my own heartbeat?

Meanwhile, Eirik moved at my side with an easy, swinging stride, utterly at home in these hostile surroundings: an alien being who was completely ignorant of everything that I was feeling.

Suddenly, to my shock, he chuckled.

"What's so funny?" I grated out, struggling to speak around the constriction in my chest.

"Harald. I'm hoping he'll be so enthralled with my flyer that he'll forget all about calling Uncle Einarr."

"Do you think he can handle it safely?" I asked in a tremulous voice.

"He'll be careful." He turned to look at me. "Are you okay?"

The laugh that I forced out sounded peculiar, even to me – and the sound was instantly swallowed up, smothered by the foliage.

"I'm fine. I guess…" I said, with a noticeable lack of conviction. "It's probably just travel fatigue."

"We aren't in any hurry. Would you like to stop and rest?"

"No!" I yelped. Taking a deep breath, I went on in a steadier voice, "It's just that I've never seen this kind of forest before. It's so… There's so much of it! How do you find your way around? People must get lost all the time!"

"It's not like this in most places." With a reassuring smile, he took my hand. "This is all second growth – in other words the trees were harvested and thinned out a couple of years ago, when the airfield was cleared. All of this stuff is just responding to the extra sunlight."

"You mean that airfield back there is new!"

"Well, the plants do take over pretty quickly."

It was not a comforting thought. Despite the heat, I shivered.

The path we were following led downhill past some large boulders and then leveled off, opening out into a park-like setting with enormous old trees and hardly any undergrowth at all. For the first time since we had left the airfield, we were able to see for quite some distance, and I discovered that once again I was able to breathe normally. Yet I couldn't completely shake off the unsettling sensation of suffocation and the feeling that these woods must go on forever.

Eirik assured me that this was not, in fact, so.

"Don't forget: Hawkness is a timber preserve. We make our living by raising and harvesting trees – so does my uncle. But adjacent to our land is Stormhaven Estate, which is mostly open rolling meadowland – famous grazing country. I'll take you there soon to visit my friend Magnus and his wife Inga. I know you'll like them."

We walked on, and before long the bulky mass of a stone wall appeared among the trees. Stepping through a pointed archway that pierced right through the middle of a building, we found ourselves in an open, rectangular clearing where, to my considerable relief, I was once again able to see the sky.

"Here it is: the Government Center of Valhalla," Eirik announced, and I looked around with interest.

A row of massive structures, crenellated fortresses of hewn rock, formed the remaining three sides of the rectangle. They looked unimaginably old.

An image of Caliban's pristine governmental center immediately came to mind. There was no way to compare the two, yet I instinctively knew that this architecture was wholly appropriate for this particular place.

"Each province has its own Thane's residence: Hawkness House is the fifth building on the left. The *Hövding's* Palace is down there, at the far end. And that's the council building." Eirik indicated a square, graceless hulk immediately to our right. "Of course, hardly anyone's here right now because the council doesn't meet in summer, except for emergencies."

"Are we going to stop at Hawkness House?"

"I'd rather not. My uncle might find out we're here, and I'm not ready to face him just yet. If you're not too tired, I'd like to walk a bit further before we stop for lunch."

I agreed, but without much enthusiasm. It seemed utter madness to wander off into these impenetrable woods. Yet I comforted myself with the thought that Eirik must surely know where he was going.

By lunchtime, I had completely lost my sense of direction, but fortunately my earlier, panicky feeling had not returned. For all I knew, we could have been walking around in circles for the past hour: there were neither signs nor guideposts that I could see – just narrow lanes which occasionally intersected with ours and then vanished into the trees.

Eirik was amused when I told him my impressions. "It's hard for me to imagine how this must seem to you, since every one of these trails is a familiar old friend."

Once Eirik had divested himself of our belongings, we sat down on a log that had been carved into a rustic bench alongside the path.

"What if you've never been in this part of the country before?" I asked. "How would you find your way?"

"Excellent maps are available and there are markers if you know where to look for them – small rune signs carved into the stones at path intersections."

He took a large bite of one of the energy bars we had brought along from the ship's stores. Chewing slowly, he examined the remainder with obvious distaste. "Disgusting!" With a flick of his wrist, he tossed it into the bushes. "It will be a pleasure not to have to eat any more of that crap. Once we've reached the Sanctuary, I promise we'll have some real food!"

I looked at him in surprise. The ship's rations, while not particularly inspired, was certainly adequate.

An ominous rumble interrupted before I could voice my opinion. Although the ground didn't actually shake, the air was disturbed by a noticeable vibration. The hair on the back of my arms and neck stirred as if they had been brushed by a cold hand.

"What – what was that?" I stammered, barely able to get the words out.

"Sounded like thunder."

He said it so casually!

He stood up, glancing at the sky, which was almost hidden by leaves. "Getting caught out in the open in a thunderstorm isn't my idea of fun, but fortunately I think the storm's going to miss us."

His words sent a chill down my spine. "You *think* it's going to miss us! You mean no one's directing it? There's no weather control!"

"Don't be afraid, Janne." Sitting down beside me, he slipped an arm around my shoulders, his expression full of concern. "I suppose all of this must seem awfully strange to you. But I promise: there really isn't much on Valhalla that's dangerous. The colonists brought only benign life forms with them, and none of the indigenous stuff is harmful to humans. A little weather won't hurt you, will it?" His eyes searched mine.

"You're asking me to be logical about this?" I protested, but I managed to give him a shaky smile.

He pulled me to my feet. "Come on, brave adventurer! Let's go. In an hour or so we'll be at the Sanctuary."

However, that last part of the trip seemed to take forever. It was hard to believe that Valhallans regularly walked this far – or for that matter, preferred walking to most other means of transportation.

Several times I doubted my ability to go on. But Eirik was considerate and we traveled slowly, stopping every so often to rest. As we walked, he entertained me with stories about his childhood, pointing out special places as well as interesting plants and woodland creatures – and I didn't spend too much time wishing for an air taxi or ground car.

After a while we crossed a crude wooden bridge, high above a roaring, rocky creek. On the opposite side, the path wound slightly uphill between several large boulders, coming at last to a place where a massive stone dwelling with wide wooden eaves had been set into a rocky outcrop on the very edge of a cliff.

"The Sanctuary," Eirik announced with obvious pride. And then he added, "My father intended that we should be self-sufficient, so besides the main house, there's also a small farm. You can't see it from here: it's off by itself, over there." He gestured casually.

"Will anything be left after eight years?"

"Certainly. The Pederson family lives there and manages the estate. Ironically, as things have worked out, they essentially own the place, while I'm just a visitor... I suppose we really should speak to them before we go inside – otherwise they might think we're trespassers." He set down our luggage, and then turned to go on.

I followed him on aching feet, too tired to protest.

A narrow footpath skirted around trees and even more boulders, eventually leading to a cottage which, like the main house, was constructed of heavy wooden timbers and stone blocks, and so cleverly designed that it seemed to melt into its surroundings. Nearby, in a flood of sunlight, flowers and vegetables grew in orderly profusion, and there was a small orchard and a pen for animals. The yard itself was overrun by a restless swarm of white and rust-red creatures that were everywhere underfoot, scratching and grubbing in the rich black soil, muttering to themselves like fussy old women.

Through the middle of this pleasant place a creek ran, widening into a deep, round pool that reflected the sky like a mirror before it flowed over a stone dam to drop soundlessly off the cliff edge in a perfect, glass-smooth curl. Beyond, the tops of enormous trees swayed, their trunks and roots more than two hundred feet below what was to us ground level.

To complete this idyllic if archaic scene, a man and two young children were digging in the garden. Moments later, a woman emerged from the cottage to join them. But all four stopped and stared the instant they noticed us: the adults with undisguised interest, while the children ran, clinging to the safety of their mother's knees.

The man put down his shovel and approached, rubbing the dirt from his hands and examining us intently.

"*Goddag*," Eirik began, and followed this up with something that sounded very solemn in his rhythmic Norsk language. He held up both hands, palms-outward, in the same curious salute that the boy Harald had performed when we had first encountered him.

The man stopped in his tracks. The expression on his face could only be interpreted as open astonishment, and he had to clear his throat several times before he was able to respond. His speaking voice was rough – although perhaps this was due to emotion – and then he also extended both hands in the same distinctive gesture as Eirik's, but I noticed that neither man actually touched the other.

While this was occurring, the woman came over to stand beside her partner, greeting us with a shy smile; but the children hung back, their eyes wide, guileless as young animals.

Eirik made another short speech, in the course of which I was fairly certain I heard my name mentioned.

Then he turned to me. "Janne, this is Sven and his wife Astrid. They don't speak Galach, but you can greet them as I did: put your hands out – that's right – just make sure you don't actually touch anyone."

A rapid conversation, of which I understood not a word, ensued between the three Valhallans, with Eirik gesturing towards his house and telling them, I supposed, about our intended stay. Excluded, I attempted to make friends with the children and quickly discovered that they were just like youngsters everywhere: curious and not at all timid once they were sure their parents had accepted us. Our lack of a common language and my clumsy attempts at communication quickly became a hilarious joke that sent the two of them into giggles and then riotous shrieks of laughter.

Eventually, Eirik called to me that it was time to leave. However, it soon became apparent that the farmer and his lady intended to accompany us.

Eirik protested.

They argued amiably for a short while, but finally both men bowed politely to one another, palms extended, and we were free to go.

"What was that all about?" I asked, as we retraced our steps, now loaded down with a wicker basket full of fruit, vegetables, and several loaves of homemade bread which the couple had insisted that we take.

"Sven and Astrid were embarrassed because the house hasn't been prepared for our arrival."

"How could they have known?"

"I pointed that out... Regardless, they wanted to come over and open up the place for us. I told them it wasn't necessary. You don't mind, do you? I thought we'd rather be alone."

I was very grateful for his sensitivity. Spending time with strangers I couldn't understand would have been a strain, and I was already exhausted.

When we reached the main house, Eirik put his palm up to a scanner that seemed completely out of place alongside the heavy wooden door. With a muted click, the door swung open.

He caught me staring and grinned. "My father wanted all the latest gadgets for his new house. Remind me to log your handprint on the master console," he added as he picked up our abandoned luggage and escorted me inside. Then we paused in the entry vestibule.

The interior walls were constructed of the same rough-hewn stone that I had noticed on the outside, but everything else within sight – the floors, the trim around the windows and doors, the doors themselves and even the furniture – was made of dark, faintly spicy-smelling wood. This struck me as odd until I reminded myself that Hawkness was a timber preserve: no doubt plastoid and cerosteel would have been as peculiar choices of building materials on Valhalla, as wood would have been on Caliban.

From the entryway, steps led up to an enormous room that was study, living, and dining area combined. Massive wooden furniture – none of which appeared to be collapsible – softened by deep cushions, was casually arranged. But rather than impart a cluttered look, as I would have expected, it created a harmonious feeling that somehow managed to reduce the place to a more human scale. The far wall was entirely made up of windows, many of which, I later learned, could be pushed aside, giving access to a deck that looked out over the Sanctuary treetops.

"Let's leave this here for now," Eirik said, easing the farmer's basket onto the entry floor beside my guitar. "We'll take the food and your guitar upstairs later."

I followed him down wide stone stairs that descended into the lower part of the house which, I soon discovered, was divided into five bedrooms, each with its own en suite bathing area.

Eirik carried our baggage into the largest bedroom. "Well, we made it." I noticed that even he looked a bit weary as, with a smile, he turned to place his hands on my shoulders. "Home at last."

I gave him an answering smile, not trusting myself to speak.

"I've brought you a long way and put you through some strange and not very comfortable experiences, haven't I?" He searched my face for an answer.

"It's been a long day, but I'm glad we're here."

He kissed me quite gently and, for a blessed moment, I leaned against him, utterly relaxed in the circle of his arms.

"There's nothing else we have to do. We can rest for as long as we like." His voice was a deep rumble against my ear.

"That sounds like heaven! My poor feet are threatening to fall off."

Immediately, he picked me up and carried me over to the bed. "Relax and let me take care of you. You should be proud: not every off-world visitor could have walked as far as you did today."

With great tenderness, he removed my shoes, then spread a light blanket over my feet. Excusing himself from the room, he returned several minutes later with two cups of some sort of heated liquor, which at that moment tasted like ambrosia. Side by side we sipped our drinks, talking quietly about the day's events until at last both of us drifted off into a peaceful sleep.

***

When we awoke, the afternoon was almost over. After a leisurely romantic interlude, we bathed and dressed and then, barefoot, went back upstairs, where we gravitated outdoors to the deck. Entranced by a gorgeous sunset and the eerie calls that emanated from the trees, we stayed outside until every last bit of color had left the sky and the first stars were peeking out.

Back inside again, I prowled around the main room while Eirik went into the little area he called the galley, to see what kind of supplies were in storage. When I joined him, lights were blinking on the food processor. He had also taken out all sorts of unfamiliar objects.

"You have an impressive collection of ancient books," I began. "My god, Eirik, what are you doing with that vicious-looking knife?"

"Chopping."

"I don't understand…"

"Cooking," was his next, equally unenlightening response.

Just then the door of the processor popped open to reveal a most unappetizing pink object.

"What *is* that?" I touched the thing gingerly with one finger. "Ugh, it's cold!"

"Of course it's cold: it just came out of storage."

"But what *is* it?"

"A chicken. You saw some at the Pederson's farm this afternoon."

"I did? And we're going to eat it? Just like that?" Despite my best effort, I was unable to suppress a shudder.

He grinned. "Of course not: first we have to cook it."

"Is something wrong with the equipment?"

"No… Oh, I see: you think this is a food processor."

"It isn't?"

With a wry smile and a sweeping gesture: "Allow me to introduce you to our deep-freeze. The food is flash-frozen, then stored, and thawed out when we call it up. But then we have to cook it. You can help. It's more fun than pressing buttons on a food processor."

I was skeptical, but interested.

It was not at all a pleasant sensation, touching unprocessed food. Yet I didn't want Eirik to think I was squeamish, so I pitched in as instructed, trying not to dwell on the fact that we would have to do this every day, for every meal we ate. By the time we finally sat down at the table, I was hungry enough to eat just about anything.

"I bet when you met me, you never suspected that cooking was one of my many talents," Eirik boasted.

I thought it best not to comment when my mouth was full.

10.

The next two weeks were idyllic. As my senses opened to the almost indescribable beauty that was all around us, Valhalla ceased to be an alien place and instead began to feel, if not exactly like home, at least pleasantly familiar.

Practically every evening produced a spectacular sunset, which we viewed from lounge chairs on the deck. We spent hours exploring the Sanctuary and its exotic plant and animal life, and more than once we made the long trek down the cliffs to the sea beyond, and back.

I had never felt healthier or more alive.

Having decided that a crash course in the Valhallan language was a basic necessity (Galach only being regularly spoken only by the wealthy and well-educated, and then only when dealing with off-world visitors), I spent hours studying Norsk tutorials, which we downloaded from Valhalla's central library.

Structurally, Norsk is a fairly straightforward language: its real challenge lies in its singsong inflections and highly articulated vowel sounds. Often my lips and tongue were numb by the time I had finished trying out my new vocabulary on a very patient Eirik.

As my ability to speak the language increased, we began paying social calls on friends and relatives. Just about everyone I met knew at least some Galach, and everyone was more than kind. The Valhallans made me feel very welcome indeed: they were delighted to see Eirik again and insisted on giving me the credit for his return.

Later, when we visited Stormhaven, the estate immediately to the southwest of Hawkness, I fell in love with its rolling hills and windswept grassy vistas. This was the home of Eirik's closest friend Magnus, a boisterous, red-haired giant of a man, his wife Inga, and their adorable and precocious one year-old son Trön.

We stayed with them for nearly a week, hiking, picnicking, and sailing during the day, and debating politics, the arts, and philosophy long into the night, our discussions lubricated by Magnus' potent home brew. They even talked me into playing my guitar for them, something which I would ordinarily have been too shy to do.

I was sorry when our visit with Magnus and his family was at an end, for I felt that I had made some very special new friends. But I was also looking forward to the peace and privacy I had come to expect and treasure at the Sanctuary. Unfortunately, before we could take advantage of that refuge, we first had to face Eirik's uncle Einarr.

The morning after our arrival on Valhalla, Eirik had used the planetary comm net to contact his uncle. I remained in the room just long enough to catch a glimpse of a grey-haired, heavy-jowled man who never ceased scowling and who spoke to Eirik in angry, insolent tones. Afterwards, Eirik told me that his uncle had claimed to be deeply insulted by his failure to call him the moment he set foot on Valhalla. Yet in the end, Uncle Einarr had allowed himself to be placated by Eirik's promise to come visit once he had settled in. However, since neither of us was at all anxious to fulfill that obligation, we kept putting off the inevitable until at last the situation had become extremely embarrassing. Now, whether we liked it or not, before we could return to the Sanctuary, we would have to go directly from Stormhaven to Uncle Einarr's residence.

To make our social duties a bit more palatable, Eirik suggested that after visiting his uncle, we should spend the night at Hawkness House and host a party the following afternoon. But during our last morning at Stormhaven, in the midst of packing, I was suddenly struck by the realization of how little time we actually had left on Valhalla. I had no idea where the days had gone, yet I realized that I had been acting as if I expected our visit to last indefinitely.

"You're very quiet," Eirik said, looking up from his carryall. "Is something wrong?"

I opted for a partial truth. "I was just thinking that vacations are never as long as anyone would like them to be."

His answering smile was rather wistful. "I know what you mean. It's hard to believe that in a little over a week we'll be back to processed food, canned air, and artificial daylight."

For several moments, neither of us spoke. Was he, like me, thinking about the less-than-ideal realities of 'civilized' life?

"Oh well, I guess we'd better be going," he said at last. "Uncle Einarr isn't known for his patience. Besides, it isn't as if we're really saying goodbye to Magnus and Inga since they'll be at our party tomorrow."

He picked up our bags – but then, with a sigh, he put them back down again and came over to take me in his arms. "Janne, whatever happens, don't let my uncle upset you." His breath stirred my hair. "I wouldn't want your last few memories of Valhalla to be unpleasant ones."

I hugged him, hard. "I already have so many good memories that there's nothing he can do to ruin them."

I felt the muscles in his arms tense, and when he spoke, his voice was grim. "But he'll try. Surely he'll try…"

***

After dropping our belongings off at Hawkness House, we walked the short distance to the *Hövding's* residence, where Eirik's aunt met us at the door.

"*Goddag, Tante Helga,*" Eirik said with remarkable composure, offering her a warm smile.

Both of them bowed, hands extended in that peculiar, non-contact style.

"Your – Uncle Einarr – will – join us –shortly." She had a peculiar way of speaking: her words came out in ragged gasps, as if she was short of breath, and her eyes darted about, looking everywhere but at us. Still, it was a relief to discover that I had no trouble understanding her Norsk.

The formalities concluded, without another word she turned and scurried off down a rather grand but dimly-lit hallway, obviously expecting us to follow her – yet she never once looked back to make sure that we were doing so. There was no one else around, not even servants: the whole place, every room we passed, the decor, the furnishings – all of it – had a faded, neglected appearance. Even the study, where we arrived at last, had the same vacant, threadbare look that made it seem more like an abandoned museum than a residence. A large wooden table stood at one end of the room, heaped with papers and work slates. It seemed to be in use, and it was the only real sign of life in the entire building.

Aunt Helga offered us seats, and then stood awkwardly by making slow, stilted conversation with Eirik. However, I was far too nervous about our impending interview with his uncle to be able to sit still, so I got up to inspect the antique tapestries which were the room's sole decoration. Every so often, while I was examining them, I saw Aunt Helga glance furtively in my direction, but she quickly looked away whenever I caught her eye.

She seemed pathetic – as faded and dull as the rest of the place. Her body was thin and angular, her hair a dull, lifeless tan streaked with grey, and her plain face was careworn. When the study door opened suddenly, she flinched.

There was no doubt in my mind that the man who came striding into the room was Eirik's Uncle Einarr. Unlike his wife, he was a large, vigorous presence. I was not at all surprised to see that he was scowling: from what little I had seen of him during his call with Eirik, I suspected that the frown was habitual.

Upon his entrance, I had started forward but, seeing his expression, it would have taken more courage than I presently possessed to brave attracting his attention by crossing to Eirik's side. Instead, I retreated back into the safety of my tapestry-hung corner.

Eirik got slowly to his feet and just as slowly raised both hands in the formal Valhallan salute. "*Goddag, Onkel Einarr. Får jag presentera—*" he began, but his uncle interrupted.

"So you're here at last." Einarr glanced at Eirik's extended hands, but failed to make the appropriate response. "You took a damned long time coming home, and even more time finding your way here!"

Eirik lowered his hands. "I'm sorry if I've offended you, Uncle Einarr, but a man must follow his conscience in these matters."

"Ha! A fine world this would be if we all had consciences like yours. You have a duty to Valhalla, as well as to me and you've neglected them both – badly."

Aunt Helga shot a worried glance in my direction. "Einarr," her voice was so quiet that I had to strain to hear her, "Eirik has come to us from so far, and he's brought…"

"Silence, woman! This business is between me and my nephew." He glared at her in disgust, and I was certain there was a long and bitter history behind that look. "Go make yourself useful. Bring us something to drink."

He turned his back on his wife in pointed dismissal, and she scampered from the room.

"I see that coming here was a mistake," Eirik said with great dignity – and then to me, in Galach: "Janne, I think we should leave."

Quick as a cat, Einarr spun around. Apparently he really hadn't known I was there. His angry expression shifted to surprise, and then to something far less easy to read. "Why, Eirik, you didn't mention that you'd brought a friend – and a beautiful one at that."

"You didn't give me a chance."

Einarr chose to overlook his nephew's sarcasm. Instead, a glittering intensity crept into his eyes and his lips slowly parted in a lascivious smile. When he moved in my direction, the sight of his flushed face was even more unsettling than his anger had been.

At once, Eirik was at my side. "Uncle Einarr," he said, still in Galach, "I'd like you to meet Sera Janne Trellerian of Caliban."

"It's certainly my pleasure," Einarr said, raising his hands in the salute which he had denied his nephew.

I only hesitated a moment before responding. "I'm pleased to meet you too."

"You rascal! No wonder you were so secretive – and so busy." Einarr leered at Eirik. "I would have kept her locked up myself, if I were in your place."

"I'm afraid it's my fault that we stayed away, not Eirik's," I said, confident that I could play this game every bit as well as he. "You see, I insisted on sightseeing before I'd let him fulfill any of his family obligations."

Behind Einarr's broad shoulder, Eirik stifled a smile.

"And who can resist the demands of a beautiful woman, eh, Eirik?" Einarr turned to his nephew with a conspiratorial wink. Then, suddenly transforming into the gracious host, he offered me his arm, and the three of us walked over to the chairs by the fireplace.

Once we were comfortably settled, Einarr spoke again. "So you're from Caliban. Imagine traveling all that way just to see a primitive little world like Valhalla. Now Caliban – well, that's another story. Everyone says it's worth visiting. Unfortunately, my duties here keep me so busy that I seldom have time to go off-planet."

I mumbled an appropriate response.

"Now tell me: what has my nephew taken you to see since you've been with us? Surely Valhalla can have little to offer compared to Caliban."

Of course, I denied it.

When Aunt Helga returned bearing a tray laden with an earthenware pitcher of ale with a matching set of mugs, fruit, cheese, and *flatbröd*, I think she was shocked to find us chatting away like old friends without a trace of animosity.

Eirik gave me a grateful, private nod while Einarr was filling our glasses.

I felt as shaky as if I had been outside during one of their violent Valhallan thunderstorms, but the storm around Einarr and Eirik seemed to have abated – at least for the moment.

Einarr's geniality lasted through dinner, eaten amidst much hearty laughter (Einarr's), and many sexual innuendoes (also Einarr's), and well into the early evening. But it wasn't until it was time to bid our hosts goodnight and return to Hawkness House, that disaster struck.

"Well, Eirik, I must admit that until now I've had my doubts about you," Einarr was saying. "Heaven knows, we've had our differences. But perhaps enough time has passed, and we can sit down again tomorrow afternoon and discuss some of my ideas for Valhalla's future."

"Certainly, Uncle Einarr. I'd be pleased to do that."

The men bowed a bit stiffly to one another, yet this time they both raised their hands in the Valhallan salute.

As Eirik began to pay his respects to his aunt, Einarr turned to me with the same suggestive smile he'd plied me with all evening. "Ah, lovely lady… It's been a very special pleasure meeting you."

"Thank you. We've enjoyed our visit."

I held up my hands.

But instead of doing what I expected – what I'd seen every other Valhallan in a similar situation do – Uncle Einarr astonished me by pressing his palms directly against mine, pushing his fingers aggressively between my own, and crushing them in a powerful grip. I was so taken aback that I just stood there, staring stupidly at his flushed face, unable to react in other any way to this aberrant behavior.

"Einarr!" Aunt Helga gasped with tears streaming down her cheeks. Abruptly, she turned and fled from the room.

"How dare you!" Eirik snarled at the same moment, giving his uncle such a violent shove that he staggered backwards, releasing my hands.

For what seemed like an eternity neither man moved.

I held my breath, shocked by the raw hatred in their eyes, afraid of what might come next.

Suddenly, unnervingly and for no apparent reason, Einarr chuckled. He looked over at me and actually winked!

His face contorted in fury, Eirik grabbed my upper arm, his fingers digging painfully into my biceps, and whirled me around, practically lifting me off my feet. And without another word, he dragged me from his uncle's presence.

Einarr's mocking laughter rang in my ears, taunting us all the way back to Hawkness House.

11.

In a daze, I stumbled along beside Eirik, my stomach clenched in a queasy knot, sickened by the bitter passions that been unleashed around me. I had to trot to keep up with his angry, long-legged strides, and several times I was on the point of begging him to stop. But all the way back to Hawkness House, neither of us uttered a single word, although my mind was seething with questions that I didn't have the courage to ask.

Once we reached the haven of Eirik's familial home, I expected him to say something – anything would be better than this brooding, tight-lipped fury! But it wasn't until we were alone in the privacy of his bedroom, with the servants dismissed and the door securely closed, that I learned what was on his mind – and by then I was close to tears.

"Why the hell did I agree to see him?" Eirik slammed a white-knuckled fist so hard against the door that I winced. "It was madness: madness to go there – madness to even speak with him!"

My own hands were trembling, but I forced myself to speak calmly. "I'm sorry if I've done anything that…"

"You!" He turned quickly towards me, his eyes wide with astonishment.

"…Please just tell me what I did wrong and get it over with." I choked back a sob. "I can bear it."

"My god, Janne – you think I'm angry with *you*?" He pulled me hard against him, and I could feel the pounding of his heart and hear the ragged rasp of his breathing. "How could you ever think that?" He stroked my hair. "Oh, that sick, sick man!"

For several minutes, we just stood there, drawing mutual comfort from each other, but at last I broke free of his embrace. Holding him at arm's length, I studied his face.

"All right, Eirik – if it isn't something I've done, then what exactly is wrong? What happened back there – I mean besides his inexcusable rudeness to your aunt?"

"He touched your hands!"

"I admit he surprised me – it was so unexpected and really quite painful. But what's so terrible about that? I don't understand."

"No…" He passed one hand tiredly across his eyes, "No – you wouldn't. Sit down, Janne." He strode over to a tall narrow cabinet, took out a cut crystal decanter and two glasses, and poured a stiff drink for each of us. Then, handing me one of the glasses, he came to sit beside me on the edge of the bed.

"How can I explain?" he muttered, more to himself than to me. "It would be so obvious to a Valhallan…"

"Please try."

He sighed. "Well… In the first place, as part of our early education, every Valhallan child is taught to meditate, beginning at the age of three or four. You might say it's our way of learning to understand ourselves and how our bodies work…"

"What does that have to do with…"

"You'll see…" He continued, "In fact, this training continues all the way into our late teens. And once we've mastered the basic techniques, we progress to deeper biological work: the girls learn to control their ovulation and their monthly cycles, and the boys to control the production and the sex of the sperm their bodies produce."

I was so startled that I started to speak, but he silenced me with an upraised hand.

"Wait – there's more to it. So much more… You see, by the time we're adults, this training has become an integral part of both our natures and our self-esteem. Our whole society is based on this learned self-control."

"You're telling me that Valhallans have developed their own method of birth control that doesn't require medical intervention?" I interrupted, no longer able to contain my incredulity.

"Exactly."

"Then no one on Valhalla has an implant?"

He nodded.

"That's amazing!"

My fingers sought the slight swelling on my upper arm that marked the site of my birth control device. How proud I had been the first time the doctor had inserted it there! It was my eleventh birthday, and I had been so excited that I had scarcely noticed the slight pain of the incision.

What would it be like not to need one, I wondered? If I were Valhallan, would I have felt equally proud, knowing that I was able to regulate my own hormones?

"For us, birth control is the responsibility of both parties," Eirik was saying, "and that demands self-control. After all, it would be unthinkable for one of us to become so carried away by passion that an unwanted child was the result. And because each Valhallan is only allowed to have one child as a replacement for him- or herself, no one would dare to make a mistake about such an important matter. It's our way of ensuring that our planet doesn't become overpopulated – and it's also our way of making sure that every child that's born is really wanted."

"But, Eirik, people must have affairs."

"Of course they do – and we're as safe with our prevention methods as the rest of the Concorde is with its anti-fertility drugs and implants."

"But what does this have to do with what happened tonight?"

"I was just getting to that… You see, with all of that self-control we're taught, there has to be a way to overcome it at the proper time. Or maybe it happened the other way around: perhaps because of our peculiar biology, we first had to learn to keep ourselves under control and then we had to be able to forget what we've learned."

"What are you talking about?"

"Valhallan biology. During the centuries that people have been relatively isolated on this planet, some very subtle biochemical changes have taken place that make us slightly different from the Concorde norm. The most obvious one is that when two people place the palms of their hands together, a chemical reaction can take place – and remember: I said 'can'. Supposedly it starts as a mild intoxication: a kind of tingling that begins in the palms of the hands and spreads to the rest of the body. We call it the 'Ekstase'."

"How odd! I've never heard of anything like that."

"I'm not surprised. Concorde scientists call it the Valhallan Reaction because so far it's only manifested here."

I put my palm against his. "It doesn't happen with us."

"Of course not – you're not Valhallan. Besides, not all Valhallans react to one another. And even if you were Valhallan and we were both reactive, the *Ekstase* wouldn't start right away: it takes a while for it to build up. But the more frequently and the longer two reactive individuals join hands, the more rapid and intense the *Ekstase* becomes – which eventually allows us to ignore our trained childhood inhibitions and reproduce. In other words, we have to overcome our self-control in order to have children."

"But if this *Ekstase* is so exciting, it must be awfully tempting to experiment."

"Not true. Certainly there's a healthy amount of sexual activity going on between consenting Valhallans, but we can also enjoy sex without the added stimulation of the *Ekstase*… Don't forget, Janne, there's a very real danger that the lovers might end up with an unwanted child."

"I guess that *would* be a deterrent."

"And think about this: you've seen that when Valhallans meet, we always extend our hands to each other, palms held out, but we never actually touch."

"I assumed it was just a matter of custom."

"It is – in a way. But there's also a very real biological reason behind it. The Valhallan greeting isn't only an expression of politeness, it's also the ultimate act of trust."

"Are you saying that anyone – a man and a woman, or two men or two women – might set off this *Ekstase* in each other?"

"Yes – if they've both reached sexual maturity. But it takes sustained contact before the reaction can even start. To actually touch someone else in a social situation isn't really dangerous – it's just not done."

"So when Einarr grabbed my hands…"

"…He was being deliberately provocative," Eirik finished for me, "in more ways than one."

"But maybe… I mean, he must have known I wouldn't be affected. Maybe he was just trying to be polite by Concorde standards." Yet even as I said this, I realized it didn't ring true.

"He's Valhalla's *Hövding*!" Eirik spat out. "He's required to uphold our standards, not the Concorde's. And what he did was an inexcusable breach of Valhallan custom! Ever since childhood, we're taught that the only ones who may touch that way are lovers who intend to have a child."

He got up for a refill. The decanter clinked harshly against the rim of his glass.

Meanwhile I sat on the bed, trying to assess the damages. "Okay – so now what?" I asked. "He upset your aunt, and he deliberately insulted you. Is there something you have to do in response according to Valhallan customs?" I had to brace myself to ask, "Something like revenge?"

"Ha! As I told you previously, the *Hövding* has the right to do – or have – anything or anyone he wants. That was one of the many things my father and I were trying to put a stop to." Picking up his glass, he started to take a sip, and then hurled it into the fireplace instead, where it shattered into a thousand glittering shards. "Damn Einarr!"

I went over and put my arms around him. "He can't do anything to me, Eirik. I'm not a Valhallan citizen, and I certainly don't have to comply with his wishes."

"And he knows it. But still…"

There was a discreet knock on the bedroom door.

"Come in," Eirik called out, stepping away from me.

A servant, the kind Valhallans call a 'housecarl', entered. "Thane Sanderson," he said, bowing, "young Harald Gunnarson has just called from the airfield to relay a message from the Space Guild… All off-duty personnel have been recalled. You're ordered to report to guild headquarters within five days standard – sooner if possible."

My heart sank.

"Something must have happened," Eirik ground out past gritted teeth. He turned to the housecarl. "Thank you, Bjarni. Please ask Harald to acknowledge that I received the recall."

Before the door had even closed behind the servant, Eirik had begun to pace.

"Do you think it's serious?" Fear made my mouth dry, and I had difficulty getting the words out.

"You can count on it."

"But what?"

"How should I know? Maybe they found some more of those damn mines!" His expression softened. "Don't worry, Janne. The guild doesn't take chances: they just like to be prepared for whatever might happen."

"You almost make it sound like the guild's an army instead of a pilot's organization."

"Don't be naive – of course it's an army! Who else is so well trained and equipped – and disciplined – as the Space Guild? Sure we transport people and goods from place to place, but that's just our public persona. I mean, my god, Janne, all of our pilots are ex-military!"

"But the Concorde Alliance has a standing army based on Concordia, although it isn't nearly as big a force as the guild."

"Exactly my point! Consider what you would have if you put the Space Guild and Concordian army together... Besides, who do you think the incoming guild cadets and officers pledge their loyalty and lives to? The Prime! Who do you think the leaders of the Concorde planets swear allegiance to? Ask your father about it sometime – he's involved in the Interplanetary Council." Aware of my distress, he sat down beside me and put an arm around my waist.

"What are we going to do?" I murmured.

"Maybe it isn't such a bad time for this to have happened. After all, sooner or later we'd have to leave – only now it's sooner. My uncle can't complain about that." His expression brightened and his voice took on a more cheerful tone. "Let's go ahead and have our party tomorrow. It would be a shame not to say goodbye to our closest friends. We'll end it early and leave immediately afterwards."

"And then what?"

"And then I'll take you back to University Seven, and report to the guild." He attempted a smile. "Hey, it could be worse: this way they still owe me the rest of my vacation."

"Oh..." My voice trailed off. The suddenness with which our plans had changed was shocking.

A moment later, he stood up and resumed his pacing. "The only thing I'm really sorry about is that our time here is suddenly so much shorter."

"So am I."

He stopped walking and turned to look at me.

"Janne, I've been wondering…" He hesitated, and then began again. "I realize how uncertain you were about getting involved with me in the first place. I understand. Truly I do… I know it was because of your marriage. And I could see how uneasy you were when we first got here. Valhalla must have seemed very strange, and you still weren't sure you could trust our relationship. You seem a lot more comfortable now with me – with us being together."

"I am. Valhalla has been perfect."

"I'm glad." Once again he hesitated, and I wondered what was going through his mind. "You know, it's funny – I've enjoyed my career with the Space Guild, and I never thought I'd want to live here again but… But, Janne, I don't want to leave Valhalla!" he cried. "I'm afraid that once we do, you might never come back."

"I will if you ask me." I don't know how I managed to say this so calmly.

He relaxed visibly. "Ever since Stormhaven, I've been trying to get up the nerve to ask if you'd consider giving up your job at the University for Valhalla and me. Do you think you could?"

"I've been wondering the same thing."

He came to me and put both hands on my shoulders. His gaze, as he looked down at me, was intense. "And…?"

"And I decided that I'll know for sure once I'm back at University – once I have a chance to take a look at my life there with another possibility in mind."

"That's fair. As for me, I already know what I want." His smile was genuine for the first time since we had entered the room. "My personal pledge to you is that while we're away, I'll consider what other kind of career I might possibly pursue if you decide against coming back here. I want us to be together whether or not we return to Valhalla."

By now I knew him well enough to see that he was Valhallan through and through, and that he would never be happy anywhere else but his home world. Besides, although I wouldn't have been able to explain it even if I'd tried, his 'Valhallan-ness' was part of what attracted me to him.

"Still, it seems only fair to remind you of all the things that will be expected of us if we do come back," he was saying. "The obligations. Do you remember: we discussed them on Caliban?"

"I remember."

"So perhaps it's unnecessary for me to go over them again – except this time I'll want them too." His fingers tightened on my shoulders. "Janne, I want us to marry – in a real Valhallan ceremony. And I want to give you this." He touched the black dragon necklace that he always wore. "The *Halsband Hökness* – the Hawkness Necklace: it's the symbol of my family's continuity. You'd be expected to wear it until our first child, our son, comes of age."

I couldn't help smiling. "How do you know our first child would be a son?"

"Biology." He was quite serious.

"Oh."

"…And my training. As I told you, I've been conditioned from childhood to produce a son first. Valhallans always do."

Suddenly, I realized how very little I actually knew about him and his world. *But I can learn*, I assured myself.

"Also, if we make our home here, another thing I'd like to do is continue my father's work," Eirik said. "He was determined to convert Valhalla to a democratic government rather than a dictatorship. Of course, all of that will have to wait. Because of Einarr…"

But I was unable to keep my real concerns to myself any longer. "What do you think you'll have to do once you're back with the guild? Will it be dangerous?"

"I have no idea. Janne," he coaxed, "tell me what you're thinking."

"Your recall… The risks…" I babbled. And then suddenly, "Is there a doctor here who would know how to remove or neutralize my birth control capsule?"

He stared at me until I blushed with embarrassment. "Would you really do that for me, *Kjæresta*?"

I could only nod.

He pulled me to my feet to give me a passionate kiss. Then he held me away at arm's length. "So what would you think if we turned our going away party into a spur-of-the-moment wedding ceremony?"

…A wedding! was my bemused thought. Did Valhallans actually still celebrate that arcane Earth custom? Would a Valhallan marriage be

recognized as legally binding on the other worlds of the Concorde Alliance? And why should that even concern me?

"How do you feel about that, Janne?" Eirik was asking. "Should we get married tomorrow with our friends here as our witnesses?"

Quickly dismissing my wandering thoughts, and with some trepidation I said, "I think it's a wonderful idea, Eirik! But what about your uncle? Is he going to cause trouble if we do?"

"To hell with Einarr!" His smile was radiant. "This is the happiest day of my life, and I want to celebrate with our friends! Let's have that party tomorrow – and we'll worry about dealing with Uncle Einarr if and when we ever return to Valhalla."

12.

We were up before dawn the next morning. Considering the events of the previous evening, what surprised me the most was that either of us had managed to sleep at all. But when we sat down for breakfast, one look at the food and my appetite fled.

How could Eirik sit there, calmly eating *flatbröd* and *gravlax*, sipping *kaffe* and discussing plans for our party when overnight both of our lives had changed just about as radically as it was possible for them to change? In fact, when I thought about it, I could hardly believe how irrevocably we were about to commit ourselves to a life together on what seemed, in the sober light of morning, like a moment's whim.

Could I really go through with this?

Also, there was the not-so-insignificant matter of Eirik's recall to active duty to consider, and what it might mean for the entire Concorde as well as for us personally.

Here we are, talking about having a future together, I thought, *when we might not even* have *a future!*

But the last thing I wanted to do was trouble Eirik with my doubts. So I ate what I could, and made a determined effort to keep up my end of the conversation.

Immediately after breakfast, Eirik contacted Magnus and Inga at Stormhaven to invite them to join us as soon as possible. It was a measure of their friendship that they didn't ask him to elaborate – instead, they simply acknowledged that they would start on their way within the hour, and that we should expect them at Hawkness House well before noon.

After he had broken off contact, Eirik sat staring at the comm screen for several long moments. "You know, Janne," he said at last, "to be perfectly honest, I didn't ask them here just because I want them to be the first to know about our change of plans – although I'm certainly anxious to tell them. But it occurred to me that it might be a good idea to have them around as a buffer in case Uncle Einarr decides to arrive early and stir up trouble."

"Trouble! I can't believe he'll dare to show up at all, let alone early, after the scene he caused last night!"

"Obviously you didn't know my uncle."

Coming over to stand behind him, I started to knead his tense shoulders. "And I plan to keep it that way."

"It may not be possible, especially once we're married."

"I realize that. But I don't intend to let him ruin this day. He's just a mean old man, Eirik – and there's no point in giving him the satisfaction of thinking that he has any power over either one of us."

"How wise you are – and how very difficult it will be to keep that in mind once he's actually here."

"You know, the person I really feel sorry for is your Aunt Helga," I said. "After all, she's the one who has to live with that beast."

He sighed. "Poor *Tante Helga*..."

"Cheer up, Eirik." I gave his shoulders one last squeeze. "Magnus and Inga should be arriving any time now, and we have a lot to do before they get here."

"We certainly do." He stood up and started out of the room. "Oh, by the way..." he said almost too casually as he turned back. "That business we talked about last night... If you're interested, I thought you might want to know that Inga is a healer."

"We talked about an awful lot of things last night, Eirik. What does Inga's being a healer have to do with any of it?"

He hesitated. "You know... About your implant. I thought that since Inga's a trained healer, you might want to talk to her. She might know how to remove or disable it."

Yet another one of those impulsive commitments that I had made the night before!

"Ah, yes," I said. "I'll be sure to ask her."

We spent the rest of the morning making preparations for our party, and the time passed more quickly than I would have expected. Before I knew it, our two loyal friends were entering the room, apologizing for being later than originally planned because it had taken them longer than expected to collect their son's belongings.

Soon Eirik was telling them about our previous evening's disaster with Einarr. Not surprisingly, they were every bit as scandalized as he was, and they were also disturbed to hear about Eirik's imminent return to active duty. But their mood changed abruptly when he revealed our intention to marry, and today.

"The moment you walked in our door, I knew you were the one!" Magnus exclaimed, catching me up in a fierce hug that lifted my feet right off the floor. "I don't know how to thank you for bringing him back to us."

"Magnus, *Kjæreste*, you're such a romantic," Inga teased, her sparkling blue eyes alight with laughter as she bounced their golden-haired young son Trön on her hip. "Which is why I love him," she confided to me in a very public whisper as she too gave me a somewhat awkward hug while juggling the baby.

"If you think *I'm* a romantic, what about my friend Eirik here?" was Magnus' teasing rejoinder. "Imagine: just five nights with us at Stormhaven and the next thing you know he's proposed to Janne and she's accepted. Obviously Eirik made good use of those five nights."

Which led to a great deal of predictable but good-natured banter about hastily arranged marriages, and rather predictably prompted Magnus to crack open a bottle of his special home-brew – several bottles of which he just happened to have brought along with him.

With the men thus occupied, I screwed up my courage and went over to consult Inga about the feasibility of removing my implant.

Her warm hazel eyes searched my face. "If this is what you really wish," she said at last, "I'm willing to look at your off-world device."

Leaving the men in charge of the baby, we excused ourselves and retreated to the privacy of Eirik's study.

She was very gentle and quite thorough, speaking careful Galach as she asked a great many perceptive questions while cautiously probing my arm. "Do you remember what it looked like? How big around – how long?" she eventually wanted to know.

"I think it was about…"

"Not words. Draw it for me. The actual size."

I did, as best I could recall.

"And there were no other parts to it?" she asked, examining my crude sketch. "Nothing else attached?"

"Not that I remember."

"Then it seems very straightforward. I think I can remove it. But before I do anything that can't be undone, I feel I must ask you once again: are you sure about this? Don't answer too quickly," she hastened to add, holding up a hand. "We Valhallans believe that it's a wise idea to make sure a marriage is working well before a couple conceives a child."

"You know Eirik's been recalled by the Space Guild. We may not have much time."

Her eyes were filled with unspoken concern – for me, for Eirik, and for our unborn children: I could see it all there, and I was grateful that she chose not to lecture me.

"Please go ahead, Inga," I told her. "It seems like the right thing to do."

Taking me at my word and without further questions, she went to work. She was surprisingly skilled for someone without a Concorde medical degree – which amused her when I told her so.

"Concorde training doesn't necessarily make a good healer," was her tart rejoinder.

From my own personal experience, I had to agree.

The deed done, she held up the narrow, inch-long tubule to inspect it. "Janne, I must tell you: it's very strange for me to realize that you have to rely on this foreign object and not yourself to determine whether or not you will have children." Suddenly, she smiled. "But then, I suppose it's equally strange for you to be told that we don't have any need for this kind of device at all."

We chatted amiably about inconsequential matters as she bandaged my arm. "There you are: good as new," she announced at last. "You know, although I'm not certain about these matters, I would guess that it may be a while before all of the residual anti-fertility chemicals are eliminated from your system. So don't be disappointed if you don't become pregnant right away," she added with a mischievous grin. "And don't look so worried: at the very least you should have nine months to get used to the idea."

When we rejoined the men, the baby was happily tossing his toys around, and Eirik and Magnus were still discussing Eirik's sudden recall, and our necessarily shortened stay on Valhalla. Naturally, Magnus and Inga were disappointed, but Eirik refused to allow them to dwell on it. Instead, he skillfully turned the conversation to Valhallan politics, speculating about who Uncle Einarr might name as his successor.

A short while later, to my utter amazement, Einarr himself showed up, trailed by Aunt Helga who was, if possible, even more subdued than she had been when I had first met her. As she entered the room, she looked at me so guiltily that for one brief moment she almost had me believing that it had been she, rather than her husband, who had behaved in such a boorish manner the previous evening!

Uncle Einarr greeted Magnus and Inga, and finally Eirik, with a heartiness that failed to disguise an undercurrent of nastiness. I made sure that I said hello from a safe distance, to which he responded, entirely in character, with yet another sly wink.

To my relief, several other guests arrived at about the same time, and Einarr was forced to settle for what amounted to a semi-private interview with Eirik. The two men stood off to one side of the room, beside the ornately-carved stone fireplace mantle, involved in what appeared to be an intense conversation.

I was so busy greeting our guests, all of whom seemed anxious to speak with me at length, that I only managed to catch an occasional word and phrase. However it sounded to me as if Einarr was still trying to convince Eirik that his way, the old despotic way, was best. It was an argument that I knew they had had many times in the past.

After a while, Magnus strolled over to join them. "Excuse me, *Hövding*," he said, loudly enough so that anyone in the room who was interested could hear. "I apologize for interrupting, but it seems to me that you're testing Eirik, trying to find out whether or not he's changed his political views while he's been away with the Space Guild."

"Of course I am!" Einarr growled, not bothering to hide his annoyance at Magnus's intrusion. "I'd like to think that the experience of commanding men, of actually being responsible for their lives and having to make difficult life-and-death decisions, has made my nephew a bit more realistic about what it means to be a good ruler."

"You know what I want for Valhalla," Eirik said, also raising his voice for the benefit of their audience – for by now most of our guests were unashamedly listening in. "Nothing you say will ever change that."

"Well, I don't intend to turn over the leadership of this planet to a man who doesn't share my beliefs."

"I've never doubted that for a moment, Uncle Einarr. Just as you probably have no illusions that I'll ever agree with you. In fact, I'm not really sure why we're having this conversation."

"Damn it, Eirik! We're having this conversation because I'm concerned about Valhalla's future! And so are you! But I want to know that the right person will carry on when I'm gone. I had hoped you'd be that man. I thought we might be able to reach a compromise."

"There's no way to compromise on differences as basic as ours," Eirik said with great dignity. "And now, if you'll excuse me, I think I should attend to my other guests."

Uncle Einarr remained alone by the fireplace for the rest of the party, for no one seemed at all anxious to talk to him – and whenever I happened to look over in his direction, he was watching the rest of the company with narrowed eyes and a sour expression on his face.

***

Because of the shortness of our stay, Eirik hadn't had time to introduce me to all of his friends. His solution was to throw a party.

We had opened up the formal ballroom and, with the housecarls' help, had decorated it with masses of cut flowers. A veritable feast of roasted meats and smoked fish, fresh fruits and vegetables, and a bewildering array of desserts had somehow been prepared and set out on heavy wooden tables that ran the entire length of the room. There were more guests than I could possibly keep track of, yet all of them seemed to know who I was and addressed me in carefully enunciated Norsk or else in Galach. Their friendliness was heartwarming, and they made me feel confident that I would receive an equally enthusiastic welcome should we ever choose to return to Valhalla.

As some point in the festivities, Magnus ordered that the *aquavit*, summer mead, and his home brew should be opened – and once the corks had stopped popping, he called for and somehow received silence.

"Friends," his deep voice filled the room, "it's been a long time since Eirik Sanderson has been here– much too long, if you ask me. I know I'm not the only one who's missed him, so I'd like to propose a toast to Sera Janne Arramsdotter, to thank her for giving Eirik a reason to come home. Janne…"

Eirik beamed as our guests raised their mugs and glasses.

"It hardly seems necessary to say how delighted we are to have them both here. Unfortunately, it may be even longer before they're able to return, because Eirik has just learned that due to an emergency situation, he's been immediately recalled by the guild to active duty. Let's hope it's nothing serious and that the emergency will soon be over…"

Voices rose in an uneasy babble, but all conversation ceased when Magnus held up a hand. "But if these two are leaving us so much sooner than we'd hoped, at least we can send them off knowing that they take with them the love and good wishes of their many Valhallan friends…"

Magnus raised his glass to silence the applause. "For surely they will return – because now they have a reason to… Eirik and Janne have asked us here today not just to say goodbye, but also to bear witness as they join their lives together in our Valhallan way."

By the time the commotion had died down, Eirik was at my side. As I watched, he removed his necklace – it was strange to see him without it, yet it must have been even stranger for him since I knew that this was the first and only time he had ever taken it off since he had acquired it on his twentieth birthday. And now he held it aloft for all of our guests to see.

In the hush that followed, he spoke. He had told me ahead of time what was going to happen, so I would be sure to understand, and I knew that the Norsk words he spoke were from the ancient Valhallan Ceremony of Joining.

"Janne Arramsdotter, *Kjæresta*," he said, "I, Eirik Sanderson, give you this, the *Halsband Hökness*, symbol of the House of Hawkness, as a token of my love and trust, in the knowledge that you will wear it for me, and for all the Hawkness generations past and future, until the time comes when our son is old enough to claim it from you."

I bowed my head, and he clasped the necklace around my throat. It was surprisingly heavy.

I noticed that Einarr had abandoned his post by the fireplace and was regarding me avidly.

"These links are heavy," Eirik intoned, "as heavy as the responsibilities that we now share. We have freely chosen to join our lives together. Let our guests be our witnesses."

Eirik had coached me beforehand about what to say, and I replied in Norsk as he had instructed: "I, Janne Arramsdotter, agree to take my place beside you, Eirik Sanderson, in the House of Hawkness. I will wear the *Halsband Hökness* and protect it with my life until our son is old enough to claim it from me. In this way Hawkness House will go on through the future generations."

Then, before all these people, I briefly pressed the palms of my upraised hands against his.

"Let our guests be our witnesses," we spoke in unison. And in sharp contrast to the long, stiffly formulaic and formal joining ceremonies of Caliban, this was everything that was necessary to make our marriage official.

People immediately came crowding around to hug and congratulate us, and suddenly it was like a celebration on any other Concorde world. More drinks were poured out and people toasted us, making the usual jokes about children and married life.

I felt incredibly giddy – it might have been Magnus' home brew, but it also had a great deal to do with being caught up in the happiness of the moment and the excitement of our guests. Yet all afternoon, I was haunted by a subtle undercurrent of tension.

Whenever I allowed myself to think about its cause – which was not very often – I knew well enough what it was: a mixture of uneasiness about the way Uncle Einarr kept watching me, combined with apprehension about the many uncertainties in Eirik's and my future, as well as recognition of the irrevocable step that I had just impulsively taken with a very kind and attractive man who was, however, still practically a stranger.

The first stars of the evening were just coming out when Eirik and I slipped away from the party and left Valhalla –neither of us knowing when, or even if, we would ever return.

13.

The flight back to University VII was not a pleasant one. Shortly after we lifted off from Valhalla, our celebratory mood evaporated and neither of us seemed to feel much like talking. As a result, we spent a large part of what began to feel like endless hours, eating together, sleeping together, and staring moodily out at the passing stars together – all in almost total silence. It was obvious that both of us were brooding over fears that neither one was willing to voice.

However, we had a lot less time to brood than previously. Since Valhalla and University VII are in the same quadrant of Concorde space, Eirik was able use the AI to plot a direct route, and our return trip was much shorter than our journey from Caliban had been. Unfortunately, just as we were coming out of hyperspace for the last time on the outskirts of the University system, we ran into some unexpected trouble.

We were finally speaking again – more, I believe, to distract ourselves from our worries than from any pressing need to say something significant during our last few hours together. In fact, we were discussing Eirik's link, the 'crown' he wore while piloting the ship. And although we had entered into the discussion with benign intentions, it was rapidly threatening to degenerate into an ugly quarrel.

"Is that thing really necessary?" I demanded, gesturing at his crown. "Can't you fly without it?"

I refused to look directly at him: the very sight of him communicating directly mind-to-mind with the ship's AI by means of neurological implants made me slightly queasy. But I didn't want to tell him that, just as I didn't want to hear the specific physical details of how the link was actually connected to his brain.

"Of course I can fly without it," was his rather brusque response, "but not nearly as easily."

"That doesn't make sense," I protested. "What if…?"

"Listen: the link gives me a direct connection to the ship." He sounded like he was patiently trying to explain some extremely difficult adult concept to a very young child. "It eliminates all sorts of time-consuming steps when I need to communicate with the onboard AI. Together we can make decisions – plot a course and calculate jumps – much faster and more concisely than I could possibly do on my own."

"So you're saying that…?"

"Look, Janne," he interrupted, "this ship and I have got to be able to work together as a unit and react quickly to any situation that might arise – the faster the better. And the link allows us to do just that."

"You're talking as if that AI is a person rather than an artificial construct!"

"Sometimes I think it might actually be sentient…"

A light flashed on the console.

"Hold on a minute. We're about to come out of our last jump." Even as he spoke, his attention was riveted on the instruments. "Now we'll find out just how good our calculations really were."

The shifting pearly-grayness that accompanies extended hyperspace travel vanished and was replaced by the familiar black velvet of Normal Space.

"Nice placement! And you can thank my link to the AI for that," was his smug pronouncement, as the outermost planet of the University system shimmered into focus far ahead on the holo-screen.

The next instant, he let out a yelp and reflexively flung one arm across my chest as if to protect me from an impending air taxi crash. Simultaneously, a brilliant streak of light shot across our forward screens: in fact, it was so intense that for a moment the main holo-screen overloaded and blanked out completely. At the same time, our ship banked sharply, lurching sideways as if it had been struck by a giant fist.

"Eirik!" I shrieked, as both of my hands spasmed tight on the co-pilot chair armrests.

"They almost ran us over!" he raged. "We're right smack in the middle of a bloody regulation entrance point, and they almost ran us over!"

"Who did?" I gasped, fighting to get my ragged breathing under control and rubbing my eyes to dispel the afterimage that still clouded my vision. "What *was* that?"

"That's what we're damn well going to find out!" He immediately instructed the AI to adjust our scanners to track the intruder, and then quickly became engrossed in the scanner sweep. "That bastard was in one hell of a hurry!"

I wasn't sure if he was speaking to the AI or me, but my heart rate was finally beginning to drop back towards normal.

"Got him!" Eirik announced with grim satisfaction.

The forward screens showed that we were radically changing direction, accelerating rapidly.

"What are you doing?" I cried. "Where are we going?"

"We're going after that ship! I want to give him a piece of my mind – if I can catch him that is…" His voice trailed off. "How can anything move that fast?" he muttered, obviously not expecting me to answer. Then he was silent, absorbed in the shifting dataflow.

"Interesting…" he said at last.

"*What* is?" I asked rather sharply, frustrated by how little he was actually telling me about what he was doing.

"That is." He pointed at the holo-screen. "Look: he's coming up on two more blips. He seems to be decelerating, so he's probably not planning on running *them* down." He looked over in my direction, but I knew that he wasn't really seeing me. "I wonder how close we can get. I'd love to log a visual."

"Please, Eirik, let's not do anything foolish."

"We have no choice: I have to get a look at them!"

Far out in the blackness of space, much too far away to be able to see them clearly on our screens, I could just make out three tiny dots, dully reflecting the light of the University System's distant sun.

"Come on, you bastards…" Eirik coaxed. "Just stick around for a couple more minutes… Good! I've got you now… Damn it! There they go – they must have scanned us too." He sounded bitterly disappointed. "Wow, will you look at those bogeys move! I've never seen anything travel that fast. Never!"

"What are they?" I asked in a tremulous voice, thinking about rumors of aliens.

Quickly glancing over at me, he reached out to place a reassuring hand on mine. "It's okay, Janne: they're not coming this way."

I let out my breath and gave him a shaky smile. "It looks like they ran off, doesn't it?"

"It looks that way all right... I wonder why? If they have the technology to move that fast, you'd assume they'd be that much better armed – which means that if they'd wanted to get rid of us, we couldn't have put up much of a fight. Not against whatever weapons they're probably carrying..."

He spoke so casually about our possible annihilation!

"But it seems as if they were more anxious not to be seen up close than to take us on," he continued, and then he sighed. "Oh well, at least our AI will have captured them on the video log, even if it isn't a close-up."

"You're still heading in that direction!" I reminded him, unable to keep a nervous edge from my voice. "Shouldn't we be turning back towards University?"

"Not yet. I want to check out the area. We're right near one of the standard coordinates for outward-bound jumps."

We slowed as we approached the place where the strange ships had been. Eirik still had the main holo-screen on its highest resolution, and he kept working with the AI to adjust its focus.

"Nothing," he said in disgust, and then, pointing, "Aha! Look at that, Janne. Right where I thought they'd be..."

"I don't see anything."

"There. And there – and there: mines. The mass is too small to show up on an ordinary mid-range scan, but we're getting a good signal now that we're close enough. Of course, if we weren't expecting them we'd have missed them altogether – at least, we would have until it was too late."

Now that he had shown me where to look, I could just make out a swarm of tiny spheres that were floating in the void: a treacherous, nearly-invisible web of destruction.

"Eirik, shouldn't you notify the guild?"

"I will. But first...Fortunately this is a military flier, and even the smallest units have some basic weaponry. So I'm going to clear those mines before we do anything else."

It took a while to destroy them all, but with each explosion, Eirik seemed that much more grimly satisfied.

At last, when we were finally heading back towards University VII, I let out a sigh of relief.

"Well, that does it," Eirik muttered, apparently more to himself than to me. "I'm convinced."

"Convinced of what?"

"Huh? Oh – that something unusual is going on out here, and that I'm going to have to get involved."

"Involved?" A chill shivered down my spine. "Involved in what?"

"Something your father asked me to do." The moment the words were out of his mouth, he glanced away, unable to meet my eyes.

"My father! Eirik, what's going on?"

"Nothing serious – he just wants me to check up on some mine sightings…" he responded with studied casualness, "…see who's turning in reports, where they've been found, who's keeping track of them – that sort of thing."

"Why you?" I demanded. "Why can't it be someone else?" To my own ears I sounded calm, but ice-cold fury was beginning to consume my heart.

"I'll be able to do this because I'm in a position to see any reports that come into the Space Guild."

"In other words, my father wants you to spy for him."

"Now, Janne, be reasonable. Your father's just trying to get to the bottom of all this."

"I don't understand why it's any of his business."

"It's everyone's business – and he's the logical person to pursue it! After all, he's just been re-elected to the Interplanetary Council, and he's also been asked to join the Inner Circle. Besides, the Prime has tasked him to find out what's going on. It's as simple as that."

"It doesn't sound very simple to me!"

"Why are you being so difficult?"

"Because it seems pretty strange that all of a sudden you're talking about working for my father! When did you have a chance to make these arrangements?… Oh, I know: that first evening we were on Caliban. You were in his study talking to him when I walked in on you. And stupid me: I wondered what you were doing there."

"I was there because I'd just witnessed a mine incident in Caliban air space, and your father wanted my firsthand report."

"How convenient for my father that it happened to be you! Did the two of you also decide that you should get involved with me so your communications with my father would look perfectly reasonable?"

"My god, how can you even think such a thing? In case you don't know it, life is full of coincidences, and it was a coincidence that I happened to meet the daughter of Caliban's Prime Minister. Why, you could have been anyone! And for your information, I was already in love with you by the time we reached Arcadia – despite my better judgment."

I had to look away from his fierce gaze.

"Listen, Janne," he went on in a gentler voice, "those mines are turning up everywhere. And every one of them – not just the ones we found today – has been located in heavily-traveled jump points. The lives of ordinary Concorde citizens are in jeopardy, and the Prime wants to do something about it – preferably before anyone else gets hurt."

"If the Prime and my father are so concerned, they ought to go through official channels instead of hiring spies. Instead of hiring *you*!"

"They *are* going through official channels!" He sighed. "But confidentially, nothing they're turning up makes any sense – which is why they're resorting to less direct methods." Again he hesitated. "You know, it wasn't an accident that Cristan Andebar was on Caliban."

"Andebar? Don't tell me he's part of this too!"

"Well who would be in a better position to do a bit of investigating? After all, his musicians are all over the Concorde. They see things – hear things – and they report back to him at the Music School. They always have, only now they'll be looking and listening for something specific."

"Fine. Let *them* do the dirty work."

"But I have access to information that Andebar's people can't possibly touch: Guild information. And I promised your father I'd think it over."

"Damn my father! He doesn't care about anyone but himself."

"That's not true and you know it! Your father's a very responsible and concerned citizen who's in a position of great trust. I only wish Valhalla had such a leader."

Without any warning, my eyes filled with tears. "I'm sorry, Eirik, I can't help it," I admitted. "I'm frightened. Frightened for you and frightened for us."

"Everyone's frightened, *Kjæresta*," he said quietly, "which is why I have to do this."

I understood his motives, but that didn't make it any easier for me to accept his decision. The Concorde government had always seemed so far away and impersonal. Having my father ask Eirik to possibly risk his life for something as abstract as the good of the Prime and the Concorde Alliance seemed unreasonable. Still, for Eirik's sake, I kept these uncharitable thoughts to myself. I could see that he was deeply concerned about the future – the Concorde Alliance's as well as our own.

As far as our own personal future went, Inga had been correct when she'd suggested that it might take a while for the anti-fertility drugs to be flushed from my system. Later that same day, when I kissed Eirik goodbye at Gemini Space Station, I knew – with very mixed feelings indeed – that I wasn't pregnant.

***

And so I returned to my room in the South Polar Dome. I was amazed to discover that during my absence it had apparently shrunk and become a great deal duller and more impersonal than I remembered. Even the highly-processed air that was piped into the Research Facility seemed to have gone stale.

The following day, with few regrets, I handed in my resignation and began working out my final weeks on University VII.

***

Quite naturally, the question that troubled me the most – besides the issue of Eirik's safety – was what I was going to do after I left University. Eirik had been adamant about my not returning to Valhalla to face his uncle alone, and I had to accept the wisdom of this. Besides, I asked myself, how happy could I possibly be, living on Valhalla without Eirik?

We had also discussed the feasibility of my going home to Caliban until the crisis was past, and he was able to resign his commission. This second alternative was Eirik's preference, but I had balked at the idea of once again being subjected to my father's whims. Sad to say, it was yet another thing we had quarreled about just before we parted.

"Maybe I'll petition Andebar to enroll in his Music School," was my sarcastic retort. "If he agrees to let me in, I'll certainly be his oldest undergraduate student ever – and if I'm really lucky, maybe he can even turn me into your fellow spy!"

***

Several weeks had passed since our final argument, and I still hadn't heard from Eirik – not since he had called to tell me of his safe return to guild headquarters. And what little information the news services broadcasted about the developing situation was not encouraging: mines were turning up on an almost daily basis now and several of the resulting explosions had resulted in massive fatalities. I worried constantly about Eirik's safety, and I was miserable whenever I allowed myself to dwell on our last, angry conversation. It hurt to know that our idyllic vacation had ended on such a sour note.

Finally, mere days before my position was due to terminate, I received a call at my workstation. When I punched it up on my console, hoping that it was Eirik and requesting 'visual only' so as not to disturb my co-workers, the following message appeared, projected in the air above my comm unit:

*Private communication for Statistician Janne Trellerian.
Access only through personal comm unit + scramble*

How odd! I thought. *More secrecy.*

Back in my room, I eagerly accepted the call, but my disappointment was impossible to disguise when my father's face, not Eirik's, appeared on the holo-screen.

"Janne, Eirik asked me to get in touch with you," he announced without preamble. "He said to apologize for not calling you himself."

My mouth went dry. "Where is he? Is something wrong?"

"I'm afraid there's been some trouble. But don't worry, he's fine," he immediately added. "Someone must have realized he's doing intelligence work for us – and that someone tried to stop him."

"Oh, no!" I gasped. "What happened?"

"I'd rather not discuss it on the comm."

Ah, the self-discipline that's drilled into every politician's child! Instead of protesting, instead of howling with frustration or voicing any of my angry thoughts, I found myself stoically replying, "I understand, Father. Is there anything I can do?"

"There most certainly is! I want you – Eirik wants you – to book yourself onto the next flight to Caliban. Neither of us will feel safe until you're back here with me. Whoever's behind this business definitely won't think twice about kidnapping or murder... Janne, are you still there?"

I eased back into range of the holo-camera.

"It sounds so melodramatic, Father: kidnapping and diabolical plots. Can't you tell me anything?"

"I'm sorry – not over the Net."

I sighed. "Very well. I'll see what I can do about booking passage."

"Janne, there's one more thing I'd like you to consider."

"Yes?"

"I know how difficult your relationship with Karle was – and I realize I was to blame for forcing you into it. At the time I did what I thought was best. I'm just sorry you had to suffer for my political ambitions..."

I was so astonished by this admission that for several moments I lost track of what he was saying. I had never expected to hear such a confession from Prime Minister Arram Trellarian!

"...At any rate," he continued, "what I'm asking you to do now is to put all of that behind us. I'd like you to come home and work with me. There's an enormous backlog of highly sensitive information that has to be processed and put into some sort of meaningful order before it can be passed on to the appropriate parties. TiAnn and I are doing our best, but to be honest, we're overwhelmed. What I need is a confidential assistant who's an expert statistician like yourself. Will you help us?"

In spite of the seriousness of the situation, his humble request gave me such a giddy sense of pleasure that I actually laughed aloud.

"Why not?" was my immediate, unquestioning response. "I've been brooding about what to do with myself once I'm finished here – and now you've given me the answer."

His smile was warm. "Thank you, Janne. I can't tell you how much this means to me – and to a great many other people."

After the screen went blank, I went on sitting there, staring at the console for the longest time. Finally, rousing myself from my musings, I logged back on and messaged a local travel agency to book me one-way passage to Caliban.

14.

And so I returned to my father's house. How strange it was to find the three of us there – myself, my sister and my father – together again after so many years!

TiAnn was doing legal research: searching for precedents, anything that might help the Prime wield his power more effectively. She was also compiling weekly summaries of the musicians' reports, which were forwarded to us by Cristan Andebar.

My job was more interesting than I had expected: I had to process and make sense of the staggering volume of data that was coming into our office from all of our other, non-Music School sources. And to my surprise, I discovered that working with my father was a pleasure. Now that we had a common goal, it seemed that our philosophical differences weren't so great after all.

I sat at a desk in his study, reading field reports and logging them into a special secure data bank. Some were from Eirik, but most were from other sources, many of them submitted by coded informants. Accounts came flooding in from every sector of the Concorde Alliance. And at first, due to their sheer numbers, they were a meaningless jumble. Many nights I went to bed with my head throbbing and my thoughts churning, only to chase troubled dreams down the corridors of my mind as I tried to make sense out of chaos, even in my sleep. But after a while definite patterns began to emerge, and at that point I asked my father to take a look at what I was doing.

"There seem to be several different things going on," I said when he joined me at my console, "all at the same time."

"Educate me."

"Okay – let's start with the mines, since that's by far the largest category... You wouldn't believe how many sightings we've had so far, and they just keep pouring in..."

"Unfortunately, they do."

"At any rate," I continued, "the first and most obvious thing the majority of them have in common is that they're turning up within the boundaries of fixed air routes, even though the systems where we're finding them seem, at first glance, to be scattered randomly throughout the Concord worlds. But in fact they're mainly being set in busy places – planets like Valhalla, where air traffic is light, haven't reported a single mine."

"Can you figure out why?"

"It's almost as if whoever's setting them isn't bothering with places that won't attract attention. Look here..." I pulled up a summary of incidents by location ."Two from Zenith, which is pretty far out of the normal traffic patterns, but twenty-three in Caliban alone – after all, this planet is much closer to the Hub. Six from Gateway – that's another outlying planet; thirty-one from New Egypt where Andebar played last month; twenty from Galleron Six, and so on. You get the idea. Now look at this: forty-two in the air space right around Concordia itself. Further analysis shows that nearly eighty percent of all reported incidents occurred within a sixty parsec distance from the Hub. And more than half of those were within three days' travel. In other words, the closer you get to the Hub, the greater your chances of hitting a mine."

"Good work, Janne! This is going to be very useful. But you said there was more. What else have you got?"

"Well, in addition to the mine reports, there are several other, lesser categories. Disruptions of public services, satellite networks, and air traffic schedules – you name it. By the way, I've included riots in this one, and unfortunately it's a rapidly-expanding category. I think we're going to see a lot more of them in the weeks to come..."

"Then there are the assaults. The majority of them are on individuals – similar to what happened to Eirik – but mixed in with those are perhaps half a dozen or so real oddballs."

"Oddballs? In what way?"

"I know this is going to sound strange, but there are a number of fairly well-documented sightings within Concorde space – things you'd almost be forced to conclude are non-Concorde starships."

"Enemy or alien?" I admired how calmly he accepted this bizarre information.

"Eirik told me he doesn't believe in the existence of aliens – and frankly, at this point, there isn't enough data to draw any conclusions about that. However, there is a common thread that runs through all of these incidents: those unidentified objects – starships or whatever – are fast! Whoever built them has developed what one source calls 'a hell of a hyper-drive!' He even gave them a nickname: IFOs – Incredibly Fast Objects."

"Didn't you and Eirik spot several on your way back to University Seven?"

"It seems we did."

"And it sounds to me like they're going to be a real headache for everyone concerned... By the way, are these IFOs attacking anyone?"

"Not so far. It's weird: almost as soon as one of them is spotted by our ships, it tears out of the area at incredible speed – which is exactly what happened when Eirik and I almost literally ran into one. Of course, Eirik was convinced that the IFO we saw was setting mines... Oh, and I nearly forgot to mention that whatever these things are, they don't respond to calls on any of the standard frequencies."

"Well, then all we can do is hope they continue to run away," was my father's grim assessment. "The other thing we need to hope for is that if we *are* being observed by aliens, they decide to wait for less troubled times before they decide to try to make contact."

"So you think the IFOs aren't part of this mine business?"

He shrugged. "Who knows? Has anyone seen an IFO actually setting mines?"

"Although we saw them near the mines, Eirik and I weren't sure *what* they were doing. And no one's reported anything definite either."

"One question I'd certainly like to have answered: if these IFOs *are* setting mines, why run away when we spot them? Why not use the element of surprise to attack us?"

"Maybe they just want to frighten us," I suggested.

"It's possible... Or maybe whoever's setting the mines is taking advantage of the IFO sightings – which actually aren't connected with them at all – hoping to look even more powerful and mysterious than they really are."

"So what do you want me to do with the IFO reports?"

"For now, let's keep them separate from the rest and continue to log in any new ones on the sector maps."

"Good idea. By the way, I think we should also separate out the attacks against individuals. If we get enough of them, we may be able to find something: a pattern or central location that would help pinpoint the source or even the agenda of the enemy agents – if there are in fact enemy agents. And if we're very, very lucky, we might even catch someone."

"Hopefully not an alien!"

We both laughed. It helped to ease the tension.

***

Because we were hesitant about broadcasting our preliminary findings over the Net, we requested a special courier to fly our report directly to the Prime on Concordia. And when the courier arrived, it turned out to be Eirik.

My heart contracted when I saw him. He looked exhausted and very thin, but seemed to otherwise be in good spirits.

"I have a feeling I'm closing in on something important," he said, settling down beside me on the sofa, and accepting the drink my father offered him.

"Closing in on what though?" My father looked tired too. He'd been up all night editing our latest report, and now he and TiAnn sat opposite us in comfortable matching armchairs.

"Our culprit," Eirik said, looking extremely pleased with himself.

I noticed that TiAnn was watching him intently.

"Would you care to elaborate?" my father asked.

Eirik shook his head. "I haven't got enough hard evidence. But I will stick my neck out so far as to say that I have it on good authority that our troublemaker is probably going to turn out to be one of your fellow members of the Interplanetary Council, if not the Inner Circle itself."

"You're going to have to have extremely hard evidence to make *that* kind of accusation stick!" was TiAnn's comment.

"I realize that – which is why I'm here… Arram, I want you and the Prime to come up with a good reason to send me out to inspect orbital shipyards. It has to be something that looks official."

"Any place in particular that you want to check out?" my father asked.

"I'd rather not say."

"And you won't tell us who you suspect?"

"No. But I will speculate that it's someone who'd benefit from throwing the entire Concorde Alliance into a panic and would like to see the Prime lose control. Someone who might be able to take over if the right situation arises."

"I'm going to look into possible legal ramifications," my sister announced, keying on her data slate. "For example, under what conditions might the Prime be forced to resign? And who's next in the line of succession after his son Ferrin? Is there anyone who might benefit substantially from a change of government?"

"One thing's certain," my father said, "it would have to be a person who already has a great deal of power and the resources to create this mess."

I was unable to remain silent any longer. "Father, don't you think it's time someone besides Eirik was looking into this? After all, by now everyone must be aware of his connection to our family. Any involvement he has in tracking down the troublemaker is sure to be noticed by your enemies."

Eirik placed his hand over mine. "I know you're worried, Janne. But there are plenty of other agents besides me who are out there, all of them looking for answers. No one will notice one more."

"Agent? It sounds more like a spy to me!"

"Your father has designated me as one of his agents," was his patient reply. "I need to be officially attached to him in order to do this, and I assure you there's nothing to worry about."

"I don't agree! I suppose acting as my father's agent had nothing to do with your being assaulted by that thug on the *Solar Eclipse*."

My father and Eirik exchanged glances.

"Well, she has to read the reports..." My father's voice trailed off.

"And I want both of you to know that I don't like any of this!" I cut in angrily. "Not one bit! Whoever's doing this is starting to get suspicious. Eirik, I think you're taking far too many risks!"

"I understand why you feel that way," my father said before Eirik had a chance to respond, "but it can't be helped. I have to have someone I can trust implicitly working for me."

"I still don't understand why you won't let me spy for you," TiAnn interjected.

"You!" I cried.

"I could be very effective. If father would just let me go to Concordia, there are all sorts of things I could find out."

"TiAnn, that's quite enough!" my father snapped. "The answer is still no. We're dealing with ruthless criminals here, not courtroom opponents."

"I can be every bit as ruthless as any criminal!"

"I have better ways to use your talents other than spying and intrigue," he told her.

"Ha! You call that stupid legal stuff you've been foisting off on me useful? You can't fool me, Father: I know busywork when I see it. You're hoping to keep my mind off more important things."

"Don't be ridiculous."

"Why do you insist on treating me like a child when I could be a real asset for your investigation?"

My father stood up. "TiAnn, I'm too tired to discuss this any further. If you have some specific proposals, write them up and I'll consider them. But remember: I won't compromise your safety! And now I think we should adjourn for the evening. Eirik and Janne must surely want some time alone."

***

We walked in silence towards my room. In many ways, Eirik and I were still strangers. We had spent so little time together, and now it seemed unlikely that we would have many more opportunities to do so in the near future. At this point, I wasn't even sure what to say to him.

The moment my bedroom door closed behind us, I sat down on the edge of my bed and watched him walk over to the window and look out at the night. From where I sat, I could see Sycorax City's glittering lights beyond the Government House gardens, yet I doubted that he noticed the view.

"There were so many things left unsaid just now when we were talking to your father and sister…" He turned to face me. "But I don't want to leave it that way. Who knows when we'll see each other again."

"Don't say that, Eirik! It sounds so final."

"But, Janne, the ideas we were tossing around so carelessly tonight – attacks, spying, and the Concorde succession – those things all have deadly consequences. I don't know if you realize it, but at this point the person who started this insurrection can't afford to lose."

I shuddered. "Is it really an insurrection?"

"You've read the reports. What do *you* think?"

"I have to admit that you're probably right."

"Which is one of the reasons why I agreed to join your father's investigation," he said. "Believe me, I want this thing to be over as much as you do! Spying isn't my idea of fun. I want to go home and lead a normal life. I want to be with you! But if I don't see this through first, I'll never forgive myself. The survival of the Concorde Alliance as we know it may depend on someone – perhaps even me – finding the right answers. My god, I've hardly dared to admit to myself some of the thoughts I've had lately!"

"Tell me – that is, if you're able to talk about it."

He began pacing around the room – I was coming to realize he did this whenever he was agitated. Perhaps it helped him concentrate.

"Well, some of my thoughts concerned your father. When he asked me to work for him, I had to ask myself why…"

"What!"

But he went right on as if he hadn't heard my outburst. "…He said he needed someone who was in the Space Guild and traveled a great deal – said he wanted a person who could collect reports from all over the Concorde. That sounded reasonable until I asked myself: why not have Andebar do it?"

"Andebar."

"Yes: Andebar. Because the one thing I realized almost as soon as I joined the guild was that everywhere I went there were musicians – and I do mean everywhere. Every flight I was on and every planet I've ever visited had at least one or two and usually a great many more Journeymen musicians in residence. We're always picking them up and transporting them somewhere else – for free, of course, since they entertain the passengers and crew. And before long it occurred to me that Andebar has the most mobile group of informants in the entire Concorde… Janne, that man knows everything!"

"But my father's already using him."

"Not to the extent that I think he should. All Andebar's doing right now is exactly what he's always done: gathering random information. Wouldn't it be reasonable to ask him to really dig into this?"

"Are you saying that you're suspicious of my father for not making better use of Andebar, or are you implying that my father doesn't – or for some reason shouldn't – trust him?"

Eirik stopped pacing. "Janne, don't look at me like that! Try to bear with me. I have to ask these questions: my survival depends upon knowing the answers. What I'm doing right now is describing my thought process, not making accusations... And of course your father isn't our troublemaker."

I hadn't realized I was holding my breath.

"First of all, he couldn't be," Eirik was saying. "He has so many responsibilities here on Caliban and to the Interplanetary Council that I doubt he would have the energy to organize and carry out a rebellion of this apparent magnitude. Besides, he wouldn't. I've studied him, and he's the kind of person who accepts power but isn't greedy for it. Both the Prime and Andebar have a great deal of faith in him, and I have no reason to disagree with them."

"Well, that's a relief!" It was a sarcastic remark, but I was only half-joking. "Now tell me more about Andebar."

"Oh, yes indeed, I've thought about Cristan Andebar... A lot. You know, in some ways he has every reason to want to take over... He already has an incredible amount of clout...

"Imagine this, Janne: he knows almost everything that's happening all over the Concorde, all the time! Few people would dare to speak a word against him for fear that some random musician might overhear and report back to him. I'll even go so far as to say that I suspect Andebar uses everyone's uneasiness about him as a way to bring pressure to bear, to help him acquire funding for his Music School – which brings me to the main reason for not suspecting him: his Music School...

"He has an all-consuming passion for that institution. It's the love of his life and he'd never give it up – which is what he'd have to do if he was going to try to take control of the Concorde Alliance."

"Besides, he's been extremely cooperative," I reminded him. "His people are constantly feeding us information. Unless he was feeding us false information, I doubt he'd go out of his way to be so helpful if he was acting against the Prime."

"Exactly. So that means he's highly unlikely to be the culprit... By the way, have you had a chance to take a look at his musicians' reports?"

"TiAnn started doing a weekly summary before I even got here. According to Andebar's musicians, citizens from all over the Concorde are complaining. They feel the Prime isn't doing enough to solve this problem."

"Which is exactly what I think someone out there wants them to believe."

"But who? You've said it's someone who has power, but not enough to satisfy him or her; someone who has resources, but not enough for a direct confrontation. Someone who would look good if the Prime could be made to look bad. A person who would like trade and transportation to break down... But who would benefit from all that?"

"I thought of Tropi," Eirik said.

"Tropi? Isn't the Tropi system pretty close to Concordia and the Hub?"

"Yes. And Tropi has a huge export business in certain drugs – special medications, but also in aphrodisiacs and other stimulants. Just suppose their leader, the Tropi, thought her profits could be improved if she were to gain control of the Space Guild freighters and even Concordia?"

"Is that possible?"

"That's why I've been away for so long: I've been investigating the Tropi."

"And what did you find out?"

"That she's a very powerful, not to mention extremely busy and intelligent woman. As Tropi's planetary and religious leader, she has a following of priestesses who help her, but she still has a workload that would do in the likes of you and me...

"It's hard to imagine, Janne, but she has total responsibility for every aspect of her people's lives: their economy, harvests, festivals, general health, industries, reproduction – everything! She's far too involved with her own planet to even have time to join the Interplanetary Council, although Andebar's been urging her for years to do just that: in the past, she's simply sent a personal representative to the Council meetings...

"She's also very knowledgeable and extremely convincing: she certainly convinced me that she's a devout pacifist, and therefore totally opposed to violence of any sort. I guess I should have believed Andebar's assessment of her as absolutely trustworthy, but I admit I haven't felt much like trusting anyone lately."

"You say she's knowledgeable. Do you think she has any idea about who's causing the trouble?"

"I asked her that. But in the process of telling me her thoughts on the subject, she said some things that have given me more than one sleepless night..."

"Such as?"

"Well, when I asked her if she knew where to find the troublemaker, she went into some sort of trance and said in this really eerie voice that I should look within the Interplanetary Council, or possibly even the Inner Circle, for that person."

"A trance? That seems awfully melodramatic!"

"Which is why, when we were talking with your father and TiAnn, I chose not to say how I'd gotten that information. And the Tropi also told me that there are far greater forces at work here than anyone imagines or even suspects."

"That's all? Wasn't she willing to elaborate?"

"She wasn't – except to say that eventually, before this is over, I'll need her help."

"Why? When? Where? Surely you must have asked."

"Of course I asked! But she just smiled this perfectly inscrutable, sphinx-like smile and said that throughout history, oracles have never bothered to explain their prophecies to anyone, and that it was one of the few traditions she didn't think she was ready to break just yet."

"She sounds unfriendly – and not terribly helpful."

"You wouldn't say that if you'd met her, Janne. She's the most remarkable woman I've ever met."

I threw a pillow at him.

"Except for you, of course," he hastily amended.

"So what did you do next? I'm sure you didn't waste time sitting around, daydreaming about her beautiful blue eyes."

"Actually they're the most incredible shade of violet." A smile quirked the corners of his mouth.

"Be serious, Eirik. All you've done is talk about everyone you think is innocent. Don't you think it's about time you told me who you think is guilty?"

"Well, after my session with the Tropi, I spent quite a few hours reviewing information about the members of the Interplanetary Council and the Inner Circle, and although nothing jumped out at me, I kept asking myself who would benefit most from what's happening."

"Casting suspicion on the Interplanetary Council and the Prime's Inner Circle? The Tropi must be mad! Every single one of those advisors is loyal to the Prime – at least, my father thinks so. And if you're willing to go to the extreme of vetting the Prime's councilors, why not check out his son Ferrin? After all, he's the one who would benefit most if his father was ousted: he's second in line to the throne."

"I did look into him," Eirik reluctantly admitted. "He's an obvious suspect. And I also had to consider that if he wasn't the actual troublemaker, he might be in league with whoever is."

"And?"

"And what I quickly discovered is that unless he's a remarkably skilled actor, Ferrin's having way too much fun chasing women and living the good life to be interested in shouldering his father's responsibilities any sooner than he has to. He may feel differently someday, but after our interview, I reached the conclusion that he's a lecherous bon vivant, but not a scheming villain."

"He actually agreed to sit down and talk to you?"

"In fact, he seemed to think that having me question his intentions was all great fun."

"Very well, Eirik – if not Ferrin, who certainly has the most to gain from his father's demise, what possible motive would anyone else on the council have to start a rebellion?"

"That's the crux of the matter, isn't it? Which is why I need to look into this further."

"And expose yourself to even more danger!"

"That's certainly not my intention. But, Janne, I have to do this! All the evidence that I've been able to gather thus far has been circumstantial – until now – although I think I may have finally turned up a potential lead…"

"Which is…?"

"Don't ask! At present it's just a suspicion, but if I'm lucky it could prove to be a turning point in my investigations – or not…"

"But you won't tell me who it is."

"I'm sorry, Janne. I'm not willing to accuse anyone – or even name a probable suspect – not until I have concrete evidence that I can present to the Prime."

"Can you at least tell me if you think it could be more than one person?"

"It's quite possible – although I do have someone definite in mind as the ringleader."

"A mysterious master criminal!" was my wry response. "So what are you going to do? Knowing you, I'm sure you won't sit around waiting for something even worse to happen."

"I have to get out there and do more fieldwork: inspect a number of space docks – look for signs of suspicious activity. That, as I suggested to your father, seems like a good first step towards solving this mystery."

"Space docks? What exactly do you think you're going to find: some evildoer standing there with a smoking mine in his or her hand?"

"I'm going to Concordia – and then further afield – to follow up on a new lead," was his patient reply. "What I'll be looking for – and what I expect to eventually find – is a small fleet of starships – nothing big enough to call attention to itself, but assuming there are a couple of modest fleets which could be combined into a larger one scattered across the Concorde– well, the conclusion will be obvious."

"But why does it have to be you?" I pleaded.

"Because if I'm able to locate what I suspect is out there, it's something I have the expertise to recognize no matter how cleverly it's disguised. And if my hunch proves out, I promise I'll immediately turn the information over to your father and the Prime and let them deal with it any way they choose. I want this thing to be over! I want to go home!"

He came to sit beside me on the bed, his eyes searching mine. "There's something else I need to tell you."

I studied his face, trying to determine whether the news was good or bad.

"Uncle Einarr is dead," he said without apparent emotion.

"How? When?"

"He had a heart attack shortly after we left Valhalla. Magnus messaged me."

"So there's nothing to stop us from going back."

"Janne, we need to talk about this. I'll only return if you're sure it's what you want. I'd never forgive myself if I took you back to Valhalla and you were miserable there."

"And where else could you possibly be happy? I knew that when I agreed to marry you. I've always expected we'd return to Valhalla."

"Then there's more you should know. Right up to the end, Einarr refused to name a successor. The Council of Thanes has already met to determine who their next *Hövding* will be... And they chose me. I'm sure Magnus was behind it. Anyway, they've agreed to wait until I've finished my work for your father and the Prime, and Magnus has offered to fill in for me until then."

"It could be a long time."

"It won't be if I have anything to say about it! If a fleet is gathering out there, as I suspect it is, I intend to find it and discover whoever's building it, make my report, and get the hell out of this mess – and that should be the end of it."

"Aren't you forgetting the Tropi's mysterious prediction?"

"Since I haven't the vaguest idea what she was talking about, I have no intention of wasting my time worrying about what she may or may not have meant. She said I'd know what to do when the time comes – which is fine with me. In the meantime, I'd feel a whole lot better if you'll continue to wait for me here, with your father."

"I will, as long as he needs me."

"I need you too," Eirik said, pulling me into a sudden, fierce embrace. "It's been way too long, *Kjæresta*." But then, quite unexpectedly, his ravenous expression transformed into a mischievous grin. "Besides, when we go home to Valhalla, the Council of Thanes will surely expect us to bring them a child."

I placed the palm of my hand against his. "And how do you think we're going to accomplish that without the help of your Valhallan Reaction – without your *Ekstase*?"

On one level, I was teasing, but on another the thought of having children now, when we hardly knew each other, with the future so vague, was terrifying – and the only way that I could possibly deal with it was with humor.

"Why, Janne." He looked so serious! "Despite all previous evidence to the contrary, I have the impression that you think I don't know how to lose my self-control…"

15.

Several days later, when Eirik left for Concordia, he did so with the rank of Space Guild Commodore, the assumption being that this would make it easier for him to move around without attracting unwanted attention. Hopefully his new mobility would also give him an excuse to inspect starships: those currently in use as well as those under construction – in addition allowing him to be in a position to personally investigate any new leads that might turn up.

Another benefit of his elevated status was that he could now attend Interplanetary Council meetings without having to request special permission – which I knew he was anxious to do so he could study its various members, and most particularly his number one suspect – whoever that might be.

At the time of his departure, Eirik had warned me that he might not be able to contact us as often as he'd like, since he didn't want to remind our enemies of his connection to Caliban. And for a while his reports came back to us at regular intervals – but then, as his information grew ever more sensitive, his communications became less and less frequent until at last, one dreadful day, I was shocked to realize that we hadn't heard from him in nearly a month.

Although I knew that I was being selfish, my immediate reaction wasn't concern for his safety – instead I felt abandoned. Eirik didn't want me and neither would anyone else! Feeling utterly alone and bereft, I wondered what kind of future I could possibly have without him.

After even more time had passed, I came to the harsh realization that he was truly gone, vanished without a trace. And then came fear: what horrible fate had befallen him? Was it possible that he might still be alive?

I tried to convince myself that I was overreacting, that I was foolish to worry, and that my nervousness and depression were the result of the early stages of pregnancy – but it was useless: I knew deep down that I had good cause to be afraid for him.

I don't know what I would have done without my father. He was extremely sympathetic and supportive, although I knew he was taking Eirik's loss as hard as I was. He pulled every string he could think of and called in every political favor he was owed, trying to locate him – but to no avail.

TiAnn was scornful. Now more persistently than ever, she pestered our father to allow her to go to Concordia where, she assured us, she would soon solve the mystery of Eirik's disappearance as well as track down our elusive saboteur.

Most of our information on the current situation now came from Music School informants and a number of Space Guild personnel who had been recruited by Eirik. Once word of his absence leaked out, many of his associates contacted us to express their concern. My father and I tried to reassure them, although neither of us felt at all optimistic about his chances for a safe return.

Little by little, as further reports came in, our picture of the events that were threatening the Concorde Alliance came into sharper focus. Pressure was increasing at an alarming rate as still more mines appeared and more ships were damaged or destroyed.

Musicians relayed the information that many Concorde citizens were postponing their travel plans, hoping for safer times. Other agents reported general malaise and a feeling of helplessness. And from everywhere came the question: why wasn't the Prime doing something to remedy the situation?

Now there were constant rumors of alien sightings, and when several influential members of the Interplanetary Council disappeared as mysteriously as Eirik had, there were even whispers of alien abductions.

At last the Prime made an official statement. Expressing concern for his people, he assured us that he understood our fears and frustrations, and that he was doing everything within his power to restore peace and safety to the Concorde. To accomplish this, he said, all military and Space Guild personnel had been recalled to active duty. Patrols were being increased throughout the Concorde, particularly in especially sensitive areas. As an added safety measure, he was placing an embargo upon space travel: only important business trips and in the case of emergencies would it be permitted. Even though the musicians had reported that citizens were already doing this on a voluntary basis, it was nevertheless chilling to have it made official government policy.

The Prime also informed us that Space Guild personnel would monitor all travelers, keeping a sharp lookout for unauthorized flights and passengers. He added that these measures could only be effective with our cooperation.

Finally, the Prime announced that he was calling an emergency session of the Interplanetary Council to review the current crisis and propose further action that would put a rapid end to what he called the "unconscionable piracy" to which we were all being subjected…

"…And I truly do mean piracy, because I am certain that an individual or group of individuals is behind this insurrection. Do not give in to unreasonable fears or make the mistake of attributing these attacks to an alien enemy," he told us. "For our enemy is real enough, and he most certainly comes from within the Concorde and not from some far-distant galaxy. I assure you that his reign of terror will be short-lived…

"In conclusion, I promise you, my fellow Concorde citizens, that I am using every available means to find and punish our enemy – and I will not rest until he or she is brought to justice, and the lives of my people are once again safe. Peace will be restored to the Concorde."

And thus he ended his transmission.

"Let's hope he really can do something concrete," was my father's grim comment to TiAnn and myself as we sat in his study at the conclusion of the broadcast of the Prime's speech. "Enough damage has been done by now that he won't last much longer unless he can restore public confidence."

"I suppose this means we'll be called to Concordia to present our reports in person to the IPC," TiAnn gloated. Obviously this was exactly what she'd been hoping for all along.

My father responded that he expected it was so.

Not long afterwards, while we were still awaiting the Prime's summons, my father received an unexpected call from his longtime friend Rigel Hafiz, who said he was messaging us because, as a fellow

Interplanetary Council member, he was anxious to learn my father's reaction to the Prime's speech.

They talked on the Net for quite a while, Rigel expressing what sounded to me like sincere regrets for having neglected their friendship in recent years.

"In these troubled times," Rigel told my father, "friends have to stick together for moral support."

He also mentioned that he'd heard a rumor that my father was gathering information for the Prime about the present situation. He offered to join us on Caliban to share his own insights, which he had gleaned as chairman of the Inner Council.

My father said he'd be delighted to have his help.

I was torn between silence and telling my father about Eirik's suspicions – that someone on the Interplanetary Council was the guilty party, and thus any of its members – even my father's old friend Rigel – might be implicated. But since Eirik hadn't been any more specific, in the end I decided to wait and watch. Yet it was painful to see that extremely charming and charismatic man, who might know more than he cared to admit about the insurrection and my husband's disappearance, enjoying my family's hospitality, talking and laughing with my father and sister.

TiAnn seemed particularly enthralled. To my knowledge, she had never before taken such an intense interest in anyone, either male or female, and she somehow managed to be available to him at every possible opportunity.

Was it because she suspected he had inside information regarding the rebellion, I wondered?

I longed to question her about her sudden fascination with our guest, but was leery of her volatile temper and sarcastic tongue. However, it wasn't long before I gave in to temptation and confronted her while we were out walking in the Government House gardens.

"What makes you think I'm interested in Rigel?" was her tart response.

"Oh, come on, TiAnn, you've stuck to him like a shadow ever since he arrived last week, and you've just spent an entire day showing him around Sycorax City. Don't tell me you aren't interested."

"Is that so? Well, if you ask me, you seem pretty interested yourself!" She paused to pick a lovely blossom from one of the manicured flowerbeds that we were passing. "I've been watching you too, and you've been hanging on his every word."

Blushing like a schoolgirl, I stooped awkwardly to pick up the gorgeous bloom, which she had kept just long enough to sniff before dropping it carelessly onto the gravel path. "It isn't what you think."

"Oh, it's exactly what I think! And you can bet that Rigel isn't interested in a twenty-seven-year-old woman who's four months pregnant! But *she* might be interested in *him* because she suspects he might know something about her missing husband."

"TiAnn!"

She let out a short, bitter laugh. "You think I can't figure it out? I know exactly why Rigel might have been one of Eirik's suspects!"

"Eirik never said anything of the kind!"

"He didn't have to! But like Eirik, I'm well aware that as the Prime's first cousin, Rigel is third, not first in the Concorde succession, and neither the Prime nor his son is likely to die in the foreseeable future. Not to mention that if the Prime's son Ferrin were to have a child in the interim, Rigel's hopes of inheriting would be finished forever."

"That doesn't mean Rigel is plotting to take over the entire Concorde, and you know it!" I protested. "Eirik had no way to prove that, and neither do we! Besides, Rigel is one of father's closest friends. Why, he was an honored guest at my first wedding!"

"Which counts for absolutely nothing! And if you think you can ferret out Rigel's secrets – if he actually has any – and discover what happened to Eirik, let me assure you that you won't get a thing out of him. He's far too clever and much too careful to be tricked into revealing anything to the likes of *you*!"

"TiAnn, what are you planning to do?"

"It's none of your business!" She started to turn away.

"*Wait*!" I clutched her arm. "You think you can handle this yourself, don't you? TiAnn, be careful! Don't do anything stupid."

She snatched her arm from my grasp, drawing herself up stiffly. "I never do anything stupid. I leave the stupidity to the rest of my family!"

"I'm sorry – I didn't mean that the way it sounded! It's just that I'm worried. I've been worried about Eirik, and now I'm frightened for you!"

"Save your worries for your husband: he's the one who's gone missing." She started to walk off, but then swung back around and marched right up to confront me. "Let me tell you something, Janne. In case you don't realize it, I understand Rigel: he's at a crucial point in his life. He's almost reached middle age but is still full of passion and vitality, and he's not about to throw it all away – which is why it's conceivable that he might indeed be the one who's trying to pull off a coup – or that he might have vital information about whoever's behind it...

"And what could be more tempting than a young woman who appears to have fallen under his spell? He might be drawn in by that: let down his guard enough to tell me what he knows, if anything, about the rebellion – and maybe even his plans if he actually is behind it. And if he is, I'll have something valuable to report to the Prime that none of his flunkies, including your Eirik, were able to ferret out...

"And in the meantime, I'll continue to investigate Rigel's fellow councilors... Because, believe me, I'm not about to sit around on Caliban for the rest of my life, playing legal secretary to father and breeding babies!"

I watched her retreating back as she walked away, her stride graceful and sure, wondering if she was really as self-confident inside as she wanted everyone to believe.

"Oh, TiAnn," I whispered, "please be careful..."

***

I watched with fear and interest as TiAnn captured the attention and admiration of our jovial guest, and I watched in silence as she, my father, and Rigel went off to Concordia to attend the next Interplanetary Council meeting. And after they returned, I asked TiAnn what if anything had happened between herself and Rigel on Concordia, or if she'd learned anything incriminating about any of the other Interplanetary Council members – but her only response was a smug smile.

And so it went.

Week after week I sat there correlating the data that was still pouring in at the rate of several dozen items per day, wondering where and how Eirik was, and trying not to give in to despair. But as the weeks turned into months and there was still no word from my husband, my fear dulled into resignation. And in my darkest moments, I felt sure that he would never return.

During this time our son Bran was born, named as Eirik had requested, after his deceased paternal grandfather. With a sense of dismay, I watched as Bran cut his first tooth and made his first awkward attempts to roll over...

And now at night, I often dream of Valhalla and the blissful interlude we spent there. But each morning, when I awake to feel once again the mounting tension all around me as the Concorde Alliance descends into chaos, I can't help wondering whether Bran will ever see Valhalla for himself, and if he will ever meet his father, whom I try to keep alive – as much for myself as for our son's sake – with stories which Bran is still far too young to understand.

So here I sit like Penelope, the wife of another wanderer in an ancient tale from Old Earth. And like Penelope, all I can do is wait and hope that someday my wanderer will return to me.

II.

TiAnn

1.

Janne is a fool! She always lets people use her and control her life…

Just consider this! Incredible as it may seem, when she was eighteen, she actually allowed our father to marry her off to cement a dubious political alliance. No one in her right mind – no one but my stupid older sister –would have agreed to such a barbaric pact!

And to make matters worse, the man my father sold her to (and I use that term advisedly)was a sadistic beast. I saw the bruises! And my poor naive sister went along with it – the arranged marriage *and* the brutality!

'But why?' you might legitimately ask.

And the answer is: because our father told her she should!

So then, after years of humiliation, when she finally had the good fortune to be rid of that animal, did she take advantage of her freedom? Oh no, not our Janne! Instead, for the next four years she went into exile, living like a nun on University Seven: no parties, no flirtations, no lovers, no travel, no fun – nothing anyone would be even remotely tempted to call a life!

And when she'd finally gotten *that* nonsense out of her system, just when you'd think she might have come to her senses and learned to take better care of herself, what did she do? She went right out and got involved with another loser – only this time it was some pretty-boy Space Guild pilot from a backwater planet way out on the Fringe. Really, it was incredibly pathetic and all too predictable – yet so like Janne.

But rather than having an enjoyable fling – I mean, there's no denying that he's a very attractive man – and then walking away, she took the whole affair oh so seriously. Believe it or not, she actually went and married the guy! Marriage – which everyone knows is just an archaic form of slavery disguised as a social contract!

So I ask you: what does my darling sister have to show for her lifetime of selfless sacrifice? Oh, the irony of it all! Now this latest fellow has vanished – leaving her pregnant and presently in charge of a fatherless little brat!

Can anyone really be that dumb?

As far as I'm concerned, my sister might as well have given me a tutorial on what *not* to do with my life, because there's no way I'm going to repeat her mistakes!

In fact, I realized long ago that if I wanted to be free, to remain in control my own destiny, I'd have to choose an independent profession and become really good at it: the very best. Law seemed ideal because it offers a unique perspective: a way of studying people to observe how they manipulate each other, and then using that knowledge to manipulate them.

And to be perfectly frank, it all comes down to a matter of self-preservation – because I have no intention of letting my father or anyone else take advantage of me!

Ironically, in the course of my law studies, both my father and my teacher Drexel have stressed a sense of what they call 'fair play and decency'. But they've had a devil of a time coming up with examples of how fair play and decency work in real life – particularly in politics and law!

As I see it, in order to be successful you have to know what you want and be ruthless about going after it. Another thing you have to do is look out for yourself, because no one else is going to do it for you... Let's face it, even my father, the honorable Arram Trellerian, Prime Minister of Caliban, didn't rise to his present office without getting his hands dirty...

Which brings me around to the man I presume was probably high on my latest (or perhaps it would be more accurate to say 'late') brother-in-law Eirik Sanderson's list of prime suspects: Rigel Hafiz, chairman of the Prime's Inner Council...

Rigel is third in line of succession to the Concorde Throne, and all things considered it might be an interminably long wait – and perhaps to no avail – before he can ever hope to acquire the throne by more legitimate, peaceful means. So I ask you: is there any reason why he should be content to sit around, watching life pass him by? And even more to the point: is there any reason why any of his fellow Inner Council members should continue to support the Prime rather than him?

So suppose Rigel does prove to be responsible for the disturbance that's tearing the Concorde Alliance apart? Can anyone blame him for trying to become something more than the Premier of an insignificant little planet like New Egypt?

Personally, I don't have much sympathy for the Prime, the Concorde Alliance's supreme leader. He's gotten himself into this mess by consistently failing to take decisive action to put a stop to the escalating acts of terrorism that are tearing the Concorde Alliance apart. In my opinion, he has only himself to blame if he loses first his credibility and then the throne.

He should have shown his strength – assuming that he has any – long before now. And by now it's almost certainly too late to do so...

Several months ago, the Prime made a public statement to the effect that he was going to hunt down and eradicate the Concorde's enemies.

And how did he propose to do that? Why by calling a special session of the Interplanetary Council to advise him on emergency measures.

What a meaningless gesture! Not to mention that it took him forever to make it. Still, I really can't complain because it got me what I wanted: a trip to Concordia...

***

By the time the Prime got around to actually setting a date for the IPC meeting, Janne was too far along in her pregnancy to go anywhere. So it turned out that Rigel, who happened to be visiting us at the time (and how much of a coincidence that could possibly have been is a matter of considerable conjecture!), father and I traveled together to Concordia.

Getting anywhere these days was difficult, what with the extra precautions the Space Guild is taking. However, father and Rigel are important people, so it wasn't long before we were berthed in the most luxurious accommodations the Space Guild has to offer, heading inward towards the Hub.

***

I hadn't been to Concordia in several years, but nothing there ever changes: it's all glitter and flash and political intrigue – and smooth going for those who are either lucky or clever enough to have the right connections.

Rigel, I noticed, was keeping a watchful eye on me, observing my reaction to it all – no doubt expecting the backward little Country Girl to be awed by the magnitude of our surroundings.

Needless to say, I was my usual cool, level-headed self, and I made sure that I continued to treat him with all of the considerable charm at my disposal – with a tantalizing hint of romantic interest thrown in for good measure…

But as for the Prime, he disappointed me. Although he was the one who had called the IPC session, he couldn't seem to retain control of it. Instead, he allowed Councilor Rigel to dominate the proceedings – Rigel, who earnestly advised the group to postpone their talks until as many planetary rulers and wise men as possible could be assembled on Concordia!

And since he was also chairman of the much smaller and far more influential Inner Circle, Rigel lobbied there as well for adjournment until a later date, suggesting that this would give each councilor a chance to form a committee to prepare an efficient and constructive plan for dealing with the crisis. As if twelve different plans would do anything but create mass confusion!

It occurred to me that Rigel was either incredibly stupid or else diabolically clever.

Not surprisingly, a few of his fellow councilors were bright enough to recognize the shortcomings of Rigel's proposal, and they argued bitterly – and I believe correctly – that even the briefest delay would make the Prime appear weak. Yet Rigel managed to carry the day: he defended his recommendations in a very convincing manner. And that fool, the Prime – not to mention a majority of the Inner Circle – fell for it! It certainly heightened my suspicions that, with or without Rigel, more than a few of those Inner Circle members might be working together to foment the current insurrection.

At the session's end, Rigel was practically glowing with triumph, and I must admit that it was gratifying to have him make a most charming and eloquent request that I accompany him to his home planet, New Egypt, for a brief vacation.

It wasn't easy, but I managed to put him off.

After having watched him operate within the IPC, I was now nearly certain that he had to be involved in or at least sympathetic to the person or persons who were responsible for the Concorde's disarray. However, as my sister had correctly pointed out: much like my late brother-in-law, I lacked hard evidence. Of course, I might have been able to acquire exactly that on New Egypt – yet something caused me to hesitate...

Although I admired Rigel for his cleverness and his ability to manipulate people, I nevertheless hadn't made up my mind about him. If he should prove to be the rebellion's chief instigator or was part of a cabal, I needed time to assess his – or their – chances of success. After all, I have no intention of coming out on the losing side of this seemingly inevitable confrontation!

Besides, I didn't want Rigel to think that I was ready to swoon into his arms the moment he beckoned. So, professing concern for my sister's health, I chose to return to Caliban with my father, telling Rigel that I wanted to be present at the birth of Janne's first (and almost certainly only) child.

As if that was really an issue!

In parting, I made sure that I left Rigel with the strong impression that I was interested in continuing and deepening our relationship in the very near future. And then I went back home to Caliban to continue my research...

***

By the time all of the preparations and negotiations had been completed for the continuation of those meaningless Interplanetary Council meetings, months had passed and the Prime's political situation had deteriorated even further.

Shortly after the council adjourned, there were major demonstrations on a number of planets. On Xerxes, the offices of the Concordian Ambassador were picketed – on Gamay, they were actually bombed. And when Cristan Andebar gave a command performance on New Egypt, Rigel's home planet, the number of mine incidents in that Sector tripled (but could that have been a clever ploy, I wondered, orchestrated by Rigel himself, to reinforce his façade of innocence?).

There were riots on Zenith, and when a fleet of six unidentified ships attacked and destroyed a guild freighter, the Prime was burned in effigy.

Commentators from the news services denounced him, not only for failing to stop the attacks, but also for allowing the crisis to escalate to the point where these attacks were becoming almost commonplace.

Throughout the Concorde Alliance, citizens were frightened, not only by the threat of terrorists, but also by persistent rumors that the events we were witnessing were the work of hostile aliens. And as a result, there was a sense that the whole system as we knew it was falling apart.

During those long months of IPC inaction, Rigel kept in touch, sending me amusing messages and reminding me to keep a positive attitude in these trying times. Gift after tasteful gift arrived at Caliban's Government House, all originating from New Egypt – as if this was necessary to sustain my interest in him!

In retrospect, I doubt that Rigel realized the depth of my understanding of Concorde affairs, or how aware I was of the ever-increasing evidence of the Prime's crumbling power.

***

At last my father and I were once again bound for Concordia, this time without Rigel, but with Janne and her baby in tow. I suspect that she had decided join us because even at this late date she was hoping to hear some news of her vanished partner.

Actually, I was glad that she was with us. If things went as I planned, she would be useful: she could keep father company and help present our reports to the council if I was otherwise occupied. With Janne at his side, I reasoned, father might not be as likely to object if I happened to go off on my own to pursue other, more interesting and productive leads.

For it was my intention to investigate Rigel and his fellow Inner Circle members firsthand to see what, if anything, any single one, or all of them together, might be up to…

2.

Concordia was different this time. Although it still retained its outward veneer of sophistication and splendor – the elaborate ceremonies and fantastic costumes, the bustling crowds of exotic visitors from countless distant worlds, the vibrant colors, and diverse entertainment venues – beneath this glittering exterior there was a hint of terminal decadence setting in, of frightened people scurrying about, anxious to give the impression that their lives were continuing on as usual.

There were definitely a great many more people about than there had been just a few months earlier: most notably swarms of dignitaries of every rank and function, from worlds great and small, accompanied by their vast retinues – all of whom were taking up space that was normally unoccupied. The palace guestrooms were filled to capacity, as were all of the hotels. From the Concordia Grand right down to the humblest hostel, every place I inquired into was booked solid.

And still more visitors kept arriving.

What a stroke of genius! With this many people jammed into Concordia's limited accommodations (although they had certainly never seemed limited before!), with conference rooms packed to bursting, and with each contingent pursuing its own special interests, tempers would be short and disagreements were sure to flare up like wildfires at the least provocation. The IPC would be virtually paralyzed, unable to accomplish a single objective.

This, I realized, would surely be a visit to remember.

***

It had been my intention to call Rigel immediately upon my arrival on Concordia. I was anxious to talk to him, curious to learn his impressions of the current situation, and to ascertain whether they coincided with my own.

Also, this might prove to be an ideal opportunity to gain some further insight into his possible innocence or guilt. However, before I had a chance to put my plan into effect, my father summoned me to a strategy session.

How strategic can you get, I wanted to ask him? As far as I was concerned, the most we could possibly hope to accomplish in the way of 'strategy' was to decide upon that terribly non-critical issue of exactly how we were going to present our reports at the next Inner Council meeting.

Still, despite my gloomy prognosis, I consoled myself with the thought that there might be some useful information to be gleaned. Besides, I didn't want to alienate father, so I went as cheerfully as was possible under the present circumstances...

***

My father, Janne, the baby and I were all crammed together into a tiny and rather old-fashioned apartment in a little-used wing of Concordia Palace: two bedrooms and a small sitting area were to be shared among the four of us. It was worse than inconvenient, yet I was well aware that this deplorable situation must be playing out to someone's advantage. After all, if people of our social status were this poorly housed, then every other visitor to Concordia, whatever his or her rank, must be that much more discommoded.

Shortly after the appointed hour, I joined Janne and my father in our sitting room. My sister seemed preoccupied: apparently she had put the baby down for a nap in our bedroom and was compulsively listening for the apartment's AI to alert her to any possible sounds of distress. To my considerable annoyance, Cristan Andebar was also present.

"TiAnn!" my father exclaimed, glancing up from his work slate, which he had been scanning with Andebar. "Where have you been? I was beginning to think you'd forgotten our meeting."

"You know I wouldn't do that," I protested. "Actually, I was out sightseeing – and you won't believe how many people are visiting here right now."

"Oh, yes we would." Andebar's mouth was pinched in a grim line.

I may as well admit it at the outset: I've never liked that man, even though he *is* father's oldest friend. He knows too damn much! He's so

152

deceptively candid and pleasant, yet all the while you're speaking with him, his yellow cat's eyes never leave your face, noticing everything, analyzing every word you speak and every nuance of your expression.

Thank heavens he's not a lawyer: he's the one adversary I'd hate to come up against in a court of law!

Now, turning from my father, Andebar crossed the cramped sitting room in several long, angry strides. "I warned the Prime this would turn into a circus if we allowed all those delegates to participate. But would he listen?" He gave a disgusted snort. "Now nothing will be accomplished, for all of Rigel's arguments to the contrary! Damn the man – what was he thinking?"

A premonitory chill shivered down my spine. What did Andebar know or suspect about Rigel? It occurred to me that it might be worth something to Rigel to know Andebar's opinion of his tactics: a valuable bargaining chip…

With a sigh, my father shut off his slate. "Well, Cristan, there's nothing to be done about it now. It's far too late to send them all packing. We'll just have to make the best of a bad situation and hope that your plan works."

"What plan is this?" Janne piped up.

Bless her! It was exactly the question I wanted to ask, yet I feared calling attention to myself by doing so.

"Cristan thinks we should urge the Prime to continue to convene the Inner Circle even while the IPC is in session," our father said. "That way we can still make progress, even if everyone else is bogged down in all sorts of unproductive talks."

"That seems quite sensible," I ventured, anxious to appear supportive.

After all, while it was true that I was impressed by Rigel – regardless of whether or not he was involved in the insurrection – I was far from ready to commit myself to anyone's cause, including Rigel's *or* the Prime's. Also, there was still some question in my mind as to whether or not the Concorde Alliance was actually vulnerable to a takeover. And since I didn't yet have enough data to make a reliable assessment of that possibility, I was determined to keep all of my options open.

Then, too, there was the issue of the Prime's son, Lord Ferrin, a rather attractive fellow (with quite a reputation as a ladies' man!) who was first in line to inherit the Concorde's throne and the substantial fortune that comes with it. Like Rigel, he was high on my list of prime suspects.

Suppose, I thought, *that by stepping in at a crucial moment, Ferrin was to hasten his father's demise?* In fact, that very possibility might have been temptation enough to cause him to have fomented the current rebellion (assuming that Rigel was innocent, or alternatively that the two men were colluding). And if Ferrin was a good tactician, adept at strategic plotting or otherwise able to take advantage of his father's weakness, people might soon come to regard him as their savior.

Furthermore, it had occurred to me that since Ferrin was apparently unattached, he might become a Concorde hero, skilled tactician or not, if he had the guidance of some clever person such as myself behind him. And no matter how accomplished a lothario he might be, I was quite sure I could use that to my advantage too!

I would definitely have to find a way to evaluate Ferrin's potential...

This was one of the many things I had come to Concordia to assess, and I was resolved to be every bit as watchful and alert as Andebar.

"I agree with TiAnn," Janne was saying. "Since the Inner Circle has only twelve advisors, they're far more likely than the IPC to help the Prime devise a viable plan."

"Actually," my father said, "Cristan wants to ask the Prime to include one more person."

"Really?" Janne's innate curiosity was definitely turning out to be an asset. "Who is it?"

"The Tropi." It was Andebar who replied.

"The Tropi!" The words were out of my mouth before I could stop them. "The leader of the Tropian people? Isn't she supposed to be psychic?"

"Well, that *is* her public image..." Andebar admitted, smiling his inscrutable smile. "And it can't be denied that she has a great deal of insight, as well as training in what you might call the psychological arts. But that's beside the point... What's important right now is that the Tropi strongly feels that she should forgo her traditional policy of political neutrality in order to help the Concorde Alliance resolve its problems."

This one factor alone could turn the tide in favor of the Prime! I thought, dismayed.

"Has the Prime agreed?" my father asked.

Exactly what I wanted to know!

"The Tropi and I are scheduled to have a private audience with him within the hour. We thought she'd be the best person to explain how she could be of use. She'll be joining us here shortly, on her way to his chambers."

"She's definitely a force to be reckoned with," my father said. "I, for one, have always admired her."

"Eirik was impressed too," Janne replied. "Apparently he had a long talk with her. Maybe she'll have heard some news of him." Her face was alight with pathetic eagerness.

"I wouldn't get your hopes up, Janne, because—" Andebar began in a kindly voice, but I interrupted. After all, why waste everyone's time by encouraging my sister's naïve fantasies?

"Judging by the Tropi's reputation for effective government," I said, "she should be an extremely valuable asset – particularly if she can convince the Prime to take a more active role against his enemies. He has to make the kind of grand gesture the public will understand. And he's got to do it before it's too late!"

Andebar shot right back at me with: "You surprise me, TiAnn. You know very well that the Prime is doing everything he possibly can. Why, in the last month alone, he's tripled the number of agents out in the field."

"And you know that's not the sort of information he can publicize without jeopardizing their effectiveness," my father admonished.

"With your law background, TiAnn," Andebar continued before I had a chance to reply, "you more than most, should appreciate that the Concorde Alliance can't be ruled by any one person. The entire system is predicated on a balance of power: the Space Guild, the Traders' Guild, the planetary rulers, the ship builders – why, even my musicians are all part of that single sprawling organism we call the Concorde. The Prime is merely the symbol of their union…"

And a poor one at that! However, I kept this less than charitable thought to myself.

Meanwhile, Andebar was droning on, "…And those disparate entities must cooperate, because the Concorde Alliance is far too vast and complicated an arrangement for a single person to control. So if any one or several of those parts fail, or if one or more of them tries to sabotage the workings of the others, they may succeed for a time – yet eventually balance will be restored. The Prime would be the first to admit that it's a ponderous system – but it does work in its own, inevitable way."

"And while the gears are slowly grinding," my father added, "it's up to those of us who are his advisors to help him make the hard decisions."

"What will you advise him to do?" Janne asked.

My sister was turning out to be a useful asset indeed!

"Your father and I are of the opinion that he should definitely allow the Tropi to join the Inner Circle," Andebar responded, "and that the Inner Circle should then pursue certain leads we've uncovered which we hope will point to who the culprit might actually be."

Now that could spell trouble for the troublemaker – whether it turned out to be Rigel, Ferrin, or both in collusion – or someone entirely different...

And if it *was* Rigel... He was the chairman of the Inner Circle. Perhaps, I thought, it would be an excellent plan to charge that group to investigate the Concorde's troublemakers. After all, it wouldn't be the first time in history that a guilty person had led an investigation aimed at himself. In fact, as chairman, Rigel would be in the ideal position to insure that the accusations never found their mark!

This was yet another small but perhaps crucial piece of the puzzle for me to ponder...

Besides, because of my work with my father and Janne, I knew that I probably had as much hard evidence as anyone concerning the guilty party's identity. And although I had my suspicions, I definitely wasn't ready to accuse someone! Neither could the Inner Circle – at least, not without additional information – and it would take them far longer to gather it than it would take me.

"But, Cristan, what if Rigel won't accept our proposals?" my father was asking. "He's been quite adamant that the IPC as a whole should work on this together."

"I believe Rigel will go along with our suggestions," Andebar said.

Unfortunately, he didn't elaborate.

"Sera Trellarian, your infant has just awakened and has commenced to cry," the palace AI's impersonal voice suddenly announced rather loudly, startling all three of us.

"Oh my!" Janne scrambled to her feet. "I need to see to Bran! Are we finished here?"

"I guess there's nothing more we can accomplish until the Tropi and I have spoken with the Prime," Andebar told her.

As far as I was concerned, there was no point waiting around for Andebar's famous guest to appear. I was sure that I could put my time to far better use by pursuing my own investigations.

"In that case," I said, also rising, "I think I'll be on my way. I have some shopping to do."

No one objected when I left.

3.

However, I hadn't gone more than a short distance from our apartment when I was confronted by a most extraordinary apparition. Three women were headed down the hall in my direction, each of them so striking that I hardly knew where to look first!

The two on the outside were more or less a matched pair. Their tall, muscular bodies were completely covered in short blonde fur and both of them wore blood-red kilts belted with golden girdles which sported what I could only assume was ceremonial weaponry, since real weapons would never have been allowed in Concordia Palace! Knee-length capes, edged in gold, were the same color as their kilts, and their generous chests and upper arms were encased in heavy gold plate armor. Gold caps fitted with bristling red plumes adorned their heads, and gold sandals laced with red thongs that crisscrossed up their calves completed this unlikely vision of picturesque if barbaric splendor. Everything about their costume and demeanor screamed 'Bodyguards!' – and archaic ones at that! Yet incredibly, their otherwise completely outlandish appearance was totally eclipsed by that of the woman they were escorting.

She reminded me of those prehistoric statues of fertility goddesses that are sometimes displayed in museums of Terran artifacts. Where her companions were hard and muscular, she was voluptuous and rounded – yet there was nothing about her that suggested weakness. Indeed, she was one of the most powerful-looking women I have ever seen: and it was a power that seemed to emanate from within. She stood nearly as tall as her golden-pelted Amazonians, but in marked contrast to their brilliant coloring and outlandish garb, hers was a subtle, understated presence.

As she paced silently towards me, it was evident that her body was covered in a velvety blue pelt, as if she was wearing a form-fitting bodysuit. But her bare skin had a definite cool bluish tint where it was revealed on her lips and breasts, and on the palms of her hands. Later, when she walked away from me at the end our interview, I saw that the soles of her bare feet were also a pale, pinkish-blue.

In fact, she was completely naked, although the silky, blue-black hair that fell from the crown of her head to her ankles gave the illusion of clothing: draping around her shoulders like a cloak, it shifted in response to her every move. However, she seemed completely unembarrassed by her ripe sensuality, exposed for all to see, and this despite the fact that she was obviously in the early stages of pregnancy, if the pronounced swelling of her abdomen and the fullness of her breasts were any indication.

When she came face to face with me, she stopped.

Simultaneously and in unison, as if it was a well-rehearsed maneuver, her bodyguards also halted. Seen from this close, their golden fur appeared to be every bit as plush as their mistress's.

"You must be the daughter of Ser Arram Trellerian." Her voice was a melodious alto and her accent was unusual, as if she didn't normally speak Galach. And although she spoke quietly, her words seemed to hang, full of portent, in the air between us.

"And you must be the Tropi," I answered with a slight bow – for in spite myself I was impressed. "I am Ser Trellerian's younger daughter TiAnn. My father and Director Andebar are waiting for you in our apartment."

"Thank you," she said, turning to leave.

"Wait!" That single word burst from me, unbidden.

With feline grace, she turned back.

Our eyes met – hers were a fathomless violet, fringed by blue lashes – and then I just stood there stupidly, stunned by my own foolhardiness and daring.

"I mean, I beg your pardon, madam," I somehow managed to force out. "I'd like to speak with you – if you can spare a moment."

"I am sure that Cristan and your father can do without me for a while longer." Her smile seemed genuine.

Yet now that I had her full attention, what could I possibly say to her? She had a reputation for being a woman of keen intellect, an astute observer of people. No doubt it would be extremely dangerous to ask this woman the wrong question. So rather than commit any further blunders, I stood there in the hallway, mute as a stone, and gaping like a fool.

"Speak, child. I can sense the confusion of your thoughts. Do not be afraid of me."

"I'm not afraid!" I flared. My face felt incandescent.

"Of course not." She smiled. "So please feel free to tell me what is on your mind."

"It's just that I've always wanted to meet you," I allowed myself to admit. "And now that I have... Well, I can't think of a thing to say that would possibly interest you." This at least was true – and therefore safe.

I hoped.

"You see," I blundered on when she didn't reply, "I study law on Caliban, and I'm particularly interested in Tropi. I've always thought it sounded like a fascinating place."

Her bodyguards regarded us, impassive as statues – as if their mistress made a regular habit of wasting her time listening to the incoherent babbling of strange young women.

The Tropi's smile deepened. "Many find Tropi fascinating, and many come to study our ways. Perhaps you would care to do so."

"Oh yes! I've always wanted to visit a society that's successfully run by women without the interference of men."

"You have misunderstood us, child, if that is what you think. But do not be embarrassed: you are not the first to have done so."

Caught between annoyance and chagrin, I somehow managed to stammer out, "M-misunderstood? How?"

"Tropi is not a society without – as you put it – the interference of men," she continued with utter serenity. "Our Tropian males are every bit as important as women. It is just that the men take no part in Tropian government – for that matter, neither do the majority of women. That is left to my priestesses. We do this so our people will be free to lead fulfilling and productive lives without the burden of ruling – a burden which, in large part, falls upon me."

"Cristan Andebar says you wish to join the Inner Circle to help the Prime solve the Concorde's problems." How naive she must think me for blurting out these simple-minded pronouncements!

"It is not that I would *like* to join them, but rather a matter of what I feel that I must do. Ordinarily, I would not participate in Concorde politics, but these are dangerous times and critical matters are at stake – perhaps the

Concorde Alliance's very existence. And it is my belief that the Concorde must free itself of these inner conflicts, and quickly, so that we may go on to address more meaningful issues. But once my help is no longer needed, I have every intention of returning to Tropi and my regular duties."

Her words pricked my conscience. "Forgive me, madam, I have no right to monopolize your time. I've kept you standing here talking far too long while Andebar, my father, and also the Prime are waiting."

Although her smile was still warm, I saw an alarming hint of something akin to pity in her eyes. "There is nothing so urgent that I cannot spend a few minutes speaking with you. And you perhaps intend to have a more important role to play in this Concorde drama than you would like me to believe."

Could she read my mind?

In a way, I almost wished she could!

"I cannot read minds, as some think…" she said, echoing my thoughts with uncanny and truly alarming accuracy.

My heart began to race, and the palms of my hands were suddenly damp with sweat.

"…What I *can* do is speak mind-to-mind with my closest associates," she was saying, "those who are specially selected and trained. But I can look into a person's heart, and I see that yours is troubled and in conflict."

"I-I," I sputtered. But then words failed me entirely.

"You must learn to look beyond yourself, TiAnn," she advised. "For I am aware that you have a great and gifted mind which you can use either for self-gain or for the good of others… Also, because you are small here…" Reaching out, she gently touched my breast.

"I beg your pardon!"

"…You believe that men will not notice your other qualities and beauty," she calmly continued, disregarding my shocked outburst. "You do yourself and your admirers a great injustice."

It took all of my self-control not to abruptly turn my back on her and stalk away.

"Patience, TiAnn," she soothed. "I am almost finished… You are, I think, contemplating doing something that involves great personal risk. Consider carefully. That which seems desirable right now might not seem so later on."

I didn't dare to meet her eyes.

"In here," the Tropi's hand moved to her abdomen, "I bear a child of love – a child which my advisors have strongly counseled me against. Do you understand what I mean by a child of love?"

I nodded. I had studied enough Tropian law to know that the Tropi is only supposed to have children who are cloned from her own body – children who would be her duplicates in every way. A child of love could only mean that she had taken a lover and was pregnant by him.

"It was a difficult decision which required much soul-searching," she went on, "for this child is an unknown entity: a combination of myself and another person. And who knows what her powers will be? Still, I have chosen carefully and tried to evaluate all of the possible consequences. Be sure that you do so as well before you make any irrevocable choices... Have you heard me with your heart, TiAnn?"

My eyes finally met hers and were held. I nodded.

"Good. Ah, here is Cristan Andebar!"

He came striding down the hall towards us. When he reached the Tropi's side, he put both hands on her shoulders and lightly kissed her brow. "I'm glad you're here," he said. "And I see you've found TiAnn. Come inside and meet the others."

"As you wish," she said gravely.

"May I go now?" I asked like a small child, and was immediately furious with myself for being overawed by her.

"Certainly," she replied. And then she stepped forward and pressed her lips to my forehead, just as Andebar had done to hers.

I shivered.

"Go with my blessing, TiAnn," she pronounced, "and be safe."

I left quickly – in fact, if the truth be told, I literally ran off in a panic, not daring to look back to see if she was watching me.

4.

I fled down the corridors of Concordia Palace, past a security checkpoint and out into the Grand Concourse, my mind seething with half-formed thoughts and questions. I had intended to go directly to a public comm console and contact Rigel, but instead my feet kept hurrying me along at a relentless pace, as if they were trying to outrun my doubts.

That woman! 'Incredible' didn't begin to describe her. The Prime couldn't possibly refuse her help, I realized. He might not dare to!

I raced on, not really noticing where I was going.

It was as if she had been able to look right through me– as if I was made of glass – straight into my soul!

Could she read me that easily?

Had she found me unworthy?

Did she sense my reservations about the Prime, and did she realize that I might not support him?

The very possibility shocked me into immobility, and I stumbled to an abrupt halt in the middle of a busy intersection. Pedestrians, androids, and swarms of mechano-bots surged around me, bumping into me from all sides, grumbling, hissing and honking with annoyance, according to their inclinations or programming.

I could still feel the Tropi's kiss and the place on my chest where she had touched me, burning with each indrawn breath as if her finger had left some sort of indelible mark – as if she had branded my skin…

What had she done to me?

And could I still continue with my plan to investigate my suspects, now that I'd met her?

"Are you ill, miss?" someone asked in a kindly voice.

The words jolted me back to reality: it would be a dangerous mistake to attract unwanted attention. I hastily thanked my would-be rescuer and stepped over to one side of the thoroughfare to consider my options.

First of all, I scolded myself, *she admitted that she can't read minds – so she can't possibly know what's going on in mine... Besides, it isn't as if I've done anything wrong. I haven't formed any alliances or committed myself to anyone's cause, so there's absolutely nothing to feel guilty about! Why, I don't even know for sure if either Rigel or Lord Ferrin is the Prime's enemy... In fact, that's precisely what I'm here to find out! And the only way to do that is by conducting more research.*

Quickly, before I could lose my nerve, I located the nearest public comm console and put a call through to the Chairman's Suite: the luxury accommodations which, as chairman of the Inner Council, were Rigel's by right and which he maintained even during his absences from Concordia.

The aide who answered recognized me immediately. "Sera Trellarian, the Premier is presently in conference with his advisors, but he asked me to notify him the moment you called. Please wait while I page him."

Moments later, Rigel's face appeared on the holo-screen. "TiAnn! What a pleasure to see you! Where are you?"

"At a public comm console near Concordia Palace."

"Wonderful! I thought you'd be arriving any day now."

"We got in a couple of hours ago, and we've been very busy – but I called you at my first opportunity."

He glanced away for a moment, revealing his familiar, sharply-chiseled profile. "I suppose my aide told you that I'm in a meeting right now, but I expect to be finished soon. Would you like to come over later – perhaps for dinner?"

"How thoughtful of you to ask! But surely that would be an imposition... You must have far more important things to do at a critical time like this," I coyly suggested, determined to test the extent of his interest.

"What could possibly be more important than seeing you?" He regarded me with what I suppose was intended as an alluring smile, but the resulting deep creases around his eyes and mouth suddenly made him look much older than his actual age.

After several more minutes of inane but apparently obligatory flirtation, he suggested a time for our encounter.

"I'll be there," I told him. "And in the meantime, I have some shopping to do."

"Enjoy yourself. I'm looking forward to seeing you."

***

In fact, I really had planned to go shopping that afternoon. However my meeting with the Tropi had given me some additional ideas about what I ought to purchase.

Concordia is not just the political center of the Concorde Alliance, it's also the place where traders and merchants from every part of our galaxy gather to display and sell their wares. No other planet in the entire Concorde boasts such a variety of luxury goods from so many different worlds. And the tens of millions of visitors who pass through Concordia each year come not only to observe or participate in government operations – they also come to buy.

I left the Government Complex and took the transit tubes out to Concordia Trade Center. For a while I strolled the malls, enjoying the fantastic window displays and eyeing the exotic crowds. At last, I entered a clothing boutique where I hoped to find something special for my evening with Rigel.

However, choosing the right dress took much longer than I'd anticipated. Current styles left little to the imagination, and I had to ransack several shops before I found something acceptable. Eventually, I settled on a gown that was quite flattering without being too revealing, but which ended up costing a great deal more than I thought it should have.

My first errand successfully completed, I moved on to the Tropian Pavilion, that renowned outlet for Tropi's major export: drugs.

The Tropian retail district was a bewildering maze of crooked little thoroughfares which were teeming with people. Packed in among stores that offered a mind-numbing variety of exotic, intimate merchandise, the drug shops were distinguishable by their signs – many of them quite graphic. I negotiated the streets for nearly an hour before I finally found a place that seemed acceptable, chosen because it was rather subdued in comparison to the others.

Outside, an unadorned sign bore the single word '*Eros*' in bold black script. Upon entering the softly lit interior, I saw that the walls and ceiling as well as the floor were carpeted in a subtle, pinkish beige color which I have since learned is commonly – and vulgarly – referred to as 'Virgin's Blush'. The main room was adorned with tall, silver vases containing large trusses of white, lily-like flowers. And a wall-sized holo display of constantly shifting images provided the room's only other visual stimulus – and it was stimulating indeed!

Once I had recovered from my initial surprise, I noticed that there were a number of individual conversation nooks within the main room. Seeing that a privacy screen had been drawn across three of them, indicating that they were in use, I entered one of the vacant compartments.

The little room contained a single, deep armchair that might have been large enough for two very friendly people to sit in together, and a low counter with a built-in interface.

While I was still standing there, trying to decide whether to sit down or leave, a stocky, pale-green-pelted Tropian man in a 'Virgin's Blush'-tinted jumpsuit entered from an inner area.

The color did not suit him at all.

"Good day, Sera – and welcome to *Eros*," he said with determined enthusiasm, and I noticed that he had the same carefully enunciated accent as the Tropi. "My name is Garro." With a nod, he gestured towards the armchair. "Please sit down." So saying, he seated himself behind the counter and pressed a button, activating our privacy screen.

Feeling more awkward by the moment, I accepted his invitation.

"How may I assist you?" he asked.

I remained silent.

"Is there something particular that you wish to purchase?" he prompted, smiling encouragement. "Or would you prefer to browse? We have a very nice sample packet."

"I umm…" I took a deep breath.

Get on with it! I chided myself. *You didn't come all the way out here to waste your time.*

"I understand that you sell aphrodisiacs," I finally managed.

"The finest!" He waited expectantly, as if he thought I might want to contribute something further to our discussion.

"Well, I want some!" I blurted out.

"Of course you do! Why else would you be here?" He chuckled at his own lame joke. "Well, my dear, in order to serve you best, I will need to ask you some basic questions."

"What kind of questions?" Even I could hear the suspicion in my voice.

"For example, I have to know how much you want."

On the surface, this sounded like a reasonable request.

"Are you buying for a large party or for private use?" he pressed.

"Private use."

"So it's just for two? Three? Four…?"

"Two." To my chagrin, I knew that I was blushing.

"Very good. And how do you intend to take it?"

I must have looked puzzled, because he elaborated. "Do you wish to inhale it, inject it, rub it into your skin – or would you prefer to eat or drink it?"

"How am I…?" I strove for calm. "We'll drink it."

As soon as I said that, he activated his interface. "Intends to drink," he intoned.

"Stop!" I snapped. "What are you doing?"

"What? Oh, this…" He winked at me – I suppose he was trying to put me at ease, but his professional charm was already getting on my nerves. "It is nothing to be concerned about, Sera. I am just logging your answers into our data base so we can determine the optimal formula."

"I see."

"Shall we continue?"

I nodded my assent.

"Now: will you be drinking this with a depressant such as alcohol, something neutral like water – or are you going to take it with another stimulant such as caffeine?"

"Alcohol, I suppose… What's the purpose of all this?"

"Alcohol," he echoed with careful enunciation, for the benefit of his interface, I presumed. Then, to me: "The chemicals in an aphrodisiac will react differently with different substances, and I would not want to sell you something that would make you sick, or would fail to have the desired effect." He looked at me kindly. "Try not to let my questions disturb you."

"I am *not* disturbed!"

"It is quite understandable… No need to worry: I only have a few more questions."

What else could he possibly need to know?

"What is the body type of the person you intend to use the drug with?"

"I beg your pardon!" How had I gotten myself into this ridiculous situation?

The Tropian reached across the counter and actually patted my hand before I was able to snatch it back! "Finding the right formula for the buyer may be time-consuming, Sera, but I assure you that it is necessary in order to do this properly. And the first time is always the most difficult."

Was I that obvious?

"Let me take a moment to explain what I mean by body type…" His terminal spat out a hard copy, which he slid across the countertop to me.

It was a simple diagram of the Concorde territories.

"You see," he continued, "although the various peoples of the Concorde Alliance are humanoid, they are spread out over such a vast area that they tend to be somewhat isolated genetically. Enough time has passed for certain small and even major physiological changes to have occurred in some populations. And several of those changes could be potentially dangerous – perhaps even fatal – to a user even though, under normal circumstances, they would be quite harmless."

"I never thought of that."

"There is no reason why you should have – it is my job to know about these things. For example, I would guess from looking at you that you fall into the h-standard category – that is human standard. Most of our customers come from within this area near the Hub," his finger traced a rough circle on the diagram, "and are therefore h-standard…

"But the farther out you go, or the more isolated the population, the more deviations there are from the norm. Some of the people from the Fringe cannot take any of our common formulas, and we have to synthesize highly specialized prescriptions for them. Some, like the Soolians, are extremely challenging customers. Have you ever seen a Soolian?"

I shuddered.

"I shall take that for an affirmative. Then you know what I mean by different! Of course, we Tropians have our own peculiar biochemistry…" Grinning, he rubbed the soft, pale green fur on his forearm.

"I gather you want to know if the person I'm going to use this with is h-standard," I said, cutting off his inane chatter. "The answer is yes."

"Are you certain?"

"Of course I'm certain!"

"Please do not take offense, Sera. Some of our clients have had extensive plastic surgery. Why, you would be surprised what some people will go through in order to appear h-standard. And as I have just explained, it is very important that we be as accurate about these matters as possible."

"I'm not offended, but I *am* going to be late for an appointment if this takes much longer! What else do you need to know?"

"Just one or two more things… Approximately how old is this person?"

"Between forty and fifty."

Did I imagine a lift of his eyebrows?

"Male or female?"

Surely the man must be trying to humiliate me!

"Male – of course!"

"His height? Approximate weight?"

I told him.

"Now I need to know your age, height, and weight."

I answered his stupid questions and waited impatiently while his interface digested the data.

"That should do it," he said cheerfully. "Oh yes, I almost forgot. I need to know how many doses you want."

I said the first thing that popped into my head. "Two. We'll use it twice."

"Then you will need four doses, two for each person," he corrected. "Very good. Now, if you will wait just a moment, one of our pharmacists will prepare your prescription. Be sure to follow the instructions on the back of each packet."

I breathed a sigh of relief.

"While you are waiting, is there anything else that you would like to purchase to use with your aphrodisiac?"

"Such as?"

"Many of our customers like to buy auxiliary drugs to complement the aphrodisiac effects… Would you care to try a psychedelic?"

I shook my head.

"Fertility drugs?"

"Certainly not!"

"Please sit down, Sera. Your prescription is not ready yet."

By now I was tired of this game. I was certain that his 'pharmacist' was a medical synthesizer that was spitting out some standard pills or powders, in spite of all the stupid questions I'd just answered.

"Tell me how much this is going to cost," I snapped.

He consulted his interface, and then quoted an astronomical price.

"You can't be serious!"

"If you can find it cheaper anywhere else, I will give you a twenty percent discount," was his haughty reply. "And that is a guarantee."

I certainly didn't want to go through this all over again in another store, so I simply said, "Very well, I'll pay your extortionist price, but believe me I intend to check up on you."

"Please do."

I started to offer my wrist, so he could scan my chip.

He pasted on a smile. "Of course, we are equipped for electronic fund transfers," he said in a cool voice, reaching for my arm, "although some customers prefer to pay cash."

I snatched back my wrist. No sense in revealing any more personal information than I had to! "I'll pay cash."

"Would you like a receipt?"

"Definitely."

"You can use it the next time you want to purchase something. What name shall I put on it?"

So he really was trying to gather data about me!

"Forget the receipt!"

"Would you like to register your name and current address in our files?" he persisted. "That way, the next time you use our services, you will not have to go through all of these tedious questions."

"No thank you. I prefer to retain my privacy."

"You would be surprised how many of our customers say that the first time they come to us." He actually sounded regretful as he glanced at his interface. "Very well, as you wish... Your prescription is ready. You may pick it up at the front console on your way out. Please read the instructions carefully before using it."

We glared at each other across his countertop.

"Thank you, Sera. Please come again."

I was quite certain that I would not!

5.

I was in a vile mood by the time I arrived back at our apartment, and unfortunately it was a great deal later than I had intended. My first and only contact with the Tropian drug cartel had been frustrating, to say the least.

As I had hoped, my father had already left for an evening of socializing and political consultation with his fellow councilors, thus relieving me of the necessity of having to reveal my plans to him. His, on the other hand, were a foregone conclusion...

It is as true today as it has been throughout recorded history that the most important work of any politician is done behind the scenes. By the time the official council meetings actually begin, many key decisions and alliances will already have been made. Normally, I would have been eager to join my father in his negotiations: I never tired of watching the endless parade of self-important and flamboyant personalities posturing and strutting in their efforts to impress one another. However on this occasion, I felt that I could accomplish far more by interviewing Rigel.

Of course, it was an interesting question why Rigel wasn't participating in my father's political scene. No doubt, if I asked him, he would have a plausible excuse for his absence.

With little time to spare, I showered, fixed my hair and completed the other essentials of my toilette, after which I slipped into my new dress, taking care to transfer my painfully-acquired supply of aphrodisiacs to my evening bag. As I left, I called out to Janne that I expected to be out late and not to wait up for me. I hoped she would assume that I was joining our father.

At any rate, she didn't ask where I was going. In fact, she was so preoccupied with the baby (and those never-ending rituals of bathing, feeding, and changing said infant) that I'm sure she scarcely noticed either my arrival *or* my departure.

By the time I left for Rigel's, I was in a much better mood, filled with keen anticipation for whatever the evening might bring. Nothing could stop me now: I was intelligent, alert, and confident that I could succeed in acquiring information where others had failed. Also in my favor: I was the right age to be a considerable temptation to the vanity of an older man.

Besides, I knew that I looked absolutely stunning.

Rigel didn't stand a chance!

***

The Chairman's Suite is second in luxury and grandeur only to that of the royal family – and far more impressive than my family's pathetic accommodations. The chairman of the Inner Circle must necessarily do a great deal of entertaining, and Rigel definitely had the setting to accomplish this in style.

One of Rigel's aides, dressed in the elegant red and black uniform of his personal staff, met me at the door. On the wall behind him, facing the entry, was a portrait of the Premier, crafted by the Concorde's famed holo-artist Erementi. Life-size and nearly as impressive as the subject himself, the portrait managed to capture Rigel's essence: the proud, almost-military bearing; the dark hair, burnished silver at the temples and swept back from a high forehead; the strongly hooked nose; and the firm mouth and square chin. The eyes were particularly arresting, hyper-alert and full of intelligence. 'I am a man of consequence,' the portrait seemed to proclaim.

As I followed Rigel's aide down a mirrored hallway that was resplendent with fancy inlaid tiles and priceless artwork, I kept peeking furtively back over my shoulder at the holo. And I had the uncanny if irrational sensation that it was watching me, as I'm sure the holo-artist had intended.

Eventually, my escort opened a massive door that led into Rigel's private study and ushered me in with a deep bow. "The Premier will join you shortly," he announced. "He asked me to make you comfortable. Is there anything I can offer you while you're waiting?"

Assuring him that I was quite content, I sent the fellow away – and the moment he was gone, I strolled nonchalantly over to Rigel's workstation on the outside chance that I might discover some evidence, either of his

173

business dealings or else his political connections. Unfortunately, the only items that were lying about dealt with mundane matters, and I had neither the time nor the courage to investigate further – for I somehow felt as if the keen eyes of Rigel's portrait had followed me into his study – exactly as the vigilant cameras of the suite's AI must surely also be doing.

I had just begun to browse the titles of his rare book collection when Rigel himself entered the room, a vital and decisive presence. He strode rapidly over to where I was standing and took both of my hands in his.

"TiAnn! You look ravishing!"

"Why thank you, Rigel," I replied, well aware of the smoldering heat in his eyes that was informing me in no uncertain terms that he an entirely different sort of ravishing in mind.

"I'm so glad you're here," he continued. "I was beginning to fear that your father would never allow you return to Concordia."

"*Allow* me? I don't need my father's permission to do anything!" I turned my cheek just in time to avoid the kiss he had aimed at my mouth. "The only reason I didn't come back sooner was that I've been busy assisting him with his research."

"Research? Oh, of course: your law school training. I don't know why I keep forgetting about that. It must be because you're so beautiful that I tend to overlook your many other assets."

"Ha! I admit to being good at the law, but not to anything else. And, Rigel, I thought we were friends. Surely you don't need to resort to flattery with…"

"You know very well that I want us to be more than friends," he interrupted.

I lowered my gaze to give him the impression that I was flustered, but in my heart I rejoiced. He had never before admitted his interest so directly.

"I'm honored to know you feel that way…" I let my voice trail off.

He raised my face with his hand, and for a moment we gazed at each other intently. Then he pressed his lips to mine, briefly but firmly. He tasted like peppermint, which I despise.

"And now," he said, "we should celebrate your return to Concordia. May I offer you a drink?" He went over to a cabinet which, when opened, turned out to be full of liquor from every sector of the Concorde.

"I don't care which one," I told him when he solicited my preference. "You choose."

He came back with two glasses, filled with smoky amber liquid. "Let's drink to our future," he said as he handed me one.

"To our future."

Whatever was in that glass had a light sweetness, which unfortunately left a bitter aftertaste that I found quite unpleasant.

"We should also drink to the future of the Concorde Alliance," I said. "May it be delivered from its enemies, whoever they are. And may it always be ruled by those who have the courage to act in its best interests."

"Wise sentiments indeed. The Concorde Alliance," Rigel solemnly intoned, watching me over the rim of his glass. "And speaking of the Concorde, it seems to me there must be a great deal of planning going on in Concordia Palace tonight. No doubt your father is right at the center of it."

"No doubt."

"I wonder why you chose to be here with me this evening, rather than at your father's side."

"I might ask you the same question."

We locked eyes – sizing one another up, I was sure.

He shrugged. "Perhaps I feel that your father may be in error as to what's in the Concorde's best interests," he said at last.

"And you know better." I made it a statement, not a question. "Well, I might be of the same opinion."

Again, that watchful scrutiny.

"I wish your father would take me into his confidence," Rigel finally offered. "If I knew more about his plans, I could make a better assessment of their chances of success."

I walked over to the sofa and sat down, hoping my excitement didn't show. This was the opening I'd been waiting for: an opportunity to let him know that I was willing to divulge confidential information – which, I was sure, was at least one of his motives for courting me. And this was my chance to prove he could trust me – of course, in return I hoped that he would reveal his own plans...

"It's a pity you missed this afternoon's meeting with my father and Cristan Andebar," I said, attempting to sound regretful. "But I suppose you were too busy with your own affairs."

"I think you know that I would have been there if I had been invited," was his bitter reply. He sat down next to me rather heavily and much closer than I would have preferred. "My staff meeting could have waited."

I watched him with intense interest, thinking, *If only you would tell me a bit more about your plans, I could make a better assessment of your chances of success, if you are indeed the mastermind behind this rebellion! And if not, what, if anything, do you know or suspect about who is?*

But what I said aloud was, "Actually, you didn't miss much. By now they've surely spoken to the Prime, and as chairman of the Inner Circle, you'll certainly be briefed."

"Then there shouldn't be any harm in your telling me," he suggested.

"No, I suppose not…" I made a pretense of thinking it over.

"You know you can trust me," he coaxed.

"Well… First of all, it might interest you to know that Andebar has asked the Prime to allow the Tropi to join the Inner Circle."

"The Tropi! Good god!" He knocked back a prodigious gulp of liquor.

"Now, Rigel, I admit she's an impressive woman – I met her myself for the first time this afternoon. But what difference can one more person possibly make to the Inner Circle?"

"It depends on what they want her to do."

I looked him over, appraising. Intelligent? Yes. Clever too. But was he a match for the Tropi?

Were any of us?

"I don't think they have a clear idea about what she can do for them," I temporized, "or even if she *can* help. But she seems to think she can, so she asked Andebar to sponsor her, and he agreed to talk to the Prime."

"Still, it would be interesting to know if she has anything specific in mind."

"It's my impression that they're hoping she'll be able to use her intuition to clarify certain issues: the disappearances, for example. My sister's husband, Eirik Sanderson – you may have heard of him – has been missing for quite some time now. And there are others: people with far more

176

political clout than he ever had. I guess she'll be looking into that, although what good it's going to do, I don't know."

"Ah yes, your missing brother-in-law," he sounded almost bored. "An unfortunate business. I'm sure the Prime would like to find him."

Platitudes and evasions! Was he ever going to speak openly?

"Damn the Prime!" I spat out in frustration. "He's an incompetent old fool, and you know it as well as I do!"

"My dear TiAnn, what a dreadful thing to say!" He didn't seem at all upset by my outburst, though.

Perhaps I could convince him to be candid if I approached this more directly…

"Rigel, anyone with the Prime's leadership experience has got to realize that every now and then someone's going to come along who wants to take charge and run the Concorde Alliance him- or herself. That's what the power game is all about: having enough strength to prevent anyone else from taking it away from you. If the Prime has forgotten that – and it seems he may have – then he's a fool!"

"I didn't realize you had such a low opinion of my cousin."

"Well, now you know. Listen: Andebar and my father preach that the Concorde Alliance is a balance of power, predicated on the expectation that a diverse group of forces can cooperate with each other to make the system function… But I don't see it that way. It seems to me that it's the leader's responsibility to keep it functioning…

"And the Prime has let his power slip away, until by now he's forced to share the Concorde leadership with subordinates who should be taking orders from him – not the other way around! Just look at the mess he's in because someone has the courage to oppose him."

"It sounds like you think this hypothetical person ought to succeed."

"We're not talking about some hypothetical person, Rigel – and you know it!" I snapped – and then I waited for him to respond.

But maddeningly, he maintained his silence.

So I went on in a calmer voice, "Yes: I think this person could definitely succeed. He or she *should* succeed if they have the strength to persevere and the means to carry out a viable plan. And if that person was in a position to somehow influence the outcome of the government's deliberations – well then it shouldn't matter one iota whether or not the Tropi is part of the Inner Circle."

I left the rest unsaid. It was as close as I dared to come to the subject of his possible involvement in the insurrection.

Rigel sat beside me in thoughtful silence. "You make an interesting point," he said at last.

I could be very useful to you, I told him silently, but I didn't dare say so aloud.

"Very interesting…" he repeated. "I suppose a private investigation by the Inner Circle isn't such a bad idea…"

"My point exactly."

But that infuriating man! Just when I was sure he was on the verge of confiding in me, he changed the subject!

"My dear, what a terrible host I am! Here I've invited you to dinner and instead of entertaining you, I've held you hostage in my study for nearly an hour discussing politics."

"But politics is what I *want* to talk about, Rigel! I'm passionately interested in…"

He put a finger to my lips. "Not another word of this! I know you're just trying to be polite. You must hear all too much of this kind of talk from your father and his cronies. And you're far too lovely to be treated that badly, not when we have this whole evening to ourselves."

"But…"

"Come, my dear. We should talk about something more romantic."

I opened my mouth to argue, but before I could utter another word, he cut in.

"No more protests! Tonight is our night, and I refuse to spoil it by talking politics. I want to show you how much I appreciate your coming here to visit me. First, we'll have an intimate candlelit dinner, and then I have a favor to ask of you."

A favor! That silenced me.

Very well: if he wanted to play it that way, I could wait him out – although everything in me rebelled against doing so.

So I let him take me in his arms for yet another peppermint, and now liqueur-flavored kiss. And then I allowed him to lead me into his private dining room, where he poured out two cut crystal goblets of expensive wine while his hovering servants presented us with plate after gold-rimmed plate of sumptuous food, setting it before us with great ceremony.

I made no protest. Instead, I listened politely and with what I hoped would pass for keen interest to the ridiculous small talk he insisted on making while we ate. But beneath my pasted-on smile, I was fuming.

How dare he toy with me this way!

Yet on another level, I was impressed by his subtle self-control, as well as burning with curiosity, wondering what he would eventually ask of me.

***

It wasn't until we had finished our meal and were sipping after-dinner drinks that he once again turned the conversation to more important matters.

"TiAnn, I said earlier that I have a favor to ask."

"And you got exactly the result you wanted!" I shot right back. "All evening long I've been trying to guess what it is."

His dark eyes glittered in the candlelight and his whole face appeared to blur and shift subtly – no doubt the result of my having had slightly too much to drink.

"Before I tell you what it is," he said with maddening indirection, "I have a present for you."

To hell with your present! I wanted to shout, but instead I smiled, and said as sweetly as I could, "A present! How thoughtful."

His answering smile was rather lopsided. "Well, actually, it's for both of us..." He got to his feet – none too steadily I noticed – and started rummaging through his jacket pockets.

"Ah!" He made his careful way around to my side of the table. "For you, my dear. And for *us*..." Laying a heavy hand on my shoulder, he placed two small, flat, pinkish packets on my palm.

I sat staring down at them for several long moments.

Why did they look so familiar?

"The last time I saw you," he was saying, "you promised me we'd meet again – and after you left Concordia, I couldn't stop thinking about you – and hoping we could be together...

"So I went over to *Eros* and bought these. The salesman promised this will make both of us very happy. I've been saving them for tonight."

179

I couldn't think of a thing to say.

"You have heard of *Eros*, haven't you?" he persisted.

"Hasn't everyone?" I managed, as he pulled me to my feet, sliding his arms around my waist and drawing me close.

"TiAnn darling, let's take it now!" His kiss was passionate, insistent.

This was not going at all as I had planned! Those damn packets were still crumpled in my right hand, crushed against his chest.

I had to get rid of them – and fast! This definitely wasn't the time for erotic distractions.

"But, Rigel," I protested at my first opportunity, "you said there was something you wanted to ask me. Shouldn't we talk about that before we do anything else?"

"Don't be afraid," he said, nuzzling my neck. "Since it's our first time together, I want it to be perfect."

"I'm sure it will be," I began. "But we have so much to talk about and I..."

"Please, darling – let's do it now. It will take a while for the formula to take effect, and I'll tell you all about my plans while we wait. Besides, what I want to ask you is rather personal."

How could I back out then?

He released me just long enough to take the powder from my hand and add it to our drinks. "To us," he beamed, raising his glass.

"To us." Closing my eyes, I drained my own glass and set is aside. "Now tell me what you have in mind."

"I have a plan, my dear – one that can only succeed if I have your support and total commitment."

At last!

"You know you can count on me for anything, Rigel."

"Bless you! I'm so relieved! You have no idea what a terrible time I've had, getting up the courage to discuss this with you."

"I understand."

And really, I did.

He had to be The One! And carrying such a dangerous scheme around in his head, going for months on end without another soul to talk things over with, must have been a terrible strain.

"Your secret is safe with me," I promised.

"Secret? Well it isn't exactly a secret… Actually, I'd like to host a dinner party."

"I beg your pardon?"

"A dinner party. You see, my dear, it's essential just now that I make a good impression on all of the delegates who are visiting Concordia. And frankly, I don't feel up to tackling this on my own since it's something that requires a woman's touch."

Think, TiAnn! I prodded my muzzy-headed self. There *had* to be a hidden agenda behind his statement.

"What do you say, darling?" Rigel persisted. "Will you help me?"

Suddenly I realized what he was getting at.

"Of course: a dinner party! That's genius! And you're going to invite all of the most influential people in the Concorde – after all, it's extremely important that you have their goodwill."

"Ah, you do understand!"

"I suppose you'll have to ask the Prime and his son – it would look strange if you didn't," I hurtled on, "and the Tropi. We probably should invite my father too, since he's…"

"A splendid thought!"

I was beginning to feel very strange: far dizzier than I had been just moments ago, and my lips and the tips of my fingers were starting to tingle.

Was it the wine or that damn drug?

"Of course I'll help you," I told Rigel. "There's a lot we can accomplish."

If we worked together, we could do an extremely thorough job of assessing the current mood of the Concorde leaders! By talking to all of those important people and comparing notes later on as to what they thought about the Prime's situation, we might be able to predict how they would react to a possible coup.

How clever of Rigel to have thought of this!

"Of course, we'll have to be discreet," I said aloud.

"I knew I could count on you!" he cried, crushing me to him. "There are so many things a woman will think of in these matters of entertaining that a man couldn't possibly remember. I'll leave you to work up a guest list, although naturally I'll want final approval before you send out the invitations…"

"Send out the…?"

"And while you're at it, go ahead and arrange for a caterer and decide on a menu – will you, darling? Better not choose anything too exotic, some of the delegates are quite provincial. By the way: do you think it should be a sit-down dinner or a buffet?"

He *couldn't* be serious! Was he was really asking me to do nothing more than play hostess for him?

"TiAnn, are you listening?"

"Of course," I answered rather testily.

"Good," he went right on in the same idiotically cheerful tone of voice. "I'll leave the details to you. You can use my interface to help you get organized. Oh yes –and be sure you ask Andebar and his musicians to entertain. But don't let him overcharge – he tends to ask whatever he thinks he can get away with."

I thought things couldn't possibly get any worse. But I was wrong.

"And, darling," he added, nibbling on my ear, "I want you to go out and find yourself the most gorgeous, the most outrageous, the sexiest dress that money can buy. Something that will make what you have on tonight look like an old rag! Charge it to my account."

"Thank you so much," I sneered.

But he was too far gone on his stupid drug to hear the sarcasm in my voice.

I must have been pretty far gone too, because under any other circumstances I would have walked out on him. As it was, I didn't – and that way, I realized later, when I'd had a chance to recover and could think more clearly, I had unwittingly managed to keep my opportunities open to find out what, if anything, he knew and what he might be up to.

"I knew we were meant for each other," he crowed. "We understand each other perfectly. You're a woman I'll be proud to have as my hostess on the night of my dinner party!"

We indulged in a lengthy kiss that became more breathless and urgent by the moment. Yet even while this was happening, there was a cold, detached little voice in my mind, silently vowing that this was the last time I would allow him to get away with underestimating my abilities.

But by then the drug was affecting us both, and soon the only thing that either of us was able to think about was ripping off each other's clothing and stumbling into his bedroom.

6.

I awoke the next morning in my own bedroom with no clear recollection of how I had gotten there, and nothing better to show for the previous evening's folly than a body that ached all over and a throbbing headache. I even discovered a couple of bruises.

What's the point of taking an aphrodisiac if you can't remember the thrill they'd (presumably) given you, was the bitter question I asked myself?

When I tried to sit up, the room spun around me.

Perhaps it was the alcohol, after all.

For the remainder of the morning, doing anything more energetic than turning over in bed was out of the question, but by lunchtime I felt well enough to get up. I put on a robe and joined my father and sister in our sitting room.

Janne was feeding the baby. The sight of his gooey hands and face made my stomach churn.

"I missed you last night," my father said, giving me a searching look. "I was expecting you to join me. Some fascinating issues came up… TiAnn, are you okay?"

"I'm fine," I said, easing into a chair.

"You don't look fine. What have you done to yourself?"

"I haven't done anything to myself, Father. Rigel invited me to dinner. I guess we had too much to drink."

My father and sister exchanged what I could only interpret as a worried glance.

"How *is* Rigel?" my father wanted to know. "I haven't seen much of him lately."

"Very busy. Actually, that was one of the reasons we got together. He's planning a dinner party and he'd like me to help him."

Hearing this, Janne's eyes widened in alarm, but thankfully she kept her thoughts to herself.

"He's certainly asking a lot of you!" my father said. "Organizing even a minor affair on Concordia is a significant undertaking, and if I know my old friend Rigel, anything he puts on will be a major production. If I were you, I'd seriously consider sparing yourself the agony and suggesting that he hire a professional party planner."

I couldn't help smiling at his accurate assessment of my lover's penchant for grand theatrical gestures.

"And I hope you realize that, should you agree, an undertaking like Rigel's is going to require a tremendous amount of time and energy on your part," my father added. "All three of us are already swamped with work for the Prime's research project. I hope Rigel appreciates the sacrifices you're apparently willing to make for him."

"So do I. Planning parties is such a thankless chore, and you know how I detest that sort of thing! Still, how could I refuse? Bachelors are totally incompetent when it comes to arranging even the simplest practical details of any social function."

My father's eyebrows rose noticeably – he had certainly never heard me express such a sexist opinion before.

"Just so you'll know where I am," I said to cover my embarrassment, "I was planning on going over to Rigel's again for a couple of hours this afternoon. I need to make a start on his party…"

"As you wish. Be sure to give him my regards – and don't forget the Inner Circle meeting tonight. I'm counting on you to help present our report."

"Father, you know I won't forget. I wouldn't miss it for anything."

***

After lunch I felt much better. I dressed and left for Rigel's – rather nervously, I must admit, since I was unsure what his reaction to our previous night's escapade might be. I was also uneasy about entering his territory on the pretext of helping him when I had my own private agenda to pursue.

Rigel was in another one of his interminable meetings when I arrived, but he excused himself for just long enough to assure me that he would be finished sometime in the late afternoon. Giving me a quick, pepperminty kiss, he left me in the care of a different aide, a Lieutenant Ent, whom Rigel tasked with making sure that I was comfortable and showing me how to access his personal workstation.

If Rigel was really as clever as he thinks he is, he'd never let me anywhere near his interface! I gloated, as I followed the aide into the study. *I'll show* him *what a mistake it is to take my help for granted!*

For although it seemed apparent that at this point in our relationship Rigel had no intention of revealing any of his plans – however benign they might be – to me, I was certain that I could coax the requisite information out of his interface.

Since every law student has to master the use of the Intergalactic Net, that vast system of entangled quantum particles which links the entire Concorde Alliance together, communications node to communications node, I had quickly discovered that I have an almost preternatural aptitude for infiltrating it. In fact, when I had first started studying with Drexel, I had taken it as a personal challenge to crack his codes, and it wasn't long before I was able to ferret out the answers to all of his tests before he'd even had a chance to give them! And now, confronted with Rigel's interface, I felt confident that I could extract any data he might have cached there without arousing his suspicions – confident, but also wary because I didn't want any witnesses to my piracy.

I had to get rid of that pesky aide!

First, I let my unsuspecting helper show me how to call up Rigel's list of contacts – and then I began methodically scanning it, trying to force myself to relax and appear to be busy. After about twenty minutes, I stopped just long enough to assure the young man, who was standing at attention nearby and looking thoroughly bored, that I would be working on this phase of my planning for quite some time and wouldn't require any additional assistance for the foreseeable future.

The fellow seemed only too happy to depart, leaving me free to pursue other, more profitable areas of inquiry.

Following up on my intention to use Rigel's contacts as a jumping-off point, I continued to skim rapidly through the list, unsure what I was looking for... And eventually I found it: the name of one of his partners in the shipbuilding firm they co-owned. Their company was called the Great Egypt Starship Company, and that seemed as good a place as any to start my investigation.

At my request, Rigel's interface quickly located the GESCo files, and within minutes I was reviewing their construction costs, sales figures, profits, and pending deliveries. It made for interesting reading.

GESCo was a healthy company, although not spectacular in its success since it had competition from any number of other manufacturers. What *was* peculiar though, was that GESCo was apparently building many more ships than had been ordered. This odd fact wasn't obvious at first, but once I began looking into the figures for materials purchased and comparing units produced against units ordered, a discrepancy began to emerge.

My curiosity was piqued. What was GESCo doing with the extra starships if no one had ordered them, I wondered? If they had been built on speculation and kept in storage for future purchasers, it was an unorthodox way of doing business, to say the very least. Or were the additional ships being put to some other, undocumented, and perhaps nefarious use? If so, I wanted to know what it was.

I went back to the suppliers of raw materials, asking the interface to crosscheck the amounts purchased versus units manufactured. It was obvious that far more supplies had been bought than were needed for the recorded sales.

Had the suppliers noticed? And who were the suppliers?

By the time I had acquired that information, I was beginning to get nervous about the possible return of my unwanted assistant. Rapidly scanning the suppliers list, I was able to determine that the major source of materials was an entity called the Cairo Mining Corporation, located on one of New Egypt's six moons.

Elated by my initial success, I nevertheless realized that I had been at work for quite some time now without having much to show for it – at least not much that I wanted anyone else to see... Besides, I didn't want to run the risk of having someone walk in on me unannounced while I was still in the midst of my covert research. So I recalled Rigel's personal contacts list and buzzed for Cameron Ent. When Rigel's aide promptly appeared, I asked him for refreshments.

I was still scanning the developing guest list when he returned with a tray laden with snacks and a message from Rigel that his meeting would probably be over in an hour or so. Rigel wanted to know if I would stay and join him for a light supper before the Inner Circle meeting.

I accepted his invitation, once again dismissed his dutiful assistant, and went back to work.

Although I was tempted to continue my intriguing investigation, I resisted the impulse and instead forced myself to concentrate on my legitimate task. I wanted to have a respectable amount of progress to show for my afternoon's labors. And by the time Rigel joined me, I was fairly organized about who should be invited to his party.

"It's coming along slowly but surely," I reported when he asked how I was doing. "You know how these things are... By the way, you haven't said when your party is going to be."

Laughing, he leaned down to kiss my neck. "Ah, TiAnn, your questions never end. Oh well, I suppose I should make up my mind about that."

"I suppose you should!" I stood up and stretched. "I've been working very hard, and I'm stiff from sitting for so long. I would hate to discover that my efforts have been in vain."

"Poor darling! It *is* boring, isn't it? Come and have a drink." Before I could protest, he poured me another glass of that awful amber stuff.

"What's the soonest we can be ready?" he wanted to know.

"Well, let me think about it..." I temporized, setting my glass aside.

"Actually," he interjected with studied casualness, "it's beginning to look like it may have to happen as soon as you're able to complete the arrangements."

My interest perked up at that. I was tempted to inquire why he was suddenly in such a hurry, but I was learning not to ask him anything directly. So instead, I offered, "I'm almost ready to have you go over the list. I'll probably be finished with it sometime tomorrow morning..."

"Good work!"

"And then I'll need another day and a half or so to decide what to serve, and to arrange for caterers, who are bound to be extremely busy just now with all the delegates present and requiring their services... And you should plan on a few more days to circulate the invitations and give your guests a chance to respond… I'd say ten days is about the soonest you can reasonably hope for."

He put his arms around me and gazed, smiling, into my eyes. "Darling, have I told you how very nice it is of you to do this nasty job for me? But I promise: when you see all of those important people gathered here in my suite, you'll have the satisfaction of knowing it was a job well done."

"I won't have the satisfaction of seeing anything at all, Rigel, unless you tell me when you want the party to take place! You know I'll have to put that information on the invitations."

"How persistent you are! Very well, ten days from today sounds fine. Are you sure that will give you enough time to organize everything?"

"Yes, Your Premiership: your wish is my command! Ten days it is!" I gave him a mocking salute. "And now I think we'd better have something to eat so we won't be late for our meeting."

"Wait!" He seized my hand as I started to turn away. "Will you come back here with me afterwards?"

I placed my free hand on his chest, and gazed earnestly into his eyes. "Rigel, last night was amazing! But I think I'd better go home tonight and get some sleep."

"Must you?"

"I'm afraid so." I gave his hand a squeeze. "You do want me to make good progress on the party tomorrow, don't you? And I know I'll be awfully tired if I stay over again… Besides, I'd really prefer not to give my father any reason to start asking awkward questions."

He sighed. "I suppose you're right." Releasing his hold on me, he took both of our glasses and set them on the sideboard.

My thoughts drifted away to GESCo and the Cairo Mining Corporation, so it was a few moments before I realized that he was still speaking.

"I'm sorry, Rigel – what did you say?"

"Daydreaming, darling?"

"No. I was just thinking about your guest list."

Which was actually the truth.

He smiled. "I was saying that I may have to leave for New Egypt immediately after the party."

So that's why he wanted to know when was the soonest he could schedule it!

"…And the last time I asked," he continued, "you wouldn't accept my invitation to accompany me there. Do you think you might reconsider now?"

"I might."

A trip to New Egypt could be extremely worthwhile – in fact crucial – if my research proved out and I was able to uncover indisputable evidence of his involvement in the rebellion that would require firsthand investigation.

"Just 'might'?" Rigel was asking.

"I'd love to come with you! But I'll have to check with father. He may have some important work for me to do."

"Would you allow me to speak to him? I'm sure I can convince him to let you have some time off."

"Very well."

"I'm anxious to show you New Egypt." His eyes were alight with enthusiasm. "It's a lovely planet – and there are so many cultural events and amusements just for the taking. I know you'll be impressed."

"I'm anxious to see it for myself."

…And if my research goes well, I added silently, *by the time I get there, I may have some very pertinent questions to ask you!*

7.

The council chamber was ablaze with lights as, arm in arm, Rigel and I entered the room.

I had been told to expect an intimate setting, a small, comfortable inner sanctum where the most crucial work of the Concorde Alliance is actually done. However, on this particular occasion, I wasn't surprised to discover that the place was packed wall-to-wall with a milling swarm of people: myriad additional delegates who had come to present their various reports and futile suggestions to the Inner Circle.

It took me quite a while to locate my father and Janne, who were halfway down the room, awkwardly juggling heavy stacks of work slates, holo-maps, and printouts, and deep in conversation.

They both turned towards us as we approached.

After exchanging the customary pleasantries, to which my sister contributed scarcely a word, Rigel turned the conversation to business.

"Arram," he said, "I'd like to thank you for sparing TiAnn from what I know is her busy schedule and allowing her to act as my hostess. She's a miracle-worker. I don't know what I'd have done without her."

My father offered him a smile that didn't quite reach his eyes (or so it seemed to me). "Yes, my daughter is extremely capable."

"I don't know if she's told you, but she's helping me plan a supper party. I hope both you and your other daughter will be able to attend."

"Thank you for the invitation, Rigel. With some luck, it will fall on an evening when we're free."

"Let me know your schedule and I'll make sure that it does," was Rigel's gallant response. "I'm almost embarrassed to ask you for any more of her attention, but I hope you can do without her for a little while longer. We still have so much work to do."

"TiAnn is the one who decides how best to use her time," was my father's somewhat curt reply.

And I could almost hear Janne's unspoken warning as she shot a worried glance in my direction: *Oh, TiAnn, be careful!*

I can take care of myself a whole lot better than your stupid husband did! I was tempted to remind her. Already, in the course of a single afternoon, I had acquired more information about Rigel's personal business affairs than I suspected Eirik had been able to uncover in several months. But instead of voicing my thoughts, I smiled and watched Janne blush and look away.

Rigel turned to me. "I'm afraid I'll have to leave you now, my dear." He raised my hand to his lips. "Until tomorrow… Arram." This last was directed at my father, and then he bowed to my sister. "Sera Trellarian."

With a brisk salute, he departed.

"TiAnn, I need to have a talk with you tonight, after this meeting is over," my father abruptly announced the moment Rigel was out of earshot.

"Certainly, Father."

It would be interesting and also rather amusing to find out how he intended to approach the lecture I was sure he was prepared to deliver.

Meanwhile, out of the corner of my eye, I noticed that Rigel was bearing down on Vice Admiral Pellen of the Space Guild. The two men greeted each other heartily.

The next moment, a murmur of excitement broke out at the far end of the room and, as if on cue, everyone in the place turned to stare. Even before I was able to see who had entered, I had already guessed who it must be.

The Tropi swept into the room, accompanied by her two bodyguards and Cristan Andebar, and none of them seemed in the least bit dismayed by the sensation they were creating.

Just let the Prime try to steal the show from her' I exulted. And once again, despite my best intentions, I found myself experiencing the unsettling mixture of awe and envy that this unusual woman inspired in me.

Talk didn't resume until the Tropi and Andebar had walked the entire length of the room, the crowd parting for them like the proverbial waters, and they had taken their seats. Her bodyguards ended up standing on either side of their mistress like hyper alert, twin golden statues.

By that time, the rest of the company had begun drifting – or perhaps it would be more accurate to say shoving and jostling – towards their own places. Regular members of the Inner Circle were seated along two sides of a long rectangular table, while the visiting dignitaries had been assigned makeshift seating along the walls. Rigel had one entire end of the council table all to himself, and at the opposite end were two throne-like chairs, set somewhat back from the table – for the Prime and his son, I assumed.

"TiAnn!"

"Yes, Father?"

"Pay attention when I'm speaking to you! I need your summary of the musicians' reports immediately! Where is it?"

"I downloaded it onto your work slate right before I left for Rigel's this afternoon." I tried to keep my voice level, hoping my annoyance didn't show. "My report should be accessible in your files. You shouldn't have any trouble locating it."

"I've got to have those materials in some sort of meaningful order so I don't make a fool of myself when it's time to present them!" was his testy reply. "The Prime doesn't tolerate incompetence." Without another word, impatient or otherwise, he turned and began forcing his way through the melee.

Janne and I trailed along in his wake while he sought his designated place at the council table. Two chairs, set slightly behind his, had been provided for us – but just as he was about to sit down, my father suddenly turned to me. "I'm sorry I snapped at you, TiAnn. I'm very nervous about this meeting. As you're about to witness, the Prime has a way of putting people on the spot, and I'd hate to appear unprepared."

Someday, I knew, I would no longer be playing private secretary to my father – and then no one, neither he nor the Prime, was going to push *me* around! In the meantime, cooperation seemed the wisest course of action, so I helped Janne sort through our printouts, arranging the crucial summaries directly in front of my father, and making sure that my report was readily available on his work slate.

Then Rigel asked everyone to rise, and the Prime and his son entered from their private chambers.

I had seen them both before on previous trips to Concordia – and of course in the media – but never from this close. As everyone waited in respectful silence, the two men strode briskly to their chairs and sat down. The Prime's son, Lord Ferrin, was a pale, slender man of about thirty. He looked rather insubstantial beside his portly father.

Could he be conspiring to usurp his father's throne, I wondered, covertly sizing him up? It was one of several questions I had come to Concordia to answer.

But in order to do so, I knew that I would first have to find a way to circumvent whatever strictly enforced protocols had been put in place around him to discourage unwanted attention from potential interviewers like myself. How difficult they would be to breach was anyone's guess.

As the rest of us resumed our places, the Prime glanced slowly around the room as if he was taking stock of the assembly, and scowling as if he was not necessarily pleased by what he saw. His eyes, partially hidden beneath bushy grey brows and slightly puffy eyelids, had a glittering, almost reptilian look of intelligence. He was a man in his early sixties, strong and apparently in the best of health, despite his girth. His haughty expression bespoke authority, and it was obvious from his demeanor that he was a person who was accustomed to being obeyed.

Breaking the absolute silence, his voice rang out with surprising intensity...

"Members of the Inner Circle, and guests: I have summoned you here this evening so we may have the opportunity to discuss among ourselves, freely and in private, the present distressing state of affairs that have overtaken the Concorde Alliance...

"Those of you who are unfamiliar with this council may be surprised by the lack of formality with which we address each other. Although we do not necessarily follow strict parliamentary procedure, I assure you that I will not hesitate to impose it if I feel it is necessary to maintain order...

"Allow me to remind you that we are here to determine a course of action in response to an apparent insurrection within the Concorde Alliance, a problem which the Interplanetary Council as a whole will take up when it reconvenes tomorrow. It is my hope that tonight we can reach some preliminary conclusions as to how we will direct the council to proceed...

"Some of you have expressed concern that the IPC is too unwieldy an organization to deal with this issue. If this proves to be the case, the decisions that we make here in this confidential forum will be all the more important. I expect your full cooperation."

In spite of myself, I was impressed. This was definitely not the figurehead I had anticipated. I waited expectantly for his next words.

"However, before we proceed any further," he was saying, "I wish to bring to your attention Councilor Andebar's petition that we include the most distinguished planetary leader, Madam Tropi, in our deliberations. She wishes to join the Inner Circle as a temporary member. I will take a few minutes to consider this request. May I have your comments?"

There was an undertone of murmured discussion among the delegates. A man stood up. I recognized him from media holos as Councilor Bleery of the Traders' Guild.

"Begging madam's pardon," he began, glancing nervously over at the Tropi and then quickly away, "I would like to know exactly what it is that she thinks she can do for us." He sat down in a hurry, his face flushed with embarrassment.

In a single, graceful motion the Tropi rose and was immediately the center of attention. "Sovereign, may I have your permission to speak?" she asked in her rich alto voice.

"Certainly, madam." Did I detect a hint of amusement in the Prime's expression? If so, it was quickly gone.

"Councilor Bleery's question is a reasonable one. What can I, the leader of a politically neutral planet, possibly have to offer the members of the Inner Circle?" She glanced around the table. "I can answer that in one word: intuition.

"The very fact that Tropi has stayed out of the mainstream of Concorde politics until now has given us a unique perspective. We have no ties or alliances to any other planet or to any particular point of view. And we have dedicated our many centuries of semi-isolation to developing the intangible art of knowing what is right, just by consulting our feelings...

"I can sense the truthfulness of a person or situation without having to sort through masses of data. I can help you by listening to what you say and by giving my best, carefully considered advice. Perhaps together we can strike at the source of this problem before it overwhelms us and does the Concorde Alliance any further injury."

She sat down.

Bleery rose again. "By all means let the Tropi join! She won't do us any harm, and she might even do some good."

There was good-natured laughter as he took his seat.

"Admiral Chert and Vice Admiral Pellen," the Prime abruptly interjected, "you seem to be engrossed in a fascinating private chat. Would you gentlemen care to enlighten us with the benefit of your collective wisdom?"

Both men looked sheepish. A few more whispered words and Vice Admiral Pellen stood up.

"Sovereign, the admiral has asked me to express his approval for allowing the Tropi to join us. We would welcome any assistance she can give us." He sat back down, still looking flustered, and the Prime's son nodded as he caught his father's eye.

Ferrin rose to his feet. "Father, I think the Tropi has been most generous to offer us her help. I don't think there's any need for further discussion."

Was this true graciousness on his part or some subtle strategy? I would be extremely interested to learn his motives. Perhaps I could charm my way into an interview with him later this evening, once the meeting had adjourned.

Rigel spoke up, interrupting my musings. "I agree with Lord Ferrin. I move that we allow the Tropi to join us as a temporary council member."

Good politics! I thought.

"I second the motion." That was Andebar.

"And I approve," the Prime said. "I shall dispense with the need for a formal vote. The Tropi is now a member of the Inner Circle and we will proceed with the business at hand...

"I would like to hear the updated reports of our special investigative task force. Councilor Trellerian, you may begin."

My father rose. "Sovereign, since I last reported to the council, the following incidents of violence against the Concorde Alliance have occurred..."

I suppose I should have been paying attention to what he was saying, but I already knew the data by heart. Instead, I found my thoughts drifting off towards that afternoon's discoveries.

What was GESCo up to? Those stockpiled supplies and/or surplus ships had to be an important clue. Why hadn't anyone noticed them? Or had they? Was that what Eirik Sanderson had been investigating when he'd disappeared?

And what about that supplier: the Cairo Mining Corporation? Didn't they realize they were sending GESCo a great deal more raw material than they should have been, if GESCo was simply filling current orders?

Who was responsible for the Cairo Mining Corporation? I had a few leads, and there might even be something on Cairo Mining in Rigel's files – but would I be able to continue my investigation without getting caught? It would be much safer if I could proceed from our own interface, and I thought I might have time to do just that tomorrow morning, before I returned to Rigel's suite.

Belatedly, I realized that the Prime was addressing my father.

"Councilor Trellerian, this report sounds like all of your others: a tale of endless woe. I asked for an update, not a rerun! Haven't you gained some insight into the patterns by now? There are patterns, aren't there? Interpret them for us!"

My father's face was flushed with embarrassment as he regarded his superior. It seemed to me that the Prime was being unnecessarily harsh.

"Sovereign, such a staggering amount of information is coming to our attention every day that it's taken a major effort on our part just to log all of it in!" my father protested.

"Father, let me speak," I suddenly announced, surprised by my own daring.

I could see the doubt in his eyes as he turned slightly aside to look down at me. But then he shrugged and said, "Sovereign, my younger daughter TiAnn, who has been working directly on this issue, has asked to respond to your question. With your permission?"

"If she has something useful to contribute, by all means let her do so."

I stood, well aware that every eye in the room was now focused on me.

Come on, TiAnn, I urged myself, *be an advocate the way Drexel taught you. And whatever you do, don't let the Prime intimidate you!*

"Sovereign," I began, "while it is true, as my father has stated, that we've been receiving a nearly overwhelming flood of information on a daily basis, as you have correctly surmised, patterns have begun to appear. But until recently those patterns have been far too vague to allow meaningful analysis, and therefore we haven't troubled you with them. However, at this point, if you wish, I can give you a brief rundown of what we believe we're seeing."

The Prime nodded his assent.

"One pattern could be defined as a campaign of incidents calculated to disrupt the regular workings of the Concorde Alliance," I said. "I would put mine placement and spreading rumors in this category. The purpose of these incidents is apparently to cause such inconvenience to the general public that they will begin to question the effectiveness of your policies...

"And this leads me to the second category: personal violence. Someone is engineering those demonstrations and riots. It only takes a few well-trained agitators to get things going – and a mere handful of agents to kidnap political figures. Consider how much more organization and what vast resources are required to assemble even a small group of starships to harass Concorde vessels."

At that moment, I happened to glance over in Rigel's direction. He was watching me intently with narrowed eyes – and so was Lord Ferrin. Co-conspirators, I wondered?

I had to struggle to suppress a gleeful smile. *Maybe now you'll give me credit for being able to do more than plan your parties, Rigel!* I told him silently, with a gratifying sense of satisfaction.

However, what I said aloud was: "Sovereign, these issues have led us to suspect that a person or several persons with just these attributes – organization and vast resources – is your troublemaker. However, there is one other possibility which you should perhaps consider before drawing any final conclusions..."

"You have my full attention, young lady." The Prime was actually leaning forward in his chair. "Please continue."

"We have received numerous reports from reliable Space Guild personnel of sightings: unknown ships of highly unusual, perhaps even alien, configuration. This may be part of the terrorists' overall plan – a hoax perpetrated to confuse us – but there is also the very real possibility that these ships are of truly alien origin."

"How do you justify that assumption?" Admiral Chert was on his feet. "My people haven't reached any such conclusion!"

I turned to face him. "I'm not offering conclusions, Admiral Chert. I'm merely suggesting something that has been a very real possibility all along: that those incidents may not be related to the others – that they may represent something entirely different. We should at least consider the implications."

"I agree," the Prime stated.

Therefore I continued on without hesitation: "If they *are* part of the first group, we're dealing with an extremely well-organized and resourceful local enemy. Conversely, if those ships represent an independent group of observers or antagonists, we may be facing not just a single enemy, but rather two distinct adversaries – which means that the Concorde Alliance would have to make contingency plans subject to two entirely different sets of circumstances."

"Your point is well taken," the Prime said.

I waited for the babble of hushed conversations to die down before I dropped my bomb.

"Of course," I said, "it's obvious that none of this really represents any significant threat to the Concorde Alliance…"

That brought a number of people to their feet.

"…It amounts to little more than a systematic campaign of harassment," I continued over the roiling buzz of agitated voices, "which is admittedly a nuisance, albeit a dangerous one. In fact, there is really only one way a person or persons could possibly hope to escalate these incidents into something far more significant… And I suspect that this is exactly what my brother-in-law, Eirik Sanderson, was looking into when he disappeared: the possibility that somewhere out there in Concorde space, someone is assembling a fleet for the express purpose of spearheading a coup which, if it succeeds, will result in the overthrow of the present government."

I had to raise my voice to be heard over the rising hubbub. "Of course, all of this is merely speculation on my part. However, Sovereign, I submit that if there is in fact a fleet out there, now is the time to act. And I advise you to use every resource at your disposal to find and neutralize that fleet as quickly as possible, before it has a chance to neutralize *you*!"

For some reason, my knees were shaking and my pulse was galloping as I practically fell back into my seat.

My father leaned over and whispered, "TiAnn, that was brilliant! Whether or not they agree with your conclusions, you certainly got everyone's attention."

"Thank you very much, Sera Trellarian," the Prime was saying, "for a report that was as concise as it was startling. My other advisors would do well to learn something from your presentation. Perhaps, if a vacancy on the Inner Circle occurs, I will consider appointing you! However, for the moment, I'm afraid I shall have to put up with this contingent, fallible though they may be..."

As the babble subsided into angry mutters, the Prime called for the next report.

The Prime complimented me! I took a deep, calming breath. *Father too! I wonder how Rigel and Ferrin felt about what I said.* But I had no way of knowing the answer to that question, as everyone else's attention was now riveted on Andebar.

After several others had spoken, Admiral Chert and Vice Admiral Pellen reported on troop distribution.

"...In conclusion, Sovereign," Pellen was saying, "we have the requisite manpower, but lack sufficient ships to utilize it properly – therefore we are incapable of increasing our effectiveness against the troublemakers."

The Prime scowled. "Why is that, Vice Admiral Pellen?"

Pellen glanced nervously in Rigel's direction. "I have been in conference with Chairman Rigel on that very subject."

Rigel rose and smoothly interjected, "Sovereign, it's a most unfortunate truth that the Great Egyptian Starship Company, of which I am a director, is one of several companies which have failed to meet their guild quotas..."

But you have plenty of ships, Rigel! I silently protested, *or at least the ability to produce them!*

Rigel went on, "...Which is a source of great concern and personal embarrassment for me. I wish to assure you that I'm making every effort to speed up production within my own company – in fact, I've scheduled a tour of inspection at my earliest opportunity. However, what with the present unstable political situation and additional council meetings, I've been reluctant to leave Concordia..."

Yet not so reluctant that he didn't already plan to leave right after his supper party!

Admiral Chert spoke up. "I'm of the opinion that augmentation of our fleet is our most pressing objective."

The Prime nodded. "I agree... Mister Chairman, I charge you with the responsibility of determining why those production companies, yours included, have not met their quotas. I want them back on track immediately!"

"As you wish, Sovereign."

Did Rigel hope it would go this way, I wondered?

"I want to inspect those production facilities too!" Pellen exclaimed, surging to his feet. "I request permission to accompany Chairman Rigel."

"Permission granted. Mister Chairman, how soon can you leave?"

"Immediately, Sovereign, although I had hoped to attend the first few sessions of the Interplanetary Council: I thought my input might be useful. Also, I must confess that I've been planning a supper party for early next week... And what would a supper party be without its host?" he added with a sheepish grin. "But if you wish, I will cancel it immediately and leave for New Egypt tonight."

The Prime regarded him intently. "I'm sure that won't be necessary. I understand that, regardless of your other plans, it will take you several days to arrange the rest of your affairs. And I would hate to deprive you of the opportunity to discuss important political matters with the other IPC and Inner Circle members under less formal circumstances. You may leave directly after your party."

"Thank you, Sovereign."

"During your absence," the Prime continued as Rigel prepared to resume his seat, "it will be necessary for me to appoint someone as interim chairman of the Inner Circle. Do you have any recommendations or preferences?"

Rigel immediately glanced up, obviously taken by surprise. "Sovereign, I had assumed that the Inner Circle would suspend its activities while the IPC is in session."

Andebar bolted to his feet. "I strongly advise against that! Sovereign, I think it's of the utmost importance that these Inner Circle meetings continue uninterrupted. The IPC will need our guidance if anything worthwhile is to be accomplished."

"I agree," Lord Ferrin said. "And I nominate Director Andebar as Interim Chairman."

How interesting! Did he really support his father's cause or was this a clever smokescreen to mask his true intentions?

Rigel glanced over at Ferrin and shrugged before he turned back to the Prime. "Very well. If the Inner Circle so pleases, I have no objection to Andebar's appointment."

Andebar bowed to Rigel.

I was fascinated by the events that I was witnessing here tonight. There were so many subtle undercurrents seething within the room. This was even more riveting than a courtroom trial – and I waited with interest to see what would happen next.

"May I speak?" the Tropi suddenly asked, also rising.

Once again, every eye in the room turned her way.

"All members of the Inner Circle should feel free to voice their thoughts at any time, madam," the Prime replied.

"I sense unspoken things here, hidden motives…"

Just what I was thinking!

"…And I wish to suggest that Admiral Chert should attempt to capture one of the enemy ships – not an alien vessel, for I do believe that there is an unknown entity observing our actions – but one employed by our local troublemaker. If he can do so, a great deal might be learned if we can examine even one of those ships, with or without its crew. Of course, prisoners would make your job that much easier, but I doubt that you will be able to take anyone alive."

The Prime gave a curt nod. "Madam Tropi, you make a valid point. Admiral Chert, get me an enemy ship. Make it your top priority – and maybe, if Councilor Trellerian's daughter is correct, you'll stumble upon an entire enemy fleet."

"I have one further suggestion," the Tropi said. "I recommend that the Inner Circle should initiate an investigation to discover which person or persons within the Concorde Alliance already has enough manpower and equipment at his or her disposal to challenge your leadership."

My thought exactly!

She went on: "Require each Concorde planetary government to give an accurate accounting of their military status. When you know who the strongest is, you will almost certainly have your agitator. That is, if Admiral Chert does not bring him in first."

"We will follow your excellent advice, madam," the Prime announced. "And now, unless there is further business on our agenda, this meeting is adjourned." His eyes flicked quickly around the table. "The Inner Circle is dismissed."

To my delight, Lord Ferrin offered me a wide grin and a mischievous wink as he turned to follow his father. That smile, I thought, definitely boded well for my being able to gain access to him!

After the Prime and his son had departed, conversations began in earnest all around the room. As I collected our belongings, I realized that I'd been holding my breath, as if I had expected something dramatic to happen at the very end.

What happened was dramatic enough! I scolded myself. *What more could there have been, unless the Tropi had openly challenged Lord Ferrin, Rigel, or someone else? I wonder what Rigel thinks of me now?*

I glanced over to where he stood chatting amiably with the Space Guild contingent, apparently unconcerned and totally relaxed.

A trip to New Egypt with Rigel and Vice Admiral Pellen would be far from dull, of that I was certain. And before I left Concordia, I definitely wanted to have that friendly chat with Lord Ferrin...

"TiAnn?" It was Janne. "Thank you for helping father tonight." Her tone was gentle, almost humble. "I don't know how he would have managed without you."

"The Prime was unfair, and he was too demanding. It was the least I could do," I replied gruffly, annoyed by how embarrassed her words made me feel. "Forget it."

Suddenly my father and Andebar were beside us.

"No, I won't forget it." my father said. "TiAnn, I'm so proud of you!"

"Not everyone has the nerve to stand up to the Prime," Andebar told me with a genuine smile, "*and* get a compliment in return!"

"Girls, I have a few things to wrap up here," my father was saying. "The two of you can go on ahead if you'd like."

"I've certainly had enough excitement for one night," Janne said. "Besides, I should be getting back to Bran and the babysitter."

Unexpectedly, the events of the past two days caught up with me in a rush, and I felt utterly exhausted. And as a result, Janne and I left before I had a chance to learn Rigel's reaction to my debut into Concorde politics.

8.

I practically fell into bed the moment I reached my room. My father must have come in much later, and he didn't bother to wake me for our promised talk.

The next morning, I got up quite early to use the apartment's comm console to connect to the Intergalactic Net: I wasn't anxious to have anyone looking over my shoulder while I was investigating Rigel's business affairs! Also, I wanted to finish this aspect of my research at the earliest possible opportunity so I could arrive at Rigel's place before he had a chance to leave for the first Interplanetary Council session.

Using a data scan routine to request information on the Cairo Mining Corporation, it came as no surprise that the files were quite uninformative. The company was located on New Egypt's moon – which I already knew – but neither its owners nor its board of directors was available. General production figures were given, but no specific details of its operations.

Another possible approach was to request information on the moon itself. I had better luck with that.

I learned that New Egypt's third moon, Anhur, was named after an ancient Egyptian god of war because of its reddish appearance as seen from New Egypt. And it turned out that Anhur had extensive mineral deposits. The presence of certain elements that could be converted into starship fuel was also noted, although for some reason this potentially valuable resource had never been exploited. So whoever had those surplus ships, probably also had the fuel to operate them – which was a crucial bit of information.

I read on.

There was a description of the mining colony itself and its facilities for processing and exporting ore. This was followed by a statement that Anhur also housed a branch of New Egypt's military academy. It was a rather small outpost – nevertheless this was another important piece of the puzzle because it provided Rigel with a connection to the military. Anhur's surface, I was told, was inhospitable to unprotected human life, which I realized would make it especially useful as a military training ground.

The report contained little else of value.

Now I had several interesting new leads, but if I was going to pursue them I knew that I would have to do so from Rigel's interface. It was a risk that I was willing to take – after all, at the very least I might be able to further impress the Prime with my detective abilities!

While I was still in the process of signing off the Net, my father came out of his bedroom.

"Good morning, TiAnn. You're up early."

"I wanted to read about New Egypt. I thought it might be a good idea to know something about it before I go there."

"You're going to New Egypt? This is the first I've heard about it."

"Rigel asked me yesterday. I didn't have a chance to mention it to you last night. Somehow the Inner Circle meeting didn't seem like the appropriate place."

My father pulled a chair over and sat down beside me. "I'm sorry to have to say this, TiAnn, but I don't approve of your going off with Rigel like that."

"Isn't that a bit old-fashioned?" I asked, trying to tease him past this awkward moment.

"I wasn't thinking of it in those terms at all. I'd hoped we'd have a chance to talk about this last night..." He hesitated and I just sat there, unwilling to make this any easier for him.

"I'm not sure how to begin," he said at last. "I'm afraid this is rather awkward... You see, Cristan and the Tropi are suspicious of Rigel. They don't think he's being completely honest with us."

"Based on what evidence?"

"That's the problem: they don't have anything definite. Right now it's just a hunch on their part."

"I'm not surprised."

"I hate to have to mention it at all because I realize you like him... And he's my friend! I've never known him to lie."

"Is it because of the slowdown in starship production?" I asked this coolly yet beneath my (hopefully) calm exterior, I was quite excited.

What exactly did they know?

"The slowdown is one of several issues," he admitted.

"But couldn't that just be an unfortunate coincidence?"

"Don't you think I've reminded them of that?" I could hear the anguish in his voice. "But they're stubbornly convinced that there's more to it than meets the eye."

"Are you?"

"No. Not really. But…" He sighed.

"None of this seems like a good reason to ask me to turn down Rigel's invitation."

"Perhaps you could just postpone your trip?" It sounded like a plea.

"I'm sorry, Father, I can't do that. Unless you can tell me something definite, I intend to go to New Egypt with Rigel."

He looked so unhappy that I took pity on him. "But I promise I'll be careful. I'll keep my eyes open and let you know if I see anything unusual."

"Oh, TiAnn, please don't go looking for something unusual! Just have a good time."

"That's exactly what I plan to do."

For several moments, neither of us spoke.

"Well, if you must go…" he began.

"Yes?"

"If this doesn't sound too melodramatic, I'd like to authorize Concordia Central Communications to give you an emergency frequency to call in on if you need help."

"All because of some overdue starships?"

"Please humor your nervous old father."

"Oh – all right." I smiled to ease the tension. "I suppose it can't do any harm. But please be discreet when you make the arrangements: it would be extremely embarrassing if Rigel found out."

He reached over and ruffled my hair. "I promise I'll be discreet. I realize it's probably very foolish of me, but after all, you *are* my little girl."

I immediately drew back from his hand. "You needn't worry, Father. I'm quite capable of taking care of myself!"

"I don't doubt that for a moment! The way you presented our report last night proved just how capable you are. It was far beyond anything a 'little girl' could ever hope to accomplish. I was very impressed, and so were many others."

His praise made me uncomfortable – but also pleased. "I did what I had to," I told him with an awkward laugh.

"And you did it very well indeed!" He stood up and then leaned down to kiss my cheek before he left me to prepare for that day's IPC meeting.

After breakfast, I headed for Rigel's suite – somewhat nervously, if the truth be told. I wondered what his reaction would be to last night's activities.

***

Rigel was in his study, apparently organizing material for the upcoming IPC meeting. He watched me enter without rising to greet me, as he previously would have done. "Well, TiAnn, that was quite a dissertation you gave the Inner Circle last night," was what he said instead.

"Someone had to get that nasty old man off my father's back! But I'm almost sorry I did. Everyone's been making such a fuss over me that it's become extremely embarrassing. I hope you're not going to start in too."

"I was especially interested in your conclusions," he went on, deadly serious, his eyes tracking my every move.

"Both the Prime and my father could have figured them out for themselves if they'd bothered to think things through." I settled into one of his enormous, overstuffed armchairs.

"But they didn't – at least, not in quite the way you did. I'm impressed by your grasp of a complex situation, TiAnn, and it's made me realize that you could be an extremely valuable asset to the Inner Circle: a person of your intellect could be instrumental in helping us track down and apprehend this cabal."

His pronouncement shocked me to the core of my being and caused me to immediately question every assumption I'd ever made about him.

Could I really have been that wrong? But I gritted my teeth and decided to tough it out – to see where he was going with this.

"Then I suppose I ought to remind you once again that I'm trained to do exactly that: grasp complex situations! My law studies – remember?" was my huffy retort, fueled as much by resentment that until now he had persisted in badly underestimating my abilities, as by my sudden uncertainty as to the validity of my suspicions about him.

Rigel was shaking his head as if to clear it of unwanted thoughts. His expression softened as he said, "Forgive me, darling. I'm under so much pressure right now to get certain things done before I have to return to New Egypt, and I guess it's making me edgy and forgetful."

"That reminds me," I said, regrouping with an effort, "I talked to father this morning and let him know that you'd invited me to go with you. He was rather reluctant at first. Can you imagine: he was worried about what other people might think!" I lied, passing it off as a joke.

He hesitated, so I quickly added, "You do still want me to come, don't you?"

Even if he didn't turn out to be the actual culprit, perhaps I could make use of the trip to continue to mine his database to search for damaging information about someone else – perhaps a partner in his starship factory.

"Of course I want to take you to New Egypt! How can you doubt it?" he protested.

"I thought you might be annoyed because I didn't come home with you last night."

"Nonsense! As it turned out, it was probably better that you didn't: I was up half the night working." He stood up, rubbing his eyes, and then began storing data cubes and his slate in an open carryall. "And now I need to get ready for the council meeting – not that anything worthwhile is going to happen there... Still, I make it my business to keep an eye on the proceedings."

And on Andebar! I thought, as suspicions about his involvement with the troublemakers once again reasserted themselves.

"TiAnn, there are aspects of last night's meeting I'd like to discuss with you sometime soon. That is, if you're interested..."

He seemed a bit dazed. I decided it must be from exhaustion – he was certainly having difficulty communicating.

So I went over and put both hands on his shoulders.

"I'd love to discuss anything that interests you, Rigel, any time at all – especially politics and the current political situation. I've told you that before." I kissed his cheek. "It's too bad we both have other commitments right now, but I hope to be able to show you a preliminary plan for your party when you come back after the meeting."

"You'll wait? I may be quite late."

"Of course I'll wait. And I don't think father will ask questions if I don't come home tonight."

His tired face lit up, and he took me in his arms. "I still have some more stuff from *Eros*," he said, kissing me quite forcefully. "See you later, darling."

As soon as he left, I activated his interface. I was no longer nearly as sure that there was any connection between Rigel, Anhur's mining industry, and the rebellion – and perhaps it was sheer pigheadedness on my part, but if there was any link at all, I intended to find it.

This time, I was more nervous than I had been the day before, probably because of my uncertainties – and at first, I had trouble concentrating. But at last I found what I was searching for: information about the Cairo Mining Corporation.

Well, well...I gloated, my confidence growing exponentially with this new discovery. *What a coincidence!*

It seemed that Rigel was also on Cairo's board of directors – which meant that he had one manufacturing company that made ships and another to supply the necessary raw materials, and no questions asked. All he needed now was fuel, which I somehow doubted was going to be an issue.

The production files for Cairo told the story. Cairo mined fuel ore, but didn't sell it: they stockpiled it instead. Starship fuel is an extremely valuable commodity throughout the Concorde. Why not sell it – it would net you trillions of credits – unless, of course, you intended to use it yourself.

And why hadn't anyone else – except possibly my brother-in-law – looked into this? Was someone high in government circles, perhaps even Ferrin, suppressing the information? This was definitely going to require further investigation…

Now more than ever determined to follow the clues to their logical conclusion and prove that my suspicions were correct, I asked myself: *So if I was plotting a coup, and I had sufficient ships and fuel, what else would I need?*

Manpower: people who were loyal and well-trained, who would not ask awkward questions, and who would faithfully follow orders. In other words, Anhur's military academy.

At that point, I wondered if Rigel's pal, Vice Admiral Pellen, might not also be involved in this too. Was that the real reason he wanted to go to New Egypt with Rigel?

The aide from the previous day entered the study, startling me. I felt my face flush a guilty red.

"Sorry to bother you, Sera Trellarian. The Premier told me to make sure you're comfortable and have everything you need."

My heart was still racing, but I realized that fortunately he couldn't see the holo-screen from the doorway – and hopefully neither could the room's AI cameras!

"I nearly had a heart attack when you came in like that! You might try knocking next time," I told him, but I smiled to soften the implied criticism. "And yes, thank you, I'd like something to drink."

"Coffee? Tea? Something else?"

"Thank you. Coffee would be fine."

I worked on the guest list while I waited for him to return. It was just about complete.

And I felt wonderful! I was now quite sure that I knew how Rigel was operating. It wouldn't be much longer before I had all of the answers.

The aide knocked and entered with a tray, apologizing all over again for having interrupted me.

The moment he was gone, I went back to work.

Information about Anhur's military academy was even more accessible. As a graduate of that institution, Rigel made no effort to conceal the fact that he was one of its major supporters. It would be an excellent place to obtain recruits for his personal army – but I wanted to prove it.

Acting on an impulse, I requested a list of persons currently enrolled at the academy and began scanning it, hoping something would catch my eye. However, nothing of interest turned up: just name after name, planet of origin, birth date, academic standing, and so on. I was disappointed when I reached the end of the list.

Next, I investigated the staff. Another long list scrolled down the screen. I came to the end of that too, discouraged almost to the point of quitting, and read:

Other Personnel

Other personnel? What could that possibly mean? When I requested further data, Rigel's interface coolly informed me:

"Restricted access: enter password."

This was surely the key to something important! But how was I going to get at it?

I sat for quite a long time, contemplating my options. After a while though, I finally decided to let it go and work on my official business. But throughout the rest of that morning, during lunch, and into the early hours of the afternoon, a part of my mind kept worrying away at the question, wondering how I might manage to gain access to that particular file, even while I was going through the motions of arranging a dinner party for nearly five hundred guests.

Why would information about personnel be restricted, I wondered? Was that standard procedure for military academies – or was it an indication that that institution had something to hide?

By the middle of the afternoon, I had accomplished enough of my legitimate work to make another stab at my illegitimate research. My new approach went well, and I was just beginning to think that I had managed to get around the intricate privacy protections, when the screen suddenly went blank.

"The information you have requested is classified," the interface responded in its impersonal voice, once again grinding my sleuthing endeavor to a frustrating halt. "Please enter your password."

I was too close to give up. For several tense minutes I simply sat there, starting at the holo-screen without really seeing it.

I had already amassed a great deal of information, every bit of it circumstantial. I had to have something more concrete, something akin to Rigel's fingerprints that would link him to the insurrection. Perhaps this particular file held it – perhaps not – but I couldn't afford to forgo at least trying to gain access.

I had to get in!

What kind of password would Rigel use? What kind of monumental ego would store potentially damning information in an otherwise vulnerable location? I knew that I might have just one chance at this…

Taking a deep breath, I entered the only password I could think of that made any sense: Rigel.

A moment later, the interface was displaying all of the answers I could possibly have wanted and more…

The 'other personnel' consisted of a staff of thirty-two, carefully chosen for their loyalty and discretion, I was certain, who were in charge of several dozen 'detainees'.

You mean prisoners! was my silent, scornful amendment.

Perhaps, I thought, some of these prisoners had been detained for political reasons. On a hunch, I asked for the records on Eirik Sanderson. The interface didn't hesitate for an instant, as these grim words appeared, projected above the screen:

> **Sanderson, Eirik: Space Guild Commodore.
> Detainee #2175
> Apprehended in the New Egyptian Sector 5.23.52
> Interrogating officer, Clode, G.S., #SIO72016

Notes:
> Detainee remained uncooperative during successive interrogation sessions.
> Interrogating officer recommends termination.

Status:
> Solitary confinement since date of last interrogation**

My god! No wonder no one had been able to find him!

Continued attempts to pry anything more about my brother-in-law's fate out of the prison files – such as whether or not he'd actually been 'terminated' – were in vain. Next, I tried the names of several other important political persons who had been reported missing, and got replies for every single one of them! Unfortunately, quite a few of them were no longer alive, according to their records.

What next?

One possibility, which I considered briefly, was to make hard copies and then go to my father or the Prime and tell them what I'd discovered. But what would that accomplish? It probably wouldn't help Eirik, and it would certainly upset my family – because if Rigel realized what I had done, he could easily arrange for Eirik to be executed long before anyone could rescue him.

That thought stunned me into stillness.

Was I was in danger too?

I had to admit that it was a possibility, especially if Rigel became aware of my unauthorized research before we had reached some sort of understanding. On the other hand, he had mentioned that there were matters he wanted to discuss with me – which could mean that he was finally going to take me into his confidence. And if he did, I would have to weigh his chances for success – for I no longer had any doubt that he was involved in, if not actually masterminding, the rebellion.

As for the identity of possible co-conspirators – well, that was an issue that I would just have to set aside for the moment until the right opportunity presented itself.

In the meantime, I decided, I would stay alert and keep all of the damning information to myself – including my knowledge of Eirik Sanderson's whereabouts – thereby holding my options open.

And I would definitely be ready to move quickly if I had to, if and when the time finally came for decisive action!

9.

That evening, as I had promised, I waited for Rigel to return to his suite. I thought this would be an excellent time for us to have a frank talk that would establish an atmosphere of mutual trust.

However, Rigel apparently had other ideas. To begin with, he didn't get back until quite late and upon entering his study, he collapsed with a groan into an armchair and demanded a stiff drink. Even after I'd served him, he was unwilling to tell me a single thing about the Interplanetary Council meeting that had just ended. Nor would he discuss the previous night's Inner Circle session. In fact, he answered all of my questions in monosyllables and grunts, and not long afterwards he fell asleep in his chair, gently snoring and with his empty liquor glass in one hand, while I was still speaking.

As hurt and annoyed as I was, nevertheless I tried to be understanding. After all, he had undertaken a hectic schedule that would have challenged a man half his age – and he was surely under an inordinate amount of stress as a result of his covert operations. Naturally he was exhausted.

Not knowing what else to do, I summoned my loyal assistant, Lieutenant Ent, and told him to put Rigel to bed. Then I returned to our apartment.

***

The next morning, I had a chance to see Rigel for about half an hour while he was getting ready to leave for yet another round of IPC talks. He was apologetic and obviously quite embarrassed about his lapse of manners the previous evening.

"That damn IPC!" he grumbled. "They insist on having far too many public and private meetings! I'm sure you must be tired too, what with all of the tedious planning for my party… Before we're through, we'll both

215

need a vacation! And I promise it will be one you'll never forget – just as soon as we can get away from this dreadful place."

With a rueful glance at the stack of data cubes that had accumulated on his desk, he added, "Unfortunately, I'm afraid I'll still have plenty of work to do, even on New Egypt." He sighed. "I suppose we'll just have to make the best of it."

I strode over to him and gripped his arms, forcing him to look directly into my eyes. "Rigel, listen to me!"

"Do I have a choice?" A smile curved his mouth.

"Your work doesn't have to be a burden – not if you share it with me. Yesterday morning you said you were impressed by my grasp of the Concorde's present situation. You told me there were aspects of the problem you'd like us to discuss."

"I remember. I *am* tired – but not that tired! Try to understand, darling: there's so much I have to do just now, so many people asking difficult questions, so many issues demanding my attention. I never have a moment's peace, and when I'm with you I don't want to discuss politics: I want to enjoy our time together."

"So you're not interested in having my help?"

"I didn't say that. You've already helped me immensely. Surely you realize that I wouldn't be able to pull off this party if it wasn't for you?" He held up his hand. "Now, don't interrupt..."

I bit back an angry retort as he went on: "You mustn't belittle your contribution. I know you'd like to do more for me, but this just isn't the right time. Please try to be patient. And later, when we're on our way to New Egypt, we'll have plenty of opportunity to talk – then I promise I'll give you all the attention you deserve." His gaze was intense. "Can you wait?"

Incapable of suppressing a frown, nevertheless I nodded agreement.

"Good!" He gave me a perfunctory kiss. "And now, unfortunately, I have to leave you."

As I watched him collect his things, it was all I could do not to say aloud: *You don't fool me for one minute, Rigel Hafiz. I know what you're up to... Once we've left Concordia, you think I'll be cut off from outside help. And then, if you actually do let me in on your plans and I don't approve, you think you'll be able to keep me quiet someplace safe –*

somewhere where I won't be able to tell anyone else what I know about you. Perhaps in your Detention Center on Anhur, in a cell right next to Eirik's...

How very nasty of you!

And how extremely wise!

***

Over the course of the next few days, besides finishing my preparations for the party, I spent several hours gathering additional details about Rigel's affairs.

I took a careful look at the layout of Anhur's military academy, trying to assess whether or not personnel in the legitimate part of the installation might be aware of the illegal presence of political prisoners. I reasoned that the prison would have to be completely hidden or very well-disguised to be overlooked to that extent.

Maps of the academy told the story. The brig was set slightly apart from the main barracks, yet within easy reach. Any military unit would require a brig for the punishment of misdemeanors, and the real prison could be contained within, kept isolated without arousing the suspicions of anyone who didn't know its true purpose. The prison had its own airfield and separate entrance, so both the brig and prison could operate simultaneously but in isolation from each other.

I downloaded hard copies of the maps and other critical information, and stored them in my personal effects for later perusal.

Another angle I considered was whether or not all or some of the academy staff might be involved in Rigel's schemes. It seemed to me they would be in an excellent position to screen possible recruits into Rigel's elite corps.

Further research revealed that several staff members were also on the board of directors of one or the other of Rigel's companies. It seemed safe to assume that they were working directly with him. I wasn't sure yet whether Vice Admiral Pellen or Ferrin were cooperating, but it seemed a likely possibility.

Eventually I succeeded in making a very rough estimate of the number of ships Rigel would need to have at his disposal in order for his plans to succeed. I hoped to be able to fill in the details later, when I accompanied him to his orbital Space Docks, in the skies above New Egypt.

Having obtained this information, I felt confident that I was ready for any new developments that might turnup. My only frustration was that so far Rigel himself had told me nothing of his plans. Everything I now knew about him was either pirated information or speculation.

As for my own plans, I was now certain that having an emergency frequency was an absolute necessity. I decided to take several additional precautions as well. After all: *You can't be too careful,* I advised myself. *Not when the person you're trying to outwit is Rigel Hafiz!*

***

I must admit that I was a bit jittery the night of Rigel's supper party. However, everything went off according to plan: there was plenty of excellent food and drink, the entertainment was first-rate, and the decor was as elegant as even the most refined and fastidious socialite could wish. All of our guests came – everyone who had been invited and several who had not – and I received lavish compliments and thanks for a splendid evening. In addition, I had the satisfaction of knowing that Rigel heard them too.

Initially, while the party was still getting under way, I was busy greeting our arriving guests and making sure that everyone was comfortably situated. But after a while, I stepped back from the center of activity, and moved off to one side of Rigel's ballroom to get an overview of the party.

The Prime and his son had made their grand entrance escorted by no less than six bodyguards, and there were undoubtedly any number of additional undercover agents among the guests. Lord Ferrin remained close to his father's side but also managed to keep an attentive eye on the female contingent, I noticed. Once I even caught him looking me over, and he answered my raised eyebrows with a shrug and an unrepentant, roguish grin – which made me think that he was either a totally innocent playboy, or else that his demeanor was the carefully calculated camouflage of a practiced deceiver. I knew I'd have to look into that further once I'd returned from my trip to New Egypt.

Rigel greeted the Prime and his son effusively and personally offered to see to their every need. However, his gallantry was short-lived: in actuality he spent very little time with them before he went off to charm his other guests, leaving the royal contingent to their own devices and me wondering if I was seeing connections where none existed.

Andebar had been our earliest arrival, accompanied by a group of his Journeyman musicians. He must have been keeping a wary eye on the royal party too, because no sooner had Rigel abandoned them than Andebar found an opportunity to approach.

Before long, the Tropi joined their group, accompanied as always by her ever-present bodyguards.

Seeing her, I had to suppress a wry grin – obviously she cared little for either social conventions or current fashion – she had come to the party dressed in her standard outfit: bare feet and basic blue fur. However, she was apparently one of those rare people who are comfortable wherever they are, whether it was nude at a fashionable party, in private conversation with a dignitary, or at a conference table. Watching her with the three men, I couldn't help but admire her. Her lovely face was expressive and alert, and I was fascinated by her graceful movements as she swept her long, dark hair back from her face.

After a while, Andebar excused himself to undertake his musical duties, and my father strolled over to talk to the Prime. Meanwhile, Lord Ferrin had drifted a short distance away, and was none too subtly ogling a famous actress who was emoting over the décor while flagrantly flaunting her astonishing and almost certainly augmented cleavage.

Janne and the Tropi now stood side by side, part of the group who had gathered to listen to Andebar and his musicians. And on the far side of the room, Rigel was involved in an intense conversation with Vice Admiral Pellen, who was making sweeping gestures with a cocktail in one hand and a plate of hors d'oeuvres in the other.

"Your party seems to be going quite well, Sera Trellarian," someone said from just behind my right shoulder.

Startled, I turned to discover Rigel's attentive young aide, Lieutenant Cameron Ent, standing beside me.

"It does indeed," I told him. "I think it's going to be a success."

"I never doubted it for a moment, considering how hard you worked to make it happen."

"Why thank you, Lieutenant Ent! I've certainly appreciated your help."

"*Me!*" He was so fair-skinned that his blush was painfully evident. "I didn't do anything."

"I may be the one who did the actual planning, but I would have passed out from hunger and exhaustion the very first day, if you hadn't been so considerate about seeing to my needs," I teased.

And he laughed. But then his expression changed to chagrin – he was so easy to read that it was pathetic. "I-I really shouldn't keep you standing here talking like this, S-Sera," he stammered. "You probably want to get back to your guests."

"Don't tell anyone I said so, but you're not the only one who's happy standing on the sidelines, watching the show," I admitted.

His answering smile was as guileless as a young boy's.

I sighed. "Unfortunately, I suppose I don't really have that option."

As I walked away, I thought, *Yes indeed: the friendship and goodwill of Rigel's aide might be a very useful thing to cultivate.*

But the next moment, I found myself face-to-face with the Tropi. Somehow, up close she was always rather intimidating.

I put on my best smile. "I hope you're enjoying the party, madam."

"Are you?" she asked as her eyes scoured my face like sentient searchlights.

"Why I… I mean… I don't…" I knew I sounded stupid: every bit as green and awkward as Rigel's young aide. With a tremendous effort of will, I drew upon all the dignity I possessed. "Surely, madam, you realize that as the hostess of such an elaborate party, I don't really have time to enjoy myself. I'm far too busy making sure that Rigel's guests are happy."

"I noticed when I came in that you were greeting people alongside Rigel. So you are acting as his hostess… How do you feel about that?"

"I beg your pardon. I'm not sure I understand."

"Are you content being Rigel's hostess?" she pressed.

She was certainly an irritating woman, with her piercing eyes and probing questions!

"Of course I am!" I snapped.

Her eyebrows, dark blue-black against her lighter blue pelt, rose in apparent surprise. "Really? Then why are you angry?"

"I am *not* angry! At least I wasn't until I started talking to you!" I retorted, shocked by my own daring – yet I wasn't about to back down.

The look in her eyes softened. "I did not mean to upset you, TiAnn – only to make you think about what you are doing."

I didn't know what to say to that.

"Consider very carefully," she went on. It almost sounded like a plea. "The situation that you are getting yourself into is unpredictable and perhaps extremely dangerous."

"I appreciate your concern, madam, but I think it's misplaced," I said, proud of myself for managing to sound so calm.

"I disagree. But I see that you must prove something to yourself. You want to show that you can make your own decisions and be responsible for your own destiny. I respect you for that."

I nodded, not trusting myself to speak.

"May I give you some advice?" she asked.

Again, I nodded.

"Stay alert. If you insist on going to New Egypt with Rigel, remember that you cannot afford to lower your guard – not even for a single moment. Be careful, TiAnn, and go with my blessing."

Before I could respond, she leaned forward and planted yet another kiss on my forehead. And then she was gone, trailed by her bodyguards and leaving me with a mystery.

How had she known about my impending trip to New Egypt?

Well, perhaps that wasn't such a mystery after all: my father must have told her.

I realized that my hands were clenched into fists. Taking a deep, shaky breath, I forced myself to relax – outwardly if not within.

Who does she think she is, giving me those dire warnings? I'll show her that I can take care of myself! I swore.

However, in the most private part of my thoughts, a part that answered to no one else, I acknowledged to myself that she was right: I had good reason to be afraid.

10.

We left for New Egypt the next morning in Rigel's private starship, the *Meteor*: Rigel, myself, and a two-man crew, plus three servants and Rigel's young aide, Lieutenant Ent. Vice Admiral Pellen and his staff were to follow later in a much larger cruiser.

Rigel's main interests during our journey were reading and writing reports, and sex. These activities kept us in his cabin for extended periods of time, and left me unsatisfied and restless. Whenever possible, I escaped, putting my freedom to good use by investigating the layout of the ship. However, as the *Meteor* wasn't very large, I soon ran out of places to explore – at which point I transferred my attention to the cockpit, where I watched the two-man crew carrying out their duties. I also spent hours in the tiny aft observation lounge, viewing the never-ending parade of stars glittering against the black backdrop of space.

Lieutenant Ent also seemed restless and bored, and both of us were apparently inveterate stargazers. It wasn't long before we had drifted into a casual sort of friendship, either as a result of loneliness or else because we were the youngest persons aboard. In any case, whatever the cause, neither of us had anything more meaningful to do to keep ourselves occupied.

Actually, I was glad of his company. During that long, uneventful trip, we did a great deal of talking – at least he did, and I practiced being a good listener, hoping to win his trust .He told me he'd been recruited directly onto Rigel's staff from Anhur's Military Academy, far too recently to have accumulated any leave. He was apparently quite homesick, and his rambling reminiscences about his home world, Fornax, helped pass the time.

Meanwhile, since Rigel still hadn't taken me into his confidence, I continued to make my contingency plans. The most important of these, as far as I was concerned, was to complete what I had come to think of as my survival kit.

Before we left Concordia, I had managed to assemble the basics: dried rations and other foodstuffs, a whole series of maps of the New Egypt Sector, a weapon that could be set for anything from 'stun' to 'kill', an impressive medical kit that included a hypodermic needle and several doses of stimulants – and of course the emergency frequency my father had obtained for me.

All of this had been relatively easily obtained on Concordia. However, I wanted to be prepared for anything, including the possibility of having to exit New Egypt in a hurry without being recognized. What was required, I decided, was a foolproof disguise – and for that I was going to have to enlist the help of Lieutenant Ent.

A direct approach seemed wisest, but I waited until we were alone in the observation lounge before I broached the subject.

"A favor?" he echoed. "Sure, Sera Trellarian. What can I do for you?"

"Come on, Cameron – I must have told you a million times to call me TiAnn."

"I'm not sure the Premier would approve."

"You have a point. Well then, call me by my formal title in public – but for pity's sake, not when we're alone."

"I guess I can do that."

"Good. Now about that favor…"

"Yes?"

"I need a staff uniform, and I'm prepared to pay well for it."

"A uniform? Why?"

"Well, this is kind of embarrassing…" I paused, yet I had known all along that I would have to tell him something. "You see, it's to wear for Rigel."

"For Rigel? I don't get it."

"No, I didn't think you would. You're much too sweet." I sighed. "You see, to be perfectly honest, Rigel has this thing about costumes. He likes me to wear different things for him when we're umm… Well, you know: fooling around…"

I could just make out his blush in the lounge's dimly-lit interior.

"Gosh, Sera… I mean, TiAnn. If it's for the Premier, I think he should be the one to get it for you."

"I'm sorry, Cameron." I placed a hand on his arm. "I wouldn't mention it at all if I wasn't desperate. You see, if I ask Rigel, he'll know all about it ahead of time, and it won't do any good. It has to be a surprise or he won't – umm – react." My hand tightened on his sleeve and I leaned forward to gaze deeply – and I hoped earnestly – into his eyes. "You know what I mean?"

Slowly, reluctantly, he nodded.

"Please, Cameron, you've got to help me! You're my only hope."

"What do you expect *me* to do?" was his peevish reply. "I can't just go out there and ask someone for a spare uniform."

"But you can – if you have this..." I held up one small beige packet, right in front of his nose where he couldn't possibly fail to see it. "Do you know what this is?"

He peered closely at the bold black script. "*Eros*! Sure, I know what it is! That stuff would cost me at least two months' pay – maybe more. How'd you get it?"

"Let's just say that I have my ways... And don't you suppose that when we get to New Egypt, someone there might be very happy to trade this for a spare uniform?"

"Well sure, but I..."

"And wouldn't you like to have some too? I have another one just like it." I was counting on his ignorance: that he would be unaware of the fact that the packets were normally sold in pairs, one for each user. After all, why advertise that I had more if I could split one dose and still get what I wanted? Besides, I intended to keep the other two for myself – they might come in handy at some future time.

"For me?" He reached out and reverently touched the packet I was offering. "Really? Hey, I'm sure I can get you a uniform – maybe more... Is there anything else you want?"

"A uniform cap, a pair of boots, and one of those utility pouches that you aides wear," was my immediate response. "They'd make the whole thing look much more authentic. Of course, it all has to fit someone my size."

"You've got yourself a deal! I'll have them for you as soon as we get into port."

"Excellent!" I smiled at him, although I realized that he probably couldn't see my expression very well in the semi-dark. "And in the meantime, I'll keep this in a safe place until you're ready to close the deal. You can have your share when you bring me the gear."

"I think I already know who to ask."

"I thought you might."

We concluded our negotiations with feelings of goodwill on both sides.

***

New Egypt. We had reached our destination, and Rigel still had yet to confide in me – and it certainly wasn't from lack of opportunity! His latest mania was touring me around: sightseeing, plus reading and writing reports, and even more sex.

I had hoped that actually being on New Egypt would provide me with further insight into the size and location of Rigel's fleet. But to my frustration, I made no progress on that front either. When I informed him that I would like to accompany him on a tour of his shipbuilding facility, Rigel replied with some surprise that it was an orbital factory.

"...Which operates under zero-grav conditions, TiAnn – to facilitate construction," he explained, as if I was either an idiot or else completely ignorant of anything of a practical nature. "Unfortunately, that doesn't make for a very pleasant experience for us landlubbers."

"I'm well aware of..."

"And, the inspection is bound to take quite a while," he interrupted. "Several days – most of it spent in zero gee. You'd be extremely uncomfortable, and I doubt you'd find it very interesting."

"But I *am* interested!" I insisted. "I'd really like to go with you."

He laughed. "Aren't you tired of floating around in a vacuum, darling? I know I am. Besides, I can't do anything until Pellen gets here – which is lucky, because there's so much I want to show you right here on New Egypt. So let's spend a few more days in the city before we head to my country estate. Believe me, I won't have time for sightseeing once Pellen arrives."

So I let him drag me out to museums and art galleries, the opera, ballet and theater, to luncheons, dinner parties, and private suppers in exclusive clubs. Our schedule was exhausting, but I did my best to perform as required, with all the grace I could muster. However, I promised myself that once Vice Admiral Pellen arrived, I wasn't going to miss any of the really important things.

And this wasn't my only frustration…

Now that we were planet-side, I couldn't get at Rigel's interface! Security was tight and I no longer had the luxury of the hours of free time which I had enjoyed on Concordia. I had come to New Egypt, I discovered, to be shown off as well as entertained.

Cameron Ent didn't disappoint me though: he came through with his part of our bargain late on the second day after our arrival on New Egypt. I complimented him heartily on his skill as a trader when I paid him off. As far as I was concerned that was two *Eros* packets well spent – and I still had two more in case of emergency.

Cameron was far too tactful and much too inhibited to ask me directly about Rigel's reaction to the aide's uniform, but the next time he had to escort us somewhere, I noticed that he kept sneaking covert glances at Rigel whenever he thought no one would notice.

My survival kit complete, I packed it carefully away in the aide's pouch that had been part of our bargain.

***

About a week after our arrival, just as we were about to embark upon yet another one of Rigel's tedious junkets, Cameron Ent hurried in with the news that Vice Admiral Pellen had just landed at the spaceport, and was at that very moment on his way to join Rigel at his city residence.

"Damn! That means we're going to miss the reception at the Botanical Gardens." When Rigel turned to me, he actually seemed disappointed. "I'm so sorry, darling, but it can't be helped. I told you beforehand that I'd have to give up everything else when Pellen got here."

"I really don't mind." I wasn't about to tell him how relieved I was not to have to fritter away another day. "Some other time will be just as good. I know you're anxious to see the vice admiral. Let's go inside and I'll help you prepare for his arrival."

"That's very thoughtful, but I know how Pellen operates. He's all spit and polish, and Space Guild protocol and punctuality. He'll want to get right down to business and he won't expect anything fancy."

"I wasn't planning on fixing him lunch!" I snapped, my patience finally at its limit. When was he going to think of me as anything other than a pretty decoration?

"I meant that I'd like to be present at your meeting," I amended with all the calm I could muster.

With a rueful grimace, Rigel glanced over at Cameron. "How about it, Ent – have you ever known a woman who didn't want to be involved in everything you do?"

The young aide looked extremely uncomfortable.

"Listen, darling," Rigel draped an arm around my shoulders and began rapidly ushering – actually almost shoving me – back into the house, "I have an idea. Why don't you go to the reception without me? I know you'll enjoy the flowers. Take Ent with you – I'm sure he won't mind." He released me with a dismissive pat on the butt.

"But, Rigel…"

"Now, TiAnn dear, I don't have time to argue. Just run along like a good girl, and do as I say." Without waiting for my reply, he turned and strode off down the hall in the direction of his conference room.

As I watched him go, cold fury settled like a stone in the pit of my stomach.

"G-gosh, TiAnn, I-I'm s-sorry," Ent stammered. "I'm sure he didn't mean that the way it sounded."

I whirled around, all set to vent my wrath on him – but then I bit back my angry retort. After all, he was just trying to comfort me. And I remembered the Tropi's advice, her melodious voice a whisper in my mind: *Stay alert and be careful.*

Well, I *would* be careful! And being careful meant that I certainly didn't want to have Rigel's aide as my enemy.

"Thanks, Cameron," I said, making an effort to sound sincere. "I really appreciate your concern."

"Please don't let what he said ruin your afternoon." His expression was so earnest! "We don't have to go to the Botanical Gardens if you don't want to. There are lots of other interesting places we can visit."

"You're very kind. But to be honest, I really don't think I can work up much enthusiasm for going anywhere right now. I hope you won't take it personally."

"Of course not. Say, how about a walk in the Premier's park? For my money, it's every bit as beautiful as the Botanical Gardens."

That wasn't at all what I had in mind, but I needed to get rid of the fellow without hurting his feelings – or arousing his suspicions…

And I *had* to find out what Rigel and Pellen were up to!

"Sure, Cameron, a walk in the park sounds great. But first I'd like to change my shoes. These shoes are giving me blisters." I turned away.

"Hey wait! Let me get whatever you need. If you tell me what to look for, I'm sure I can find it – that is, if you don't mind me going into your room…"

"How thoughtful!"

Damn the fellow! His face positively glowed with pleasure.

"But actually," I added, "I have to go back to my room anyway .I'd like to get out of this party dress."

"Are you sure you really want to go for a walk? We can do something else if you'd rather. I…"

"A walk will be fine, Cameron – but first I have to get comfortable. You go on ahead, and I'll catch up with you."

"Oh, I don't mind waiting."

"That's very sweet, but it isn't necessary."

"You might get lost."

"Look outside!" I commanded, trying to keep exasperation from creeping into my voice. I pointed out the door. "Do you see that path right there: the one that goes straight down to the river?"

"Yes, but…"

"Good. You start walking and don't turn off anywhere, and I promise I'll find you."

He still looked uncertain.

"Get moving!" I ordered.

He went.

***

Of course, I had no intention of going back to my room. Instead, my plan was to make a quick check on Rigel, and then rejoin Cameron before either of them realized what I was up to. However, things didn't work out quite as I expected…

No sooner had Cameron left me, than I turned and began walking down the hall, following in Rigel's footsteps. At that point, all I was hoping to accomplish was to eavesdrop on whatever might be going on between Rigel and Pellen so I could later make use of it as a bargaining chip to negotiate my way into the proceedings.

I slowed as I approached the massive door to Rigel's conference room. Since the hallway was obviously deserted except for myself, I stopped when I came abreast of it.

There was definitely a conversation going on inside. Unless Rigel was talking to one of his own people, it seemed that Pellen had indeed made excellent time getting here. I leaned closer, attempting to look casual in case anyone happened along.

At first, I could only hear a low rumble of male voices, but before long, those voices rose in anger, and soon I was able to distinguish every word.

"…And I say we act now!" someone – Pellen? – shouted.

"I say we wait – and that's final!"

"What's wrong with you, Rigel? I bring you fifty more ships than I originally promised, all of them manned by loyal personnel, and you have the gall to say that you expect me to tell them they're going to have to wait?"

"Tell them whatever you like! I'm sure you'll think of something – you're good at making excuses."

"I resent that!"

"Easy there, Pellen," someone else interjected. "We need to discuss this rationally. What you're suggesting doesn't time out. As I see it, it's a matter of being able to surprise…"

Their voices sank lower, making it impossible for me to hear what they were saying.

I had to know more! I edged closer to the door.

Abruptly, the voices grew louder again.

"…And I'm telling you we have plenty of time!" This was definitely Rigel. "I'm not about to jeopardize our plans by rushing into anything."

"Plenty of time! How can you say that when that horrible blue woman is practically breathing down our necks?" Pellen demanded.

"For that matter, what about Andebar?" someone else asked. "He and the Tropi have the Prime's ear. If we wait much longer, they'll be knocking on our door!"

My stomach did a nervous little flip-flop. I glanced up and down the corridor, but no one was in sight.

"I say we act now, while the element of surprise is still in our favor!" This was delivered in a shout.

"Pellen, you idiot, if we go charging in there like a troop of Space Cadets, they'll swat us down like flies! We have to wait until we're sure we have tactical supremacy."

"And I keep telling you we don't need tactical supremacy with our latest design. Our new starships can outmaneuver anything the Space Guild has to offer."

"So you say. But we don't know that for sure, now do we?" Rigel's voice had taken on a nasty sarcastic bite that I'd never heard before. "There hasn't been nearly enough time to complete the field tests."

"Well *I* know it," was Pellen's sulky rejoinder. "Besides, haven't those ships already proved themselves? They've been one hundred percent successful in avoiding contact while they're out setting mines. No one's been able to get more than a glimpse of them. Why, some of those dopey guild flyboys are actually convinced they're seeing aliens! Doesn't that prove anything to you?"

This statement met with total silence. It seemed that the conspirators had reached an impasse.

Perhaps they would appreciate an unbiased opinion...

But the argument was picking up again.

"You know, if we wait much longer they're going to catch us with our pants down," an unfamiliar voice cut in. "Is that what you want, Rigel?"

There was a loud crash, as if someone's fist had slammed into a hard surface.

"Are you implying that I'm trying to sabotage our mission?"

Would they be interested in hearing my thoughts? I had studied the situation as thoroughly as any of them, of that I was certain – and I could contribute a unique insider's knowledge of their enemy's point of view.

I gave myself a pep talk. *It's probably now or never, TiAnn! Rigel isn't going to let you participate unless you force him to.*

I took a deep breath and knocked on the door.

The voices inside cut off abruptly. For a moment nothing happened, and then footsteps approached.

The door swept open. I caught a glimpse of dark-paneled walls and a long conference table where a dozen or so men were seated, occupying most of the places. Faces stared out at me with startled expressions. But no one looked more surprised than Rigel himself. It was he who had opened the door.

"Hello, Rigel," I said in my warmest voice.

"TiAnn! What the hell are you doing here? I'm very busy right now."

"I know. I'd like to join the discussion."

"I don't have time to humor you. Go away and we'll talk about this later." His tone was anything but friendly, and his face was flushed an angry red that was deepening by the moment. He loomed over me, a menacing figure, as if he wanted to blot out the sight of his allies.

Quickly, before he could close the door, I stepped across the threshold.

"Stop right there!" he roared, grabbing my arm in a punishing grip.

I tried to pull free, but to no avail. "You can't send me away!" I protested, attempting to maintain my poise. "I could be very useful if you let me stay. I promise you won't regret it."

"Get her out of here!" Pellen growled from the foot of the table.

I glared at him until he looked away, embarrassed. He was the only man present who was at all familiar to me.

"TiAnn, I realize you're accustomed to helping your father with his work," Rigel said in a deadly quiet voice, tightening his grip on my arm, "and he's made you feel that you're a valuable part of his team. But that's not true here. The matters we're dealing with are far beyond your scope of expertise."

"Is that so? What makes you think…?"

"Stop this nonsense! You're acting like a spoiled brat!"

"How dare you!"

"How dare *you!*" Rigel spun me around to face him. "You are *not* welcome here!" he gritted out between clenched teeth, forcing me backwards from the room. "Is that clear?"

Cameron Ent was standing in the hall outside. His face was white with fear, and his eyes were staring in shock as he glanced anxiously back and forth between Rigel and me.

"Ent – I thought I told you to keep her busy!" Rigel thundered, releasing my arm with such force that I stumbled against the aide.

"I-I'm s-sorry, s-sir!" he cried, catching me just in time to prevent me from falling. "I don't know how it happened. W-we got separated, and the next thing I knew she was h-here."

Too furious to speak, I stood glaring at the two men and rubbing my bruised bicep.

"Let's see if you can get it straight this time, mister," Rigel snarled. "I want her out of here – out of the palace! Take her anywhere. Take my flyer and show her something she'll never forget. I don't care what it is or how long it takes – just get her out of my sight! Do you understand?"

"Yes, sir!"

"And you!" He gave me a withering glance. "I'll deal with you later!" Abruptly, he turned and strode back into the conference room.

The next moment, I heard him say to his visitors in quite a different tone of voice: "My sincere apologies, gentlemen. Please excuse the interruption. I assure you, it won't happen again."

Someone in the room remarked, "Serves you right, Rigel. That's what you get for screwing around with a younger woman."

There was a spate of nervous laughter, and then another voice piped up, "Reminds me of something my old grandfather used to say: 'All women should be born with a mattress on their backs…'"

"…And a cork in their mouths," another wit finished for him.

The door closed on their hearty guffaws.

Cameron Ent groaned.

"Let's get out of here," I snapped, and then I strode off down the hall without waiting to see if he would follow.

"I-I'm sorry, S-Sera!" Cameron sputtered as he scampered after me. "So s-sorry!"

But I barely heard him. Rigel would live to regret this day – of that I was certain!

"Please, Sera," Cameron moaned. "Please don't be angry with me. I didn't mean for this to happen!"

As if he was responsible for the ugly scene back there!

There was no longer the least doubt in my mind whose side I was on. Rigel was going to pay for this if it was the last thing I ever did!

Abruptly, I halted my headlong flight and swung around to face my companion. "Listen, Cameron," I said, feigning calm to the best of my ability, "it's okay. What happened back there wasn't your fault…"

I offered him a reassuring smile. "And you know, maybe Rigel's right. Maybe we *should* do as he suggested. Let's take his flyer and go somewhere."

"W-we should?" he stammered, caught completely off-guard by my sudden change of demeanor.

"Absolutely! Just give me a couple of minutes to get a few of things together and I'll be ready to go. Why don't we meet at Rigel's ship on the airstrip – say in ten minutes?"

He made no move to leave.

"Honest, Cameron," I coaxed, "I won't disappear on you again. I know it was a rotten thing to do. This time I'll be there. I promise."

"I-I'm sure you will. But where are we going, Sera Trellarian?"

"It's just TiAnn, remember? We're going sightseeing… And it really doesn't matter where we go. We'll make up our minds when the time comes."

But I knew exactly where we were going and why…

11.

I went back to my room and grabbed my precious survival kit. Then I left Rigel's palace (forever, I hoped) and joined Cameron Ent aboard the *Meteor*. But it wasn't until we had cleared ground control and were soaring through New Egypt's sunny skies, that he turned to me and said, "Any ideas about what you'd like to see?"

"Well... While I was collecting my gear, it occurred to me that this might be as good a time as any to pay a visit to Anhur."

"Anhur? That's New Egypt's moon!"

"So I've been told."

"But why do you want to go to Anhur?"

"Rocks and minerals."

"Huh?"

"Rocks. Minerals. Haven't I mentioned that I'm a passionate gem collector?"

"No, you sure didn't!"

I forced a laugh. "I can't believe I forgot to tell you something as important as that! Mineralogy is my favorite hobby. I wish you could see my collection back on Caliban."

I lapsed into somber thoughtfulness (at least I hoped it came across that way). "I guess I had a few other things on my mind while we were enroute to New Egypt."

"Listen, TiAnn, I'm really sorry about what happened just now with the Premier..." His voice trailed off in uncertainty, and his face was creased in a worried frown.

"I know you are, Cameron. And I appreciate everything you've done for me. You're a real friend, and a true gentleman – unlike Rigel and the rest of his cronies."

"I don't understand what went wrong back there."

"It isn't exactly a matter of 'back there'." I offered him a rueful smile. "You know very well that Rigel and I have been having trouble, even on the way to New Egypt."

He nodded, looking unhappy and extremely embarrassed.

"Well, this was just another unfortunate incident…" I pretended to sigh. "Anyway, why don't we agree to forget about that fiasco and enjoy our day together? To be perfectly honest, I'd rather be sight-seeing and rock collecting on the moon with you instead of sitting around in a stuffy conference room with Rigel and his pals."

Poor Cameron Ent, he was so easy to read. As clearly as if it were a holo-screen, his face reflected his latest concern. "Gosh, TiAnn, I'm not so sure we should be doing this."

"Doing what?"

"Leaving New Egypt."

"Why?"

"Well, I sort of got the impression that the Premier meant for us to stick closer to home. He was awfully mad – and I'm not sure he'd like the idea of us going all the way out to Anhur without his permission."

"Hey, Cameron, where's your sense of adventure?" I teased, hoping to shame him into cooperating. "Don't be a spoilsport."

His uneasiness was palpable.

"Okay," I amended, "if you think Rigel might object, why don't we call and ask him?"

He looked as terrified as I had hoped he would be.

"You want *me* to ask him?" I demanded, reaching for the comm link and hoping that my bluff would work.

"Never mind!" he cried, swatting my hand away. "I've got a better idea: we'll go now, and tell him about it later."

"An excellent plan. I like your attitude."

So Cameron Ent called air traffic control and requested permission to fly out to Anhur.

"Just tell them it's the *Meteor*," I whispered. "Don't mention that Rigel isn't aboard. That way they're sure to give us clearance."

He gave me a thumbs-up and followed my suggestion.

Shortly afterwards, we were on our way to Anhur's third moon.

Our troubles apparently behind us, he stretched out his legs and laced his fingers behind his head. The very picture of relaxation, he smiled over at me from the pilot's seat. "So why do you really want to visit an airless desert like Anhur? Come on, TiAnn – let me in on your secret: what exactly are you looking for?"

"Shouldn't you keep your hands on the controls?" I asked, feeling a bit anxious.

"Nope. This beauty is the most state-of-the-art piece of materiel the Concorde Alliance has ever seen. All air control or her pilot has to do is give her a destination and she practically flies herself there. In fact, this baby has an on-board AI that can do everything but tap dance and write science fiction. The pilot is almost superfluous."

"If you say so."

"So isn't it about time you told me what kind of rocks we're after?" he persisted. "Or is it some kind of rock hunter's secret?"

"Well, it *is* something rare. But it's not a rock, it's a mineral – a very beautiful one called Borealis Anhurite," I improvised, hoping for the best.

"That's a pretty technical sounding name. Doesn't it have a common one?"

"What! You think something as rare as Borealis Anhurite would have a common name?"

"I suppose not… So what does it look like?"

"Why should I tell you? You'll see some and grab it for yourself before I can even get a chance to look at it."

"I wouldn't do that!" he protested.

"I know that, Cameron. I was joking."

"So how about giving me a clue? Or are you going to let me wander all over the lunar landscape in an EV suit, picking up rocks and hoping to find some?"

"Exactly." And then I burst out laughing at his dejected expression. "You know what, Cameron? I really like you! Hey, don't worry: I promise I'll tell you what to look for when we get there."

That cheered him up instantly.

***

Cameron cleared us through Anhur air control too.

"So where to now?" he asked as soon as he'd signed off.

He was so nice and so painfully naïve that I was starting to feel guilty about what I was planning to do to him. But I had more urgent things to think about than the fate of one overly-trusting aide, and I told myself sternly that it was time to get down to business.

"Can you get us into some sort of medium-altitude orbit?" I asked.

"No problem." He promptly instructed the ship's AI – and moments later: "Right you are, TiAnn: one medium-altitude orbit coming up. Now what?"

"Now we sit here and watch the moon go by, and look for a likely spot to land."

"Yes, ma'am!" Grinning, he gave me a jaunty salute.

And I did sit for a while and watch the moon passing by beneath us. I also asked several pertinent questions, and when we flew within visual range of the military academy, I asked a few more. But after a while I excused myself and headed back to Rigel's cabin.

Okay, TiAnn, this is it! I told myself. *From here on out, there's no turning back.*

In fact, if I was honest with myself, it had been far too late to turn back for quite a while now…

Opening my survival kit, I removed the gun, carefully checking that it was set it for the heaviest stun. Then I put it on the bunk beside the pouch.

Next, I stripped down to my underwear and laid my discarded clothing on the bed, directly over both the pouch and the gun, making sure that everything was within easy reach.

Much to my annoyance, I discovered that my hands were shaking.

So: do you want to go back to New Egypt and face Rigel – or would you rather get even with him instead? I chided myself.

And then, before I could talk myself out of my next step, I quickly reached over and pressed the intercom button.

"Hi there, TiAnn," Cameron's cheerful voice sounded tinny over the cabin speaker. "What can I do for you?"

"I was wondering if it's okay for you to leave the cockpit for a couple of minutes."

"Sure. Why?"

"I'm having trouble opening my travel pack. Could you come back here and help me?"

"Not a problem. Be right there."

While I was waiting for him to arrive, I fussed with my lacy lingerie, arranging it in what I hoped was an attractively disheveled manner. I also concentrated on keeping my breath deep and even.

"Hi, TiAnn, what seems to be the...?" Cameron Ent came to an abrupt halt in the doorway.

"Come in, Cameron," I said in as inviting a voice as I could summon up.

"S-sorry! I didn't mean to walk in on you l-like..." His face was so red that he looked almost apoplectic. "W-what did you say?"

"I said come in."

He started to back off.

I quickly stood up, almost knocking my survival kit off the bed in my haste. "Cameron, wait!"

"W-what do you w-want?"

I held out my arms. "I want you!"

"M-me! Sera Trellarian, w-what are you t-talking about?"

"Cameron, how can you ask? You've seen how Rigel treats me. I'm so lonely and you've been so very kind. I've tried not to think about you and how I feel about you, but I just can't help myself."

His face went through the most complex changes: from confusion and worry, to uncertainty – and then, suddenly, desire flared. "I want you too!" he cried.

Crossing the room in three quick strides, he grabbed me in his arms, almost knocking the breath out of me. His kisses were hot and eager on my throat, and his fingers tore at my flimsy underwear.

"Whoa, Cameron!" I pushed against his chest. "Stop!"

Immediately he relaxed his stranglehold, and then he stood looking down at me, his face more flushed than ever, obviously at a loss for words.

"Don't be in such a hurry!" I told him, forcing a laugh. "We have plenty of time."

His blush deepened. "I-I'm sorry, I didn't mean to..."

"Now don't start apologizing again. I like you much better when you don't."

"What do you want me to do?"

I sat back down on the bunk. "Take off your clothes."

"W-what?"

"Take off your clothes! I want to watch."

He began tugging at his trouser buttons.

"Not so fast!" I quickly amended. "There's no need to rush. You wouldn't want to tear your uniform, would you?"

Reaching beneath my discarded clothing to place my hand on my gun, I waited until he was down to his underwear and then I said ever so gently, "I'm sorry I have to do this, Cameron. You'll never know how sorry…"

He looked up at me, a questioning expression on his innocent face.

And I shot him.

He slumped to the floor, his puzzled frown softening into repose.

I let out a shaky breath. "Poor Cameron," I whispered. Then, before I could succumb to the jitters, I forced myself to continue with my plan.

Taking some heavy-duty bandaging tape out of my medical kit, I knelt down beside him. I had known he would be heavy, which was why I had gone to all the trouble of having him undress himself before I'd stunned him, but I hadn't counted on having to move him around so much in order to bind him securely. At last though, I was finished.

There he lay, peacefully slumbering, wrapped in yards of adhesive, with his mouth taped shut. I wasn't sure how long the stun would last, but since I couldn't drag him out of sight, I just left him where he was. Then I picked up his uniform, carefully folded it, and stowed it away in my aide's pouch.

Next, I put on the uniform Cameron had gotten for me. And after that, I spent several minutes in front of the mirror, removing all traces of cosmetics and twisting my hair into a tight knot on top of my head. Last, I put on the aide's cap, pulling it down low on my forehead so most of my face was shadowed by the brim.

For a long moment, I just stood there, surveying the results in the mirror. *Not bad. Not bad at all if they're expecting to see a young man and they don't look too closely,* I told my reflection.

Fortunately, just then I remembered the I.D. badge on Cameron's uniform and retrieved it from the pouch. As a finishing touch, I hung my weapon in plain sight on my belt. Then, picking up the aide's pouch with my survival kit inside, I left the cabin, carefully locking the door behind me.

It was time for the most audacious part of my scheme.

***

"Anhur Detention Center, this is *Meteor*. *Meteor* calling Anhur Detention Center. Come in Detention Center. Do you copy?" I made an effort to pitch my voice as low as I could possibly manage.

"*Meteor*, this is Anhur Military Academy. You're calling on the wrong frequency." The fellow on the holo-screen looked perplexed.

Damn! What an inauspicious way to begin. Well, there was nothing for it now but to try to tough it out.

"Anhur Military Academy, this is the *Meteor*. There must be a glitch in my comm link. Can you patch me through to the Detention Center?"

"Affirmative, *Meteor*. I'll have your connection for you in just a moment…"

As the static on the screen cleared, a new face appeared. "*Meteor*, this is Anhur Detention Center. How may I help you?"

"This is Lieutenant Cameron Ent calling on the Premier's behalf. He's instructed me to notify you of his intention to visit the Detention Center. He wishes to carry out a final interrogation of detainee number two-one-seven-five, Sanderson, Eirik."

"*Meteor*, please stand by while I run a check on the status of detainee number two-one-seven-five."

"Standing by, Detention Center," at least I hoped that was the proper response. I held my breath. *Please don't call New Egypt!* I prayed silently. *And Eirik, please still be alive.*

The wait seemed interminable.

"*Meteor*, this is Anhur Detention Center. Detainee number two-one-seven-five can be made available for interrogation, but it will take us a while to prep him – he's, errr… The guard says he'll need a bit of cleaning up."

"Roger, Detention Center. It should take us …" (I consulted the readout on the forward screen)"… about thirty minutes standard to reach your airfield. Will that be sufficient time to get him ready?"

"Affirmative, *Meteor*. Detainee two-one-seven-five will be prepped for interrogation. You're cleared for landing at the Detention Center airfield. Dock at gate number six. Do you copy?"

"Roger, Detention Center. Gate six. This is *Meteor*, signing off."

So far, so good. As soon as the man's image had disappeared, I requested a review of the flight plan.

By the time I could see the airfield, I was feeling jittery again. Everything was going to depend on timing, I realized.

I let the ship fly itself. Cameron hadn't exaggerated when he'd said she was state of the art – and I was very grateful. I'd previously done a bit of flying, but not much solo, and certainly not in a ship of this advanced design.

As we touched down to an ultra-smooth landing, I could see a long, low, bunker-like building jutting right up out of the ground at an angle, its sides bristling with retractable airlocks. Knowing that the main part of the prison complex was underground, I reasoned this must be the landing dock, and I tried to recall the exact layout from the plans I'd pirated from Rigel's files back on Concordia.

What I saw now seemed to confirm my memory.

Fortunately, I felt comfortable about taxiing the ship myself. I guided her right up to the area that was marked with a large number six.

A moment later, an extensible airlock glided out to make contact with the *Meteor*. The ship rocked slightly when the lock touched her side and pressure equalized.

I had arrived.

12.

Feeling terribly small and vulnerable, not to mention conspicuous, I walked out of the ship, down the slanting airlock ramp, and into the Detention Center. The heels of my military boots clicked loudly on the cerosteel floor, and my survival kit in the aide's pouch and my weapon bumped like dead weights against my hip.

At the foot of the ramp, an armed guard saluted me with brisk military precision. "Welcome to Anhur Detention Center..." He paused and I realized he was scanning my badge, "...Lieutenant Ent. I was told to expect the Premier's party."

I returned the salute. "Thank you, errr..." Now it was my turn to do the badge reading bit, "...Corporal Marz." My mouth was so dry that I had difficulty forming the words.

For several long moments we both stood there, stiff and awkward (at least that was how I felt), while my pulse beat an erratic, adrenalized tap-dance in my ears. When my palms began to sweat, I decided that it was time to put an end to our impasse.

"Corporal Marz, where will I find the detainee?" I demanded as if I had every right to know.

"Find the...?" His eyebrows rose. "Where's the Premier? I was told he wanted to interrogate a prisoner."

"Umm... The Premier has been delayed, Corporal. He's still aboard the *Meteor*."

"But where is the officer who usually accompanies him?"

"I haven't the vaguest idea," I admitted. And then hastily improvising: "Actually, I'm new at this job. Someone told me to come out here and make sure all the necessary preparations were made while the Premier was getting ready."

"You say he's been delayed? That's odd. He's usually quite punctual."

Uh oh. This wasn't going at all well.

Placing one hand on my weapon and hoping that the fellow wouldn't recognize the gesture as a threat, I stepped closer and said in a conspiratorial whisper, "To tell the truth, Corporal, the Premier hasn't exactly been delayed. That's just what they told me to say…" I purposely kept my face averted, hoping he wouldn't get too good a look at me.

My fingers trembled on the butt of my gun. How quickly could I pull it on him, I wondered?

Probably not fast enough…

But: "Really?" Corporal Marz said with obvious interest. His voice dropped to a conspiratorial whisper: "Why'd they want you to lie?"

"Well… See, he's got this girl with him – in his cabin. And they're having a little party back there… You know what I mean?" I risked a quick peek at him and winked.

His answering grin caused the knots in my stomach to loosen noticeably.

Lowering my head again, I leaned closer still. "Can you believe it: they sent me out here to take care of the preparations so he can finish up whatever it is they're doing back in his cabin?"

The corporal gave a low whistle.

"Some people have all the fun, don't they?" I ventured. "And meanwhile, all us poor grunts ever get to do is the dirty work."

"Ain't it the truth."

"So give me a break, Corporal," I went on in a slightly louder voice. "Just tell me where I'm supposed to go, and let's get this over with."

"Sure thing, Ent. They're gonna deliver the prisoner to room three – it's right down the hall there. Take the first left, and it's the second door on the right."

"Thanks. Say, do me a favor, will you?" I dared, acting on a sudden inspiration. "Keep an eye on the ship and holler real loud if it looks like the Premier's coming out."

"You bet!" was his jovial reply as he waved me along.

Well you got yourself in… Now all you have to do is get back out! was my ironic comment to myself as I strode purposefully down the hall.

Oh yeah: piece of cake!

Before I turned the corner, I risked a glance back the way I'd come. Corporal Marz was standing like a statue at the point at which the airlock ramp joined the main corridor, dutifully watching for someone to leave my ship.

Let's just hope no one does! was my silent prayer, thinking of the real Ent, trussed up like a package on the cabin floor.

I had no trouble finding room three. When I opened the door and stepped in, it appeared to be some sort of operating room or medical lab. A shiny metal table stood dead center with an ominous-looking drain in the floor beneath it. Metal cabinets with glass doors lined the walls, filled with bottles and unrecognizable equipment. The counter bristled with nasty-looking implements: silver cutlery arranged in precise rows, a large hypodermic, and an array of what I realized with queasy certainty were electrodes. The only other furnishings were two metal chairs and a small metal desk. Otherwise, the room was empty.

I barely managed to stifle a shriek as the door behind me banged open. I whirled quickly around, weapon in hand.

"Sorry to burst in on you." The speaker wore a guard's uniform, and he was supporting a second, taller man who was slumped over, obviously unable to stand unassisted.

"No harm done," I said, forcing my fingers to relax. Clipping my gun back on my belt, I stepped closer to the center of the room, where the overhead lighting would throw the deepest shadows on my face.

"This here's detainee two-one-seven-five," the guard said. "Where do you want me to put him – over there?"

Glancing in the direction he indicated, I noticed the restraining straps dangling from the sides of the table.

"No!" I fought to suppress a shudder. "I mean – that won't be necessary. Just put him in that chair. I'll take care of the rest."

The guard tried to do as I'd requested, but his unwieldy burden was so limp that he immediately started to slide out of the chair. A brief struggle ensued as the guard attempted to rectify the problem by wedging the chair and its unresisting occupant into one corner of the wall.

"Guess this one won't be giving you any trouble." The guard straightened up and glanced around the room. "You alone?"

"They sent me ahead to get things ready."

The man shrugged. "Fine with me. Inspector Clode said to tell you he'll be right along."

"Very good."

I waited for him to leave, but the man stood his ground.

"Is there anything else I can do for you?" I asked, anxious to send him on his way.

The guard's eyes darted nervously around the room, skittering over the gleaming instruments. "You umm – you want me to stick around?"

"I don't think that will be necessary." Obviously he was uncomfortable with the idea of being asked to be present at an interrogation. "Unless you'd like to watch…?"

His eyes rolled, showing white. "No thank you! No."

"You're sure? Because…"

"Real sure! So I guess if you don't need me, I'll be going." He tore out of the room.

Now if only that Inspector didn't show up too soon!

I approached the prisoner somewhat apprehensively. At close range, he stank. "Eirik?" I queried.

But instead of answering, he was groaning quietly to himself, apparently lost in his own private hell.

I knew how to deal with this. Reaching into my aide's pouch, I pulled out the medical kit, loaded a heavy dose of stimulant into my own hypo, and shot the stuff directly into his arm, right through his filthy shirt. Then I put my hand under his chin and tilted his face up to the light.

Beneath the matted tangle of hair and grizzled beard, I saw the gaunt face of a battered old man.

"Oh shit!" Panic hit me like a gut punch, and I almost dropped the hypo. "Oh god, no!" I groaned. "They sent the wrong man! What am I going to do?"

It was too much: I retched, overcome by the nauseating combination of his stench and my own fear. "Who the hell are you?" I wailed, not expecting to ever learn the answer.

The old man's eyelids flickered, and his eyes slowly opened, faded blue-grey against his sickly, jaundiced skin. He blinked, licking his cracked lips with a parched tongue.

"Aaargh…"

I realized that he was trying to speak.

The next sound that came out was also a croak, but halting words soon followed: "Sanderson… Eirik. Guild – Commodore. Serial number S-G-O-three-five-four-seven-three-five."

"Eirik?" I breathed.

His eyes narrowed and grew slightly more alert. "Who – are you?" His voice was so hoarse that I could barely understand him.

"It's me: TiAnn. Janne's sister."

He put up a hand to shield his eyes from the light. "TiAnn? How…?"

"My god, Eirik!" My voice broke and it was a moment before I could continue. "What have they done to you?"

A fleeting grin moved across his ravaged face, making him look more like a death's-head mask than ever. "What – haven't – they done?"

Get hold of yourself, TiAnn! I scolded.

"Okay, Eirik," I said in the most matter-of-fact voice I could summon, "I've come to get you out of here. We haven't got much time, so we'll have to move quickly."

He was obviously still dazed, but I could tell that the stimulant was taking effect because he could now sit up unassisted, and his eyes were tracking my movements.

"Here's what we're going to do," I hurtled on, "so listen carefully… I've got a uniform that should fit you – more or less. And once you're dressed, we're going to walk right out of here… Rigel's ship is parked a short distance away – and with some luck no one's realized it's missing. Yet…"

Even as I was speaking, I was pulling Cameron's clothing out of my pack. "Do you think you can make it?" I asked, never doubting for a moment that he would try.

In the end, he was so weak that I had to help him get dressed. He did as much as he could, but I could tell that it cost him a terrible effort. I hadn't realized it was possible for the human body to become so emaciated.

When I finally stepped back to take a look at him, it was painfully clear that the uniform didn't fit at all well.

"This isn't going to work…" Eirik mumbled, swaying unsteadily on his feet.

"Don't you worry about a thing!" I told him with a great deal more confidence than I actually felt. "I've got you covered. Watch this!"

I picked up his grubby prison uniform and stuffed it down the disposal chute. And before it was fully out of sight, I was rummaging through my survival kit.

"What are you doing?" Eirik asked, reaching out a visibly shaking hand to clutch the back of his chair for support.

"Looking for this!" Triumphantly, I held up a square green bottle. "It was supposed to be for an emergency – and I guess this qualifies!"

"What the hell is it?"

"Denovian Brandy. We're going to convince everyone that you're stinking drunk!" And I emptied the whole thing right over his head.

"I don't understand," he mumbled, scrubbing at his eyes while rivulets of alcohol trickled down his neck, soaking Ent's abused uniform.

"Listen, Eirik: even if you *could* stand up and walk out that door by yourself – which you obviously can't – you look like hell. Especially in a uniform. Anyone who saw you would immediately be suspicious: they'd smell you coming if they didn't see you first…"

"I really do stink, don't I." It was a statement, not a question.

"Well, now you smell like you've had way too much to drink. And I'm hoping that might just get us through… Besides, anyone who was that drunk couldn't possibly walk by himself – which happens to be very convenient for our purposes."

"Do you have a gun?"

"Yes, but I'll only use it as a last resort. Although if we don't start soon, I'm afraid it may very well be our last resort!"

"Let's go then."

I slipped an arm around his waist, and he draped one skeletal arm across my shoulders. It was a bit awkward, but it worked. We shuffled over to the door, and I peeked out.

The hall was empty, but I thought I heard footsteps.

"Quick Eirik! It's probably Inspector Clode."

Beneath my hand, I felt him flinch.

Without another word, we were out the door and heading towards the exit.

Now there were definitely people behind us: voices as well as footsteps.

When we turned the corner, I was dismayed to see Corporal Marz still standing in the corridor, waiting for someone to come out of Rigel's ship.

I swore under my breath.

"What's the matter?" Eirik breathed in my ear.

"That damn guard!" I hissed back. "I was hoping he'd be gone by now. Shit, we'll have to try it anyhow." I put a finger to my lips, hoping Eirik would realize that I didn't want the guard to notice us until the last possible moment.

Eirik nodded, and together we inched forward.

But just as we came abreast of Marz, Eirik staggered, either on purpose or else by accident – I never found out which – and the guard whirled on us.

"Hey, what's going on here?" he demanded. "Where do you two think you're going?"

"Sorry, Corporal Marz. Can you believe it: the guy who was supposed to bring in the prisoner turned up without him – and drunk as a skunk!"

"Is that you, Ent?" The guard examined us warily.

"Sure is. Looks like this character must have found himself a whole closet-full of booze."

Marz started towards us, and then quickly backed away. "Phew! I'll say he's drunk: he smells like a brewery!"

"I thought I'd do a good deed and take him back to the barracks before he gets into even worse trouble." While I was speaking, I slid my hand off Eirik's waist and lowered it to the grip of my weapon. Fortunately, the guard was on Eirik's other side and couldn't see what I was doing.

I hoped.

At the same time, Eirik squeezed my shoulder and leaned slightly away from me, giving me room to maneuver.

"Can we go now?" I whined. "This guy's awfully heavy."

"He's not your problem. I'll call someone to come and get him." As he spoke, Marz started to turn to a comm unit on the near wall, but he must have seen me moving out of the corner of his eye. "Hey, what the hell do you think you're…!" he yelped.

I hit him with the first blast of the stunner.

"Nice shot," Eirik said, grinning lopsidedly.

From somewhere down the corridor, I heard the sound of running feet.

"I think we're in trouble," I told Eirik. "You and I had better get going… Now!"

Skirting the fallen guard, we stumbled up the ramp towards the ship. Somehow Eirik managed to run, even though I had to support him. The moment we staggered into the *Meteor*'s airlock, I palmed the hatch shut and sealed it. Then I helped Eirik into the cockpit.

He collapsed into the co-pilot's seat. "Quick thinking, TiAnn! Now get us out of here!"

He might just as well have sucker-punched me in the gut. I stood there gaping at him open-mouthed, feeling suddenly sick. "I umm… I-I'm not sure I can do anything on such short notice," I finally confessed.

Eirik blanched. "You mean you don't know how to fly this thing?"

"I can!" I blustered. "A little… But it's going to take me a while to figure it out."

Eirik swore. "How the hell did you get here?"

"Auto-pilot."

"That's just great! Okay, where's the crown?"

"The what?"

"The damn AI crown!"

I felt really stupid, just standing there, but even as he spoke, his hands were clawing at the instrument panel.

Something thumped against the outside of the ship.

"Thank god!" Eirik pulled open a shallow compartment and extracted a shining wire ring that had several terminal patches attached to it.

As he settled it around his forehead, I experienced a shock of déjà-vu: the first time I had ever seen him, on the shuttle from University VII, he'd been wearing one of those crowns – and he'd certainly been in a whole lot better shape than he was right now!

By the time I refocused on the present, Eirik's fingers were dancing madly across the controls even as he accessed the onboard computer. "Strap yourself in!" he barked.

I barely had time to throw myself into the pilot's seat.

With a jolt that tore the couplings loose, we shot right off the ground and directly into space.

As Anhur dropped rapidly away beneath us, both of us breathed a sigh of relief.

Eirik turned to me with a shaky grin. "My, that was exciting! By the way, I hope you have another shot like the one you gave me back in the Detention Center…"

I could see that his hands were trembling.

"…Because I'm pretty sure that before we go much further, I'm going to need it."

13.

By then, warning lights were flashing all over the cockpit.

"Ignore that!" Eirik swatted my hand away as I reached over to press a glowing button on the comm unit. "Anhur Traffic control is probably trying to find out what the hell we think we're doing."

"What *are* we doing?" My stomach felt as if it was being assaulted by swarm of angry bees. If Rigel caught us now, I realized, I would probably end up in even worse shape than Eirik! I tried to suppress a shudder.

"What we're going to do, as soon as we can, is jump."

"Doesn't that take lots of planning?"

"Usually – except right now we don't have that luxury." He gestured at the ship's holo-screen.

Several fast-moving blips were closing in on us.

"Police?"

"Probably. Or a military patrol. Luckily, I'm prepared for an emergency like this." Even as he spoke, his hands were flying across the boards. "To tell the truth, though, I've never heard of anyone jumping from within a solar system," was his casual addendum.

"Advisory," the disembodied voice of the ship's AI suddenly announced. "The procedure that you are requesting is not recomm—"

Eirik silenced the voice with a slap of his hand.

My mouth went suddenly dry. "Are you sure this is such a good idea?" I managed to ask.

He shrugged. "Unless you have a better plan, we're about to find out."

"Wait!" I protested.

"Sorry, TiAnn, I don't have time to discuss the pros and cons of jumping blind, because I think they're about to open fire."

"Eirik!"

"Here we go!"

Abruptly, everything on the screen blurred and vanished – the lunar landscape, the other flyers, and the bright disc of New Egypt – to be replaced, first by the shifting grey veils of hyperspace, and then by a black void with a light dusting of stars.

"Where are we?" I whispered, scarcely daring to believe our incredible good luck.

"The Corona Gap."

"I've never heard of it."

"Hopefully neither have they. It's just a bit past the standard jump distance from the New Egypt system, and in an unlikely direction. It's kind of an in-between place – not very close to anything of importance, and quite far from the Hub. These coordinates aren't used much by guild navigators. I thought it might be a good idea to have them memorized…"

My breath came out in a whoosh. "Thank goodness you did!"

He turned to regard me, his expression sober. "I was beginning to think I'd never have a chance to use them." He was obviously exhausted: his eyes stood out like bruises against his clammy skin, his breathing was shallow and ragged, and his mouth was pinched in a harsh line, as if he was suppressing intense pain.

A walking corpse.

"TiAnn, I need something to keep me going," he said very quietly.

"I have more of what I gave you in the Detention Center, but I don't think it's a good idea for someone in your condition."

"I can't afford to collapse now."

"I suppose you're right. But first let me get you something to eat."

He simply nodded agreement. It probably took all of his remaining energy to do so.

I brought hot broth from the processor, hoping it wouldn't be too much of a challenge for his empty stomach, and then I shot him with a half-strength stim.

He gave me a weary smile. "Thanks, TiAnn. Thanks for everything."

"Let's agree not to thank each other until we're safely out of this mess," I replied rather testily. "After all, it isn't over yet."

"That sounds eminently practical."

It was several minutes before he spoke again. "I think I'm starting to feel better."

His color was definitely improving.

"I'm glad to hear it. What are we going to do now?"

"Well, I'm sure it will be quite a while before they figure out where we are – if they even bother."

"Why wouldn't they try to find us? They must be mad as hell about the Detention Center. Not to mention that I've run off with Rigel's favorite ship – and you."

"Oh, they'll try to find us all right, but only for a little while. It's not as if they don't realize where we're ultimately going. They just don't know how long it will take us to get there."

"Concordia?"

He nodded. "Unless you had other plans?"

"Not really."

"Then I'm going to try to contact my commanding officer. I'm sure the Prime will want to know that I'm still alive and where I've been all this time. And you can bet that my escape is going to push Rigel ahead in his schedule – whatever that is."

"It might be worse than you think." And I told him what I'd learned about Rigel's schemes over the course of the past few weeks. In a strange way, it was a relief to get it off my chest. I'd kept everything to myself for so long that I'd somehow begun to feel guilty by association. It was almost as if, by knowing Rigel's plans, I'd become a party to them.

"…So I went with him to New Egypt to try to discover how many ships he actually has," I concluded. "But it didn't work out the way I hoped. Rigel didn't trust me enough to tell me anything, and I couldn't find out any more than I'd already learned on Concordia."

Eirik had been watching me intently throughout my recitation. And now he said, "You've certainly taken quite a risk! As far as I know, Rigel has always been a very private person. I imagine he's had a hard time deciding what to do about you – whether or not he could trust you. And maybe it's a good thing he decided not to, because if he had, he might have forced you to go along with him whether you wanted to or not. Anyway, he certainly would have kept a closer watch on you…" He paused. "By the way, how *did* you manage to get away from him – and with the *Meteor* too?"

I told him that also, but I was careful to downplay my initial ambivalence in my dealings with Rigel. That was none of Eirik's business – or anyone else's for that matter! Besides, by now I was anything but ambivalent. Just telling Eirik about how Rigel had humiliated me during our last confrontation made my blood boil!

"And you say his aide helped you fly out to Anhur so you could look for me?" Eirik wanted to know.

"Well, he didn't exactly realize he was helping me," I admitted, "or what I was after. For that matter, I don't think he was even aware of Rigel's illegal activities. You see, Cameron Ent is really a very naive... Oh no!"

"What's wrong?"

"Cameron Ent: Rigel's aide. I stunned him and left him trussed up in Rigel's cabin. You're wearing his uniform. I forgot all about him."

"I hope you aren't expecting me to thank him for the loan of his clothing."

"No." I managed a rather ragged smile. "But please don't be too hard on him. I'm sure he was totally unaware of Rigel's plans. And I've treated him terribly. I hope he's okay."

"If you just stunned him, I'm sure he'll be fine. I'll take a look at him a little later. But first I'd better put that call through to the guild."

"I forgot to mention that I have an emergency code we can use to call the Prime's staff directly."

He whistled. "You really thought of everything! That will save us a lot of time."

I could feel myself blushing. "Actually, it was my father's idea. He was worried when I insisted on going off to New Egypt with Rigel."

"Your father cares a great deal about both of his daughters," Eirik said, and then he hesitated. His next words were spoken almost in a whisper, and I had the definite impression that he was afraid of what my reply might be.

"Janne... How is... I mean, is she... okay?"

For some reason, his sudden change of mood irritated me, and I answered a bit more harshly than I'd intended. "Of course she's okay! Why wouldn't she be? She's so cautious about everything she does that she couldn't possibly get into trouble. Besides, she spends all of her time fussing over that stupid baby, and..."

When I saw his eyes widen in surprise, I realized that he had been trapped in Rigel's prison for a very long time indeed.

"A baby?" His voice was full of awe.

"Congratulations." I sounded cold, even to myself. "You have a son."

"Then we really will have something to celebrate when we get back to Concordia!" He seemed oblivious to my lack of enthusiasm.

"If you don't hurry up and call Concordia," I told him, "we might not have anything at all to celebrate. Not if Rigel gets there first."

Of course, Eirik knew as well as I did that Rigel couldn't possibly be on his way to Concordia yet, but it was true that the information we each possessed was of the utmost importance. He entered my emergency code into the comm unit, and our call went through at once.

The communications officer recognized the urgency of our situation, and patched us directly through to the Prime. Within minutes, that familiar pugnacious face had appeared on the holo-screen, and we were making our report.

At first I was the one who had the most to say, because Eirik had been a prisoner and out of touch for so long. I didn't hesitate to reveal everything I'd learned, just as I had recounted it to Eirik.

The Prime listened without comment until I reached my arrival on Anhur. "Pardon me, young lady," he interrupted, "it occurs to me that you might have saved yourself a great deal of trouble, and your father a great deal of anxiety, if you had simply informed either him or myself of your suspicions about Rigel."

"But they were just that: suspicions. And I didn't want to trouble you with them until I had solid facts. You see, I kept expecting Rigel to take me into his confidence at any moment. If he had, I would have advised you at once."

"Would you, Sera?" His stern look and pursed lips underscored his skepticism.

I met his challenging stare with one of my own. "As you may recall, my proper name is Sera TiAnn Trellarian," I replied coolly. "And the answer is yes: I had every intention of telling you – just as soon as I had something worthwhile to say."

He glared at me a moment longer, and then his expression softened. "Very well, Sera Trellarian. Please go on with your report."

It occurred to me that he actually seemed amused.

"May I continue instead?" Eirik asked.

"Please do."

When he began describing our escape, I sat there beside him, not really paying attention. I felt as if I had just passed through some sort of final ordeal. From now on, I knew, no one would question my official version of the story. If the Prime believed me, so would everyone else.

Except perhaps the Tropi, I reminded myself. She would certainly feel the need to ask any number of probing questions before she was satisfied.

Well, I would deal with her when the time came...

"How do you feel about that, TiAnn?" Eirik was asking.

"I'm sorry – I'm afraid I wasn't paying attention."

"The Prime wants us to check up on Rigel's fleet before we return to Concordia."

"That could be very dangerous, couldn't it?"

He nodded, his eyes giving nothing away.

"It's okay with me," I said at last. "What about you? How are you feeling?"

"Pretty worn out – but I'll manage."

"I realize that what I'm asking is an imposition," the Prime cut in, "but the more you can tell us about how many ships he has, how soon he's likely to move out, and in what direction, the better prepared the guild will be to meet him."

"Sovereign," I interrupted, "I'm not sure you realize how ill Eirik is."

"But I do, Sera – and I'm asking him to make a sacrifice for the good of the Concorde, even though both of you have already made substantial ones. Can you help him – give him a chance to recover?"

"We'll work something out, Sovereign," Eirik interjected before I could begin to form a reply.

"Excellent. Take a few hours' break – no need to rush – and then contact me for further instructions. In the meantime, I'll consult my advisors. I expect Admiral Chert will back me up on my request that you take a quick look at the New Egypt Sector before you start for home."

"A quick look!" I muttered. "He makes it sound so easy."

Eirik glanced over at me and shook his head in warning.

"We'll call in on this frequency at twenty-one hundred hours, Concordia time, Sovereign," Eirik said, and then he signed off.

"There's no point in antagonizing him," Eirik told me without the least trace of rancor.

"He's so damn free with our lives!"

"Never fear: he knows the value of having us return alive. But there won't be much to return to if Rigel destroys the Concorde fleet first."

I sighed. "You're right. And if Rigel wins, I'm sure you and I will be at the top of his blacklist."

"I imagine we already are," Eirik said with a wicked grin.

After that, he managed to drink a bit more broth.

"The AI is programmed to run the ship," he announced as soon as he'd finished eating, "so I guess I'll try to get some rest." But when he took off his link and attempted to get out of the co-pilot's seat, he was unable to do so.

"You're going to need a whole lot more than a few hours' rest!" was my blunt assessment. "You should be in a hospital."

"Well, until you can get me there, the only alternative I have is to rest here."

I hauled him to his feet, but he was so shaky that I had to half-carry him all the way back to the cabin.

***

When I unlocked the cabin door, the first thing I saw was Cameron Ent, lying exactly as I had left him – but now he was wide awake. His eyes regarded me accusingly from his bandaged face.

After I'd helped Eirik lie down, I went over and knelt on the floor beside Cameron. "I know you hate me for what I did to you, but I couldn't think of any other way," I told him. "I doubt it will make you feel any better, but I'm sorry, Cameron. Really, really sorry…"

It must have been the strain, because before I knew it, first one and then a second tear trickled down my cheek. I stood up quickly, scrubbing angrily at my eyes, embarrassed by my moment of weakness. And then I changed the subject.

"Cameron, I'd like you to meet Commodore Eirik Sanderson. Eirik, this is Lieutenant Cameron Ent."

"Pleased to meet you, Lieutenant," Eirik said. And then: "For pity's sake, TiAnn, take that tape off his mouth. I'm sure he isn't going to talk us to death!"

I crouched back down and did as Eirik had requested.

Cameron still didn't utter a single word – he just glared at me as if he wished he could somehow incinerate me on the spot.

Eirik spoke from the bunk. "Don't be too hard on her, Lieutenant. Whatever TiAnn did to you, it was because she felt obligated to get me out of Rigel's prison."

"Prison!" Cameron exclaimed.

"The Anhur Military Academy brig has a Detention Center for political prisoners," I told him somewhat stiffly.

"I don't believe you! Why would the Premier do a thing like that?"

Eirik was the one who answered. "I'll leave you to think about that, Lieutenant, while I try to get some sleep. Maybe we can talk about it later. TiAnn, you really should get him something to eat…" His voice trailed off.

By the time I returned with the food, Eirik was sound asleep, tossing and moaning on the bunk.

"He looks awful," Cameron said. "What happened to him?"

As I fed him, I gave him a brief account of Eirik's unfortunate dealings with Rigel.

Cameron asked several pertinent questions, but mostly he just listened, and when I reached the end of my story, he shook his head.

"I haven't always agreed with the way the Premier does business, but I can't believe he's involved in all the terrible things that you say he is… Still, I have heard of him," he nodded in Eirik's direction. "Back at the guild, he's practically a legend, and after all this time, everyone was sure he was dead. Do you think he'll be okay?"

"Oh god, I hope so… Listen Cameron, I can't stay away from the cockpit too long. We've been talking to the Prime, and I don't want to miss him if he calls back… Is there anything I can do to make you more comfortable before I go?"

"Sure: get rid of this damn tape! But you won't, will you?"

I shook my head, not trusting myself to speak. How could I have done this to him? He had been my friend.

And how could I not? For Eirik's sake as well as my own, I couldn't afford to give in to sentimentality or take any chances.

"Do you want a pillow or would you like to sit up?" I finally asked.

"A pillow would be nice." He sighed. "I guess…"

Here I was, responsible for two men: one of them dangerously ill, and the other a captive with questionable loyalties. If anyone could convince Cameron of our good intentions, I thought it might be Eirik. For some reason, I felt that I would rather have Cameron Ent on our side than on Rigel's.

***

I spent the next two hours alone in the cockpit. It was hard to sit there in the Gap with nothing more diverting to do than watch the stars wheeling slowly past on the holo-screens.

It wasn't that I was eager to return to the New Egypt sector to carry out the Prime's mission. I wasn't at all anxious to do that! But it was nerve-racking, waiting to see what would happen next: whether it would be orders to move out or the discovery of our position by Rigel's scouts.

Naturally, that thought made me wonder what Rigel might be doing at this very moment. Pushing his fleet into attack readiness, I suspected, and cursing himself for ever having invited me to New Egypt. By now, he must have heard about my raid on the Detention Center. It gave me a great deal of pleasure to imagine what his reaction must have been when he discovered that his sweet young lover had run off with his favorite ship, his trusted aide, and one of his most dangerous political prisoners.

Suddenly I had an irrational urge to contact him via the Net. How satisfying it would be to see him, angry and humiliated, and to remind him that I was the one who had put a serious crimp in his precious plans!

But calling Rigel was definitely out of the question, no matter how tempting the thought might be. There was always the possibility that someone on his communications staff might be able to trace the *Meteor* – which would bring us nothing but trouble…

I must have dozed off, because the next thing I knew, the intercom buzzed, startling me awake.

"TiAnn – are you there?"

"Yes, Eirik. How are you feeling?"

"Marginal. But I've had a chance to talk to Cameron, and I think we've reached an understanding."

"I'm so glad!" I exclaimed, surprising myself with the intensity of my reaction.

"How about bringing us something to eat?" Eirik suggested. "Unfortunately, I think I'm going to need help getting up."

I ordered up all sorts of food – a real feast by food processor standards – and then I headed back to the cabin.

"I hope you left something for later," Eirik teased when he saw me coming.

Although Cameron was no longer glaring, his expression was still extremely guarded.

"Now, Cameron... I'm going to ask TiAnn to take off the rest of that tape," Eirik said, giving the young aide a reassuring smile. "But you understand that I can't trust you one hundred percent yet. I don't suppose you feel much like trusting us either."

"That's correct, Commodore." This confession was accompanied by a familiar telltale blush.

Meanwhile, Eirik had managed to prop himself up in the bed. "TiAnn, do you still have that gun?"

I nodded.

"Good. Give it to me, and I'll keep you covered. Is that acceptable, Cameron?"

No prisoner had ever been treated with more consideration – of that I was certain – and Cameron must surely realize it too as I began unwrapping his ankles.

"When we're through here, TiAnn and I are going to call the Prime," Eirik explained, for Cameron's benefit I knew, rather than mine. "He's supposed to give us instructions about checking up on Rigel's troop movements. Cameron, Rigel is preparing to attack Concordia."

"I can hardly believe what you're telling me, sir, but I suppose it must be true if you've convinced the Prime."

Now that Cameron's legs were free, I glanced over at Eirik before continuing.

He nodded almost imperceptibly.

"You're going to be a bit stiff," I warned. "Don't try to stand without my help."

The young aide studied me intently as I removed tape from his wrists, but for once his face didn't betray any emotion. When I was finished, I sat back on my heels and watched him rub the sore places. Then I stood and held out my hand. His expression remained uncharacteristically neutral as he allowed me to help him up.

Eirik spoke from the bunk. "I've always prided myself on my ability to judge people, Cameron, and I truly believe that you had no knowledge of Rigel's plans. I'd like to be able to call you my friend…" He held the gun out, butt first to the aide. "I believe this is yours. I'm sure I won't be needing it."

Cameron couldn't have been any more surprised than I was. His eyes suddenly blazed with undisguised admiration as he reclaimed his weapon. I recognized a hero worshipper when I saw one.

"T-thank you, Commodore! I'll try to be worthy of your trust." He hastened to Eirik's side. "Here: let me help you up."

As Eirik got to his feet, he flashed me a dazzling smile over Cameron's shoulder and said: "Now, let me at that food!"

***

The Prime regarded us from the holo-screen. "I gather that the young man who is standing behind you is Rigel's aide."

"Former aide," Eirik corrected. Lacking a change of clothing, he had insisted on showering in what used to be Cameron's uniform, shaving, and pulling his unkempt hair back into an untidy ponytail. He now smelled significantly better, although he was still rather disheveled and awfully pale. "This is Cameron Ent," he went on. "He's a good man, Sovereign. I'll vouch for him."

Cameron, who was now dressed in some of Rigel's things that we had liberated from his onboard wardrobe, never took his eyes from Eirik's face, not even to look at the Prime.

"Very well: his past associations will not be held against him," the Prime stated.

"I appreciate that, Sovereign," Eirik said.

"Since we last spoke," the Prime continued, "I have conferred with several of my advisors: Admiral Chert and his staff, Cristan Andebar and the Tropi, as well as Prime Minister Trellerian. And we've reached consensus on a course of action. Admiral Chert has offered to brief you... Admiral?"

Admiral Chert came onscreen, intently examining a data slate. "Commodore Sanderson, I..." Glancing up, he stopped short. "Errr...Sorry, Commodore! I, uh... I wasn't expecting to see you looking so, umm...?" His voice trailed off.

"You wouldn't look any better than I do, sir, if you'd been Rigel's guest for as long as I have." Eirik was definitely amused.

"No doubt. Now where was I? Ah, yes. After evaluating your report, we've decided to recommend that you hold your present position for another twenty-six hours – that is, if you have sufficient rations."

"We do, sir."

"Excellent. Give yourself another day to rest, then we'd like you to go back into the New Egypt Sector to scout out Rigel's activities. We need as much information as possible on fleet distribution, the number and configuration of his ships, plus any guesses you might have as to their embarkation schedule and possible jump routes...

"Naturally, if at any time you feel endangered, we expect you to use your judgment and take whatever evasive action you consider necessary, up to and including leaving – although we're hoping it won't come to that...

"What we *are* hoping is that you'll be able to infiltrate Rigel's system without being detected. We'd like you to evaluate his fleet and trail it in towards the Hub, reporting back to us as you go. The longer you're able to monitor them, the better. Follow them all the way in if you can. Will you be able to work with that plan, Commodore?"

"We'll do our best, Admiral Chert."

"Thank you, Commodore Sanderson – and good luck."

"We're going to need it..." I muttered to myself as the two men saluted each other.

The Prime reappeared on the holo-screen. "Admiral Chert speaks for all of us in wishing the three of you the best of luck. Your help has been invaluable to the Concorde."

I thought he was going to sign off, but instead he said, "Commodore Sanderson, your wife wishes to speak with you. I've warned her that you've been quite ill but are on the road to recovery, and that she shouldn't be alarmed by your appearance."

"Thank you, Sovereign." Out of sight of the camera, his hands spasmed shut on the seat's armrests so tightly that his knuckles turned white.

Janne appeared onscreen, holding Bran in her arms.

Neither she nor Eirik said a word.

"Come on, TiAnn!" Cameron hissed, plucking urgently at my sleeve. "Let's give them some privacy."

So we left the bridge before I had a chance to discover what, if anything, Eirik and my sister had to say to each other after all this time.

14.

The next day we returned to the New Egypt sector. Fortunately, by then Eirik had regained some of his strength and no longer needed quite so many stims. Meanwhile, Cameron and I had managed to establish a rather wary truce after several hours of cautious conversation.

Coordinating with the AI, Eirik jumped us to a location outside the main area of activity in the New Egypt system – and right away we almost ran into a military patrol. If he hadn't taken the additional precaution of positioning us behind the protective bulk of one of the outer planets, we would surely have been detected by the enemy's instruments.

"Rigel isn't taking any chances, is he?" was Eirik's cool assessment. "Looks like he's been expecting us to come snooping around."

"Isn't that going to make it awfully hard for us to carry out the admiral's orders, Commodore?" Even as he spoke, Cameron was fiddling nervously with an adjustment on the holo-screen.

"Relax, Cam. I'll let you know when it's time to start worrying," Eirik teased. "At least wait until someone spots us."

"Yes, sir." Judging by his expression, Cameron didn't find Eirik's words reassuring.

My sentiments exactly.

Miraculously – for the moment at least – we seemed to have avoided trouble. It wasn't easy to sneak into Rigel's territory, but Eirik apparently had an uncanny instinct for choosing the right places to hide. I never felt completely safe while we were there, yet I realized that I would have felt far less so if anyone else had been at the helm.

A little more than two hours into our mission, we finally located the fleet, cruising just beyond New Egypt's asteroid belt.

"My god, Eirik, does the guild have that many ships?" My voice came out in a mere whisper, as if I thought someone out there might overhear my question. "Does the Prime?"

"It doesn't look good." His expression was grim. "And we don't even know if this is the entire fleet…"

That was a sobering thought.

"All right, folks," abruptly Eirik's voice was brisk and full of authority, "let's get down to business. What I believe we're seeing here is an excellent ratio of heavy battleships to smaller, more mobile units although I don't recognize some of the configurations. How about it, Cam: have you ever run across anything like this before?" His finger traced the outline of a slim, needle-nosed flyer.

"Negative, sir."

"I think it may be similar to what Janne and I saw on our way back from Valhalla," Eirik remarked, "but we never got close enough to log a good visual."

I told him, "Back on New Egypt, I overheard Pellen telling Rigel that he'd designed a small, ultra-fast ship that could outmaneuver any of the guild's more conventional ones. I'm not sure Rigel believed him."

"It doesn't look good," Eirik repeated.

"Neither does that!" Cameron pointed to a wedge of five ships that had just emerged from behind the moon we had been using for cover. "Uh, oh – they're heading our way!"

"Let's hope Pellen gave the *Meteor* that extra dose of speed too," was Eirik's stoic response. "Hang on everyone!"

Banking sharply, we sped off in the opposite direction, rapidly accelerating to jump velocity. Moments later, when we cleared hyperspace, I recognized the now-familiar barren reaches of the Gap.

"That was too close," Eirik announced. "I'm not willing to risk it again. We'll have to call the admiral and give him our best estimate based on what we've just seen."

"You mean we're not going to follow them in, sir?"

"I don't think we have much choice about that. After all, they're between us and Concordia. If we're lucky, we may be able to leave before most of them are ready to move out – although I seriously doubt it. And I don't want to risk jumping into them on the way home."

I shuddered at the thought. Now that Rigel's scouts had been alerted, they would certainly be on the lookout for the *Meteor*.

"So how will we get back to Concordia, sir?"

"I'm afraid we'll have to opt for a more roundabout approach. But before I start working on that, we'd better make our report… How about it, you two: what do you estimate you saw in the way of ships back there? I have my own ideas, but I'd like to hear your impressions. We need to agree on what we're going to tell Admiral Chert."

We spent so much time debating numbers that I was beginning to get jittery, but eventually Eirik announced that it was time to call Concordia. He gave the admiral a concise summary of what we had seen, and said that in his opinion, Rigel was already on the move, but that we were unable to determine exactly what route or routes his fleet would take. He also reported our run-in with the enemy scout ships, and that he felt it was unsafe to risk another encounter. In summary, he told Admiral Chert that we were on our way home, and they both agreed we would maintain radio silence for the time being.

No sooner had he signed off, than Eirik began consulting with our AI to plot a safe series of jumps back to Concordia.

Cameron and I tried to stay out of the way while they were working. Since we were far too nervous to concentrate on anything more constructive, we spent the time talking in the observation lounge. And by the time we were ready to begin the actual transit towards home, we had managed to convert our truce back into friendship. I was glad: it was the first time we had felt at ease with each other since Anhur.

***

It would have been impossible for anyone who hadn't known our flight plan to have traced us through the complex series of jumps that Eirik and the *Meteor's* AI had devised. However, in any jump sequence it's only safe to go so far before stopping to take star fixes and make the inevitable course adjustments. Because of this, our journey seemed to take forever – and knowing that Rigel was out there somewhere and almost certainly hunting for us, only served to increase the tension. Every time we jumped, all three of us literally held our breaths, half-expecting to find ourselves materializing in the midst of the enemy fleet.

Before long, Eirik was exhausted.

He and I had a brief, bitter argument about the wisdom of my giving him any additional stims – but then he abruptly capitulated and agreed to leave the responsibility of flying the *Meteor* in our current, obscure no-man's land to Cameron and myself for the present, rather than trying to attempt any more jumps. And once he'd satisfied himself that there were no enemy ships in our immediate vicinity, he retired to the privacy of his cabin.

Our plan was to join the branch of the Space Guild fleet that would be responsible for defending Concordia itself. Eirik and Cameron said they were determined to participate in whatever fighting occurred, but they offered to take me to a place of safety if I was reluctant to stay aboard.

I told them that since I'd already come this far, I would remain with them. The risks of battle seemed minor compared to the possibility of missing something of truly historic importance.

Admittedly, I was nervous – but then, so was Cameron – and I reminded myself that Eirik wouldn't take unnecessary risks. He had far more to lose than either of us: a wife and an infant son, plus the responsibility of ruling an entire planet upon what we all hoped would be his safe return to Valhalla.

***

While Cameron and I continued to practice our navigational skills, closely supervised by the ship's AI, Eirik contacted Admiral Chert from the haven of his cabin, and over the course of the next several hours I assumed that they were discussing the deployment of the Concorde fleet, debating various strategies and assessing the readiness of each squadron, down to individual ships and their crews.

Eirik was apparently quite familiar with a large number of guild personnel, and Admiral Chert seemed to place great value on his recommendations. I soon realized that Cameron wasn't the only one who was impressed by my brother-in-law.

At this time, the admiral also gave us the coordinates for a rendezvous point, several days and jumps distant, which hopefully would place us well within the Concordia system and the Space Guild's sphere of influence.

But before we were able to reach our destination, we had the extreme misfortune of running into Rigel's advance guard...

Eirik was once again resting, and Cameron and I were at the controls when they came out of hyperspace, two dozen of Rigel's ships flying in tight formation, materializing directly ahead of us and traveling in the same direction as we were. At our urgent summons, Eirik staggered from his cabin and joined us in the cockpit.

"Where did they come from?" he demanded, strapping himself into the pilot's chair and slapping the crown on his head.

"N-nowhere, Commodore!" Cameron sputtered. "They jumped out right in front of us!"

"My god, Rigel's certainly taking chances – it's sheer madness jumping this close in!"

"He must believe it's worth the risk," I said. "After all, he has to have some element of surprise, now that we've made his agenda public."

"I don't think they've realized we're here yet," Cameron added. "But it won't be long..."

I pointed to the screen. The ships on the trailing edge of the formation were already veering around to face us.

"There goes our access to Concordia," Eirik announced with apparent unconcern. "Looks like we'll have to make a run for it... And even if we do get out of here in one piece, we're going to have a hell of a time reaching our own fleet."

"Shouldn't we make that emergency call to Concordia?" I suggested.

"Do it! And be sure to give them our present coordinates. The least we can do is warn them that Rigel is practically on their doorstep."

"They're firing at us!" Cameron's voice was edged with fear.

"They can only hit us if they get close enough," was Eirik's grim reply. "TiAnn, strap yourself into the comm bay."

And he plunged the *Meteor* into a series of high-speed evasive maneuvers that left me clinging to my seat and gasping for breath, even with the ship's grav-gens at full strength.

But three small flyers were still on our tail.

"Let's see what they make of this!" Eirik threw the *Meteor* into what my queasy stomach apparently construed as a somersault, flipping us over and behind them.

Two of our original pursuers tried to compensate and nearly collided with the third.

At which point my poor, befuddled brain seemed to believe that I, rather than our ship, had been doing acrobatic tricks.

"TiAnn – you're not calling!" Cameron cried, grabbing my arm to draw my attention away from the main holo-screen.

"Sorry!" I punched in the emergency code. Almost immediately, I was describing our unenviable situation to a startled guild officer and giving him our coordinates, as Eirik had instructed.

"Stand by, *Meteor*. We'll see if we can get you some help," the man responded.

Somehow, I didn't feel the least bit reassured. "I think I've decided to skip the battle after all," I muttered, not really caring whether or not the others heard me.

"Uh oh – here come some of the big guys!" Cameron warned.

"No problem." The worse the situation got, the calmer and more focused Eirik seemed to become. "I think I can outrun them…"

We began accelerating away from the enemy ships.

Suddenly up ahead of us, in the direction of our escape, the blackness of space shimmered as hundreds of Rigel's ships came out of hyperspace.

Eirik hit the reverse thrusters.

At the same instant, my screen went dead and the guild officer's image disappeared, replaced by Rigel's all-too-familiar face. He was in full dress uniform, and his expression was anything but friendly.

"*Meteor*, this is *Avenger*. Pellen and I thought we might find you here."

"Hello, Rigel," I said, attempting to emulate Eirik's cool demeanor.

"It's a pleasure to see you, my dear." His voice was heavy with sarcasm. "I hoped we'd meet again – although I must confess, I would have preferred it to be under very different circumstances."

I noticed that Cameron had switched on the co-pilot's comm screen and was staring, fascinated, at his former boss.

"I'm not at all happy about the way we parted," Rigel was saying, apparently unaware of his new audience.

"Neither was I," I responded. "But I've done everything I could since then to make up for it."

Out of the corner of my eye, I noticed that we were rapidly being hemmed in on all sides. To my dismay, ships continued to materialize on our holo-screens, both above and below the first group.

"*Meteor*, you are now surrounded by the New Egypt Liberation Fleet," Rigel gloated. "Escape is impossible – we can destroy you before you're even aware of what's happened." He paused. "However, since I want my ship back, I'm willing to negotiate. Let me talk to Sanderson."

Eirik reached over to switch on his own comm screen. "*Commodore* Sanderson here."

"Well, well…" Rigel sneered. "I didn't expect to see you again. I was sure Inspector Clode would have finished you off long before now."

"Cut the crap, Rigel. What do you want?"

Rigel's face contorted in fury, but he managed to keep his voice level as he replied, "Very well. These are my conditions: I'm willing to spare your lives if you will surrender my ship. Take it or leave it."

For several long moments, neither man said a word – they simply glared at one another in mutual hatred.

"I've already had a taste of your version of sparing my life," Eirik said at last, "and frankly, I'd rather be dead."

"Have it your way," Rigel growled. "Although a quick death is not what I'd prefer for any of you!"

Cameron's face went quite pale.

Suddenly, Eirik's lips pulled back from his teeth in a wolfish grin. With his colorless face and feverish eyes, the effect was truly unnerving. "If I were you, Rigel," he said, "I wouldn't write us off so quickly."

He gestured towards our main screen.

Cameron gasped.

I tore my eyes away from Eirik's fiercely triumphant face and looked at the screens. Slicing through space at right angles to the plane of Rigel's fleet, ships bearing the welcome insignia of the Space Guild had appeared as if from nowhere.

"Thank you, Admiral Chert!" Eirik muttered under his breath as he pulled the *Meteor* up into a steep climb.

Cameron let out a yelp – either out of fear or excitement – as we flashed up into the guild ranks and reversed direction, meshing perfectly into their formation.

"Nice flying, Commodore!" Cameron crowed.

The holo-screen had blanked out as we entered the ranks of the guild forces. Now it lit up again: a serious, dark-skinned man appeared where Rigel's face had been just moments ago.

"*Meteor*, this is the guild flagship *Victor*. Admiral Ivar speaking."

"Delighted to see you, Admiral," Eirik replied, with that ghoulish smile still pasted on his face.

"If you will switch to guild inter-ship frequency, we can stay in touch without risking further interruptions," was Ivar's calm and very sensible suggestion.

"Do it, TiAnn, and stay on the comm. Cameron, you're in charge of weaponry. I'm going to have my hands full just flying this thing."

In a few terse words, Ivar briefed us on the overall plan of attack, giving us specific instructions as to which ships we were to work with. By now, the guild ships had cleared the New Egypt fleet and were regrouping for a frontal attack.

In the ensuing lull, I couldn't stop myself from asking, "Eirik, did you plan for this to happen?"

"Not exactly." He actually seemed amused. "But Admiral Chert and I hoped that somehow things would work out so we'd meet Rigel far enough from Concordia that we'd have more room to maneuver and no civilian targets to endanger."

"We were acting as a decoy?" I knew how angry I sounded, but I was still very frightened by our narrow escape.

"We accepted the possibility that we might find Rigel before the rest of our fleet did. And Admiral Chert and I agreed that if that happened, we would send them our coordinates and they would try to jump out to meet us."

"I'm not sure I approve of your plans."

"They worked, didn't they? We're safe."

"For now..." I glanced at the main screen and shuddered.

Even as we spoke, the Concorde fleet was continuing to materialize around us. Yet they were so well-coordinated that there were no overlaps to their jumps, and the extremely difficult maneuver of transferring a large body of ships from one location to another was accomplished without any losses.

And so the battle of Concordia began. I have since read many accounts of what transpired that day, and each makes sense in its own way. Some evaluate the tactics: the strategic maneuvers executed by each side, others calculate the balances and imbalances of the opposing forces, while other analysts describe the individual engagements, encounter by encounter.

I was not in any position to form an overall picture, either of the fighting or the grand scheme of things because I was caught up in one small portion of the battle, unable for the most part to see what was happening anywhere beyond the space immediately surrounding our ship.

However, one thing that all of the accounts agree upon – and my own experience confirms – is that Eirik Sanderson was a tremendous asset and source of inspiration for the entire fleet. Cameron and I were not the only ones who were impressed by his outstanding abilities, both as a pilot and a leader. That day he saved more than one ship and its crew with his fast thinking and daring tactics.

From the outset, Eirik realized that we could best serve Concordia by utilizing the *Meteor's* unique swiftness to first scan for hot spots, and then dart in to give aid wherever it was most needed. Our operations soon fell into a distinct rhythm: scout for trouble, swoop down into the midst of it to assist our beleaguered colleagues, resolve the conflict, and then dart back out again for another overall scan.

During our overviews, I had a chance to gain some perspective on the fighting, which was intense, shifting first one way and then the other, as the struggle ebbed and flowed around us.

The losses on both sides were staggering. The carnage went on for hours, with no time out and not a moment's respite: it would have been far too dangerous for any ship to jump out of the area and expect to be able to jump back in again without hitting something.

There were no sidelines in this battle.

How Eirik managed to stay alert and focused, I will never know. Twice I had to give him stims to keep him going.

***

After several hours, I began to feel as if the slaughter had been going on forever – it was hard to think back to its inception. And an alarming suspicion was beginning to grow in me that there were more and more enemy ships in our sector of space, and fewer and fewer of our Concorde allies. However, I kept these ominous thoughts to myself, hoping that in the long run they would turn out to have been a figment of my imagination. And Eirik and Cameron were so engrossed in their maneuvers that I doubt they noticed any changes.

The nightmare went on and on.

And then something totally inexplicable happened…

We had just disengaged from yet another skirmish and were taking a short breather and a quick look around for more potential trouble spots when, far off in the distance, out beyond the limits of the fighting, I noticed an object hurtling towards us at incredible speed. I remember thinking that whatever it was must be truly enormous because our scanners picked it up at about the same time that it became visible on our holo-screens.

I pointed out the newcomer to my companions.

"What *is* that thing?" Cameron breathed. "No starship I know of is *that* big…"

For several long moments, the three of us just sat there in stunned silence, watching it come on. It occurred to me that because of our unique situation, it was possible that no one else in either fleet was aware of the intruder.

When this strange apparition reached the edge of the battle zone closest to the main concentration of Rigel's ships, it slowed and its form became apparent. It was a dull grey sphere, pocked with indentations containing what could only be interpreted as instrumentation or else huge shuttle bays. Incredible as it seemed, this was definitely a ship – one that was nearly the size of a small moon!

"My god, what *is* that thing?" Cameron repeated in a hushed voice.

Eirik glanced over at me, an awed look on his weary face. "TiAnn, I think your reports of alien starships have just been confirmed."

In unison, we once again turned to gape at the main holo-screen.

Cruising even more slowly now, the alien visitor was sailing directly into the midst of the battle, where the fighting was fiercest. It was apparently surrounded by some sort of force field, because the space around it shimmered with a bluish-white haze every time it was struck by a random shot. As we watched in disbelief, that terrible object cut a swath across the battlefield, like a boulder rolling down a hill, annihilating everything in its path. But it was a boulder from Hell: whatever had the misfortune to come in contact with the alien sphere, sizzled briefly against its protective corona and then disappeared.

By now everyone was aware of the intruder: every ship in its vicinity had come to a complete and sudden halt. The comm link buzzed with confused chatter. And like all the others, we waited, hanging suspended in the void. I had the sensation that every person aboard every ship was holding his or her breath, just as I was.

"W-what are we going to d-do, sir?"

Eirik glanced briefly over at Cameron. "I haven't a clue," he admitted with a frown.

Just then, I noticed movement out among the enemy ships. Eirik saw it too, and swore. "What the hell does Rigel think he's doing?"

From our position, it was obvious that Rigel and the part of his fleet closest to the alien were regrouping.

"I don't believe it!" Cameron cried. "It looks like they're going to attack."

"TiAnn, get Rigel on the comm!" Eirik roared.

But when I tried to raise our nemesis, there was no reply.

As we watched, Rigel's force swung around in a perfectly coordinated arc to confront the alien. Bolts of energy arced from his ships, slicing through space between themselves and the sphere, everything concentrated on a single point on its hull.

"They're insane," I commented to no one in particular.

The shots glowed briefly on the surface of the alien's force field and then flickered out, apparently without effect. The next instant, there was a tremendous surge of energy, obviously far more powerful than that of the attackers. Lancing out from the alien vessel, it played over the nearest ships, incinerating whatever it touched.

"I can't watch!" I cried, covering my eyes.

But then Eirik gasped, "My god – Rigel's going in for a direct attack!"

And I forced myself to look.

Slow and ominous, the alien juggernaut was still moving forward, decimating the ranks of starships in its path. One flash, and the *Avenger* was gone as if it had never existed.

"Rigel!" I whispered.

"TiAnn, get on the comm and call the Prime! Now!" Eirik barked. "And let's hope Ivar has the sense to tell everyone to get the hell out of here!"

Cameron glanced down apprehensively at his weapons board.

"Don't touch a thing, Cameron!" Eirik snapped. "That's an order!"

Cameron flinched as if he'd been stung.

Meanwhile, I was trying to obey Eirik's command, but my fingers wouldn't cooperate.

"Hurry up, TiAnn!" Eirik prompted. "Use the emergency frequency. We've got to warn the Prime!"

Outside, ships were scattering in every direction, guild ships alongside Rigel's fleet, everyone jumping out in wild confusion. And none of the remaining New Egypt forces were attempting to fight the alien.

At last, my connection went through and the Prime appeared on my holo-screen.

"Sera Trellarian, why are you calling?" he demanded. He and his son Ferrin were surrounded by a crowd of advisors. I caught a glimpse of my father and Andebar in the background. "I was expecting to hear from Admiral Ivar."

"Stand by and I'll switch you over to our main screen so you can see this for yourselves," was my terse explanation.

The alien ship was gliding through the last of Rigel's ranks, systematically obliterating everything that stood in its way. Some ships were destroyed before they could complete their jump preparations, while others – the lucky ones – somehow managed to escape.

Meanwhile, back in the Prime's audience chamber, pandemonium erupted: people were jostling to get a better view of his holo-screen, horrified looks were on every face, and everyone was talking at once.

"What *is* that thing?"

"Where did it come from?"

"How did it get here?"

"How many ships have we lost?"

"Silence!" the Prime roared, his expression livid.

The babble cut off instantly.

"Sera Trellarian," the Prime went on in a calmer voice, "would you be so kind as to tell me what we're witnessing? Is that Rigel's secret weapon?"

"As far as we can determine, Sovereign, it's an alien starship. It showed up just a little while ago, approaching at incredible speed. Rigel attacked it, and it wiped out most of his fleet, including his ship. We lost some of ours too... There doesn't seem to be any way to stop it." I hated the way my voice cracked. "Nevertheless," I went on, "Commodore Sanderson wants Admiral Ivar to order all guild ships to clear the area immediately."

In the midst of my recitation, a staff member handed the Prime a message slate.

"I've just received a communication from Admiral Chert at Space Guild Central," the Prime announced. "Admiral Ivar has recalled all Concorde forces from the battle zone. The fleet is to rendezvous just outside Concordia airspace at the earliest possible opportunity."

He looked up, directly into the camera. "Of course, I imagine that 'the earliest possible opportunity' is going to take considerable time. Not only does our fleet have to regroup, it also has to come back in at sub-light speed."

"Commodore Sanderson, how fast would you say that alien ship can move?" Lord Ferrin suddenly asked.

Erik switched his comm screen back on. "I have no way of knowing... Its approach was almost instantaneous, from the moment we first spotted it. I can attempt to make some calculations if you insist."

"That won't be necessary... More important: do you believe it's on its way here?"

"God, I hope not!" I blurted out.

"I don't know," was Eirik's stoic reply.

"Sovereign." The Tropi stepped into view, hurrying through the crowd to address the Prime, "may I make a suggestion?"

What a relief it was to see her!

"Please do!"

"Perhaps I can contact the aliens." She appeared calm, although I could hear the urgency in her voice. "It may be possible to use the *Meteor*'s communications system, simultaneously with my ability to mind-speak, to channel a message through to them."

"Why should they listen to you?" someone demanded.

"And what makes you think they'll understand?" someone else wanted to know.

"The next person who interrupts the Tropi will be thrown out of this room!" the Prime bellowed.

In the absolute silence that followed, he said very quietly, "You were saying, madam?"

"Let me try to contact them, Sovereign. If I greet them as friends, I may be able to convince them of our peaceful intentions. At the very least, I might be able to determine why they are here, and if they mean to do us further harm."

I glanced over at the main screen and shuddered: the area was now clear of every ship except ours.

And the alien was cruising slowly in our direction.

"Whatever you decide to do, you'd better be quick about it," Eirik announced. "I'm not willing to stick around much longer."

"Sovereign," the Tropi said, "if I have your permission, I am ready to proceed."

When the Prime nodded, she moved to occupy a central position on the screen. "TiAnn, please open all of your communication channels."

As I complied, she paused and seemed to gather strength. Her serene face grew even calmer, until she appeared to be almost in a trance – perhaps she was summoning her mind-speaking abilities… But then her eyes slowly opened, and she began to speak aloud in a warm, friendly tone…

"The people of the Concorde Alliance welcome our visitors from beyond. I am the Tropi, one of the planetary leaders of our Alliance, yet I speak for all when I greet you…"

The alien ship was still coming on.

I tore my eyes away from the main screen and went back to focus on the Tropi.

"You have arrived at a very difficult time," she was saying, I presumed also in her mind-spoken language, "when some of our people, with evil intentions have chosen to strike out against the majority of us, who are law-abiding, non-violent citizens. We regret that you have had to witness the ugliness of our conflict – but we are grateful for your help in destroying our enemy and ending this battle."

Once again I glanced away towards the main screen and noted with considerable relief that the alien was no longer in motion: it hung immobile, its shields shimmering eerily in the absolute blackness of space.

"We offer you friendship and a meeting of minds," the Tropi continued, her voice gaining in intensity. "Will you join us in peace?" She stretched her arms wide as if to embrace the alien.

"It's moving again," was Eirik's unemotional statement.

At his words, my heart, which was already racing so fast that I felt slightly out-of-breath, seemed to jump right out of my chest. "What will they do to us?" I whispered, more frightened than I would ever have thought possible.

No one spoke: the answer was obvious.

"Sir – it's going back the way it came!" Cameron's sudden shout was the most beautiful sound I had ever heard. "It's moving away from Concordia!"

It was true: the alien ship was gathering speed with breathtaking swiftness. One moment it was there – and the next it was a mere blip on our screens...

And then it was gone.

On my holo-screen, the Tropi stood motionless. As I watched, a single, bright tear brimmed in the corner of one eye and trickled down her cheek. "Come back," she whispered. "Please come back."

I doubt anyone shared her regret.

In silence, we survivors surveyed the area which only moments before had been a desperate and bloody battlefield. But there was no one left and nothing to fight for.

"Let's go home," Eirik said quietly.

And so we began the long sub-light flight back to Concordia.

15.

It's a well-known fact that the citizens of Concordia are pragmatic folks. Living as they do near the center of the Hub, they are constantly exposed to strange visitors and unusual situations. Threaten them with danger or even destruction and they simply dig in and continue to go quietly about their business. Still, when we returned to Concordia, I must admit that I was expecting some kind of public reaction, be it outrage or celebration – some response to the Armageddon which had so narrowly been avoided.

But there was none. And while no effort had been made to hide the truth that something extraordinary had occurred in the outer reaches of the Concordia System, nothing much had been done to advertise it either. Apparently neither the media nor the public was anxious to examine the implications of what had just transpired.

Of course, everywhere we went, people were talking about the recent battle and the unexpected advent of the aliens, yet the whole, bizarre incident was spoken of in such an abstract way that the subject under discussion might as well have been the most recent political polls, the Moonball Finals score, or the latest fashion trend. Furthermore, as time passed and the aliens failed to reappear and no drastic changes actually took place in anyone's lives, people conveniently began to forget about the recent disturbing events. And as normality returned, complacency set in.

Over the course of the following weeks, one by one the ships of the Concorde fleet straggled in with tales of fierce fighting, narrow escapes, and the loss of brave comrades, yet crew members were already speaking of their adventures as if they had happened to someone else, in some distant, heroic past.

The survivors of Rigel's fleet also started turning up, at first somewhat sheepishly, docking at Space Guild bases or the facilities of their various home planets. However, few received more than a short confinement and a severe reprimand. It seemed that no one besides Rigel and Pellen was destined to go down in history as a villainous traitor – and since both men had conveniently been dispatched by the aliens, they were certainly beyond retribution or (apparently) even interest.

As for myself and my two companions, no sooner had we docked at the Grand Concordia Space Station than a team of medics arrived to rush Eirik straight to Concordia Hospital where he underwent a cursory examination and was immediately admitted. My father, Janne, and her baby met Cameron and me there – and before long there wasn't a dry eye in the house. Eventually, my sister settled in to remain with Eirik, while the rest of us returned to our humble abode. And since Cameron had nowhere else to stay, my father invited him to join us there, even though all we had to offer him in the way of accommodations was a sofa.

***

At first it was a letdown to be back. However, our apartment soon became a welcome refuge from the storm of publicity that our return had unexpectedly unleashed. Yet of all the people who had been involved or caught up in what the media was now calling Rigel's Rebellion, the only one who ultimately captured the imagination of the general public was Eirik Sanderson – and ironically, he was the one person who least craved the attention. The news hounds gave his story exhaustive coverage, from the time he was admitted to Concordia Hospital, right up to the day he left Concordia.

My father, Cameron, and I were constantly pestered for interviews: Father because he had worked closely with Eirik before his abduction, and Cameron and I because we had been with him during the battle and the days leading up to it.

Janne was far less accessible because she never left Eirik's bedside, but what must have finally amounted to hours of holo-vids of their son Bran toddling around the palace grounds, were recorded and shown to a seemingly insatiable public. We were also treated to glimpses of Eirik resting in his hospital bed and taking his first unassisted walk down the hospital corridors, accompanied by my sister and a team of beaming doctors and nurses. Before they were through, the reporters had managed to distort the whole story to the point where it sounded as if Eirik had single-handedly defeated both Rigel *and* the alien intruders!

Cameron and my father were amused by the news coverage.

I was not.

To put it mildly, it was embarrassing to have every last detail of my rescue of Eirik from Rigel's prison talked about and analyzed – and extremely unnerving to hear my methods and motives speculated about by commentators and the public alike.

I wanted my privacy back!

And then, just when the fuss had finally started to die down, it was stirred up all over again by rumors that the Prime had offered Eirik the rank of vice admiral in the Space Guild and that Eirik had turned him down.

That was one story I simply couldn't ignore!

I had no trouble believing that the Prime might offer Eirik such a promotion – he had more than amply demonstrated how truly he deserved it – but what I couldn't believe was that Eirik would refuse the honor! I had spent enough time with him to know that he was a natural leader, and I also knew that as a vice admiral he would be in a position of much greater power and influence than he could ever hope for as the ruler of a backwater Fringe planet like Valhalla. Accepting the Prime's offer would only be common sense.

Up to that point, because of the omnipresent reporters, I had avoided going out of our apartment except when it was absolutely necessary, and I hadn't visited Eirik in the hospital because I felt that what he needed most was a complete rest, not a swarm of well-wishers. Besides, I admitted to myself, I felt a bit shy about seeing him again. Some of Cameron Ent's hero-worship seemed to have rubbed off on me, and if the truth be told I was rather in awe of him.

But now the visit had to be paid. And so, braving the reporters and their ever-present drones and holo-cameras, I fought my way past them and boarded the air taxi I'd hired to take me to the hospital. However, to my annoyance, when I arrived there, I was greeted by a whole new contingent of reporters and their nosy questions. It seemed like forever before I was ushered into the welcome haven of Eirik's private room.

Right away I noticed that he looked much better than when I had last seen him. The deeply-etched pain lines were gone from his face and he no longer had a corpse-like pallor, although he was still terribly thin. He started to get up to greet me, but I waved him back to bed and pulled up a chair beside my sister's.

Janne, too, seemed transformed. I couldn't remember when I had last seen her looking so radiantly happy – and for some reason, I found this quite disturbing.

"Hello, stranger," Eirik said. "I was beginning to think I'd have to wade through all those media folks out there if I ever wanted to see to you again."

I turned my attention from my sister in time to receive his warm smile, and felt myself blushing like schoolgirl. "I thought you needed rest more than you needed visitors," I said, trying to disguise my embarrassment behind a gruff tone of voice.

"Maybe other visitors – but never you!" Janne cried. "We wanted to thank you. We're so grateful for what you did for Eirik!"

"Hey, don't get carried away," I protested. "I did what I had to do. Thanks aren't necessary."

"I disagree," Eirik said, and he looked at me so intently that I finally had to look away. "You know as well as I do that I'd be dead by now if you hadn't risked your life to get me out of that hellhole."

"Rigel certainly wasn't going to free Eirik of his own accord," was Janne's unnecessary addendum.

"Can't you just forget it?" I snapped. "I didn't come here to be praised – I came to ask Eirik a question."

"Ask away." He seemed amused by my (unfortunately) obvious discomfort. "That's the least I can do for you."

"It's just that I heard the craziest story."

"Which is...?"

"That you'd turned down the Prime's offer to promote you to vice admiral in the Space Guild. It sounded so ridiculous that I had to come here and ask you about it myself."

"It isn't ridiculous," he said with great seriousness. "He did ask me – and I refused."

"Why!"

"Because I want to go home! I have unfinished business there – and I also have an obligation to my family." He reached for Janne's hand, and their eyes met and held.

"Come on, Eirik!" I scolded. I hadn't come all this way to waste time on their romantic nonsense! "Don't you think the best way to honor your commitments to your family and the Concorde Alliance is to accept the Prime's offer?"

"If I believed that, I would have accepted. Surely you know me that well, TiAnn."

For a moment I studied his familiar and undeniably handsome face – then I shook my head. "I still don't understand."

"It seems to me that the Prime can always find someone else to serve as vice admiral," Eirik patiently explained. "But the people of Valhalla can't find another leader so easily... And since they've asked for me, I think I have an obligation to go home and finish my father's lifework."

"Which was?"

"To free Valhalla from the cruelty of a despotic government: a government ruled by self-interest rather than democratic principles."

"You sound like a revolutionary!" I accused. "But I've often heard it said that the common man can't be trusted to decide what's best for himself."

"I'm surprised to hear you repeat that nonsense, TiAnn: that's Rigel's kind of thinking! You know very well that within the Concorde Alliance, power is spread out over such vast distances that each planet actually ends up being more or less autonomous. Not even the Prime can dictate the rules that govern the everyday lives of its citizens."

"And you want Valhalla to be self-governing like the rest of the Concorde," I retorted.

How much more comfortable it was to be arguing with him, rather than blushing like a star-struck teenager at his every glance!

"I do. My father believed that a government should reflect the will of the people rather than those of special interests or an absolute ruler. Of course, my Uncle Einarr didn't agree – and neither have many of our past leaders. But times change: maybe now Valhallans are ready to have a say in their own government. At least, that's what I'll try to give them."

"And I suppose you told all of this to the Prime."

"I did. And as you can probably guess, he wasn't happy to hear it. But what could he do?"

"Not much, I imagine."

"Well, he did use his influence to get me to make a commitment after all." He smiled as if at some private joke.

"Which is?"

"It concerns the Tropi. She thinks the aliens will return."

"Return!" I shuddered. "She can't be serious."

"Well, if not immediately then sometime in the near future. And when they do, she wants us to be prepared to meet them."

"By the way, where is the Tropi?" I interrupted, for I suddenly realized that I had neither seen nor heard news of her since our return to Concordia.

"She went home," Janne answered. She had been so quiet that I'd almost forgotten she was still in the room with us.

I wondered what she thought of Eirik's decision to return to Valhalla. Even though she was obviously very much in love with him, did my sister really want to spend the rest of her life marooned on some primitive planet? However, this didn't seem like the appropriate time to question her.

Meanwhile, Janne was saying, "…The Tropi asked me to tell you that she's sorry she missed you. Her child is due any day now, and she wants to be with her own people when she goes into labor."

Once again, I felt the confused and confusing mixture of reactions that the Tropian leader always inspired in me: relief when I realized that I wouldn't have to face her again anytime soon – and a sense of disappointment because she was no longer on Concordia.

"She left immediately after the battle," Janne was saying. "But before she did, she convinced the Prime that it would be in the best interests of the Concorde Alliance to form a permanent committee to try to establish communication with the aliens. She thinks an active attempt to make a peaceful connection with them will prevent them from taking an aggressive stance when they return."

"When they return!" A chill shivered down my spine. "She really thinks they'll come back? And Eirik's going to be on her new committee?"

"We both are," Janne said. "Cristan Andebar too. The Tropi has volunteered to act as chairperson. She'll call meetings whenever she thinks it's necessary – for example, if there's another sighting or if any new information turns up."

"And the Prime agreed to let you return to Valhalla if you join her ridiculous committee?" was my incredulous question for Eirik.

"He didn't have much choice. And the minute those damn doctors release me, we're going straight home!"

For several long moments, I simply sat there beside his bed, trying to imagine what would influence me personally, TiAnn Trellerian, to throw away a promising government career like that. And I couldn't think of a single thing: there was no doubt in my mind about where I preferred to be.

"By the way," the sound of Eirik's voice recalled me to the present, "be forewarned: you should expect to be hearing from the Prime too."

"Me! I'm not going to join any stupid alien contact committee, even if it *is* the Tropi's!"

They both burst out laughing.

"I doubt that's what the Prime has in mind," Eirik finally said.

"Well, what *does* he want then?"

"I haven't the slightest idea. But he did ask a lot of questions about you."

"What kind of…?" I began, but Eirik interrupted.

"He didn't confide in me, TiAnn. Still, whatever he wants, you can be sure it will be interesting."

While I was still pondering this surprising news, he added a bit too casually, "By the way, I almost forgot to ask: how is Cameron?"

I thought I detected a note of interest in his voice that had nothing at all to do with that young man's state of health. "He's fine," was my rather tart reply, "although he's certainly at a loss for something to do. I think he's so used to taking orders from other people that he doesn't know how to manage his time unless he has a boss."

Eirik looked startled, but before he could respond, I hurried on: "Anyway, he sends his regards. Neither of us wanted to disturb you."

"He seems like such a nice young man," Janne mused, "although I really haven't had much of a chance to get to know him. But Eirik speaks very highly of him… I wonder what's going to happen to him now that Rigel's out of the picture."

"I have no idea. It's my impression that he'd jump at a chance to go to Valhalla as Eirik's aide if he was asked. And I wouldn't be surprised if father offers him a job too."

"What do *you* think he should do?" she wanted to know.

"M-me?" I sputtered, caught completely off guard. "How should *I* know?"

"Well, we couldn't help wondering…" Janne said. "That is, Eirik mentioned that Cameron seems to be very fond of you and we thought you two might be…"

How insulting that they should presume to encourage a romance between Cameron and me!

"I have neither the need nor the income to hire a private secretary," I interrupted, not bothering to hide my scorn, "which is the career that Cameron is undoubtedly best suited for."

"Don't be angry, TiAnn," Janne hastened to say, "we were only thinking about your happiness."

"*My* happiness! Well, for your information, Cameron Ent is probably the last person who could make me happy!"

But then I relented. This whole thing was undoubtedly her foolish fantasy, not Eirik's: I knew very well that he didn't think so little of my abilities that he would presume to match me up with Cameron. And in truth, I really didn't wish to fight with either one of them.

"Sorry, Janne," I said, suppressing my annoyance. "I didn't mean to snap at you. I guess I'm still tired. I've had so much on my mind lately. Mostly, I've been wondering what I should do now that Rigel's rebellion is over and I'm out of a job."

"That's a question all of us have been asking ourselves," Eirik agreed, obviously relieved that the conflict between my sister and me had been averted. "Which reminds me: if you don't have too many other things on your agenda, we'd love to have you visit us once we're back home."

I thanked him, although I wasn't at all comfortable with the idea of visiting Valhalla. From what I'd heard, it didn't sound like a planet that would appeal to me. However, I was too polite to say so.

Still, I had to admit that I was curious about what kind of place would have such a hold on a dynamic and talented man as Eirik Sanderson. There had to be some reason, beyond what he'd revealed, for his loyalty and devotion. Something special must be drawing him back, luring him away from an extremely lucrative and promising career with the Space Guild.

"I might take you up on your offer," I told him as I rose to leave. "But first I'll have to find out what the Prime has in mind for me."

***

The Prime and Ferrin greeted me warmly in their private reception room. A summons to appear at the palace had been awaiting me upon my return from the hospital – and I had responded immediately.

"Father always expects people to drop whatever it is they're doing and rush right over here the instant he calls," Ferrin said, offering me a chair. His eyes sparkled with boyish mischief and when his father wasn't looking, he winked at me! And at that point, I finally admitted to myself that he was obviously far too lightweight a personality to have ever been involved in plotting a rebellion against his own father.

"The expectation of prompt obedience to one's summons is one of the many privileges of being Prime," I replied, and I felt myself relax a bit. Their courtesy in greeting me indicated that they apparently hadn't called me in to complain about the way I had handled Rigel. "…And of course I'm honored to do whatever I can for your father," I made sure to add.

The Prime was already seated in a comfortable armchair, and now he crossed one leg over the other, steepled his fingers and said: "How would you feel if I asked you to do something, not just for me, but for the entire Concorde Alliance?"

It seemed imperative that I give him exactly the right answer, so I chose my next words with care. "It would be my pleasure, Sovereign…" And then, high on a heady rush of self-confidence I added: "Although it seems to me that I've already done a great deal for both you *and* the Concorde."

His shrewd, grey eyes narrowed. "Yes, that's quite true – which is why I've asked you here today… It has come to my attention that in the course of rendering your extremely valuable services to the Concorde Alliance, you have inadvertently deprived me of a vital member of my Inner Circle."

"That *was* a rather unfortunate side-effect of Sera Trellarian's actions." Ferrin said this quite seriously, but the corners of his mouth quirked upward in a truly wicked grin.

"You must learn to stop interrupting, Ferrin," the Prime chided. "You'll make me lose my train of thought."

"Sorry, Father." But he didn't look at all contrite – rather, I sensed that he was enjoying himself immensely.

"Now where was I?" the Prime said. "Ah, yes. I also seem to recollect that I once threatened those exceptionally lazy advisors of mine with the possibility of appointing you to a position of great responsibility on my Inner Circle. Isn't that so, Ferrin?"

"Yes, Father, you did."

I gripped both arms of my chair tightly to keep my hands steady. This was a most unexpected turn of events!

Suddenly the Prime grinned, and for an instant he looked every bit as youthful and mischievous as his son. "I seem to recall that my advisors weren't at all pleased with the prospect."

"I seem to remember that too, Sovereign," I dared to say, hoping that my rising excitement wasn't too obvious.

"I rather thought you would... I also understand from your father and from several other sources as well, that you have been trained as a lawyer."

"I have, Sovereign. Very well trained."

"The merit of that training shows in the way in which you were able to grasp the various elements of the developing conflict and put them to good use. You were quite effective against Rigel where many others failed."

"Thank you, Sovereign. I'm glad you think so... But speaking of the developing conflict, there's a question I've wanted to ask you – that is, if you're willing to discuss the matter."

"Please feel free to ask questions about anything that concerns you. And I shall feel equally free to answer – or not."

"In that case, I've wondered all along why you apparently made no effort to stop the attacks and sabotage as soon as they began: why you let Rigel have his way for so many months. At the time, it made you seem terribly weak."

"A fair question – and since you're a highly intelligent young woman, I think it's also fair to assume that you have already worked out the answer... So tell me: what would the early suppression of Rigel's rebellion have accomplished?"

"Probably nothing except driving it underground. Therefore, I assume you allowed the situation to escalate, hoping that whoever was behind the incidents would eventually tip his hand and reveal his or her identity. At least, that's the only reason I would have waited as long as you did."

"Correct. By the time you left for New Egypt, Andebar, the Tropi, Admiral Chert, and I were all pretty well convinced that Rigel was our troublemaker yet, like you, we lacked hard evidence. We hoped he'd be less cautious if we allowed him to leave Concordia. Fortunately, you were in a position to observe him and could supply us with that crucial data."

"Extremely fortunate," Ferrin amended.

"And now, back to the matter at hand," the Prime said. "Although it is my intention to offer it to you anyway, I think you should know that my son feels that you are too young to take the position of legal advisor to the Inner Circle."

For several moments I didn't say a word. It took all my powers of concentration to register what he'd just said – and when I did, I almost gasped aloud.

Legal advisor to the Concorde Alliance's Inner Circle! This was a heady prospect indeed!

"Father, I didn't exactly say that!" Ferrin was protesting. He glanced over at me, a most Cameron-like flush spreading across his fair skin.

"But you did, Ferrin! I want this out in the open. I won't have any more factions and undercurrents within my Inner Circle! After all, someday Sera Trellarian may end up as *your* legal advisor, so I strongly suggest that you'd better make your peace with her right now."

"Very well, Father… Forgive me, Sera," Ferrin said with great dignity, "but I think Councilor Andebar should be the person to appoint the new legal advisor, and that it should be someone with more experience. However, I would definitely approve of you being that person's second in command."

"I disagree!" was my bold rejoinder as I locked eyes with him. "Cristan Andebar already has enormous influence – perhaps too much. It would be a mistake to provide him with even more, which is what allowing him to name the Inner Circle's legal advisor would certainly do."

The Prime nodded – a quick, curt gesture – as he gave his son an 'I-told-you-so' look.

"Perhaps you have a point," was Ferrin's rather sheepish admission.

"As a matter of fact, Andebar has already approved my suggestion to appoint Sera Trellarian," the Prime announced with a certain gleeful malice.

"You could have told me sooner, Father, and saved me from making an ass of myself!"

"Son, there are some things that I prefer to keep to myself. And I reserve the right to inform you about them whenever I see fit."

They had forgotten me for the moment. This was apparently an old argument – one which, I realized with a thrill, I was likely to hear far more of in the future.

"Well?" the Prime was asking me. "Will you accept my offer – or are you going to follow in your illustrious brother-in-law's footsteps and turn me down?"

I burst out laughing – I couldn't help it. "Sovereign, whatever else I may be, one thing I am *not*, is a fool!"

"Then I take it you accept."

"With pleasure!"

***

When I told my father about the interview, he didn't seem at all surprised. Apparently, the Prime had asked so many questions that my father had already guessed he was going to offer me some sort of position on his staff.

"But legal advisor to the Inner Circle – that *is* a coup! Drexel will be very proud. And so am I!" His expression sobered. "But that's a tremendous responsibility, TiAnn. The Prime is going to expect a lot from you. Do you think you can handle it?"

"Of course, I can handle it!" If I had any doubts, I certainly wasn't going to make them public! "Besides, the Prime has given Ferrin the task of supervising me, so it's not as if I won't have some guidance."

"I guess this means I'll be losing both of my girls," was my father's rather wistful reply. "Still, I'm glad you'll be doing something challenging and enjoyable."

"I suppose someone else is going to have to help you with your own work now. You know, Father, you really should take Cameron home with you."

"Don't you care about him?"

Not that again!

"Of course I care about him!" I snapped. "Which is why I'm suggesting that you give him a job!"

My father sighed. "Very well, if that's what you think is best, I'll ask him. But what about you? Won't you need an assistant?"

"Yes, Father, I will need an assistant. But how could I possibly work with Cameron? He has no legal training and frankly, I need someone I can think with – not for."

"My dear, you badly underestimate his intelligence."

"Try working with him for a couple of months, and then *you* decide how bright he is!" I sneered. "Anyway, what kind of a man is he: letting others decide his fate for him?"

"I don't think he's doing that."

"Ha! If he had any kind of gumption, he'd decide what he wanted out of life and then go after it. Just look at Eirik! Do you know he actually turned down the Prime's offer so he can go home and fulfill the obligations that he…?" I stopped mid-sentence, startled to find myself defending Eirik's decision, which I had earlier ridiculed as foolish.

"There aren't many men like Eirik Sanderson," was my father's unfortunate comment.

"I'm quite aware of that!" I retorted, knowing how bitter I must sound.

Still, as I walked down the halls of Concordia Palace later that same afternoon on my way to inspect my impressive new office and sumptuous living quarters, I managed to subdue those annoying thoughts. After all, I had little reason to envy anyone, and certainly not my sister – except perhaps for the man that Fate had given her. Besides, there were plenty of other attractive men to be had: Ferrin for example, if I wasn't very much mistaken…

As for myself, I was ready to take on whatever challenges that might come my way – Ferrin and the Inner Circle included – anxious to test my abilities against whatever the Concorde and the Prime might have in mind for me to do.

16.

The next year was one of the busiest of my life – and also one of the most rewarding. My responsibilities as the legal advisor to the Inner Circle were demanding but stimulating, and it was gratifying to be a vital member of the Concorde Alliance's single most important governing body. The verbal and mental exercise was exhilarating, and my abilities were tested as they had never been before.

I got along well with that crusty old man, the Prime, once I discovered that he appreciated people who weren't intimidated by him. He detested servility and respected anyone who had the gumption to stand up to him. In addition, he thoroughly enjoyed a good debate.

That made two of us, and we argued for hours at a time – much to the dismay of Ferrin, who conscientiously courted his father's approval, despite all of my eminently sensible advice to the contrary.

As for Ferrin himself, he was something of a disappointment. While he had a good sense of humor and a definite flair for mischief, he was clearly incapable of standing up to his father. He was handsome enough, and a satisfactory if uninspired lover, but he certainly never made me feel as if he was the one who was in control of our relationship. He was useful, even necessary for my future – yet I couldn't help but feel a certain dissatisfaction, as if some crucial ingredient had been left out of his character.

To tell the truth, I couldn't get Eirik Sanderson out of my mind. It was annoying to realize that whenever I met a man, I automatically compared him with Eirik – and no one passed the test. Ferrin kept a close eye on my activities, so it wasn't as if I had much opportunity to indulge myself. But I really didn't want to. No one I met seemed worth the trouble.

And so it came to pass that once my responsibilities to the Inner Circle had settled into a fairly comfortable routine, I considered the possibility of making the trip to Valhalla. I had kept in touch with the Sandersons after they had left Concordia the previous year – for some perverse instinct made me want to know what they were doing, even though I was sure it would have been more sensible to forget them entirely.

Janne sounded happy and content with her life. Her second child, a girl, had recently been born – which seemed a plausible excuse for paying them a visit.

Still, I hesitated.

What was the point of it? I asked myself. Yet I kept toying with the idea.

***

At last, the announcement by the Prime that he would be taking a two-month-long vacation, thereby suspending the Inner Circle meetings for that period of time, tipped the scales in favor of a visit to Valhalla. Ferrin was disappointed when I announced that I wouldn't be accompanying the royal party, but I told him that I felt it was my duty to see Janne's daughter, reminding him that I hadn't spent any time with my sister in well over a year. However, Ferrin was remarkably persistent about wanting me with him – which was actually quite flattering – so I finally promised that I would spend only half of my vacation on Valhalla, and the rest with him.

Yet it was not without some misgivings that I made travel arrangements and packed my luggage. More than once I asked myself why I was pursuing some romantic fantasy halfway across the Concorde. Besides, I was quite aware that Eirik might prove to be a disappointment. A year was a long time, and he might have changed a great deal since returning home.

Surely I had idealized him.

Eventually I calmed down, reassured by the thought that if I went to Valhalla and found Eirik dull, it would be exactly the medicine I needed: reality would have cured my infatuation. After all, everyone knows that it's not practical to live on dreams.

***

The trip out to Valhalla was incredibly boring. The planet is in such an out-of-the-way sector of our home galaxy that I had to change starships more times than I care to describe. And the latter part of the journey was especially bad when I found myself on a puddle-jumping little dump of a ship that stopped at nearly every inhabited planet known to man. The ratty thing could never have survived a hyperspace jump – if its second-rate pilot had even dared to attempt one! When I finally arrived on Valhalla, I was so relieved to have reached my destination that it took me a while to register what a primitive place it was.

The first person I saw was Janne, running towards me across the airfield as I emerged from the small flyer that had brought me there. I barely had time to inhale one breath of Valhalla's sultry air before I was caught up in her embrace.

Dazzled by the bright sunlight, at first I didn't notice Eirik – but then I realized that he was standing just a few paces behind my sister, watching our reunion with amusement.

He looked well, I thought – very well indeed… The months of rest at home had put flesh on his bones and healthy color back in his face. In fact, he looked even better than I remembered! I studied him covertly – or so I thought – peeking around Janne's shoulder while she hugged me, laughing and babbling about how happy they were to have me with them at last.

"You're staring, TiAnn," Eirik chided. A teasing smile quirked his mouth, creating attractive crinkles at the corners of his eyes. "I suppose you're amazed to see me standing on my own two feet."

Curse the man: he seemed to have a genius for making me blush!

"You're looking well," I admitted. "I'm impressed."

They both grinned.

"How was your trip?" my sister wanted to know.

"Not too bad, considering…"

"Considering that Valhalla is at the hindmost end of everything," Eirik finished for me. "Come along, you two. I'm sure this shuttle has other stops to make, and you'll have plenty of time to talk once we're home."

It was at this point that I finally took note of our surroundings. The surface of the airfield was cracked and uneven, suggesting either gross neglect or disuse. Wisps of greenery sprouted from every crevice, threatening to eradicate all traces of human presence.

Beyond the field, blocking the skyline, was a solid wall of dense foliage, shot through with every imaginable shade of green. Strange noises – the muffled sounds of alien creatures – drifted in the air. The forest pressed against the open clearing we were standing in, exuding an unhealthy stink of rotting vegetation. And not a building was to be seen anywhere except for a moldering hangar. Furthermore, there was no visible ground transportation, just a small air sled standing off to one side of the paved area. The place reminded me of Arcadia – without the AdventureWorld amenities.

"I'm afraid it's not very impressive by Concorde standards," was Eirik's matter-of-fact comment when he noticed me taking silent inventory.

By then, the pilot was dragging my things out of the flyer's hold and piling them on the pavement beside his ship.

"Is all of this yours?" Eirik asked, dismayed.

"TiAnn never travels light," my sister said, before I could respond.

"I don't know what you're going to do with that stuff," he said, shaking his head. "You certainly won't have any use for fancy court dress here."

I told them about my promise to join the royal party after visiting Valhalla.

Meanwhile, Eirik was piling my things onto the sled. "How's that going?" he asked, pausing for a moment in his efforts. "Are you glad you took the Prime up on his offer?"

I gave them a brief run-down of my work while he stowed the last of my belongings on the undersized sled.

"And Cameron?" Janne wanted to know. "Have you heard from him? Father said he was very homesick and left Caliban shortly after we came home."

"He called once or twice, but I've been too busy to keep in touch," I said, not bothering to add that I also wasn't interested in keeping up a correspondence with him.

They let the matter drop. And by then, we were preparing to leave the airfield.

It turns out that on Valhalla, almost everyone walks nearly everywhere. If Janne and Eirik are to be believed, most of the time no one is in much of a hurry to get anyplace. They claim that Valhalla has a whole network of inns and hostels, located at convenient intervals for pedestrians and other travelers.

What a ridiculous system! At the time, I assumed it was one of those antiquated things about the Valhallan lifestyle that Eirik was trying to change, but in retrospect, I think he actually prefers it that way. It's hard to believe that such a well-traveled person would tolerate the inconvenience, but I suppose we all have our blind spots when it comes to our home worlds.

By the time we arrived at the government center, I was pretty tired. The Valhallans don't have weather control either, and the air was disgustingly hot and muggy. Who knows – if you asked them, they would probably claim they like that too!

Janne showed me to my room in their decadent stone palace. She said to make myself comfortable, that I should take time to rest and relax, and that she would come back later to check up on me.

I lay perspiring on my bed for more than an hour, wondering what insanity had led me to this dreadful place. But eventually, I decided to get up and take a look around.

There wasn't much to see. I walked up and down long, cool corridors that were decorated with old paintings, carvings, and tapestries, enjoying the feel of my bare feet sinking into the thick carpet runners, but I never met another soul.

At last, I came across what I assumed was their family room. As I stepped through the doorway, I realized that the place was occupied, although it quickly became apparent that neither Janne nor Eirik was present.

A bright cotton rug had been spread out on the floor in a patch of warm sunshine, and a baby sat there amidst a scattering of toys, a riot of coppery red hair framing her elfin face.

"*Goddag, Tanta TiAnn…*" a serious child's voice said from the far end of the room.

"Speak Galach, Bran!" a second young voice interrupted. "Your aunt doesn't speak Norsk."

Startled, I looked over and discovered that two boys were standing there, side by side. One was small and sturdy with dark hair – and I immediately recognized the resemblance to my father, Arram. The other was quite different.

He was taller and slimmer than my nephew, with a shimmering halo of golden curls that tumbled all around his face. His beauty was striking, and the poise and grace of his young body would have been arresting in a male of any age.

"Hello, Sera Trellarian," the golden child said very politely. I noticed that he spoke Galach with a subtle but very charming accent.

"You surprised me," I told them. "I wasn't expecting to find anyone here."

"My mother and father are in the library," my nephew announced.

"Thank you," I told him, and started to turn away.

"Wait, Sera!" the other cried. "Wouldn't you like to see Janna?"

I turned back, wondering who this child could be. I guessed from his way of speaking that he was somewhat older than my nephew – and he was also quite a bit taller.

"I'd like to meet all three of you." Smiling, I held out my hand to my nephew.

His dark eyes widened in surprise, and he regarded my outstretched hand with apparent revulsion. "I'm not allowed to touch anyone that way!" he scolded. "Father says it isn't polite."

"That's rude, Bran!" The other boy gave my nephew a fierce shove. His marvelous sky-blue eyes moved to my face. "Please don't be angry with him, Sera. Bran isn't old enough to realize that off-world customs aren't the same as ours."

My sense of shock dissolved in the warmth of his bright smile. "And how is it that you know so much about off-world customs?" I asked. "You can't be much older than Bran."

"I'm almost five!" was his indignant reply. "I go to school."

I tried very hard to suppress a smile.

"Aunt TiAnn?" My nephew looked down, studiously avoiding my gaze. "I'm sorry about what I said." And then he glanced up at me. "Do you want to see my sister?"

I supposed that was his way of trying to make up for his social gaffe.

"Yes, I do – but not until you've introduced me to your friend," I said with a laugh.

"Oh! This is Trön. His father Magnus is my father's best friend, and he's mine too. Trön stays with us a lot because his mother…"

A cloud of worry instantly shadowed both boys' faces.

"My mother is sick," was the golden boy's grave admission.

"I think I'm ready to meet your sister now," I said quickly, to distract them.

They both perked up at that.

The baby burbled happily, watching us with interest as we approached. A wooden block was clutched tight in one tiny fist, and she gnawed on it wetly with four opposing front teeth.

"Here she is!" Trön announced, his voice full of pride.

"Her name is Janna, and she's kind of boring," Bran said. "She can't do anything yet: she's too little to play and she drools a lot."

I opened my mouth to say something very grown-up and tolerant, but before I could begin, Trön said, "I already explained about that, Bran. Janna can't help it that she's little. Pretty soon she'll be big enough to play with us, and then you'll be her most special person. You're lucky to have a sister. You should be nice to her."

Bran scuffed a bare toe along a seam in the floor. "Yeah, I know. But it sure is hard. Babies are so dumb."

The blonde child actually looked up at me and shrugged.

"I'm not really a baby person either," I found myself admitting.

Just then, Janne walked into the room. "There you are!" she said brightly, and for a moment I wasn't sure whether she was referring to me or the children. "Thanks for watching Janna for me, boys. You can go out and play now."

Both youngsters raced out of the room, whooping with glee and pent-up energy.

The baby remained sitting in the middle of the room where they had left her, dropping her block and reaching out after the retreating children, opening and closing her little hands in obvious distress. She began to whimper.

"There, there, Janna," my sister crooned, gathering the baby in her arms and bouncing her up and down until she giggled. "Before you know it, you'll be running after them too… Did you have a nice rest, TiAnn?" she asked, turning to me. "I remember how exhausting Valhalla was for me at first."

I was still looking in the direction of the retreating boys, and her question barely registered. "I'm okay. That's quite a best friend your son has!"

Janne sighed. "Trön's been spending a lot of time with us recently because his mother is sick."

"The boys told me. Is it serious?"

Janne nodded, and suddenly she looked as if she might be about to cry.

"Why doesn't she go to a medical center at the Hub? Concordia has the facilities to treat almost everything. For that matter, so does University Seven, and it's even closer."

"She and Magnus have decided against that," was Janne's somber reply. "Inga says that if she's going to die, she'd rather do so at home."

I shrugged. What could you say to illogic like that? "Is Trön going to live here then?" I asked instead.

"Oh, no! His father loves him very much and needs him to help on their estate. We're just trying to give him some time off to get away from the sickroom atmosphere – and time to be a carefree child." She gestured that we should both sit on one of the sofas.

"I see you've named your daughter after yourself – even though she looks much more like Eirik," I said to change the subject.

"Oh, I don't know… I think she resembles you quite a bit too, when you were little."

"I never looked like that!"

Janne laughed and gave the baby another bounce. Her daughter reached out, grabbed a handful of Janne's thick auburn hair, and pulled.

"Ouch! Oh yes, you did! Anyway, Valhallans don't name children after living relatives. But Eirik insisted that we had to choose a name that was close to mine, and the only compromise he was willing to make was to change the final letter of her name. And of course the Valhallans pronounce it 'Yah-na'." She kissed the baby's forehead. "Do you want to hold her?"

I looked with some distaste at the soggy front of the baby's dress and her slippery, clutching hands. "No thank you!" I blurted out. And then, so as not to appear rude: "I think I'll wait until later."

Janne chuckled. "You can't fool me: I heard you telling the boys that you're not a baby person."

Her teasing was beginning to annoy me, so I hastily changed the subject. "Where's Eirik?"

"In the library doing research. He's always doing research! One of these days, he might even find what he's looking for!" She stood up, balancing the baby on one hip. "Come on. He told me to bring you to see him when you were up."

Their library was lined with books from floor to ceiling. I can't imagine why anyone would want to store information that way – it's terribly inefficient.

Eirik, who was sitting at a long table with a portable interface on it, noticed me inspecting the room.

"My father's collection," he said by way of explanation. "We have even more books out at the Sanctuary. But don't worry, TiAnn, even Valhallans can access the Net."

"What are you doing?" I asked, peering over his shoulder.

The screen projected a lengthy text. "Looking through the original founders' notes. I'm trying to find a legal precedent for turning Valhalla into a democracy," he said with a wry grin.

"You're still at it?" I asked, with a mixture of wonder and dismay.

"Of course! I'm a very single-minded fellow. I won't give up until I find what I want, even if it takes years."

"But I thought your father spent his whole life doing that to no avail."

Eirik laughed: a short, bitter bark. "You're right. My whole family is famous for our pig-headed stubbornness!"

Janne gave him a warm, loving smile. And then she went over to sit down on an upholstered window seat and began to play with the baby.

"Listen, TiAnn, I don't want to turn your vacation into a work session…" Eirik actually seemed embarrassed. "But I was wondering if you've studied any Valhallan law."

"It wasn't considered to be one of the essential parts of my education," I said dryly, reminding myself, even as I spoke, of the Prime.

"No – I don't suppose it was." He hesitated and then began again. "Listen, stop me if you're not interested – but I was hoping you might be willing to discuss a few legal points with me. A fresh opinion would be very helpful and I'd really appreciate your insight."

I wondered briefly if he was trying to flatter me in order to get some free legal assistance, but as I stood there watching him, I didn't get that impression at all. Instead, I was reminded once again of what it was that I admired so much about the man: he had an unerring ability to make people feel valuable, and he somehow let you know that if he respected you, then you were indeed worthy of respect.

"I'd be glad to help," I found myself answering.

Janne stood up. "And I'd better go and see about getting this girl ready for her nap."

But before she left, Eirik insisted on holding the baby. He tossed her into the air and tickled her, much to the child's delight.

It wasn't until Janne had taken her away that Eirik and I finally got down to business.

17.

And so I began my study of Valhallan law. With each passing day, I learned more about the inner workings of their planetary government – and Eirik's plans for changing it. Yet study as I might, I never did comprehend his reasons for wanting to alter a perfectly functional system.

With the death of his uncle, he had acquired absolute power. Why would any sane person choose to give that up? Accepting it didn't necessarily imply abusing it…

We had several long, late night sessions, debating that very issue. However, despite the fact that our philosophical differences ran deep, I never lost my admiration for him – and I thoroughly enjoyed every moment that we spent together.

Here's a man who knows what he wants, I found myself thinking on more than one occasion. *Why couldn't he have been the Prime's son instead of Ferrin?*

But fate isn't necessarily fair, and neither is love. I could hardly fault Janne for being attracted to him – I certainly was! But I found it terribly frustrating, working with him so closely, yet he never seemed aware of me: TiAnn, the woman.

I'm quite sure my father would have found it ironic if he had known that I, who complained so often and so bitterly about men who refused to take me seriously, was unhappy when the opposite occurred.

How strongly was Eirik attached to his ideals, I couldn't help but wonder? How strongly was he attached to Janne? And could he be lured away from either one of them?

It seemed obvious that I would never have an opportunity to find out.

***

A week or so after my arrival, Janne and Eirik apparently started feeling guilty about how much time I was spending on Eirik's democracy project, and they insisted that I take a break to go sightseeing.

Frankly, I would rather have skipped the experience. There's no doubt about it: travel is extremely unpleasant when all you have are your own two feet to take you anywhere!

Nevertheless, walk we did: all over their vast, empty estate and its neighboring lands. We visited the timber and wildlife preserves near their vacation home, the Sanctuary, and from there we progressed to the seaside. We also toured a number of the primitive little villages that are scattered across the Valhallan countryside like pimples on a teenager's face. We even paid a brief visit to Stormhaven, the estate of Trön's father Magnus and his dying mother Inga.

And while we were there, the Sandersons proposed to take me on a three-day cruise on Magnus' sailboat – but that was where I put my foot down. It had been bad enough, trekking around with the boys and Janna, who rode in a pack on her father's shoulders; but it was only too easy to imagine what life on a tiny sailboat would be like, cooped up with three noisy and extremely energetic young children!

By comparison, work seemed relaxing.

Unfortunately, by the time we arrived back at Hawkness House, my visit was almost over. In a matter of days, I would be leaving to join Ferrin and the rest of the royal party.

You should be satisfied with what you already have! I chided myself, as night after night I found myself lying alone in my bed, speculating about what Janne and Eirik might be doing in theirs.

Frankly, I was miserable. The more time I spent with him, the more attractive Eirik seemed to me – and the more wasted on my sister.

Why was he so resistant to even a mild flirtation?

Of course, I knew very well that a flirtation would only have made matters worse, but it might have helped to ease the tension.

The whole situation was really very frustrating.

***

All too soon it was my last evening on Valhalla, and I still wasn't sure what to do about Eirik. Sitting on my bed with my luggage spread out on the floor around me, all I could think about was how, in a few short hours, I would be boarding the shuttle that would take me back to my everyday life and routine commitments.

Oh, how I wanted to leave Valhalla with better memories than dusty footpaths, sore feet, noisy boys, and a slobbering baby! And it was at that late hour when I finally realized that I would never forgive myself if I didn't at least try to approach Eirik.

Besides, if the truth be told, there was also a certain element of temptation involved in my decision: for whatever reason, I was still carrying around my remaining two doses of Tropian aphrodisiacs, left over from my fiasco with Rigel. Up until this point (after having traded the first two packets to such good effect), I had never had any occasion to consider using them, and I certainly didn't need an aphrodisiac to get Ferrin's amorous attention!

Did I dare try them now on Eirik? And if I did, would it mark the beginning of a new relationship or the destruction of our present one?

A small voice (which sounded suspiciously like the Tropi's) in the back of my consciousness asked, *What can you possibly expect to gain from this, TiAnn? Is it worth the risk?*

I chose to ignore the voice.

What would really mean the most to me, I knew, would be for Eirik to admit of his own accord that he was attracted to me. But apparently that wasn't going to happen. Time was running out, and by now I was ready to take him on whatever terms I could get him.

But first, I was going to have to overcome his inhibitions...

Earlier that evening, when we had parted for the night, I had overheard him telling Janne that he intended to stay up for a while longer to do some further research. My decision, when it came, was that I would proceed to the library and if I found him there alone, I would do whatever was necessary to accomplish my objective.

I removed a single packet of the drug from my toiletry kit, for I knew very well that my plan would require only one dose: his. Then, pulling on a robe against the night chill, I left my room.

The corridors of Hawkness House were deserted, inhabited only by deep shadows that were cast by glow globes set in hand-wrought iron sconces. The massive walls and thick carpet runners muffled every sound, and I felt as if I was the only creature alive in that vast stone edifice.

At last I reached the library. Lamp-glow created a pool of warm yellow light on the hall rug outside. I had thought I was calm, but to my surprise I discovered that my heart had begun to gallop as I peeked inside.

He was there, deep in thought, apparently mulling over an old text – but somehow he must have sensed my presence, for he looked up immediately, his face alight with welcome.

"Janne? Is that you?"

"No, it's me: TiAnn."

"Come in! What are you doing up at this ungodly hour!"

I walked into the room – and with each step, my sense of commitment grew. I knew the time was right: I would never have another chance like this.

"I couldn't sleep." I offered him my warmest smile. "I guess it's because I'm feeling sorry that I have to leave you tomorrow."

"We're sorry too. Having you here has meant a lot to us – especially Janne."

Why did he always have to drag my sister into it?

"But it's meant a great deal to me too," he added.

My hopes began to rise.

"I don't want to embarrass you," he was saying, "but I have to tell you that having you here and being able to work with you has meant more to me than you'll ever know."

"Why, thank you, Eirik!" I felt positively radiant with pleasure.

"Just when I was the most discouraged, when nothing seemed to make any sense, you came along and gave me the inspiration to carry on. I don't know how to thank you."

"Thanks aren't necessary – but I'm glad to know I've been of some help." By now I was standing right in front of his large wooden desk.

"*Some* help?" he protested. "Without you, I would never have understood the legal ramifications of what I'm trying to accomplish. Your analysis is flawless, TiAnn. You have a truly amazing way of grasping the essentials of a problem."

Complimentary: yes – but decidedly not romantic. It was disappointing, but I had already accepted the fact that if anything was going to happen, it was probably up to me to make the first move.

"Well, I've enjoyed working with you too," I told him. "How about it: what do you say we have a drink to celebrate our joint efforts – and our last evening together?"

"An excellent idea. I was just about to pour myself some tea, but I can get you something stronger if you'd like."

"Oh, don't go to any trouble just for me. I'll drink whatever you're having. And don't get up!" I quickly added. "Let me get it for you."

As I filled two mugs from a teapot on the sideboard, I silently cursed him for his stupid, unsophisticated Valhallan tastes. At the same time I was desperately trying to remember exactly what that obnoxious Tropian drug salesman had told me about the aphrodisiac.

Was it safe to take with a non-alcoholic beverage?

I couldn't remember.

And what exactly had he said about body types? Something about special formulas for people who weren't h-standard...

Were Valhallans h-standard?

To hell with it: I was too committed to my plan to hesitate now!

My back was towards Eirik when I emptied the packet into one of the mugs – and I made sure I kept track of which one was his! "Here you are," I said, coming around to his side of the desk and handing him his tea. "Let's drink to our future good relations."

"To good relations," he said with a smile. He took a cautious sip and made a face. "Ugh! I'm afraid this has been sitting around too long. It's lukewarm, and it tastes strange. Throw it away and I'll send for more."

"Oh no! I prefer it this way!" I cried, taking an enormous gulp of the foul brew.

"Really?" He shrugged. "I guess I can stand it if you can." He took another mouthful and set his mug aside.

"You really should drink it all before it gets completely cold," I urged.

"I suppose you're right," he said, not bothering to retrieve his mug. "You know," he continued, "I really wish you could stay with us a while longer. Talking to you definitely sharpens my wits."

"I wish I could stay too. If I did – who knows – I might end up convincing you of my point of view." Even as we spoke, I was watching anxiously for any sign that the drug was beginning to take effect.

How long had it taken with Rigel? And how could I get him to drink more tea?

"Not a chance!" he was saying. "Besides, I know you: you'd get bored with Valhallan life – probably sooner rather than later. Admit it, TiAnn: by your standards, we're a pretty dull lot. And you know very well that nothing here is nearly as exciting as your life on Concordia."

"Oh, I'm not so sure about that…"

He laughed. "Well, I am! Why don't we just agree that I'll call whenever I come across something I need to discuss with you."

I leaned against the desk, trying to look casual and – hopefully – desirable. "Don't wait for that," I told him, lowering my voice, "call me whenever you feel lonely."

"Lonely?" Abruptly he sneezed: two short violent explosions.

"Bless you!" I decided to move even closer: it might hasten the aphrodisiac's effects. "You know, sometimes it's nice to have someone to talk to, someone who really cares."

He smiled. "I suppose it is! I guess I'm lucky that way: whenever I need to talk, there's always Janne. No: I'll save the long distance calls for more urgent things."

I seated myself on the desktop, taking care that my thigh ended up resting against his forearm where it lay along the tabletop. Even through the fabric of my robe and nightgown I could feel his body heat on my skin.

I tried another tack. "Caring about someone can be urgent too. And tonight Eirik…"

He sneezed again, only this time he did it five times in succession. "Speaking of tonight, suddenly I seem to be getting a cold," he said as soon as he could speak. He sniffled wetly. "Strange: I felt fine earlier."

"Sick?" Surely, the drug wouldn't make a person sick! "If you have a cold coming on," I told him, "maybe you should have some more tea."

"Don't want it!" Abruptly he was agitated. "I'm hot enough as it is." He began tugging at his shirt collar.

That was definitely a good sign.

"Here, let me do that for you," I soothed, leaning against his shoulder, certain the effects would intensify the closer I got to him. I started to place a hand on his chest, but he shoved me rudely away, tearing at the neck of his shirt until the fastenings broke.

"Can't... breathe..." he gasped.

I noticed with some alarm that his eyes were streaming, and his nose was running profusely. This was certainly not the reaction Rigel and I had had to the drug. Perhaps Valhallan s *did* respond differently – and that could mean trouble.

Now Eirik was coughing and choking – and still sneezing.

"Air," he cried. "I need... air!" His eyes begged me for help. "TiAnn!"

Now thoroughly alarmed, I slid quickly off the desk and hauled him to his feet. He was gasping and wheezing as I half-carried, half-dragged him over to the window seat. With a sickening chill of déjà-vu I vividly recalled a similar situation at Anhur prison.

What had I done?

Eirik collapsed onto the window seat, and I hastily pushed open the windows. He slumped against the paneling, not quite sitting, but not quite lying down either. His breath rasped in and out in harsh, labored gulps, and his face was a sickly ashen color.

Was he about to pass out? For some reason, just then it seemed very important that he remain conscious.

"Try to relax," I urged, lifting his feet off the floor. "Eirik, you've got to stay awake!"

I shoved a pillow behind his head to make him more comfortable. His breathing steadied and became a little less strained.

Gently, so as not to disturb him, I felt his pulse. One moment it was racing and the next it was faint and erratic. "Please don't die, Eirik!" I whispered, choking back a sob.

His eyelids flickered open. Slowly, the blue-grey eyes focused on me. "TiAnn? What...?" His voice was so faint that I could barely make out the words.

"I don't know! You seem to have had some sort of violent seizure."

He continued staring at me until I finally had to look away.

Did he suspect that whatever this was, it was all my fault?

When I looked again, his eyes were closed and he was breathing a bit more normally. Perhaps the crisis was over.

Slowly, I stood up, wondering what to do. I couldn't just leave him there in that condition – which meant that I had to summon Janne. But I would only tell her as much as I had to, I quickly decided: basically that Eirik had collapsed while we were drinking tea.

However, before I left the room, I went over to his desk, picked up his mug, and threw the rest of that damn stuff out of the library window.

***

We ended up staying up all night with Eirik: Janne, their local medic and myself. For a while, his condition was so critical that I came very close to telling them the truth – but fortunately, the danger point eventually passed, leaving Eirik weak but definitely recovering.

The doctor told us that Eirik seemed to be suffering from shock caused by an extreme allergic reaction to a foreign substance that he had either breathed in or ingested. He went on to say that in many such cases, the victim is never able to determine afterwards what set off the reaction in the first place (and I certainly hoped that was true!). To prevent a possible relapse, the doctor put Eirik on a strict diet for the next couple of days – and banned that particular type of tea from the house.

I stood by, watching them in silence, thankful that Eirik was going to be subjected to nothing worse than bland food, and quite relieved that I had been able to keep my secret.

By morning, the medic told us there was no further need to keep watch over Eirik, and he prescribed sleep for everyone.

I returned to my room to finish packing.

***

Later that same afternoon, as I sat in yet another little flyer, watching Valhalla falling away beneath me, I felt as if a chapter of my life was also dropping away forever. And in acknowledgment of that passage, I made several resolutions...

309

First, I promised myself that I would never again take a chance on anyone or anything that was likely to result in my own personal embarrassment. And if in the future I found myself in a position where I had to participate in any covert activity, I would make very sure that nothing incriminating could ever be traced back to me.

I also thought about Eirik, and I reached some conclusions about him too. I wouldn't dare to try another dose of aphrodisiac on him – not even if I could hire Tropi's most skilled biochemist to prepare a special Valhallan formula. I had learned my lesson: although Eirik Sanderson might continue to be a standard against whom I judged all other men, he was definitely not for me. The best thing I could do was forget about him and look to my own future.

And it was a promising future indeed.

As I headed towards my rendezvous with Ferrin and the Prime, I stretched my enervated body, finally able to relax after the night's ordeal.

It had been a worthwhile trip after all, I decided, a refreshing break from Concordia's incessant demands. I sensed that in the course of my adventures, I had grown up: the Sera TiAnn Trellerian of today was no longer the naive young woman who had so recklessly launched her own private investigation into that charismatic troublemaker, Rigel Hafiz.

So as I watched that intensely blue and green globe shrink into insignificance behind me and then vanish entirely from sight, swallowed up by the vastness of space, I knew that although my thoughts might occasionally stray there, I would never again return to that tranquil, primitive world: the planet called Valhalla.